Rawlins touched his pistols, making sure they could be pulled out easily, and made sure his knife and tomahawk were in place. When he closed in on the trio, he saw that the one pinned against the adobe wall was Diego.

The two robbers looked up at his approach. "Move on, *Americano*," one snarled in poor English. Both were short and stocky. Their faces were scarred from dozens of fights. Each had a deadly look in his eyes.

"Ye two boys think you're enough to handle that critter?" Rawlins asked sarcastically.

"This is none of your business *marrano*—filthy pig," the second said.

"Let the boy go," Rawlins growled.

One grinned, said something in Spanish to his partner and then advanced, knife in hand.

Rawlins pulled out a pistol. The man stopped. He looked disappointed. "And here I thought you had some *cojones, amigo*."

Rawlins nodded. "Hell, shootin' a critter like you'd be a waste of damn good powder and ball." He shoved the pistol back into his belt and pulled out the big, wicked knife. "I got the *cojones*, hoss," he said flatly. "But ye won't have yours much longer."

The Mexican advanced slowly, with his knife darting little circles ahead of him. Rawlins stood there cockily, waiting. Then the Mexican charged, and his knife cut vicious arcs as it moved toward Rawlins's chest.

Look for these books in the
MOUNTAIN COUNTRY series

SOUTHWEST THUNDER
WINTER THUNDER

Available from HarperPaperbacks

MOUNTAIN THUNDER

JOHN LEGG

HarperPaperbacks
A Division of HarperCollins*Publishers*

This is a work of fiction. The characters, incidents, and dialogues are products of the author's imagination and are not to be construed as real. Any resemblance to actual events or persons, living or dead, is entirely coincidental.

HarperPaperbacks   *A Division of* HarperCollins*Publishers*
10 East 53rd Street, New York, N.Y. 10022

Copyright © 1994 by John Legg
All rights reserved. No part of this book may be used or reproduced in any manner whatsoever without written permission of the publisher, except in the case of brief quotations embodied in critical articles and reviews. For information address HarperCollins*Publishers,*
10 East 53rd Street, New York, N.Y. 10022.

Cover illustration by W.A. Dodge

First printing: July 1994

Printed in the United States of America

HarperPaperbacks and colophon are trademarks of HarperCollins*Publishers*

❖ 10 9 8 7 6 5 4 3 2 1

Once again:
For my brother,
Joe Legg,
whom I look up to
in more ways than one.
Thanks.

1

THE GOOD CITIZENS OF TAOS THOUGHT for a few moments that a large war party of Comanches was attacking the brown adobe town again. They looked up, startled and worried, from their work or play, fear striking into their hearts and souls. The few soldiers stationed in the drab little Mexican town tumbled out of their quarters, hoping that they had remembered their powder and ball and bayonets and praying that they would not be the one to fall to a Comanche lance or, worse, be taken off to be tortured.

There was anger, but more relief, when the people saw that it was only three *loco americanos* making their usual raucous, frightening, and flamboyant entrace into town. Once the people had seen this, they made sure their children and sheep and chickens were out of the path of the wild men, and then they watched, more often than not cheering the Americans on.

Abe Rawlins, Ezra Early, and Lucien Chardonnais screeched and roared as they thundered on their horses down the dusty street toward the plaza. They had fired their rifles to announce the commencement of their hell-for-leather ride, and then war-whooped as they spurred their horses.

They circled the plaza, whooping at the señoritas, and then pulled to a stop in the center of the plaza, rearing their horses.

From one side of the plaza, Hobart Adams watched them. Though it had been almost three years since he had seen them, they had changed little.

"You fellows sure are a noisy bunch of bastards," Adams shouted when the mountain men's horses had finally come back to earth.

"Where's the chil' said that?" Rawlins demanded, fierce eyes searching the crowd. "I'll gut the fractious chil'."

"Like hell you will," Adams said. He boldly stepped away from a building and marched toward the three mountain men.

"Well look at this goddamn dandified, peacock-struttin' ol' hoss," Rawlins said, catching sight of Hobart Adams. He grinned.

Adams smiled back, mostly in embarrassment. Rawlins had been right, though. The young man wore fine wool trousers of a deep blue hue, with a matching, short Taos-style jacket that was set off by silver buttons and thread. A light blue cotton shirt made a nice contrast. Boots with silver spurs, and a wide, dark blue sombrero and tie completed the ensemble.

"How's doin's, ol' hoss?" Early asked.

"Just fine, boys, just fine!" Adams was fairly bursting with excitement at seeing his friends.

"Is dis de same Bart Adams we left 'ere?" Chardonnais mused aloud. "'E sure don' look like 'e did."

"Goddamn, ye little frog fart, I'm thinkin' ye're right," Rawlins offered. "He looks more like a tight-ass citified chil' to this ol' hoss. Goddamn, the Bart Adams we left was a shinin' chil', with the hair of the b'ar about him."

"I'll raise your hair anytime you want to come against me, Abe," Adams said, laughing. It was not true, but he had to try giving back verbally as best he could.

"'E's got you dere," Chardonnais said to Rawlins.

"Eat shit, ye fat little frog." Abe Rawlins was generally a joyful man. He took life as it came and tried to find some humor in it when he could. He was also a simple man, not one to complicate his life by worrying about things he could do nothing about.

Adams shook his head in amazement. The men hadn't changed their antics either.

"Well, you boys can stand here and flap gums with Bart," Early said, "but this ol' chil' aims to wrap paws 'round some *awardenty* here straight off."

"Waugh!" Rawlins growled. "Such doin's plumb shine with this chil'."

"Mais oui!" Chardonnais agreed.

"First jug's on me, gentlemen," Adams said, eliciting renewed whoops from the three mountain men.

*   *   *

"Ye know, boy, ye hurt ol' Ez's feelin's when ye didn't wait for him to stand by ye at your weddin'," Rawlins said. "Such doin's don't shine wth this ol' hoss."

The grin froze on Adams's face when he realized that Rawlins was serious. "But I—"

"But shit, boy," Rawlins growled. "After all Ez done for ye. Goddamn, ye're one lucky niggur I wasn't around when you run off with that damn trollop or—"

"That'll be enough of that talk, Abe," Adams snapped, anger crackling in his eyes. "Maybe I was wrong not to wait for Ezra, but I'll not have you speakin' of my wife in such a manner."

"She-it," Rawlins said with a smirk. "Ye gonna paint your face black agin me, ol' hoss?"

"I took care of Parfrey. I can take care of you, too," Adams retorted.

"There's a mountain's worth of difference 'tween a shit-sucker like Parfrey and this ol' chil'," Rawlins said arrogantly.

"I don't much—"

"You better listen to him, *mon ami*," Chardonnais said. "Besides, it's been t'ree year almost since you went against dat son of a bitch. Even if you could've gone against Abe den, you couldn't now."

"But still . . ."

"Maybe was ye to offer some goddamn explanation," Rawlins said, "I might see fit not to raise your hair, hoss."

Adams was about to retort, but there was nothing he could say other than to comply with Rawlins's suggestion. Trouble was, his explanation wasn't very convincing—or rational. "I just couldn't wait," he finally mumbled, face almost the color of Chardonnais's shirt.

"Couldn't wait!" Rawlins exclaimed. "Well, Jesus goddamn Christ Almighty." He was astounded, but began to grin. "You're gettin' near'bout as bad as Lucien. Think with your pecker all the time."

"Dat's because I 'ave one to t'ink wit' all de time," Chardonnais said brightly. He had no shame about his sexual appetite. "And speakin' of such t'ings . . ." He rose and approached a thin, almost attractive young Mexican woman who was serving in the cantina. Moments later he and the smiling young woman had gone off into the back room.

"Jesus," Rawlins breathed. "He's worse'n a goddamn goat." Then he burst into laughter.

Early joined in, and then Adams did, too, though tentatively.

When the laughter died down, Rawlins looked at Adams and growled, "Now, boy, ye best make things to right with Ez."

Adams nodded sadly. He felt bad that he had hurt his friend. Ezra Early had done so much for him, and he had found himself too weak a man to wait until the trapper had returned to Taos to get married.

Adams was closest to Early, if anyone could be said to be close to the three mountain men. Early had saved him from Comanches, after some Santa Fe traders had left the young Easterner out in the Cimarron desert to die. Adams was a reporter for the *New York Register* who, a little more than three years earlier, had been sent west to report on and sketch the sights of the flourishing Santa Fe Trail trade. The freighters he was traveling with objected when he tried to stop them from raping and mutilating a

Comanche girl, and had beaten him and left him to die. Several Comanche warriors found him wandering along the Cimarron Cutoff of the trail and were about to start tormenting him when a wild man on a big Appaloosa roared up. Ezra Early killed one of the Comanches and wounded another, sending the three survivors packing in a hurry. For reasons unknown even to himself, Early took to the young New Yorker and brought him to Taos. Later, Early and his two longtime friends and partners taught Adams some of the ways of the mountains.

The last time Adams had seen his three new friends, they had been heading out in the fall, shortly after the Easterner had evened the score with the men who had left him to die. Adams had fallen in love with a pretty young señorita named Dolores Ortega y Delgado, and she had consented to marry him. He had planned to delay the wedding until the next summer, when Early and the two others returned from the mountains for their annual spree in the friendly Mexican town.

"I love Dolores something awful," he said quietly, ashamed to be explaining his inner self to these hard, crude men. "Have just about from the moment I met her over in Doña Montoya's. When I got to thinking of spending the whole winter here without making her my wife, I went a little *loco,* I guess." He smiled weakly. "Besides, the Mexican authorities weren't too keen on having a vagabond American hanging around."

"Told ye that, boy," Early said with a low growl.

Adams nodded. "What really pushed me to move ahead, though, was learning of the possibility of taking a ship to New York. I wasn't about to do that and leave Dolores here. So we got married and headed south." He looked at Early with pleading in his eyes. "I never meant to hurt your feelings, Ezra," he said. "If I thought you'd be this put out, I'd never have—"

"Goddamn, boy, don't go soft on me now," Early said quietly.

"But—"

"Jesus, ye dumb little bastard," Rawlins snapped, "have some balls, for Christ's sake. Ye did what ye did for a reason. Ye ought to be man enough to tell it straight out and not like some pulin' little girl."

"But I do regret having hurt Ezra. He—"

"Oh, good goddamn, boy," Rawlins snarled. "Ye said ye was sorry once. That's enough. Ez didn't like your explanation, he'd tell ye so. Ye know that. But ye shouldn't even give a shit about that neither. Whether he accepts that or not's that ol' chil's doin's. Ye might have to defend yourself some over it, if he decided to raise hair on ye, but ye can do that. Or so I thought ye could."

"You're an annoying son of a bitch, Abe, you know that," Adams commented. "It's particularly galling when you make sense." He looked at Early, his face set in determination. "I am sorry, Ezra. And I've explained it as best I could. You don't like that, I guess we'll have to go outside."

"I'd stomp the shit out of ye, boy," Early said.

Adams nodded seriously. "I expect you would." He smiled just a little. "But you'd not come out of the encounter unscathed."

"Waugh!" Rawlins commented. "That ol' hoss still does have some of the hair of the b'ar on him. Goddamn if he don't."

Early clapped Adams on the back. "Apology

taken, ol' hoss. Now buy us another jug and tell us about New York."

"Well," Adams said after he had gotten more whiskey and filled his friends' mugs, "Dolores was the hit of New York, I can say that for certain. I was surprised at that because of her heritage. I was not surprised at it because of her beauty."

"What about that ol' hoss sent you out here?" Early asked.

"Humphrey McWalters?" Adams said with a smile. "The old reprobate was most put out that I had not sent more dispatches."

"Ye tell him to kiss the devil's ass?" Rawlins asked with a laugh.

"No, sir. I'm not that foolish. I led him to believe that I was still a loyal and hardworking employee of the *New York Register.* As such, he paid for our hotel as well as some of our other expenses, which were considerable after more than a year there. I even did some work for him."

"Goddamn fool," Rawlins muttered.

Adams shook his head. "I don't think so," he said. "The morning Dolores and I were to sail for Mexico, I marched into his office and told him that I wasn't going to work for him any longer, but that I appreciated his having paid for our stay. He was apoplectic. My God, you should've heard him bellowing."

"I think we did," Early said easily.

"I favored him with a few of the expressions I learned from you fellows and even some from Parfrey. Then I told him I'd be glad to send him dispatches—story or sketchings—for a price. And one that was well above my measly salary. He almost choked on his choler, but he finally agreed."

"Waugh!" Rawlins roared happily. "Ye sure made that ol' chil' come now. Sure as birds shit whilst flyin'."

Adams looked about proud enough to burst, but he tried to hide his smile behind his mug of whiskey.

2

RAWLINS ROSE AND STRETCHED his long, hard frame. "This chil's got a hankerin' to fill his meatbag." He grinned. "And find me some willin' señorita. Any of ye others of a mind to join me?"

"Mais non!" Chardonnais exclaimed. He had returned to the table only minutes before. "You 'ave no table manners, and if dere's anyt'ing I don' want to see, it's your skinny ass bumping on some poor little señorita."

Early laughed. "Yeah, one who's too goddamn brain-addled to spurn his crude advances."

"Bah," Rawlins said in a mock growl. "Ye boys're just afeared of learnin' somethin' from this ol' hoss. *Adios, amigos.*" He slapped his sombrero on and headed off. Then he stopped and turned back. "I'll talk to Ceran about the plews soon's I'm done." He grinned. " 'Course, that could be some time."

"Shit," Early hooted. "You'll shoot your pizzle off in your pants soon's some little señorita looks at ye."

"You're confusin' me with that little frog fart over

10

there." Rawlins pointed to Chardonnais. "But if'n it'll make ye feel better, I'll talk to Ceran first. Then when me and some señorita start rollin' in the robes, I won't have to think about ye two settin' here a-frettin' over gettin' the plews in."

Early and Chardonnais laughed. Early plucked a red chili pepper out of a bowl on the table and threw it at Rawlins, who managed to catch it.

Rawlins bit into the chili and chewed happily. "*Gracias, mi amigo,*" he said with another grin. Then he wandered outside. He stood there for a few moments, enjoying the feel of the warm summer air and the light breeze. He could still remember the first time he and his two partners had come to Taos. That was eight years ago now, but it was still fresh in his mind. The city had been surprising in its drabness, but that did not bother the three young mountain men. Not when there were heaps of pretty, freethinking señoritas to be had; not when there was unlimited quantities of fiery, home-brewed Taos lightning to be sampled; not when there were more than enough strutting *vaqueros* and *soldados* to fight; not when there were a plethora of spicy new food dishes to be eaten.

Now, as then, strings of red or green chili peppers hanging from rafters helped brighten the dull brownness of Taos. As did the gaily painted doors or bright window sashes sprinkled about town. Vendors at their carts still sold produce or tortillas or goods that they or someone in their family had made, their haggling voices rising up now and again over the noises of the city.

Despite the many years Rawlins had come to Taos, the city still had a vibrant fascination for him.

He wasn't sure what it was, nor did he really care. Abe Rawlins was a simple man, one who did not go looking for the complex in life. He was content just to acknowledge that Taos was somehow almost mystical, and accept it. Let others, men with a book education like Hobart Adams, delve into it deeply. Rawlins would rather just enjoy himself.

A friendly smile from a cigarillo-smoking señorita who passed by gave him at least one tangible reason to like Taos. Still, he knew there were other, less obvious ones.

Rawlins strode across the plaza, rifle in hand. He was a big, rangy American with broad shoulders, slim waist, no behind to speak of, and long, powerful legs. He had a long, dour face that bore some resemblance to a sad hound dog. He had a thick mane of wheat-colored hair that reached down to his shoulders and he wore a fat mustache that dropped around his slim lips and hung off the points of his square chin. He was otherwise clean-shaven. As was usual while he was in Taos, Rawlins wore his wide sombrero. He had changed his moccasins for boots, with spurs that had huge rowels. His buckskin pants were tight-fitting, with fringes and conchos alternating down the outside seam of each leg; *botas* covered the bottoms from knees to ankles. A decorated buckskin war shirt hung almost to his knees. People got out of his way, fearing a little this big, broad-shouldered man. That he was an American didn't hurt either. All the Mexicans seemed to think that all Americans were plumb *loco*. Rawlins didn't think he was, but he couldn't help what others thought.

He strolled into the store owned by the Bent

brothers and Ceran Saint Vrain. The latter, a short, dark-eyed, dark-haired Frenchman, looked up from some paperwork. He smiled widely and came from around the corner of his cluttered, fragrant counter.

"Bonjour, mon ami. Bonjour!" he said jovially. He clasped Rawlins's hand and slapped him on the biceps a few times.

"How's doin's, ol' hoss?" Rawlins responded with an almost equally wide smile.

"I 'eard you and your frains ride into town before," Saint Vrain said. "You make quite ze spectacle, eh?"

"Goddamn right. Me and the boys figure if ye cain't do somethin' up big, why the hell bother."

"A good attitude," Saint Vrain said with a firm nod. "You 'ave a good season up in ze mountains, eh?"

"Yep. Got us nine pack of plews. All goddamn prime ones, too." He glared at Saint Vrain, even though he knew the little Frenchman would not try to cheat the three mountain men. At least no more than could be expected among friends.

"Zey probably look like rat pelts," Saint Vrain said. Then he laughed. "We will get zem tonight, as usual?"

Rawlins nodded. "It won't shine with this ol' chil' to leave them plews out there too goddamn long. Me and the boys make the best goddamn cache in the mountains, but damn if there ain't always some critter who cain't up and find it."

"Zat is ze truth," Saint Vrain agreed.

"How's your business been, Ceran?" Rawlins asked.

"Doing real well, Abe. Ze company opened us a big trading post on ze Arkansas. Bill's going to run it mostly. He's ze one gets along best with ze Cheyennes. So, you will meet me here just after dark, zen?"

"Yep." Rawlins turned and walked out. He took a small, winding side street off the plaza and then turned down an alley. Through it he came to another little side street and entered a restaurant a few doors up. The place was small and crowded, but served the best *machaca de huevos* in all Taos. His mouth watered for the dish of pounded jerky, eggs, and chilies.

"Ah, Señor Rawlins!" said Manuel Gonzalez, the owner of the restaurant. His creased, chubby face was split in a broad smile, showing that several teeth were missing.

"Señor Gonzalez," Rawlins said with a grin.

"Un momento, por favor." Gonzalez chased a lingering customer from a small table, quickly swiped it almost clean, and then held the chair for Rawlins.

The mountain man took the seat and leaned his rifle against the table.

"Some *machaca de huevos,* señor?" Gonzalez asked.

"Sí," Rawlins said with a great nod. "And some of your special wine to wash it down, eh?"

Gonzalez nodded and hurried away.

Rawlins ignored everyone in the restaurant—everyone but Gonzalez's daughter, Juanita—as he filled and lit his pipe. Then he leaned back to watch Juanita at work.

She was just about seventeen, he figured, tall and slender in her simple skirt and blouse of inexpensive material. The skirt barely reached the middle of her calves, and the blouse was cut quite low, offering quite an eyeful of smooth, dusky skin. Her feet were bare, and her hair was pulled back from her face and tied with a bright yellow ribbon.

It was a delight to watch her, Rawlins felt. She moved with lithe grace and a bouncy step. Her skirt swirled around as she hurried about. She was quite busy, but she found the time twice to cast Rawlins a warm and inviting smile, which he returned with pleasure.

Rawlins had first seen her in Gonzalez's a couple of years ago. He had noted her already shapely form and her inherent allure. But he had figured that she was a little too young. He had felt the same last year. But now, now she was just about ripe for the plucking.

Then Juanita brought his food. She set the plates down and favored him with another smile. Her deep eyes smoked with desire. "One hour?" she suggested quietly.

"*Sí*," Rawlins said enthusiastically. Then he dug into the food with gusto.

It took three heaping platefuls to fill him, but finally he settled back with his pipe and another glass of harsh wine. He had no watch, but he knew when it was close to an hour after Juanita had brought him his first plate of *machaca de huevos*. But still he waited patiently.

Juanita at last hurried out of the back and up to his table. Rawlins stood and dropped some coins on the table. Together the two walked out into the warm, dusty afternoon and turned up the street. They walked slowly to the plaza and then on to Rawlins's room at Señora Rubio's house, where the three mountain men had rented rooms.

Inside, he leaned his rifle against the wall and poured two glasses of wine. Juanita took hers and drank it gratefully. Rawlins waited until she finished it.

When she set down the glass, he moved up and placed his strong arms around her. She looked up at him, lips parted, waiting. He covered them with his own, and his tongue sought out hers.

She responded, shivering a bit with delicious anticipation. But she finally broke away. Juanita swiftly disrobed. It took only moments before she was standing there naked.

Rawlins stared at Juanita's small, firm breasts and puckered nipples ringed with a deep rose color. A cross of gold dangled in the chasm between the billowing mounds of her breasts. Her dark skin was flat over the belly.

"Well?" she asked, drawing out the simple word.

Rawlins reached out for her, but her hand on his chest stopped him. "What?" he muttered, surprised.

"I'm not letting you up against me, señor" she said with mock severity, "while you're wearing that shirt."

He glanced down, realizing that the beads, porcupine quills, and other adornments would rip her tender flesh. He grinned and shucked his buckskin war shirt. He kicked off his moccasins and shimmied out of his fringed buckskin pants. He was hard.

Juanita liked what she saw. She stepped up, grasping him in one soft hand, making him jump a bit. She reached up and grabbed the back of his head with the other hand, then pulled his head down for a protracted kiss.

She finally released him, and he scooped her up.

He dropped her lightly on the bed. He bent over her, mouth descending to her bosom. His tongue flicked at a nipple, then the other. Juanita jerked at the touch.

Rawlins slid his tongue down the smooth contour of Juanita's middle, lingering an instant at the deep navel. Then he slid his tongue back up, through the valley of her breasts, over her chin, and dipped it into her mouth. At the same time the middle finger of his left hand caressed the cleft between her legs.

Juanita groaned around Rawlins's mouth as his right hand sought one of her breasts. She muttered in Spanish as she grabbed his hard lance. Juanita screamed, pulling her mouth away from Rawlins's to do so. She bucked and jerked against his hand, until the feelings subsided.

Rawlins quickly stoked her passions again. She gasped, "Now!" and tugged on his manhood. He let Juanita guide him into her. She gasped, and he moaned.

There was something special about the daughters of the *ricos* in Taos, Rawlins thought sometime later, but those rich and often spoiled women could not hold a candle to the blazing passions a girl like Juanita brought to the bed.

Rawlins had had his share of both kinds and had found over the years that he preferred a woman like Juanita. She was not as demanding of foofaraw and did not expect him to bend to his every whim. Let Ezra Early have the rich ones, Rawlins figured. He was a simple man and was content with simple women. His chest heaved a little as he fought back a chuckle when he thought about Lucien Chardonnais. The little French-Canadian would roll in the robes with any female when his ardor was up, which was about all the time.

"Is something wrong?" Juanita asked worriedly. She was lying in the crook of his left arm.

"Nope. Just thinkin' of my friends is all." He pushed himself up, pulling her with him. He rolled each of them a corn-husk cigarillo. She lit them with a candle.

"I got to go soon," he said after they had smoked their cigarillos down.

"You don't like me?" She was worried. She had heard about these big, arrogant *americanos*. So many of them would use a woman and then cast her aside. She had no real thoughts of marrying this broad-chested mountain man, but she did not want to be used and discarded either. She had thought Rawlins would be different. Suddenly she was no longer so sure.

"I like ye jist fine," he responded. "But I got work to do once the sun goes down."

"Then we have time left. *Mucho* time." She presented her lips to be kissed.

"Waugh! You're right, *señorita bonita*," he growled as he accepted her invitation.

It was half an hour before dusk when Rawlins finally rose from the bed, pulled on his fancy outfit and weapons. He bent and kissed Juanita one more time.

"Will I see you again, señor?" she asked.

"I expect ye will, señorita." Moments later he was out the door and heading up the quiet, crooked street.

3

"IT'S ABOUT TIME YOU got here," Saint Vrain scolded, not very seriously. He was too jovial a man to be angered by someone being a few minutes later than he had expected.

"Eat shit, ye black-bearded little frog," Rawlins responded. "There was this here purty little señorita just couldn't get enough of this ol' hoss. I couldn't just up and leave her."

"She must be touched by ze spirits, as my frains ze Cheyenne would say."

"She might be at that," Rawlins agreed with a laugh. "Well, your men ready to go?"

"*Oui*. I will go with you zis time," Saint Vrain said evenly.

Rawlins's eyes darkened. "Ye ain't accusin' me and my *compañeros* of tryin' to pull somethin' on ye, are ye, Ceran? Such doin's wouldn't shine with this ol' niggur."

"How long 'ave we been doing business with each other, eh? Four, maybe five years? Longer? You

should know me by now. If I suspected you were trying to cheat me, I'd tell you to your face, eh."

"Reckon ye would at that," Rawlins said, mollified.
Ceran Saint Vrain had certainly been of help to him
and his two partners more times than he could
remember. Just taking in the plews the way he did
made it easy for the trappers to keep them out of the
hands of the Mexican authorities. Then there was
three years ago, when Early and Adams had been
arrested in Santa Fe after a brawl. Rawlins and
Chardonnais had raced back to Taos and talked with
Saint Vrain. The fierce little Frenchman had assembled
a force of Americans, galloped to Santa Fe, and stood
off the entire garrison there. That was some, Rawlins
thought. No, he knew Saint Vrain would not be shy
about letting him know if there was a problem.

"I just want to get away from ze city a little, eh,"
Saint Vrain said.

"Cain't blame a chil' for that," Rawlins agreed.

It was fully dark when the men went outside,
around back of Saint Vrain's store. The French
Canadian had taken the liberty of having Rawlins's
horse saddled. It waited along with the other horses,
mules, and six workers in the yard behind the store.
They mounted up and rode out, reaching the spot
where the plews were about two hours before dawn.

"Best have your boys get some sleep, Ceran,"
Rawlins said. "There'll be a heap of work to be done
come daylight."

"Zis is nothing new for us, Abe," Saint Vrain said,
slightly reprovingly.

Rawlins nodded. "I'm jist tired and ain't thinkin'
right." He paused, then growled, "It really galls my ass
that we got to go through this goddamn foolishment

every goddamn year. Jesus, I wish those goddamn Mexicans weren't so goddamn fractious."

"But zey are," Saint Vrain said, "and our wishing it different won't make it so."

"You're a cheery bastard, ain't ye?" Rawlins complained.

"Get some sleep, *mon ami*."

Rawlins was uneasy in the morning, but he wasn't sure why. He and his partners had hidden their furs since they first went to Taos eight years ago. That had been on the advice of Etienne Provost. The next year they did it, too, and soon afterward, they had seen an American lose nearly every fur he had, confiscated by the Mexican authorities.

It had become rote by now for him and his friends to cache their furs here before going into Taos. In town, they would alert Saint Vrain. Then, under cover of night, one of the three partners would bring Saint Vrain's men out here to dig up the plews and bring them back into Taos.

Everything seemed fine to Rawlins, but still he had an uneasy feeling, and it gnawed at him. He put up with it for more than an hour. Then he jabbed his shovel into the small mound of dirt next to him. He wiped the sweat off his face and head with a bandanna and then strolled nonchalantly over to Saint Vrain. "I'm gonna take a look around, Ceran," he told the Frenchman.

"Is something wrong?" Saint Vrain didn't look very concerned.

"I ain't sure, but this critter's got a powerful itch 'tween his shoulders."

Saint Vrain nodded. "I'll have ze men keep digging."

"*Bueno.* But tell 'em to keep their weapons handy. Hell, there's always a chance I'll find some goddamn red devils out there." Still shirtless, he headed off into the bushes near where the men were digging. Once behind the brush, he moved faster, gliding silently along the dusty ground.

Rawlins headed swiftly up the mountain ridge in front of him—almost due north. From atop it, or its continuation around to the northwest and southeast, one could look straight down to where the men were working.

He stopped on the top of the rocky ridge and looked around. The southeast was dominated by Wheeler Peak. Closer to hand, the ridge and mountainous folds of land ran in a rough S pattern with Wheeler Peak in the center. South were the flats that meandered down to Taos. They continued at a northwest angle, narrowing between the ridge on which he was standing and one that ran almost straight north and south.

From the top of the ridge where he stood, it almost seemed as if he could see forever, at least toward the south. He knew it was not true—he couldn't even see Taos—but it gave the impression. There was nothing to the south but emptiness and blue sky. Such views struck some men down with their immensity, but Rawlins had never been one of those. Hell, this was a big land, anyone who was out here more than a few days knew that. It shouldn't humble a man. After all, the rocks and trees and plains and sky were not going anywhere, but man was unfettered, able to go wherever he pleased, if he had some gumption.

Rawlins turned to his left, following the ridge. It seemed as good a way to go as any. If there were Indians around, they could be anywhere among these ridges and canyons. And if there were Indians here, they would most likely be Jicarilla Apaches, men who knew these mountains intimately.

He moved swiftly but silently past boulders and trees—small cedars, junipers, and piñon pines mostly—eyes flicking back and forth, looking for sign of someone or something.

He was about to give up and turn back to check the other way when he saw a patch of dark blue. He couldn't tell what it was, but it definitely was out of place in these dull brown mountains. He moved forward, more cautiously.

He suddenly stopped and darted behind a young cedar. Then his eyes widened when he saw a Mexican soldier lying on the edge of the ridge twenty feet away. Rawlins's right hand fingered one of the single-shot pistols tucked into his belt and held in place by the iron strip that formed a clip. Then he moved his hand. If one of the *alcalde*'s *soldados* was around, there were sure to be others. He did not want to risk firing a shot that would alert them.

Instead, he pulled his tomahawk and rose. He headed toward the soldier, his movements almost ghostly. When he was only six feet away, he stopped. "Hey, *amigo*," he called softly.

The soldier jerked his head around, eyes wide with surprise and fright.

"Ye lost, ol' hoss?" Rawlins asked evenly.

"*No hablo inglés*," the soldier said.

"You don't, eh?" Rawlins mused. "Then I reckon ye won't mind was I to cut off your nuts and pitch 'em over the ridge there, eh?" He smiled to himself when he saw the light of recognition in the soldier's eyes. It had been as he expected. "Now that we got that established, hoss, how's about ye tell this here chil' just what the hell you're doin' up here spyin' on my camp."

"May I get up?" the soldier asked. His accent was thick, but the words were still understandable.

Rawlins nodded. "Throw your pistol over the edge there, hoss," he ordered. When the soldier had done so, Rawlins said, "Now the sword."

The soldier nodded and began easing out the sword. Halfway, he suddenly jerked it. With the weapon in hand, he felt much more confident. He had nothing to fear now from this foolish *americano*. "Now it is you who will throw away his weapons," he said arrogantly.

"In a pig's ass, ye bean-fartin' son of a bitch."

The soldier's eyes widened in surprise, then as quickly narrowed in anger. He flicked the sword once or twice, set himself, and then advanced, the weapon dancing ahead of him.

Rawlins waited until it was almost touching him. Then he moved. His tomahawk darted out and connected with the sword, seeming to latch onto it. With a flick of the wrist, he flipped the soldier's sword off and away. Before the Mexican could shout for help, Rawlins had split his forehead with the tomahawk. The Mexican kind of melted down to the ground.

"Teach ye to mess with this ol' chil'," Rawlins said calmly as he wiped the tomahawk blade off on the soldier's uniform front. He rose and stood a minute, wondering which way he could go. He was certain that other soldiers were around, and this bothered him. He was not afraid of any soldier, or any group of them. Their presence, though, meant that the *alcalde* of Taos suspected him and his partners of doing what they did with their furs every year. And if even one soldier got back to Taos with the news, Early and Chardonnais would be in danger, as would he when he got back to town.

He suddenly decided to head back the way he had come and follow the ridge around. He could see some distance along the ridge the way he had been going, and there appeared to be no more people in the vicinity. The other way, though, was heading generally toward Taos. If the soldiers had come up, they most likely would have stayed in that area. He suspected that the soldier he had just killed had been sent this far out to keep an eye out in case others—including Indians—came through the gap between the ridges.

Rawlins moved fast until he got to the spot where he had climbed up the ridge, then he slowed, not knowing when he would run into anyone else. Not far off, he spotted another soldier. He dropped to the ground and waited patiently. He saw no one else, though, and he crept forward.

Suddenly he pounced on the soldier's back, keeping him down. His left hand clasped tightly across the Mexican's mouth. The other hand brought his large knife up and rested it against the soldier's throat. "Speak English, hoss?" he asked in a deadly whisper.

The Mexican nodded, hoping the slight movement did not make the sharp blade pierce his neck flesh.

"How many others're with ye, hoss?"

The soldier mumbled against the hand, until Rawlins said, "Use your fingers."

The Mexican held out four fingers.

"All *soldados?*"

He held out three fingers. That surprised Rawlins considerably. One of them was not a soldier. He did not think for a moment that the *alcalde* himself had come along. So he wondered who the other man could be. He shrugged mentally. He would find out when he found out.

He slid the knife across the soldier's throat. The action was so smooth and sudden that it would have seemed to someone watching to have been casual. Rawlins continued lying across the soldier's back until the Mexican stopped jerking. Then he wiped his blade on the soldier's uniform, stood, put the knife back into his sheath, and stepped off again.

Disposing of the next soldier was as easy as the first two had been. Possibly even easier, considering that he made no effort to gain any information. He simply slipped up behind the Mexican, suddenly knelt on his back, jerked his head back with a hand over his mouth, and then made a swift, sure movement with the big blade.

Then he was on the move again, ignoring the sweat that dripped off his face and rolled down his sides and back. He was grateful, though, for the shade cast by Wheeler Peak some miles east. Soon after, he spotted two men squatting on a ridge overlooking the place where Saint Vrain's men were still working. Rawlins figured the two couldn't be more than a hundred yards from the one cache being dug up.

Rawlins paused behind a piñon to watch the two for a moment. One was a soldier, the other a civilian. There was something familiar about the civilian, but from this angle, he could not figure out who it was. The soldier had an air of command about him, and Rawlins figured he was a corporal, or maybe a low-ranking sergeant.

The mountain man pulled out both his pistols since he was outnumbered, and he no longer cared about the noise of a shot. If the second soldier he had slain had spoken the truth, these were the last two men here. If the soldier had been lying, there might be some real trouble soon.

Rawlins moved out again, heading cautiously toward the two men. Just because the first three Mexicans had been childishly easy to kill didn't mean these two would be as well.

He stopped about five feet behind the two, relishing the breeze that swept the ridge. "How's doin's, boys?" he said quietly.

Both Mexicans froze.

"Get up and turn slowly."

"Or what, *americano* pig?" the soldier asked arrogantly.

"A fifty-caliber ball'll do one hell of a lot of damage to a soft sack of shit like you at this distance, ye chili-fartin' son of a bitch," Rawlins said evenly. "It'd make a hell of a mess, but that won't bother this ol' chil' none."

"We're getting up," the civilian said hastily.

4

"YE GOT NAMES?" RAWLINS asked when the two had stood and turned to face him.

"I am Corporal Roberto Baca," the soldier said with a sneer. He was of medium height, and had a rapierlike build. His face had a hard, mean cast to it, heightened by deep-set eyes, dark skin, and a thin stripe of black mustache.

"Ye?" Rawlins asked, flicking his eyes at the other man.

"Carlos Navarro." He was a handsome man a little under medium height. His build was stocky, though not overly so. He had something of a feral look about him.

"Jist what'n hell're ye two goat-humpin' peckerwoods doin' here spyin' on my camp?" Rawlins asked.

"I owe you no answers," Baca said, his arrogance not diminished a bit. "You'll be dead in minutes." His accent was so thick as to make the words almost unintelligible.

"She-it, hoss."

"My men will—"

"Ye ain't got no more men," Rawlins said with the hint of a smile. "This ol' chil' made wolf bait of them ye brought with ye."

Baca looked shocked for a moment, then recovered. "You are good, señor," he said, his haughtiness returning. "You almost had me convinced."

"I think he's telling the truth, Corporal," Navarro said nervously, the words barely tinged with an accent.

"Bah, you are a coward, Carlos," Baca said.

"Call them," Rawlins suggested. "Bring them here to shoot this ol' hoss down." He spit. "Go on, ye goddamn arrogant walkin' sack of shit."

Baca suddenly shoved Navarro as hard as he could. Navarro gasped as he was propelled forward.

Rawlins managed to fire both pistols before Navarro slammed into him, but he was not at all sure he had hit either of his adversaries. He fell, with Navarro half on top of him. "Goddamn son of a bitch, get off me, hoss," he growled. He smacked Navarro on the side of the head with a pistol barrel and then shoved him off him.

As Rawlins got to his feet and dropped his pistols, he saw Baca just disappearing into the brush off to the side. He could hear horses there and figured that's where the man was headed.

Rawlins grabbed Navarro's collar and half hauled him up. "Get your ass up, hoss," he snarled. With Navarro standing, he ripped a couple of fringes from his pants. He tied them together and then bound the Mexican's hands behind his back. It took him only seconds, but he could hear a horse just beginning to run.

"Let's go, hoss," Rawlins said. He grabbed Navarro's collar again and dragged him toward the edge of the ridge. Without waiting, he leaped out, dragging the bound man with him.

Navarro screamed, but the sound was cut off when he hit the slope ten feet below the top of the ridge. Rawlins gave him a shove, and the two men tumbled down the banked land.

"Watch that critter," Rawlins said as he came to his feet at the bottom. He raced to where his saddle lay and yanked out his Fordney rifle. He ran straight west for some yards before sliding to a stop where he could see the flats heading south toward Taos. He swiftly checked his rifle and waited.

It wasn't long before Baca burst onto the flats from Rawlins's left about two hundred yards ahead. He was whipping his horse hard, now riding straight away from Rawlins. The mountain man fired.

A few heartbeats later—enough for him to begin to believe he had missed—Baca fell from his horse, which kept running.

Rawlins spun as Saint Vrain trotted up to him. "What ze hell . . . ?" the Frenchman said.

"Have somebody git that carcass out there," Rawlins ordered. "And the goddamn horse."

"*Oui,*" Saint Vrain said without hesitation. He turned and shouted orders in a combination of French, Spanish, and English.

Moments later two of the workmen galloped toward the body. One stopped at the corpse and dismounted; the other kept going. The second returned minutes later with the horse in tow. He stopped and helped the first throw Baca's body across his own horse. Then they returned.

While these two were on their mission Rawlins said to Saint Vrain, "There's three more of them critters up on the ridges." He pointed in the general direction. "Best have your boys fetch them down here, too, Ceran. And their horses're up that way." He pointed once again.

Saint Vrain gazed steadily at Rawlins for a moment, then shrugged. He issued more orders and the rest of his men left.

Rawlins and Saint Vrain walked to where Navarro was sitting, looking frightened and worried. There was some blood on the side of his head.

When they stopped, Rawlins began running some tow through his rifle barrel to clean it a little. Then he reloaded it.

While he worked Saint Vrain asked, "Would you mind telling me now just what ze hell all zis is about, eh?"

"I found them niggurs up there on the ridge spyin' on us. Four *soldados* and that chil'." He pointed to Navarro. "I asked the first hoss I found what was goin' on, but he pulled a sword on me. After that I wasn't so kindly disposed toward the other critters I found."

"You killed three soldiers?"

Rawlins shrugged. "Four, countin' that hoss out there."

"*Sacre bleu!* Zis will be trouble."

"Not near as much trouble as it would've been had that ol' hoss made good his escape."

Saint Vrain nodded, then sighed. "What were zey doing here?" he asked.

"I reckon this bean-suckin' son of a bitch we got here can tell us that." He glanced at Navarro. "Ain't that right, hoss?"

Navarro nodded, but looked like he had swallowed his tongue.

Soon all the men were back with their grisly burdens. The soldiers' horses were tied along with their own; the bodies were set down nearby, in the shade of some brush. Then they made a fire, roasted some meat they had brought from Taos, and made coffee.

After eating, they gathered around Navarro, squatting in a semicircle, their coffee cups in hand. They, too, seemed worried. All but one were Mexicans; this problem could have severe consequences for them back in Taos.

"Qué pasa, Carlos?" Rawlins asked. "What's up?"

"We were spying on you."

"Hell, I know that, hoss. Why?"

"Furs. I . . . I . . ." He stopped.

"Best tell it, hoss. It'll go a heap easier on ye."

Navarro looked from one hostile face to the next. He realized that his only possible chance to survive would be to talk and hope these men took that into account.

"I had heard of the way you—you and your partners—get your furs into Taos."

"Where'd ye hear that, hoss?" Rawlins asked harshly.

"Here and about," Navarro responded, shrugging. "You aren't the only ones who do it. When I saw you and the others come into Taos yesterday, I got to thinking. So I went to Corporal Baca, my brother-in-law. We worked it out that if we could find where you had hidden your furs, I would get half of them to bring in myself and sell. Roberto and his soldiers would take the other half to Taos and tell them he confiscated them from an *americano* who has no license to trap or trade in our country."

Rawlins nodded. It made sense. "You'd get yourself a heap of specie, and Corporal Shit'd be a real goddamn hero for the *alcalde.*"

"*Sí.* Everyone would be happy."

"*Merde,*" Saint Vrain breathed. "I wouldn't be happy. *Mais non!* And my frains, zey would not be happy."

Navarro shrugged. He could not be too concerned about this. A man had to worry about himself and his family first, then friends. One couldn't be too concerned about any American—he considered Saint Vrain an American—especially the swaggering mountaineers who had been invading Mexico for so many years now.

"Just how were you going to take ze plews?" Saint Vrain asked suspiciously.

"Roberto and his men were going to arrest you," Navarro said lamely.

"But how could you—" Saint Vrain stopped, his usually merry eyes flashing in anger. He let go with several long passages of French that Rawlins could not hope to understand, though he could pick out a few of them. They were not complimentary.

Saint Vrain finally wound down and looked at Rawlins. "You knew zis all along, didn't you?"

"Knew what?" Rawlins countered innocently.

"Zat zese whoremongers were going to kill us all so zey could get ze plews."

"Why would they do that? They'd just as soon arrest us and show us off to the people of Taos."

"*Merde,*" Saint Vrain muttered. "Zey could not arrest me and bring me back to Taos. I am a businessman and in ze good graces of ze *alcalde*. And if zey treat us bad zere, word will get out, and zen all ze mountaineers zat we know will pay a visit to Taos, eh. Like ze time when our frain Ezra was in ze jail in Santa Fe t'ree years ago."

"Cain't put nothin' past ye, ol' hoss,' Rawlins said with a tight grin. He paused. "Now that we all know that, what're we gonna do with this critter?"

"Zat is for you and I to decide, *mon ami*," Saint Vrain said, still angry. "Ze others, zey are just my workers, eh."

Rawlins shrugged. His face was hard. "That's up to you, ol' hoss. This chil' knows where his own stick floats."

Saint Vrain glanced up at him, stared for a moment, then nodded. *"Oui."* He turned to his men and told them to go back to their work.

"Can ye trust them critters?" Rawlins asked as he watched the workers leaving.

"I t'ink so. Zey have little reason to like ze soldiers. And zey know ze soldiers were planning to kill zem, too. Zey will keep quiet."

"Ye best hope so, ol' hoss."

Saint Vrain shrugged fatalistically. There was nothing he could do about the situation.

"Ye go on with the others, hoss," Rawlins said. "I'll take care of what needs doin' here."

"You're sure?"

"Yep."

"You will have no remorse about zis?" He seemed more interested than concerned.

"Nary a bit," Rawlins said calmly. "It don't shine with this ol' niggur for someone to plot to take my hair and steal my plews. I wouldn't have any remorse was he to come in here shootin'. I cain't think of no reason to have any just "cause we caught him aforehand."

"I suppose not." Saint Vrain walked away, muttering to himself a little, but he would do the same thing Rawlins was planning to do if the decision were up to him. It might not be a pleasant thing, but it was necessary. They couldn't let Navarro go. If they did, every soldier in Nuevo Mexico would be out after them, whether the *alcalde* of Taos liked them or not.

"Ye got any last prayers you'd like to say, hoss?" Rawlins asked Navarro.

The Mexican nodded sadly. He knew he was going to die in moments, but he could not hate Rawlins for killing him. He understood the trapper's reasoning. It could be no other way. He considered asking for clemency, telling Rawlins he would leave this area forever. But he did not. He knew the trapper would not believe him. He wouldn't if their positions were reversed.

"Best get to it then, hoss. We got us a heap of work to be done yet."

Navarro could almost hate Rawlins then. Not so much for what he was about to do, but for the insufferably calm demeanor with which he was going about it. Navarro said a prayer, addressing a silent supplication to the Virgin Mary. Finally he opened his eyes and looked up at his executioner. "I am ready, señor," he said evenly.

"Which way ye want it, hoss?"

Navarro almost smiled. "I get to choose the method of my own demise?" he responded. When Rawlins nodded, he said, "I choose old age, then."

"I can see as how you'd like that, but"—the trapper shrugged—"it ain't possible."

Navarro did smile this time. "Strangle me," he said quietly. He hoped he would see regret or fear or concern in Rawlins's eyes when the mountain man throttled him. He was disappointed.

Rawlins shrugged and stepped up. Grabbing Navarro's throat in his big hands, he squeezed. His eyes were blank. He did not feel good about this, but he had been called upon to do much worse things. All he was doing now was removing a man who had plotted to kill him, Saint Vrain, the seven helpers, and quite possible Early and Chardonnais later. It was, to him, only a matter of justice.

The deed took only moments, and then Rawlins eased the body down. He then walked back up the ridge, taking the longer but easier way around, to collect the pistols he had dropped. When he came back down, Saint Vrain's men looked to be just about done. He sat, a little away from Navarro's corpse, and reloaded his pistols.

5

THE DEAD WERE BURIED IN THE holes that had cached the furs, after Saint Vrain let his men rifle their pockets. Then everything was taken off the soldiers' horses, and whatever was of any use was divvied up by the men. The saddles, bridles, and other equipment was buried with the corpses. Then the horses were driven several miles north and sent running.

That meant they had to push it to get back to Taos while it was still dark. They also hurried in unloading the packs of plews from the mules.

"I wish we didn't have to do zis trading zis way," Saint Vrain said as he toted up what he owed Rawlins, Chardonnais, and Early.

"Such'd suit this chil' jist fine," Rawlins noted. "I don't understand these here boys makin' all this trouble for us. Jesus, we're bringin' in a heap of goddamn business for half the people in Taos, and everybody ought to know no bean-eatin' son of a bitch's gonna bring in the plews me and the other Americans do."

"Politics, *mon ami*. You know zat. And a game of

power, especially when it comes to outsiders like you and me."

Rawlins nodded. "Goddamn chili-eaters got their hands out for somethin' every goddamn minute." Then he grinned. "But as ye and Lucien'd say, *c'est la vie*, eh, ol' hoss?" Life was the way it was, and a man accepted it that way if he was to get ahead.

"Oui," Saint Vrain agreed tiredly. He was weary, not only from the long, hectic trip, but also from the press of business that made such trips necessary. In addition, he was a little worried about the trouble they had had on this trip. He was not afraid, but if it was found out, it could cause a lot of trouble for his business. He tried to push that out of his mind. There was nothing he could do to change it, and worrying about it wouldn't help. Such a thing, though, was easier said than done.

Saint Vrain finished his figuring. "I owe you and ze others t'ree t'ousand six hundred dollars, eh. Does zat sound right?"

Abe Rawlins was uneducated, but he could figure as well as anyone. He had found out some years ago that he could do most figuring in his head a lot faster than many a man could with pencil and paper. He toted the amount up quickly—nine packs of plews, each weighing between ninety and one hundred pounds. Saint Vrain was paying four dollars per pound of beaver, thus making the price somewhere between $3,200 and $3,600. Thirty-six hundred sounded fair, and that would give him and his two friends each twelve hundred dollars.

"That shines with this chil'," Rawlins said after a moment. "Pay out a few hundred now so me and the boys got us some cash to spread around. Them señoritas want their foofaraw, ye know. Damn if they ain't nearly as bad as squaws." He laughed, figuring the señoritas—and his Ute wife—were worth a fair amount of foofaraw.

Saint Vrain nodded absentmindedly as he pulled Mexican gold coins from an iron-bound wood box. He handed the money to Rawlins, who dropped it into his possible bag.

"Thankee kindly, Ceran," Rawlins said. He turned and walked out. It was close to dawn, but several gambling houses and cantinas were still going full out. On the chance that he would find his two friends in one of them, he started making the rounds.

He was a little wary for a while, just in case someone had heard of what had happened out by the caches. He figured this was unlikely, but he was wary just in case.

He did not find them in the first two cantinas he tried, nor in the first gambling house he visited. In the latter, however, a pretty young señorita caught his eye and he discarded plans to find his friends for the time being. Half an hour later, with an extra $128 in monte winnings in his pocket, he and Carmelita Ayala left Doña Montoya's.

They walked to Carmelita's darkened house, which surprised Rawlins a little. Carmelita was no tavern girl like Juanita. No, she was the daughter of one of the *ricos*, a rich man who had a large *hacienda* outside of Taos. Most of the *hacendados* also had a place in town, and they spent much of their time there in the summers, what with all the *fandangos*, balls, and festivals that were held.

His curiosity was answered when Carmelita led him into the house and put a finger to her lips.

"Your pa?" Rawlins asked in a whisper.

She shook her head. "He is at the *hacienda*," she answered, pulling on Rawlins's hand. "I don't want to wake my *tía*, Doña Graciela. She watches over me when Papa isn't here." She spoke with a strong accent, but her voice was so mellifluous that Rawlins did not care.

Then they were in her room. She lit a small candelabra, then turned and allowed Rawlins to kiss her. She stood on tiptoe and managed to get her tiny hands around his neck to hold his head close.

When she broke away, Carmelita was a little befuddled. She had heard her older friends talking about some of these wild Americans. Her friends considered most of them crude and boorish, but not nearly so possessive as Mexican men. They were also free with their money when it came to women. Her friends also had talked about the occasional American who was different—more like Mexican men in their lovemaking, while still retaining their wildness. She had not known what to believe of these tales and had waited impatiently until she was really old enough to find out.

Her first had been the suave, handsome son of another *hacendado*. The caballero had been arrogant, and impatient in their lovemaking. And he was done swiftly, satisfying himself but leaving her wanting. She was very disappointed.

Then she had tried an American, one of the traders rather than a trapper. He had been no better than the caballero, and in some ways even worse. His breath had been bad and his body reeked. He, too, was arrogant in his own way, thinking that she was receiving the best there was.

Two more Mexican men followed, one a caballero, the other a craftsman. The former had been haughty but managed to live up to it; the latter tried to sweep her away on the wings of passion, but was not up to the job. Carmelita appreciated the effort, but was still left wanting.

But now, with this large, broad-shouldered *americano,* she began to think she had found someone who could please her. She hoped so, since she had been left almost dizzy simply from one kiss.

She soon found other differences, too, between this man and the ones who had come before. Rawlins's hands were strong and rough, like the craftsman's. But they were far more knowing. His body was hard and muscular from a life of work, unlike the soft bodies of the caballeros, men who did little that was strenuous. Carmelita also found many scars on Rawlins's big torso and limbs, the record of battles with Indians and Mexican soldiers and Lord knew who else. They intrigued her, as did his pale flesh.

She had worried for a few moments that he might be impatient like the others when he placed her on the bed. Her fears fled when he began stripping her as she lay there, slowly peeling off her clothing, hands lingering here and there. Then, when she was nude, his hands and mouth and tongue really went to work on her. She soon was moaning and wriggling. She had never been made to feel like this before, and she suddenly wanted him inside her, so she tugged urgently at him.

"We got us plenty of time for such doin's, purty señorita," he said in a soft but still deep and strong voice. He kept on with what he was doing.

Carmelita bit back screams of pleasure, but could

do so for only so long. As an exquisitely pleasurable burning burst in her loins, and moved throughout her body, it forced a small, sharp scream past her parted lips. Then came a spreading warmth and contentment.

Carmelita's eyes widened when she realized that Rawlins's hands were continuing to caress her, bringing back the insistent thirst for another release.

With much regret, Carmelita finally told the trapper he had to leave. "Doña Graciela will be waking before long." She was lying on top of Rawlins, whose head was on the pillow. She rested her chin on her small hands, lying one atop the other high on Rawlins's chest.

"I reckon," the trapper said, continuing to run his hands up and down her smooth back. He lifted his head and ran his tongue around her lips. "But this ol' chil' wants another go."

A warm, sensuous smile spread across Carmelita's lips and she squiggled up along his body so she could kiss him properly.

Twenty minutes later he was dressed and being let out the back door. "Will I see you again?" she asked tentatively. The night had been incredible, but she didn't want this man thinking she was in love with him. She would love to make love with him again, but there was no way she would consent to marry him, if he ever had the audacity to ask.

Rawlins grinned. "That'd suit this ol' chil'."

Carmelita smiled back. She could see plenty of lust, but no love in the clear blue eyes. *"Bueno."*

He slipped through the gate in the fence at the rear of the courtyard and headed back toward Señora Rubio's. Just as he got there Early and Chardonnais stepped outside into the new day's still-feeble sunshine.

"Well, lookee here, Lucien," Early said. "If it ain't ol' . . ." He looked blank for a moment. "Goddamn, Lucien, he's been gone so long I plumb forgot the critter's name."

"Eat shit, *amigo,*" Rawlins said without rancor. Indeed, he was feeling pretty good, if somewhat tired. "You're jist all ruffled up 'cause I spent the night with some purty señorita whilst ye had to make do with that little frog fart over there."

"Hah," Chardonnais retorted. "You were probably layin' wit' some señora who was so old she didn't have no hair or teeth."

"No eyesight or sense of smell either," Early added. "Else she would've sent him packin' straight off."

"Goddamn," Rawlins said with a shake of the head, "I knew ye hosses envied me for my handsomeness, my trappin' skills, and my largeness." He grabbed his crotch. "But I didn't know ye was so bad off in a jealous way as to treat this chil' so poorly when he's just scored himself such a coup."

They all laughed.

"Ye critters headin' to break your fast?" Rawlins asked when the laughter faded away.

Early nodded. "How're you fixed for such doin's?"

"Ain't filled my meatbag since afore we left the caches yesterday eve. This ol' chil' could eat hisself a mule, hair and all."

They started walking down the street. "I'm about half froze for some of Gonzalez's *machaca de huevos,*" Rawlins said.

"Buffler shit," Early said with a laugh. "Ye just want to get your hands on that pretty young daughter of his."

Rawlins laughed, too. "She-it," he offered, "I counted coup on that 'un the first night we got to Taos. Afore I took Ceran and the others out to get the plews."

"Waugh!" Early said. "He is some now, ain't he, Lucien?"

"Bah, he t'inks he is de big man because he 'umps two women in t'ree days here. Hah, dis chil', he 'as had four already," Chardonnais boasted.

"Well, shit, Lucien," Rawlins countered, "if ye could keep your pizzle hard more'n two goddamn minutes, ye might not need so many 'cause the others keep throwin' ye out."

"He's got ye there, Lucien," Early said with a laugh.

"Don' you speak to me about such t'ings, Monsieur Can't Get a Señorita," Chardonnais said, as if his dignity were hurt.

"None?" Rawlins said with a laugh. "Ye been in town near three days and ye ain't humped a single señorita? Jesus, Ez, you're a plumb goddamn disappointment to this hoss. Christ, I don't know as if I even want to be seen in public with ye no more."

"Well, hell, go on and leave if'n you're of a mind to," Early said. "It don't matter none to this ol' chil'. Just 'cause ye two'd hump anything that's got tits—includin' a buffler cow—don't mean every chil's got to do the same. I'm some discriminatin' when it comes to the women I bed."

"You're only so discriminatin' because the señoritas in Taos are so choosy," Rawlins countered. "Most of 'em—the worthwhile ones anyway—got more sense than to let you hump 'em."

"Mais oui!" Chardonnais agreed. "Dem mademoi-

selles, dey like *les grands hommes.* Like dis chil',", he bragged, jabbing his chest with a thumb.

"And this 'un," Rawlins added.

Chardonnais couldn't resist. "Dey accept you and your tiny pizzle only when dey can't have me," he boasted.

"Christ, listen to the cocky little bastard," Rawlins said. "Goddamn, this ol' hoss agrees with him, and he still ain't happy. Ungrateful little frog fart."

They shut up when they entered Gonzalez's. As they sat Juanita saw them, and favored Rawlins with an inviting smile. He grinned back at her and then cast a smug look at his two friends.

Early and Chardonnais said nothing, but they soon learned to appreciate Juanita's affection for Rawlins, since it meant they got friendly, quick, and efficient service. And because the girl was the owner's daughter, the three mountain men also got heaping portions of food, and their coffee cups were never empty.

Finally, though, the three sat back. Early lit a pipe while Rawlins and Chardonnais rolled and lit cigarillos.

"How'd the doin's with Ceran go?" Early asked.

6

EARLY AND CHARDONNAIS SAT in silence while Rawlins explained what had happened. When he was finished, Early asked, "Ye sure ye made wolf bait out of all of 'em?"

"This chil' don't leave such doin's undone," Rawlins said flatly, annoyed that his partner would even think to ask.

Early nodded. "Then there ain't no chance the *alcalde* or any other goddamn greaser official'll find out?"

"Not that this chil' can figure." He paused, squinting through his *cigarito* smoke. "Based on what those critters said afore I put 'em under, weren't nobody in Taos knew what they were up to. Even if the *alcalde* figures out four of his men're gone, he won't have no inklin' of what happened to 'em."

"I expect you're right, ol' hoss," Early agreed. He and his two friends put the matter out of their thoughts.

Rawlins crushed out his *cigarito*. He reached into

his possible sack and brought out the gold coins. He counted out two hundred for Early and the same for Chardonnais. "We got credit for another thousand each over at Ceran's. I figure this much'll keep us goin' for a spell."

Rawlins rose, yawning. "Well, this ol' chil's well past needin' some robe time. *Adios, amigos.*" He awoke in time to eat dinner and then slick himself up for a *fandango* that night, held in the courtyard of Don Tomas Rojas. He joined his two friends on the walk to the Rojas's Taos hacienda.

The *fandango* was a small one—perhaps only fifty people attending, nearly equally divided between men and women. Rawlins and his partners were the only real Americans there, though Ceran Saint Vrain showed up. Charles Bent—on one of his rare stays of more than a day or two in Taos—appeared after a spell to pay his respects to Rojas and talk briefly with Saint Vrain.

Bent came up to Rawlins, Early, and Chardonnais while they were buying a jug of Taos lightning. "I hear you had some trouble gettin' your plews in this year, Abe," Bent said by way of greeting.

"Well, how's doin's to you, too, hoss," Rawlins said sarcastically. Charles Bent might be a partisan and all, but Rawlins was a free trapper and bound to no one. He didn't have to take any nonsense from Bent.

"Eh, what's that?" Bent said. He seemed almost dazed.

"Ye need to spend a heap less time on that goddamn trail, Charlie," Rawlins said, "and a heap more 'round here, with some purty little señorita."

Bent laughed a little self-consciously. "I'm thinkin'

you're right about that, Abe. But I can't afford the time."

"That's your lookout, hoss," Rawlins said flatly. "But don't you get your bowels all twisted in a knot and come 'round here botherin' me with it." Any man who put business ahead of pleasure every day of his life was a damn fool as far as Abe Rawlins was concerned.

"It is my business," Bent said sourly. "Now, Ceran tells me there was a heap of trouble up by the caches."

"Yep."

Bent waited for some seconds, until he realized that there would be no more forthcoming from Rawlins. "Well, goddammit, what happened?"

"Ceran ain't told ye?" Rawlins countered.

"Of course he's told me," Bent snapped. "I want to hear it from you."

"Eat shit, hoss," Rawlins said evenly. "I ain't of a mind for gabbin' with the likes of ye jist now." He wasn't angry, but he was going to become so if Bent kept pressing him.

"Jesus Christ, Abe," Bent retorted, "I got to know what happened." He grabbed Rawlins's arm.

Rawlins grabbed Bent's hand and peeled the fingers off his arm. "Charlie," he said coldly, "me and ye go back a ways, but if ye put your hand on me agin, I'm gonna raise your hair."

Bent looked shocked, then grinned stiffly and nodded. "You think there'll be trouble here over it?" he asked. He was not a man to apologize for anything he did.

"Nope. Not 'less'n one of your workers opens his mouth."

"That ain't likely. Not considerin' how my men feel about the soldiers and the other officials."

"My thinkin', too, hoss."

The cloud of gloom seemed to lift from Bent. He suddenly grinned for real. "How'd you boys do?"

"Better'n middlin'," Rawlins answered.

"Then how's about you buy me a drink. I'm one parched ol' chil'."

"Hell, Charlie, ye got more money'n God," Rawlins snapped, but he was smiling. "Ye can afford to buy everybody in Taos a drink and here you're tryin' to get us poor niggurs to pay for ye."

"Goddamn, you're an insufferable son of a bitch, Rawlins," Bent said with a laugh.

Rawlins and his two friends also laughed, and he handed Bent the jug. "But seein's how we're already supplied and ye don't look like ye could make it as far as yon bar, ye might's well have a taste of ours."

"Thankee, boys." Bent tilted the jug up and drank thirstily. He handed the jug back and wiped his mouth with the back of a hand. "Damn, that sets well in this beaver's stomach," he said. "Well, ye boys have a shinin' time tonight," he added just before he walked away.

"That chil's got the hair of the b'ar on him," Rawlins commented. He took another drink and then handed the jug to Chardonnais. "Now, I see me some purty señorita I'm fixin' to set my trap for." He walked off.

Suddenly Hobart Adams, an attractive young woman, and a well-dressed Mexican youth stepped in front of him. "Abe, I'd like you to meet my brother-in—"

"Later, hoss," Rawlins growled as he saw some

fancified caballero heading for the woman he had chosen for his target. "This chil's got business to tend to." He shoved on by and kept walking.

Adams's eyes widened, and his face colored with a little anger. He turned with Dolores and his brother-in-law, Diego Ortega y Delgado, to watch Rawlins's departing back. "Well that son of . . ." He smiled weakly at his wife. "Sorry, my dear."

Dolores smiled back. She was certain she was as happy as any woman had ever been, and she found it very difficult to ever be angry at her man, though she could easily be angry at others who hurt him.

"Is he one of your friends?" Diego asked, the last word contemptuous.

Adams nodded. "Yep. Abe Rawlins. He's always been a little standoffish around me, but never . . ." He suddenly chuckled.

"What's so funny, my love?" Dolores asked, confused.

"I should've known," Adams replied, pointing. "He had his eye on one of those señoritas, and she was about to be asked to dance by someone else."

"You Americans are all alike, aren't you?" Dolores said with a laugh.

"Only till we meet the one woman for us," Adams answered half-seriously. He did not see the flicker of anger on Diego's face. "Well, Diego, come on. I'll try to introduce you to the others before they're off on their quest. Especially Lucien."

"He's that little Frenchman? The one who can't stop . . .?" Dolores began.

"Yes, that's the one," Adams said hastily. Taking Dolores's arm, he steered her around people, heading for where Early and Chardonnais were still standing, passing the jug. Adams thought it so odd that Early had saved him more than three years ago now, he had been married to Dolores more than two years, and yet none of his three mountain-man friends had met any of Dolores's family. She had met them as they had pulled out that fall, but that was it. By the time the three mountain men could leave—after Adams had accomplished what he needed their help to do—it had been so late that they had little time for visiting. They simply bought their supplies as quickly as they could, packed their mules, and rode off.

As she neared the two, Dolores took stock of them. It had been almost three years since she had seen them, but she remembered them quite well.

Like Rawlins, Early was maybe an inch on the tall side of six-foot, with a broad chest, wide shoulders, and a slim waist. A wad of tobacco bulged in his cheek, as one so often did. Curly, dark brown hair tumbled thickly onto his shoulders. He was clean-shaven and, unlike Rawlins, did not sport a mustache. He had faded gray eyes, a nose that had been mashed flat, and his left cheekbone was distorted, the result of a Blackfoot war club. He wore a tight, soft buckskin shirt that his Ute wife, Falling Leaf, had painstakingly decorated with tiny bits of silver, beads, and porcupine quills. The sleeves were fringed with long buckskin whangs. His buckskin pants also were fringed along the outside seams, and the bottoms flared ever so slightly. Shirt and pants were so finely tanned as to be almost white. His soft moccasins were decorated in a pattern similar to the one on his shirt, and a tiny bell on each tinkled as he moved. A rawhide thong around his neck held a heart-shaped piece of leather through which was stuffed a small clay pipe. His crowning glory, however, was a beaver top hat, which he wore only rarely.

Chardonnais was not nearly as tall as either Rawlins or Early and was rather bowlegged. Not that such things bothered him, but it did give his two friends plenty of opportunity for ribbing him. He was, typically, the most colorful of the three. Below his red calico shirt, he wore buckskin pants that were decorated heavily with bright beads, porcupine quills, and bits of metal. His moccasins were marked with a striking pattern of blue, green, and white beads. And his omnipresent bright red sash was in place. A small patch knife dangled by a thong around his neck, as did a large, heart-shaped ornament of silver.

Rawlins's long legs carried him swiftly to the young woman. He almost gently elbowed aside the young caballero who was about to ask her to dance, smiled brightly, and asked instead.

The woman—Esperanza Quinoñez, he learned shortly—smiled a little. She figured that this big, hard-looking *americano* must want to dance with her badly if he had shoved that poor young caballero out of the way like that. She consented.

Rawlins was, for all his size, bulk, and muscularity, a far more accomplished dancer than either of his two close friends. Ezra Early was hopeless on the dance floor, and people soon learned to give him a wide berth whenever he was torturing some señorita to a musical accompaniment. Chardonnais was a little better, but only a little. Rawlins had taken more than a fair share of ribbing from his two friends about his seemingly natural gracefulness.

He surprised all the señoritas that he had ever danced with, and Esperanza was no exception. Though she had favored him with this dance, she was certain that her feet would ache by its end from being stomped on by another boorish American. The surprise, when it came, was pleasant.

After the dance, he asked for another. Esperanza nodded, but said, "The next one, *por favor*. I must catch my breath."

Rawlins nodded and escorted her back to her seat. As he straightened and turned to watch the other dancers, someone slapped him in the face with a small glove.

"I challenge you, señor," the young man he had shoved out of the way said. His face was tight with anger.

Rawlins sized up his challenger. He was about twenty years old, stood perhaps five-foot-eight, and couldn't weigh more than one hundred sixty, Rawlins figured. He had a handsome, if rather slack-looking face, with bright eyes, a long, aquiline nose, and thin lips.

"Best mosey on, hoss," Rawlins suggested, "afore ye make me angry."

The young man sneered. "You are afraid of me, then, señor?"

Rawlins laughed.

"Don't laugh at me, señor!" the young man snapped.

"What's your name, boy?" Rawlins asked.

"Raul Aguilar," he said with dignity.

"Well, then, Señor Aguilar, I'll tell ye agin— mosey on, hoss."

"You won't accept my challenge?" Aguilar asked, surprised. These Americans always seemed ready to fight.

"It don't shine with this ol' chil' to shed blood durin' a *fandango*. Especially children's blood." That was stretching it, he thought, considering that he wasn't more than ten years older than Aguilar.

The Mexican was close to tears from anger. He slapped Rawlins again. "You coward!" he said in rage. He reared back and threw a punch at the mountain man.

Rawlins caught Aguilar's fist in the palm of a hand and clamped down on it. "You're foolin' with the wrong chil' here, hoss," he said harshly.

"Either fight him or leave, señor," Esperanza said quietly.

Still holding Aguilar's fist in his hand, Rawlins half turned to look at the woman. "Ye want this boy dead?" he asked.

"Of course not, señor. What I want is to have the next dance with you. But Señor Aguilar will only persist in bothering us. I would hope that would teach him a lesson. I don't think it should be necessary to kill him."

"Expect not." Rawlins looked at Aguilar. "I'll face ye, hoss, but we'll take it outside of Señor Rojas's courtyard."

Aguilar nodded, and then rubbed his fist when Rawlins released it.

"Ye can bring a friend with ye, if you're of a mind, hoss," Rawlins said. "I'll even let ye bring two."

"I won't need them. I have my pistol."

"Ye challenged me, hoss," Rawlins said flatly. "That means I get to pick the weapons. I choose fists." A fist fight—or even a brawl—would do the least amount of damage to Aguilar, he figured. There were few men in Taos who could match him with pistol, rifle, knife, or tomahawk, and all those who could were Americans.

"So be it," Aguilar said. "Outside the courtyard. Five minutes."

"I'll be there, hoss. Don't ye fret none." Rawlins turned to Esperanza, lifted her hand, and kissed it lightly. "You'll wait for me?" he asked, keeping most of the sarcasm out of his voice.

"*Sí, señor.*" She was fascinated by this man and wanted to experience him as fully as she could. She also had no doubt, knowing how Americans were, that he would win the fight even if Aguilar brought two friends with him.

Rawlins saw Aguilar and another young man coming and stepped out from the shadows. "Ye ready, ol' hoss?" he asked.

"*Sí,*" Aguilar said tightly. He nodded toward the other man. "This is my friend, Bernardo Ruiz."

Rawlins shrugged. "Let's get these doin's over with, boys. I got me a purty little señorita in there a-waitin' for me." He paused, then added, "Ye know, this ain't necessary."

"I'm not afraid."

"Didn't say ye was. Ye want to get the shit kicked out of ye for the hell of it, hoss, I don't mind doin' it for ye."

"We will see who gets beaten," Aguilar said. He suddenly charged.

It was over in less than two minutes. Rawlins let Aguilar come at him, and then jarred him with a stiff forearm to the face. As his opponent reeled, he grabbed him and spun, shoving Aguilar away from him in the same motion.

The young man hit the adobe wall around Rojas's courtyard and sagged to the ground with a muffled groan.

Before Rawlins could turn again, Ruiz had jumped on his back and locked his legs around his middle. One arm was around the trapper's face, and the other pounded the side of his head, though the shots were weak.

"Waugh!" Rawlins muttered. He reached up, pried Ruiz's arm loose, and then by sheer strength broke it.

Ruiz's scream was partly muffled by Rawlins's back. The music from inside the courtyard would take care of the rest. The Mexican's legs slipped down and touched the ground.

Rawlins grabbed him by the shirt and sent him sailing into the wall, where he fell alongside his friend.

Rawlins shook his head at the foolishness of youth. Then he smiled. He had been even worse than these two at their age. He turned and headed into the courtyard—and to Esperanza.

7

RAWLINS GOT TO MEET ADAMS'S brother-in-law a few days later. Esperanza Quinoñez had turned out to be one hell of a woman, and Rawlins didn't get out of his room at Señora Rubio's for three days. Señora Rubio was understanding about such matters and provided food for the two. Rawlins's partners supplied whiskey, wine, and an occasional bawdy serenade from outside.

Finally, though, both Esperanza and Rawlins were sated, and the trapper escorted the woman home, spending a considerable sum on foofaraw for her. He was eating breakfast—at a place other than Gonzalez's, considering he really didn't want to see Juanita just yet—when Adams and his entourage tracked him down.

"Mind if we set?" Adams asked.

"Nope." He pointed his fork at Diego. "This here the chil' ye wanted me to meet, hoss?"

"Yes. You remember Dolores, yes?"

"Hell, boy, even an ol' chil' like me couldn't forget

57

a woman so pleasin' to the eyesight as Señora Adams."
He smiled brightly.

Dolores returned the smile, but she was stunned.
She would never have believed that a loud, uncouth
American like Abe Rawlins could be so gallant and so
charming. "Why, thank you, Señor Rawlins," she
said, still flustered.

"Name's Abe, ma'am. It don't shine with this ol'
hoss to be called señor, or even mister."

"Abe, this is Diego Ortega y Delgado, my wife's
youngest brother."

Rawlins put down his fork and looked at the boy.
He was fourteen or fifteen, of less than medium
height, and thin, though he had a certain wiriness
about him. Clear eyes gazed steadily at him. Diego
was dressed well, with expensive wool pants that had
silver-dollar-size conchas up each side, a matching
Taos jacket, and a billowy white shirt."

"How's doin's, ol' hoss?" Rawlins asked, holding
out his hand.

Diego shook the hand tentatively, but kept his
gaze on Rawlins. He was not about to be made to feel
inferior by one of these crude American trappers.
Abiding his brother-in-law was bad enough.

"This chil's fine, too," Rawlins said with only a
touch of sarcasm. He went back to eating. "Ye
folks're free to order here and fill your meatbags. I'll
pay."

"We've already eaten, Abe," Adams said, "but
some coffee'd be good." He called the waiter over and
ordered a new pot of coffee, plus cups for himself,
Dolores, and Diego.

By the time it all came, Rawlins was done and
had pushed his plate away. He rolled a cigarillo and

lit it before pouring himself a new cup of coffee. He leaned back and asked, "So what're ye doin' with yourself these days, ol' hoss?"

"Some work for my father-in-law," Adams answered with a lack of enthusiasm. "I'm still selling my drawings, too. They seem to be quite popular hereabouts." A decided note of excitement had crept into his voice. "I've been trying for some time to get paints and canvas so that I might do some real artwork. They finally arrived not long ago, so now I can get started. They should bring in a considerable sum."

"Sounds like ye made 'em come again, ol' hoss," Rawlins commented. Then he waited for one of the others to say something. He had run out of small talk, but he assumed that Adams wanted him to meet Diego for some reason. If the assumption was not correct, well, there was nothing wrong with silence.

Adams did not feel the same about it, and within minutes he was beginning to fidget. He asked Rawlins a few questions about the previous trapping season, but when he got limited responses, he gave up. Finally he rose. "Well, Abe, I think we'd better be going."

Rawlins stood, surprising Dolores again. He did it yet again when he kissed the back of her hand gently. "*Adios,* Señora Adams," he said quietly. "Maybe we can fill our meatbags again sometime when I'm a little more clearheaded." He smiled in self-deprecation. "I been wrasslin' with a little too much *awerdenty* the past few days," he lied smoothly.

"I understand, señor . . . Abe," Dolores said, trying to hide her befuddlement.

Rawlins turned to Diego. "Nice meetin' ye, hoss," he said, shaking hands with the youth again. "Ol' Bart there ary gives ye too much of a hard time, ye come see me. This chil'll fix him good.

Diego didn't know quite what to make of this man. He had never expected politeness and even joking from him. He was determined not to like Rawlins, though, and tried to keep that in mind.

Adams and his two companions left, and Rawlins sat again, relieved that they were gone. He was never comfortable in such situations, though he always seemed to pull them off with aplomb. Still, he felt much better when such things were over with.

A couple of weeks later Adams and Dolores had Rawlins, Early, and Chardonnais to their home for supper. Don Francisco and Doña Maria—Dolores's father and mother—were there, as was Diego. The three mountain men had been invited to bring women, if they so chose. All three did.

Rawlins decided to be a little perverse, and he asked Juanita Gonzalez to go with him.

She had at first refused. "I can't go to a *rico*'s house looking like this," she said plaintively, pointing to her poor clothes.

"I ain't expectin' ye to."

"But these and another set just like them are all I have." She was close to tears. She wanted to go something awful, but she would not embarrass herself, Rawlins, or her father by appearing in a house run by Hobart Adams in such poor clothing.

"Well, hell, woman, there's a heap of stores in Taos. We can get ye a fancified outfit."

"I don't have the money for that, Señor Rawlins. You know that."

"It don't shine with this chil' to be called cheap, señorita," he said a little harshly.

"You will buy me these things?" Juanita asked, tears stopping, face brightening.

"'Course I will, woman. Ye think I'd expect ye to do so?"

That's exactly what she had thought, but she was not about to admit it. "I was just making sure," she said lamely.

Juanita looked mighty good to him when Rawlins escorted her into the Adamses' home. Don Francisco looked at her a little askance, but said nothing. The only other person who seemed to think there was something slightly odd about Juanita's presence there was Diego, who kept staring rudely at her.

The looks made her uncomfortable, but it took Rawlins a little while to realize this. When he did, he excused himself. Looking at Diego, he said, "Let's me and ye go get some more wine for the table, hoss."

"No," Diego said flatly. He was not about to be ordered around by such a lout. Not when there were servants to do such things.

Adams looked at Rawlins in confusion, then figured something was up. "Go with him, Diego," he said sternly.

Diego glared at his brother-in-law a moment, then rose and headed to the other room. Just inside the door, Rawlins grabbed him by the shirt and hoisted him up and plunked the youth's rear end down on a worktable.

"Your starin' at her is makin' Juanita some uncomfortable, hoss, and that makes this ol' chil' displeased. Ye keep it up and I'll correct your poor manners for ye."

"You'd not dare to do anything to me," Diego said scornfully. "Not while my father's around."

"Your father don't mean shit to me, hoss," Rawlins said flatly.

"He has many *vaqueros.*"

"He ain't got enough to cause me any worry, hoss. I've been set after before by *vaqueros,* as well as *soldados.* Your pa and all his men don't frighten me none."

"Diego had the sudden chilling realization that Rawlins was telling the truth, and he gulped.

"Ye think ye can behave yourself, hoss?"

Diego nodded.

"*Bueno.* Now grab that bottle of wine there and let's get back to the others."

Diego spent the rest of the evening alternating between hate, anger, fear, and sullenness.

Not long after the meal, the don and doña left for their own home, taking Diego with them. The other eight decided that they would go to Doña Montoya's for a few hours of gambling.

That panicked Juanita a little. She gambled, of course, as did nearly every other woman in Taos. But she had never had the clothes or the money to go into Doña Montoya's.

Rawlins winked at her, and under cover of night as they walked to the gambling parlor, he slipped her some gold coins.

Also on the walk, Adams and Dolores moved up to walk alongside them. "You and Diego have a falling-out or something?" Adams asked. He had learned a long time ago that frankness among these men was considered proper.

"I wouldn't say that," Rawlins said.

"You had a talk with him, though, didn't you?"

"Yep.

"What about?"

"None of your concern, hoss," Rawlins said evenly.

Adams was annoyed, but there was nothing he could do about it. And, truly, it wasn't his business.

The next time Rawlins saw Diego was more than a week later. He was heading to Gonzalez's for supper—and, he hoped, a rendezvous with Juanita. The young woman was still basking in the glow of his generosity and so was disposed toward being mighty friendly. He had been with her three nights since that one.

Rawlins was alone this time. Chardonnais was off with some woman somewhere, which was often the case. Early had the remains of a hangover and was not interested in food, despite the lateness of the hour. So Rawlins had gone off on his own.

He was just entering a dark alley, lit only by a few sputtering torches on building walls, when he saw two men holding another up against the wall. The dull torchlight caught the glittering of steel blades.

Rawlins touched his pistols, making sure they could be pulled out easily, and made sure his knife and tomahawk were in place. When he closed in on the trio, he saw that the one pinned against the adobe wall was Diego.

The two robbers looked up at his approach. "Move on, *americano*," one snarled in poor English. Both were short and stocky, running to fat. Their faces were scarred from dozens of fights, and each had a deadly look in his eyes, Rawlins could see when the torchlight was just right.

"Ye two boys think you're enough to handle that critter?" he asked sarcastically.

"This is none of your business, *marrano*—filthy pig," the second said.

"Let the boy go, ye fart-suckin' scavengers," Rawlins growled. He had had about his fill of these two.

One grinned. It was an awful sight. He said something in Spanish to his partner and then advanced, knife in hand.

Rawlins pulled out a pistol. The man stopped. He looked a little disappointed. "And here I thought you had some *cojones, amigo,*" he said.

Rawlins nodded. "Hell, shootin' a critter like you'd be a waste of damn good powder and ball." He shoved the pistol back into his belt and pulled out the big, wicked knife. "I got the *cojones,* hoss," he said flatly. "But ye won't have yours much longer."

The Mexican advanced slowly, knife making darting little circles ahead of him. Rawlins stood there cockily, waiting. Then the Mexican charged, knife cutting vicious arcs as it moved toward Rawlins's chest.

The trapper fended off the blows and gave way a little bit. The Mexican was far better with the knife than he had expected, and suddenly his blade darted in and then out, leaving a six-inch gash in Rawlins's left arm.

Rawlins felt the blood, and with it rose his anger. Most of the rage was directed at himself for underestimating this man. He looked at the grinning, fat face and let the anger build a little more. "You've had your chance, hoss," he growled low in his throat. "Ye won't get another.'

The Mexican was cocky now. As had happened so often, his looks had fooled this hulking *americano*. Now he had the upper hand. He moved in again.

As the Mexican made his next move for his heart, Rawlins threw up his bloody left arm. His left hand grabbed the Mexican's right wrist—the one that held the knife. He jerked two quick punches into the man's face, his right fist made harder by the hilt of the knife it encompassed.

Rawlins spun toward the Mexican's back, twisting the knife arm up as he did. He suddenly freed that wrist and his left hand snaked up to grab the man's greasy hair. He jerked the Mexican's head back with that hand and swiftly slid the blade across his exposed throat.

Rawlins shoved the gurgling bandit away from him and turned. The second bandit spun and ran.

"Ye all right, hoss?" the trapper asked, walking up to Diego.

The youth nodded, looking sick.

Rawlins stepped between the still-gasping corpse and the youth, blocking Diego's view. "Time ye was home and in bed, boy," he said quietly.

8

THE FEW DOZEN AMERICANS in Taos held themselves one hell of a *fandango* for Independence Day. The Mexican officials were not happy with the visitors flaunting their independence in such a way, but they had little recourse other than to start a war with the United States, and that was out of the question.

Most of the other Mexicans in town—even those who were not particularly fond of Americans in general—thought it a great time, and they helped in the celebrations. For them it was as good a reason for a festival as any other.

It was a day of feasting, dancing, fireworks, and drinking. The Taos lightning flowed with a free hand, and more than one man—Mexican or American— was out of the festivities before nightfall.

Rawlins wasn't that bad, but by the time Independence Day was over, he was one of the casualties of John Barleycorn.

Rawlins awoke the next morning feeling like his

insides had been taken out and used to sweep the town and then replaced. He lay in his bed at Señora Rubio's most of the day, doing little more than moaning. He managed to keep from vomiting, but he wasn't sure that was the best idea either. Better to clean the poisons out of his system, he figured, but there was a certain point of pride in not vomiting.

Just before dark, he roused himself and staggered outside. He went to the nearest restaurant and found his two friends. He was infinitesimally cheered when he saw that they appeared to be in even worse shape than he was. He managed to down two bowls of weak stew and several cups of coffee, the first laced with whiskey. That helped settle his stomach a little.

"Ye hosses remember much about last night?" he asked.

Early and Chardonnais shook their heads.

"Must've been a hell of a *fandango*," he said, trying for a note of cheeriness. It didn't work.

"Waugh!" Early groaned. "This chil's gettin' too goddamn old for such doin's. Christ A'mighty, I feel like I was et up by a bear and shit out by the critter the same day."

His friends agreed to all points made.

Rawlins finally pushed himself up. "Ye hosses can stay here groanin' all ye like, but this chil' aims to get some more robe time. Might even try'n remember me a prayer or two to see if'n that helps." He lurched outside, grateful that it was dark. He suspected the sunlight would fry his eyeballs right out.

Two days later he—and his partners—were back to their old selves, feeling their oats and raising hell around Taos. But they knew their time was growing short. They would have to start picking up supplies and such and get ready to leave in less than a month if they wanted to find good trapping grounds before the high country started getting choked off by snow.

Nowadays, when the three partners were together, their talk almost always turned to the coming season at some point. It was usually after they exhausted their friendly insults over each other's prowess with women and such, but it became something of a cloud that hung over them.

Hobart Adams occasionally tracked them down in some cantina and sat with them, drinking or gambling. He left the wenching to the others, though, not wanting to hurt Dolores. The others, surprisingly to him, did not deride him for it, though they often made some jokes, ones that he knew were meant in a spirit of friendship.

Much to his surprise, all the talk about the mountains and Utes and beaver and Blackfeet and buffalo and high snows and monstrously cold temperatures made him feel wistful. He had become close to these three men, yet he had never really shared anything with them outside of Taos.

Such thoughts would end, though, as soon as he caught a glimpse of Dolores. He had never thought he could love someone so deeply, and he did not regret it in the least. Dolores was everything he could want in a woman and yet far, far more. There was no way he could leave her for any length of time. That was why he had taken her to New York.

Adams saw less and less of his friends as the summer pressed on. It seemed as if the three mountain men were trying to cram as much frivolity as they could into their last few weeks in Taos. They were constantly on the prowl for willing señoritas, more often than not had a jug in hand, and they ate prodigiously. Still, Adams would spend time with them when he could.

It was several weeks after Rawlins had saved Diego from the bandits that the youth mentioned the incident to his brother-in-law. He was still amazed that a man like Abe Rawlins had done such a thing.

"Those men're like that, Diego," Adams said. "At least those three. They don't go out of their way to find friends, but they'll generally help those of us who can't do for ourselves very well. If they weren't like that, Ezra would've never helped me back there on the Santa Fe Trail. Most others wouldn't have."

The next day Adams made a point of finding Rawlins. It took some doing, but late in the afternoon he succeeded. The trapper was just about to make his way to Gonzalez's. "You mind if I speak with you, Abe?" Adams asked.

"Nope. How's doin's, señora?" Rawlins said, addressing Dolores, who was with Adams.

"I'm well, Abe."

They began walking, with Adams on Rawlins's right and Dolores on his left.

"Diego told me yesterday what you did for him a few weeks ago," Adams said.

"'Twarn't nothing."

"Like hell," Adams said. It sometimes annoyed him that Rawlins and the other two couldn't—or wouldn't—take credit for things they often did, but he calmed himself. "Anyway, Diego wanted me to thank you."

"He did that his own self that night. I don't need no more."

"I wanted to thank you also, Abe," Dolores said.

Rawlins nodded. "That shines with this chil',
señora."

"He also wanted me to tell you that he doesn't
hate you," Adams added.

"That suits this chil'," the mountain man said
truthfully. The fewer enemies a man had, the simpler
his life was.

"And he . . ." Adams shut up when he saw two
men suddenly come around the corner of a building.
Each man had a pistol in hand.

Rawlins stopped and threw out his left arm.
Dolores walked into it, and Rawlins swept her behind
him, seemingly without effort. "Stay there, señora,"
he ordered.

"What the hell's this all about?" Adams demanded.

"The *americano* pig knows," Raul Aguilar said
nastily.

"Ye boys want this ol' hoss, that's one thing.
There's no need for ye to try'n come agin me when
there's others about—especially a woman."

"She does not matter," Aguilar said haughtily.
"She has chosen to consort with another damn
americano."

"You son of a bitch," Adams retorted. He took a
step and then stopped when the second man—
Bernardo Ruiz—aimed his pistol at him.

"Ye best shoot me then and get it over with,"
Rawlins said flatly. "Ye don't, I'll make wolf bait of ye
straight off."

"With pleasure, señor," Aguilar said with a flourish.
He cocked the pistol and began bringing it up.

Rawlins suddenly shoved Adams with his right
hand, knocking him sideways. Then the trapper fell
backward, knocking Dolores down. He landed on

top of her, hoping she was not injured.

Both Mexican men had fired a heartbeat after Rawlins moved. Because of this action, Aguilar's bullet went sailing down the alleyway, and Ruiz's thudded into the wall above Adams.

Rawlins rose, turned, and held out his hand for Dolores. "How's doin's, señora?" he asked.

"I'm fine, Abe," Dolores answered, taking the proffered hand and letting him pull her up. "Just fine." She was flustered but recovering.

"Bueno." Rawlins turned and saw Adams brushing himself off. Adams reached inside his jacket and pulled out a small, single shot pistol.

"Whoa there, ol' hoss," Rawlins said. "Put your pistol away."

"But those sons of—"

"See to your wife, *amigo,*" Rawlins said flatly. "I'll take care of these two fractious shit piles. Get Dolores out of here."

"I'm not going anywhere, Abe," Dolores said. "I'm—"

"This ain't gonna be pretty, señora. Now go."

"But—"

"He's right, my dear," Adams said. He put away his tiny pistol and went to her. "Come, we must leave here now." Seeing the look of doubt on her face, he said, "You remember I told you about how I was in jail down in Santa Fe with Ezra and what happened when Abe and the others came to free us?"

Dolores nodded.

"And what Ezra did to that fat jailer?"

Dolores nodded again.

"Abe's every bit as skilled in fighting as Ezra. He'll be all right, and he'll take care of this with no trouble. Now, *vámonos*." He gently herded his wife back down the alley.

Rawlins walked toward Aguilar and Ruiz. The two were trying desperately to reload their pistols. When they saw him coming, they stopped. First Aguilar then Ruiz turned his pistol and grasped it by the barrel, figuring it would make a good club.

Rawlins pulled out his butcher knife and ran a thumb along the edge. "Time to *fandango, muchachos*," he said coldly.

Aguilar managed to get in one fairly good shot with his pistol club, but the blow served only to anger Rawlins, who gutted the young caballero a fraction of a second later.

Rawlins shoved the body aside and headed for Ruiz, who spun and ran. He turned at the corner of the building and headed up the small side street, hoping to reach the plaza. He figured he'd be safe there. Not even this *loco americano* would kill him in front of all the people in the plaza.

Ruiz had not counted on Rawlins's long, loping strides, however, and within moments the trapper was on him. Ruiz fell with Rawlins on his back.

Rawlins slit the young man's throat, kneeling on him until his death throes were over. Then he wiped his blade off and stood, sliding the knife away. As the anger in him melted he felt a sense of not exactly remorse, but a little regret that what had begun as an attempt at an innocent tryst had taken so bloody and deadly a turn.

He sighed and continued on to Gonzalez's. While he might regret that the situation had turned so bad, he also knew he could not have changed it. Mainly because he could not change what other men did.

Had Aguilar and Ruiz taken their thumping and gone about their business, they would still be alive.

By the time he had finished his meal—and was heading toward his room with Juanita—Rawlins had reconciled himself to the whole thing. His medicine was strong; the other men's wasn't. He knew that someday his own medicine would turn bad, and there would be nothing he could do to change that either.

Adams found Rawlins, Early, and Chardonnais in a cantina two days later, took a seat, and helped himself to the jug.

"How's Señora Adams?" Rawlins asked.

"She's well."

"*Bueno.* As clabber-footed as this ol' chil' is, I didn't want to hurt her none."

"You saved her life." Adams smiled lopsidedly. "You seem to be making a habit of saving the lives of people in my family."

Rawlins grinned. "Somebody's got to do it, hoss." He grew a little more serious. "When did ye start carryin' that little bitty pistol of yours?"

"I bought it back in New York. I think it's less safe there than it is here. I kept carrying it when I got back. Not all the people of Taos like Americans who marry one of their prize daughters."

"Found that out, did ye?" Early threw in.

"Yes, indeed."

"You evair have call to use it?" Chardonnais asked.

"No, thank God. I've pulled it out once in a while. People've pretty much left me alone since shortly after we got back from New York. I think that's partly because they saw that I was trying to become a productive citizen of Taos. I also think it's partly due to the fact that I beat the stuffing out of a few fellows who tried to run roughshod over me. Word seems to have gotten around."

"Waugh! That's makin' 'em come now, boy!" Early whooped.

"Hell, just because I'm not as tough as you three doesn't mean I can't be of some protection to my family. Besides, I can't let all that training you gave me go completely to waste."

"Hell, we can always use a tough ol' hoss like ye when we're out amongst the savages," Rawlins said.

"Speaking of that," Adams said hastily, not wanting to think about it too much, "when're you boys leaving?"

"Couple, three weeks," Early said. "No more, though."

"Why don' you come with us, eh?" Chardonnais said with a chuckle.

"Dolores'd kill me," Adams said, though the idea intrigued him more than a little.

"Not if de Blackfeets kill you first, eh," Chardonnais said with a roar of laughter.

9

"WE'RE LEAVIN' IN THREE days, *amigo*," Rawlins said flatly, "and this ol' chil' ain't waitin' for the likes of ye."

Adams nodded his head. "I understand, Abe. I'm not going to hold you up any."

"Like hell," Early tossed in. "Christ, Bart, Lucien was just foolin' with ye when he told ye to come along."

"I know that," Adams said seriously. "But to tell you boys the truth, I had been thinking of it for a while. Lord, every time one of you mentions those mountains, you all get kind of slack-jawed and your eyes go all funny."

"Waugh! It plumb shines up there," Rawlins said. "Plumb shines. Even durin' the starvin' times."

"Well, what do you think?" Adams asked, worried and excited at the same time.

"I don't know, Bart," Early said thoughtfully. "Have you really given full thought to what all this means?"

"I think so." Adams paused to down a drink. "Look, I know it's not going to be easy up there. I've heard you all talk about it enough."

"Talkin' ain't doin', hoss."

"I know, Abe." He winced at some of the memories. "I came a lot further than you thought I'd ever do back those three years ago. Met Parfrey on his terms and put him under, right here in the damn plaza."

"Waugh!" Rawlins said with a grin. "Now, them was shinin' doin's, hoss. Damn if they weren't."

"Well, I think I can still make them come, or I wouldn't say so," Adams said, feeling a little silly about using the argot of the mountain men.

"What do ye think of all this, Lucien?" Early asked. He had about half made up his mind to give his approval.

"I t'ink he'll be made wolf bait of by de Blackfeets," Chardonnais said only half-seriously. "Or he'll make wolf bait out of half de Blackfeets. Who can say."

"Christ, ye frog-eatin' son of a bitch," Rawlins growled, "cain't ye ary give a straight goddamn answer to a question? Goddamn, if ye ain't the most annoyin' critter this ol' hoss's ever knowed."

"Dat is my job, *mon ami*. To be a t'orn in your goddamn ass all de time."

"Well, goddammit, you're doin' a mighty good job at it, too, ye fat little frog."

"Well, what about it, Frenchie?" Early asked.

"If you can put up wit' him, I can do so, too. He ain't so bad a fellow after all, I t'ink."

"What about you, Abe?"

"Hell, Ez, I don't give a shit one way or the other. He's your friend mostly. I got nothin' agin him, but like I said, I ain't fixin' to ruin my trappin' season waitin' on nobody."

"So ye two're gonna leave the decision up to me, are ye?"

"*Mais oui.* Dat way we can blame everyt'ing on you when de season gets shot in de ass."

"Hell," Early complained, "I'd do as well to have the Blackfoot as my friends as I am with ye two." He paused. "What about Dolores?" he asked. "She ain't gonna like it none you go ridin' off into the mountains with the likes of us."

"She'll have no say in it," Adams responded defiantly.

It took several minutes for the three mountain men to stop laughing. When they did, Adams conceded, "Well, so she will have some say in it. But that's not your concern."

"It ain't?" Early asked.

"No. She doesn't let me go—and I accept that—then I don't go. Shouldn't be any skin off your noses."

"This chil's got fifty dollars in Mexican gold that says he cain't talk her into it in three days," Rawlins said. "Any of ye others willin' to take that bet?"

"I'll match it," Early said without hesitation.

"And me," Chardonnais added.

"Christ, you three are something," Adams said a little angrily. Then he grinned weakly. "But I'm not so damn foolish as to take that bet myself. No, sir. Dolores can be most persuasive at times." He joined the others when they began laughing.

"Well, then I wouldn't go tellin' her about that plump young Ute squaw we'll get for ye to keep ye warm in them long, cold mountain winters," Rawlins said, still laughing.

"Mais oui!" Chardonnais added. "What you t'ink, we match him wit' Bloody Basket, eh?"

"That fat, skunk-smellin', disease-ridden ol' bitch?" Rawlins said, unable to stop laughing. "Waugh! This chil'd as soon hump a griz's put his pizzle in that fat ol' sow."

"But she will take de starch out of him quickly, no?"

"She would that," Early tossed in, tears of humor leaking out of his eyes at the look on Adams's face.

"Damn right," Rawlins added around his guffaws. "Hell, she gets wind that we're bringin' him just for her, she'll have that chil's breeches down afore he can git off his horse."

Adams was horrified, and it showed on his face, which did nothing to stem the tide of laughter from his three companions.

"Even Lucien can't keep up with that goddamn one," Early managed. "He's . . . she's . . ." He finally had to stop talking.

"I don't need any Ute squaw," Adams said stiffly. "I'll be just fine without one." But talking to them was hopeless. The three mountain men were lost to reason as they roared with laughter. Adams rose, a little angry. "I'll meet you three here tomorrow and we'll talk it out some more. When you've come to your senses," he added pointedly.

Abe Rawlins, Ezra Early, and Lucien Chardonnais roared out of Taos three days later. They left as they usually arrived—with war whoops, shouts, and gunfire. This time, though, they had a little more freedom for frolicking on the way, since Hobart Adams brought up the rear, holding the rope to the lead mule. The ten other mules were roped to that one and followed docilely along. Much the way Adams was following his friends.

Dolores had been even more difficult to persuade than he had thought. The hardest part was convincing her that he was not doing this because he no longer loved her, that he was doing it for reasons even he could not fully comprehend.

She was quite certain that he was leaving her for some savage squaw. She was sure his head had been filled with stories about those savage women by his three crude friends.

She had finally given her assent just yesterday morning. Yesterday had been a blur of buying supplies and getting a horse and doing everything that needed to be done before he could leave.

She refused to see him off at the plaza, and as he rode out of town Adams looked back several times, hoping that she had changed her mind. He did not see her, however, and he began to worry even more. Perhaps she would not wait for him. Perhaps she would have their marriage annulled and go off and marry someone else. He had not had time yesterday to think of those things. Now that he did, he worried. Those thoughts ate at him as he left, and would continue to do so for some time.

His brother-in-law Diego did come down to the plaza, and before the small group actually began leaving, he looked at Adams and said solemnly, "I'll watch Dolores for you, *amigo*."

"I'd be obliged."

"Don't worry. She'll be safe and well."

Adams nodded. "Make sure that you tell her that I love her more than anything."

"I will. And don't worry."

Adams did anyway.

For once, the three mountain men were not hungover when they pulled out. They all figured it would be a little more pleasant to spend their last night in Taos in the company of a woman rather than drinking in some cantina. Besides, they had all promised Dolores—through Adams—that they would watch over her husband. They took the promise rather seriously, despite not having made it to the woman's face.

Gone the next day were their fancy outfits, the ones with all the bangles and beads and such. The three mountain men had reverted to their working outfits, all basically the same—Rawlins and Early each wore moccasins and a set of buckskins that were so coated with grease, blood, sweat, and smoke as to be almost black. They hung loosely on the men's big, wide-shouldered frames, the fringes on the outer seams of the pants sagging and missing more than a few of their fellows. Each had a knife in a plain, hard-leather case hanging from the left side of his wide leather belt, just in front of a pistol clipped to the belt. A matching pistol was on the other side. At the small of the back, each carried a tomahawk in his belt.

Chardonnais was similarly dressed in battered old clothes. Instead of a buckskin shirt, though, he wore another bright red calico shirt. He also had his ever-present green knit cap instead of the wide-brimmed felt hats favored by his friends. He, too, favored greasy buckskin pants, but he had cut off the legs below the knees and replaced them with blanket material. A wide, red sash circled his waist.

Two big pistols were stuck through the sash, as was a colorful sheath encasing a large knife. A small patch knife dangled by a thong around his neck, as did his large, silver heart-shaped ornament.

Adams was dressed in new clothes—wool pants, calico shirt, felt hat and plain workman's boots— bought just before leaving.

They rode a little northwest, toward the Rio Grande, skirting the foothills of Wheeler Peak. They camped along the river that night, calling it an early day. Adams was not used to a saddle, and the three mountain men felt they had softened just a little after a few months in Taos. They pushed on the next day in a more northerly direction, as the Rio Grande headed slightly northwest. They went around Ute Peak and pressed on up through the San Luis Valley.

Adams seemed to fit in with them fairly well, which surprised the mountain men a little. He fell into the routine and rarely complained, even though he got the more onerous of the camp tasks.

Several days later they turned west, still roughly following the Rio Grande. A few days more and their progress slowed considerably. From the flat, broad San Luis Valley, they started making their way up into the San Juan Mountains. Once in the mountains, however, they turned southwest, away from the Rio Grande. Wolf Creek Pass had a fair amount of snow already, dazzling—and awing—Adams.

They spent a night with a small band of Utes at some springs on the western side of the pass. Adams was awed by the Indians, too, as well as by the mountains and the passes and tumbling creeks and streams. Just about everything he had seen since he was out of Taos a day had impressed him.

They pushed on a little faster the next several days as the ground leveled and stayed pretty much that way for a while. They made good time, and camped that night on the Piedra River, near Chimney Rock.

Another two days' traveling and Early—who was in the lead, as he usually was—called an early stop.

"Why?" Adams asked as they were setting up their camp.

"You've had it purty easy so far, *amigo,*" Rawlins drawled. "Tomorrow we'll head north into the heart of the San Juans. Them're some goddamn mean ol' mountains, hoss, and don't ye nary think it ain't so."

"Easy?" Adams said. "Lord, my ass is sore, my shoulders are sore. Come to think of it, there isn't a spot on my body that isn't sore."

"Jist wait'll ye get up in them San Juans again, hoss," Rawlins warned. "Ye don't know what sore is."

The group followed the Animas River north. The first day wasn't so bad, and Adams began to wonder if perhaps Rawlins and the others weren't playing him for a fool. He found out that they were not the next day. There were times he thought he would roll right off the back of his horse as the animal struggled up one grade or another.

Rawlins, who since the day after they left Taos brought up the rear, watched Adams. He was a little impressed with the New Yorker. Adams might not know much that was useful up here and might be a bit soft, but he had sand in him, Rawlins could see that. He still did not think Adams was going to survive the winter in the mountains, but he wasn't as certain of that as he had been.

When he had the chance, Adams would drop

back and talk with Rawlins. He considered Early his best friend of the three, but Early was way out in the lead. Rawlins, however, was at the back, and not too far from him. When he was able to, he peppered Rawlins with questions, doing so until either the terrain or Rawlins's steadily increasing growls sent him back to his regular position.

Adams annoyed Rawlins far more than he knew. The trapper, though, would put up with it for as long as he could. What irritated him the most was the fact that the constant questions made him think too much. Like his partners, he did much of what he did on instinct or by habit. Early had told him one time about the questions Adams often asked, of the young man's drive to put reasons to everything. Rawlins didn't like that. He tried explaining this several times, which shut Adams up for a short while, but then he would be back with more questions and wanting not just answers, but reasons, too.

Finally Rawlins had had enough of it. "Look, hoss," he said, trying to rein in his temper, "if you're going to survive out here, ye need to quit lookin' for the how or why of everything."

"But if I know the how or why of things, I can do it better."

"She-it. You'd be a heap better off if you just paid attention to what the hell ye see around ye, hoss. It don't make no difference how ye know what somethin' means. It only matters that ye know what made it."

"But—"

"Listen, hoss, the goddamn Blackfeet don't give a shit for your reasoning and such, and the Blackfeet're about the best trackin' Indians ye can find. Much as I hate those bastards, I got to give 'em that. We come on some goddamn Blackfeet, hoss, ye ain't going to give a shit about no reasons or hows or whys. And neither are they."

"I still think—"

"That's your problem, hoss—ye do too goddamn much thinkin'. Now quit pesterin' me with all these goddamn questions. Ye want to know how to set a trap or how to fix a broke trap or a rifle that's been busted, then ye come and ask me. Till then, though, ye best leave this ol' chil' alone."

In little over a week they were so high in the mountains that Adams wasn't sure he could breathe right. But then they started heading downward, at least a little. Two days later the group stopped in a meadow off a mountain trail.

"Strong Bear's camp," Rawlins said, pointing.

"That where your women are?"

"Yep." A slow, sure smile spread across Rawlins's face.

10

THE INDIAN ATTACKED JUST as Rawlins was dismounting. With a screech and a howl, he launched himself at Rawlins and clamped onto the mountain man. Rawlins spun and grabbed his attacker. Then he swung his five-year-old son high in the air, released him, and then caught the boy on the way down.

"How's doin's, li'l hoss?" Rawlins asked with a grand smile after he had embraced the boy.

"Shinin', Pa," Standing Eagle giggled. He put his chubby hands out and playfully tugged at his father's new beard, grown on the journey from Taos.

"Ye been a good little critter for your ma whilst I was gone, boy?" Rawlins asked in mock sternness.

Standing Eagle nodded solemnly.

Rawlins set the boy on the ground and then rummaged in his possible sack. He brought out two pieces of hard candy. Handing them to Standing Eagle, he said, "Ye share that with one of your *amigos*, ye hear me, boy?" He smiled.

Rawlins rested an arm on his saddle as he watched

the boy run away, whooping in delight. A small smile lingered on the big mountain man's face.

"Is that the same Abe Rawlins who saved Diego and then me and Delores?" Adams asked. He was rather shocked.

Adams and Early were standing near their horses, taking in the village. Chardonnais had hardly let his horse stop before he was off the animal and had charged into his lodge, where his wife, Looks Again, knowing his proclivities, was waiting for him.

Early looked at Adams in surprise. "Why, hell yes, he's the same. Why?"

Adams shook his head. "He sure as hell doesn't seem it."

Realization spread over Early. "You mean Standing Eagle?" he said. "Waugh! That ol' hoss is some soft inside when it comes to that boy of his. I reckon it's about his biggest flaw. I'm sure as hell glad I ain't like that."

Adams stared at Early, still in surprise, as Early swung around, crouching to embrace a four-year-old girl who came running over. "You aren't, huh?"

Early looked up and grinned.

Rawlins watched Standing Eagle until the boy had disappeared around a lodge, another boy racing after him. Then he turned and led his horse to a lodge set off just a bit from the others in the high mountain meadow.

A young woman waited almost shyly just outside the lodge. She was short and just a bit on the plump side, which was one of the many things Rawlins liked about her. She had a full, round face that was touched with a little vermilion-and-white paint. Dark, merry eyes were set deep under a broad, smooth forehead.

Her cheekbones were not as prominent as many of her Ute sisters', and her lips were thin. Her hair was parted down the center, and each side was braided, wrapped with rabbit fur, and hung down onto her breast. The part was painted with vermilion. She was smiling softly.

Rawlins stopped in front of Scatters the Clouds and ran a big, hard finger down her cheek and across her lips. "I missed ye, woman," he said gruffly. He liked his time in Taos, but it was good to be back in Strong Bear's village—and with Scatters the Clouds. This worried him just a bit, since it complicated his life a little. There was no denying, though, that his trips to Taos were a little less important these days than they used to be. He wasn't sure he liked that idea very much.

Rawlins had married Scatters the Clouds seven years ago, mostly as a matter of convenience. She was young, attractive, and, he had heard, a fine worker. All those things had proved true, for which he was glad. He wasn't sure where, when, or how he had fallen in love with her, but during their time together he had. He was sure she reciprocated the feeling.

Scatters the Clouds shuddered a little at Rawlins's touch. When she had first moved into the lodge with him, she was a mere girl. She had thought then that living with a hairy-faced white man would be almost revolting, though it probably would make her and her family much better off. She had never even seriously considered loving the man. She loved him now, though. It hadn't happened all at once, but over the time they spent together she had found him a strong man, a great hunter, a mighty warrior, and far more gentle and exciting in the robes than she had ever thought possible.

"I'll take care of your horse," Scatters the Clouds said quietly.

"There's time for that later, woman," Rawlins said huskily.

Scatters the Clouds didn't quite look him in the eyes—that would be improper—but she did look up and grin. "You're getting to be as bad as your *amigo* Lucien," she said in her passable English. Then she laughed.

"And that'd offend you?" he asked in mock affront.

Scatters the Clouds only laughed more.

"Jist get your pert little ass in the lodge, woman," Rawlins growled.

Scatters the Clouds did as she was told, as a good Indian wife should. Then, just inside, she turned and nearly dragged Rawlins to the robes.

"Missed me, did ye, woman?" Rawlins asked a few minutes later. Their lovemaking had been much like a fire of buffalo chips—of short duration, but plenty hot, and with a tinge of spiciness.

"Only a little," Scatters the Clouds lied.

"Mayhap I'll jist stay down there a wee bit longer next time, Miss Molly," he countered.

Even after all these seven years they had been together, she still wasn't sure she liked the American name he had saddled her with. She understood that her full name, in Ute, was too much for Rawlins. But she could not see what was so bad about the shortened, Americanized version. She had tried to bring it up with him a few times, but she never seemed to be able to. She shrugged it off now, glad to have Rawlins back in the lodge—and in the robes.

"You best not," Scatters the Clouds said.

"Or what?" he teased.

"Or I might go off and marry Bloody Thumb," Scatters the Clouds said, barely covering her laughter.

"Ain't he the chil' that's a dozen years older'n Manitou?"

"Yes." Scatters the Clouds laughed.

"Hell, Molly, he ain't gonna be able to put meat in your pot like this chil' can—and just did."

Scatters the Clouds laughed again. When the laughter dwindled, she pulled away from him. "I must see to your horse," she said.

"Hell, there's always time—"

"Hush now, Abe. Strong Bear's fixin' to have a feast and a dance tonight to welcome you and your friends back, dammit." Scatters the Clouds spoke English fairly well, though she had a thick accent. Still, she had learned most of that language from Rawlins, with the resultant mountain man's argot and healthy sprinkling of profanity.

Both rose, fixed their clothing, and went outside. Scatters the Clouds led his horse away, while Rawlins headed toward where the pack mules were. Chardonnais and Adams were unloading the supplies from the animals. Rawlins figured Early was still with Falling Leaf. The French-Canadian, he suspected, had finished up a round or two and was taking a short breather before he went back to Looks Again.

"Is that your wife I saw there, Abe?" Adams asked.

Rawlins nodded. "Name's Scatters the Clouds, but sometimes I call her Molly. We been together more'n seven year."

"And your son is your only child?"

Rawlins laughed. "The only one I know of for certain. Hell, no tellin' how many others is runnin' around the mountains or Taos."

"Listen to dis shit," Chardonnais threw in as he dropped a sack of beans on a piece of canvas. "Dat son of a bitch, 'e 'umps two or t'ree women in his whole life, and he t'inks he is somet'ing special. Well, let me tell you somet'ing, Monsieur Adams, ol' Abe over dere ain't no *grand homme* like dis chil'." He jabbed his chest with a thumb for emphasis.

"Eat shit, froggie," Rawlins said evenly. "You had half the pizzle this chil's got, ye wouldn't know what to do with it all."

"Things're back to usual, I see," Early said, gliding up. He joined right on in the unloading, which the others had not stopped while they gabbed.

"Ol' drippin' dick over there's bein' an annoyance like he usually is, if that's what ye mean," Rawlins offered.

"An' limp pizzle's boasting about his two conquests," Chardonnais retorted.

Early glanced at Adams and grinned. "Yep. Normal," he said.

"Seems to be." Adams returned the grin.

"Ye hear that ol' Strong Bear's plannin' a *fandango* for us tonight, Ez?" Rawlins asked.

"Yep." Early glanced at Rawlins and winked. "I figure that'd be a good time to introduce Bart to his future bride."

Rawlins fought back a snicker. "Bloody Basket?" he asked.

"Yep. I told Falling Leaf to have her get her weddin' bed ready for tonight." He looked over at

Adams. The New Yorker's face was pasty and he looked like he would be sick at any moment. "From what I hear, ol' hoss, she's got herself a powerful hankerin' for ye already."

"Looks Again says ol' Bloody Basket can hardly keep her dress on just t'inking of your lily-white flesh, ol' hoss. Goddamn, boy, I just hope you got de balls to handle dat bitch. *Sacre bleu!*"

"We ever tell ol' hoss there about the time ol' Bloody Basket saved the whole village from them goddamn Arapahos?"

"Can't say as we have, *mon ami*," Chardonnais said. How he and his two friends kept from laughing was beyond him.

"Tell it, Abe," Early added.

Rawlins quit working and leaned up against a tree. He filled and lit his pipe. Early put some fresh chaw in his mouth while Chardonnais lit his pipe. They left off their work to listen.

"Well," Rawlins said, "the goddamn village was coming back from the prairie where they'd been huntin' buffler. Christ, they only had maybe twenty warriors with 'em at the time, when all of a sudden a heap of goddamn Arapahos come ridin' up looking to make trouble for us and the Utes."

"There was what, maybe two hundred of them Arapahos?" Early suggested.

"Hell, at least," Rawlins agreed with a nod. "Maybe more. Anyway, they was about to make quick work of us and the poor Utes, since they was so many and the Utes was so few. Then ol' Bloody Basket, well, she ups and tells the skunk-humpin' war leader of the Arapahos that she didn't think him and his men was all that manly. *Los mato* all, she called to them. Well, as ye can figure, such doin's didn't sit so well with none of them goddamn Arapahos. Ye remember that ol' shit-eater's name, Ez?"

"Short Lance weren't it?" Early managed to get it out without guffawing. He wasn't sure Adams would've noticed anyway.

"Yep, that were it. Well, ol' Short Lance, he says, 'We'll just show you. If you can take on all my men, you'n your people can go free.' So Bloody Basket shucks her dress right then and there and plops her fat ass down on it. 'Bring on them boys,' she says to Short Lance."

"And while she was entertaining the Arapahos you and the Utes made your escape?" Adams asked innocently, though he didn't like where this was heading.

"She-it," Rawlins drawled. "Nosirree, them Arapahos lined up and dunked their pizzles in her one at a time. By the time the last ones was done, the first ones was ready again, so she gave 'em another round. Hell, she was enjoyin' herself so much, she even gave those that could a third humpin'."

Early and Chardonnais were sputtering as they tried to hold in their laughter.

"Well, that about did those limp-pizzled Arapahos in. 'You people can go on free,' Short Lance said. 'She has won.' Then he started leavin' with his warriors. Well, them doin's didn't shine with Bloody Basket no goddamn way at all. Damn, if she didn't get up off her fat ass and start chasin' after them goddamn Arapahos, her ponderous tits a-flapping 'twixt knees and face, ass shakin' like snow just afore an avalanche. And all the while she's shoutin' for them boys to come back, that she weren't near finished yet. Christ

A'mighty, hoss, I ain't ary seen critters move as fast as them Arapahos did when they heard that wailin' bitch comin' after them to rob 'em of the last of their manhood."

Adams looked like he had swallowed one of the mules whole. For a moment Rawlins—who had kept a straight face throughout but was having trouble doing so now—thought the younger man was going to stop breathing.

Early and Chardonnais were holding their stomachs, as if in pain. Finally, though, the dam broke, and the laughter poured forth. Rawlins could not stifle himself any longer and joined his companions.

Adams was frightened, and worried. He more than half suspected his friends had just told him a tall tale, which would explain their laughter. However, the story could be true—albeit exaggerated some—and the laughter could be due to the look he knew he had on his face. As moments passed he began to suspect the latter more and more. With a sinking, sick feeling in the pit of his stomach, he went back to work, dreading every minute that brought him closer to his doom.

It did not take the four men long to finish unloading the mules. They covered the supplies up with canvas tarps and then led the mules out to pasture with their horses and the village's vast herd.

"Well, ol' hoss," Rawlins said to Adams as they were walking back toward the main part of the village, "ye best get yourself as fancified as ye can. Bloody Basket's gonna expect ye to shine, hoss. Plumb shine!" He clapped Adams on the shoulder a good strong shot.

"I hope Bloody Basket don't expect too much

from this chil'," Early added. "Hell, he ain't got much
finery and geegaws and such."

"Dat don' matter none," Chardonnais put in.
"Wit' Bloody Basket, Bart ain't going to be wearing
anyt'ing for very long." He chuckled.

"Damn, if ye ain't right, froggie," Rawlins offered.
"He stayin' in your lodge for the time bein', Ez?"

"Yep."

"Well, whatever finery ye find for him to wear,
best make certain it ain't too costly. Hell, that ol'
bitch's just gonna rip it to shreds anyway."

"Good thinkin' there, ol' chil'," Early said somewhat seriously, trying not to laugh again. "I'll do so."

11

IT WAS A COOL NIGHT, BUT NOT so bad as to drive the celebrants inside. A large central fire was made, and meat was set to cooking—fresh elk and deer and buffalo. Then the drumming began, and soon men and women were dancing, adding the sound of rattles and whistles to the drums.

The Utes were dressed in all their finery, as were the mountain men. It was all new to Adams, but he could not enjoy any of it. His bowels were twisted into a tight knot at the thought of Bloody Basket's impending assault on him. He kept glancing around nervously, waiting, worrying.

"What's wrong with your friend?" Strong Bear asked, pointing to Adams.

"Lonely," Rawlins answered. He, Chardonnais, Early, and their women were sitting near Strong Bear. Adams was there, too.

"He has no woman?"

"He's got one all right. Down in Taos," Rawlins responded. "Misses her somethin' awful."

"That is good. It's not good, though, that he's lonely here. There are plenty of women here. He can—"

"We know all that," Chardonnais said hastily. "And we got ol' hoss there one all picked out. We're just waitin' till the proper time."

Strong Bear nodded. "Good. Who is she?"

"Bloody Basket," Chardonnais said with a straight face.

A look of puzzlement began to cross Strong Bear's face, but Adams was not looking at the Ute civil chief.

"Ye know the one, Strong Bear," Rawlins said smoothly. "That fat bitch always after one goddamn man or another."

Strong Bear's eyes widened, but he caught on right away when he saw Rawlins rolling his eyes. "Of course," he said with a nod. "Such a woman'll be good for your young friend."

"That's what we figured," Rawlins said.

"And when do you think the time'll be right?" Strong Bear asked.

"Well, I ain't exactly sure, Chief," Rawlins said. "I mean, Bloody Basket wants to have herself all painted up and shinin' when she meets her husband-to-be. And considerin' who she is, that could take a goddamn long time."

Strong Bear nodded solemnly, noting that Adams was now looking at him. The young man's face was etched in worry.

Rawlins rose and went out to dance with Scatters the Clouds. Early and Falling Leaf and Chardonnais and Looks Again soon joined them. Adams sat, arms around his knees, trying to curl into a ball and disappear. He could not eat any of the foods that were passed around, nor could he even think. His mind was too full of dread.

The moon had passed its zenith and was heading slowly downward when the three partners and their women sat near Strong Bear again.

"Well, ol' hoss, I reckon it's about time ye met your mate," Rawlins said to Adams.

Adams managed to suppress the shudder that crept up his spine and threatened to explode out his shoulders.

"Best close your eyes, hoss," Rawlins commanded. When Adams complied fearfully, everyone in the tribe gathered around, eagerly waiting to see what would happen. The three mountain men tittered, choking back their laughter.

Suddenly a screech rose up from the depths of hell and splattered vomitlike and sticky all over Adams. He almost lost control of his bowels, and he shook. Then he felt a hard, crusty palm scrape down one cheek and then the other. The action was accompanied by a disgusting, blubbery cooing sound.

Early's daughter, Straight Calf, walked up and stopped right in front of Adams. "Are you all right, hoss?" the four-year-old asked in passable English.

Adams cracked his eyes open to see the serious, pretty little face before him. Beyond Straight Calf, he could see Rawlins, Early, and Chardonnais rolling on the ground, unable to speak because they were laughing so hard. Adams looked around like he had just awoken from a bad dream. All he saw were people laughing, and the delightful chubby face of the child. There was no big, fat, man-eating squaw waiting to pounce on him.

Slowly the fact filtered into his befuddled mind that there never had been a Bloody Basket, that he had let the mountain men's tales pollute his mind until he conjured up all kinds of demons for himself.

"You bastards," Adams breathed, anger battling with disgust and relief inside him. "You bloody, stinking, rotten, buffalo-humping, whoremongering, fetid, pestilent, disgusting, worm-eating bastards." He had the sudden thought that he could probably kill all three mountain men right now without much effort. They were laughing so hard that they were helpless. Of course, the Utes—the ones who weren't laughing quite so hard—would prevent him from doing so.

Rawlins, though, managed to sit up, breathing heavily. "Welcome to the Stony Mountains, ol' hoss," he said, breaking down into laughter again.

"I swear by all that's holy, and a heap that's not, that I'll get you three bastards for this." But the hilarity of the others, plus the general humor of the situation, which had as its basis his own gullibility, began to get through to him. He chuckled a few times, but then real laughter bubbled up, and in moments he was roaring every bit as hard as his three tormentors.

Finally, though, things settled down and he was able to eat and then sit back and enjoy the festivities. He even passed around a few of the small store of cigars he had brought with him.

Two nights after the celebration, the four mountain men met in Strong Bear's lodge with the chief and three warriors—Runs Back, Bull Nose, and Iron Wolf.

"We must make meat for the winter," Strong

Bear said, speaking to Chardonnais, his son-in-law, as he usually did, in English.

"*Oui*. And we must be on de trail soon to catch de early prime bevair."

"When're you thinkin' of leavin'?"

The French-Canadian shrugged and looked at Early. If anyone could be considered the leader of the small group, it was Early. He was the most levelheaded of the three. Chardonnais went from high to low in the blink of an eye. He was passionate about life, about everything he did. Rawlins, on the other hand, was playful and oftentimes not serious about things. Besides, he didn't want to complicate his life.

"Two, three days, I reckon," Early said. "We should make a little meat for the travelin', till we can make more for the winter."

Strong Bear nodded.

"How about ye, Strong Bear?" Rawlins asked. "When're ye fixin' to pull your people out of here?"

"I think we'll leave when you do." He paused. "Tomorrow we hunt, yes?"

"Suits this chil'," Rawlins said. The others agreed.

The next morning the four mountain men rode out of the small village with Strong Bear, Runs Back, Iron Wolf, Bull Nose, and another warrior named Buffalo Heart. Adams, as both a newcomer and a novice, was in charge of the mules that would be used for packing meat.

The Utes spotted the herd of elk first, and charged off after them.

Rawlins pulled up, waiting to see where the game animals were heading. When he saw, he shouted, "Bart! Come watch these doin's."

Adams hurried up just in time to see the five mounted Ute hunters racing at full speed down a sharp slope, shouting and firing arrows at the panic-stricken elk. "Good Lord Almighty," he breathed.

"Them boys can make 'em come now when it comes to such doin's," Rawlins said.

Adams looked at Early with accusatory eyes. "You said the Utes look like shit when they ride."

"Well, hell, they do—sometimes." He laughed.

"Hell, all us ol' critters do, one time or another," Rawlins added helpfully.

"Except me," Chardonnais boasted.

"Listen to this shit," Rawlins scoffed. "Frog-humpin' little peckerwood, you're lucky you can stay on your horse, let alone look good in the doin'."

"I look better dan you at it. But dat's because I look better dan you all de time."

Rawlins grabbed Chardonnais's knit cap and whacked him with it a few times.

"Give me dat *chapeau,*" Chardonnais said in mock anger. He grabbed the cap and looked it over. "You're damn lucky dere ain't no bugs on dere, *mon ami,* he growled. "Don' do dat no more."

"What the hell do ye think I'm gonna do, hoss?" Rawlins said innocently. "Ruin my own hat beatin' some sense into ye?"

"We best go'n help Strong Bear and the others," Early interjected. "Ye two can annoy each other later."

"'E is *un fléau*—a scourge—just by being here," Chardonnais said firmly.

"It shines with this chil' to be good at somethin' without makin' an effort at it."

Early rode off, shaking his head. The others followed.

It was a long, bloody day. They killed more than a dozen elk and two dozen black-tailed deer. That took time, but the more time-consuming work was in the butchering. Working in two-man teams—with Strong Bear not doing any of the work but keeping a watch out for enemies—the work was less difficult and proceeded with as much speed as possible.

It was a bloody, tired, and hot group of hunters who rode into the village in the afternoon. Chardonnais, who was in the lead, spotted someone who didn't belong there, and pulled to a stop, signaling the others. He looked back and gestured to Rawlins, who loped up. The French-Canadian pointed.

Rawlins nodded. He rode brazenly into the Ute camp. The man looked up at the sound of the horse, then turned to wait for him, nervously fingering his pistol. He was of medium height and thin to the point of scrawny. His buckskins hung on him like rags on a scarecrow. He had a nervous tic over his left cheek.

"How's doin's, hoss?" Rawlins asked.

The man nodded.

"What the hell're ye doin' here, boy?"

"I don't think that's any of your account, hoss," the man said stiffly.

"What's your name?"

"That ain't none of your account, neither."

Rawlins moved his horse a little closer to the man and then suddenly kicked him in the face. He slid out of the saddle, dropped his rifle, and piled on top of the man and began thumping him.

The man fought back gamely, but he was no match for a man of Rawlins's size and ferocity. The trapper was about to pound him into the ground for good when there was a gunshot. Still holding the man down with one hand, Rawlins glanced up.

"Leave off that critter, hoss," a buckskin-wearing white man said as he and several others rode into the camp from the east. The man was easily as big as Rawlins or Early, and had a thick bull neck on him. "Do ye hear now, boy? What's these hyar doin's anyway, eh? Such don't shine with this ol' mountain chil' none-some-ever. Hell no, they don't."

"That you, Jim?" Early asked. At the sound of the shot, he, too, had moved into the camp from the safety of the trees. "That can't be ol' Jim Bridger?"

The new man in the camp looked around. "Well, by Christ, it's ol' Ezra Early." He looked back at Rawlins and pointed. "Then yon chil's got to be ol' Abe Rawlins."

"The same, ol' hoss. How's doin's?" Rawlins straightened.

"Ye mind tellin' this hyar ol' chil jist wha'n hell you're doin' to poor ol' Charlie Bickford thar?"

"Teachin' the critter to mind his goddamn manners." Rawlins extended his hand as Bridger dismounted.

"Well, goddammit, the critter's one of mine," Bridger said as he passed around greetings with Early's group.

"Maybe ye don't shine as a partisan no more, Ol' Gabe," Rawlins said flatly, using the appellation by which Bridger was known throughout the mountains, "if this's the kind of critter you're hirin' on these days."

"Hell, boy, I seem to recall a time when ye was a fractious little bastard, all full of yourself."

"'E still is dat way," Chardonnais said. "'E nevair gets any better. Only worse."

Rawlins turned and held his hand out. Bickford took it cautiously and allowed himself to be helped up. Then Rawlins looked at Bridger. "What the hell're ye doin' out this way? This ain't your usual huntin' grounds."

Bridger shrugged. "It ain't, but—"

"Hell, where's our own manners," Rawlins said. "Come on, Gabe, ye and your boys get over to the fire. Meat's on." He led them toward his lodge. The women, meanwhile, had come out and took the horses and meat-laden mules away.

At the fire, Bridger continued, while chewing on some elk, "It ain't my usual huntin' grounds, but this ol' chil' goes where the beaver is. I hear tell there's aplenty beaver in the Humboldt River out west of here—out by that goddamn big salt lake, the one I thought for a spell was a piece of the ocean, I found that one time. Ye remember that?"

Rawlins and his friends nodded.

"Anyway, the goddamn Blackfeet've been fractious as all hell since a bunch of the boys whupped their asses good and proper up in Pierre's Hole just after the doin's year before last. So I figured this'd be a hell of a good time to check out the Humboldt."

"This's kind of the long way 'round, ain't it?" Rawlins asked.

Bridger nodded. "I was hopin' to hire a couple goddamn Utes to guide us out there. We rode in a little bit ago. Heard we're supposed to talk to a Strong Bear, but he wasn't hyar."

Rawlins pointed to the chief.

Bridger nodded again. "Since he weren't hyar, I left Charlie whilst me and the other boys went off to do a little huntin'. Reckon I best go talk to ol' Strong

Bear soon's I can. He cain't help us, we'll need to get back on the trail first thing."

"I figure Strong Bear ain't gonna be too cooperative, though."

"Trouble?" Bridger asked.

"Nope. Just needs to make meat, and he's our friend." There was no threat implied, just a statement of fact.

"He thinks he'll be goin' agin ye if he was to have some men guide me and my boys?"

"I think so."

"Then we'll mosey on to the next place. But ye don't mind I was to ask him first to be sure?" He grinned.

"Nope." Rawlins smiled back. He liked Bridger, and had nothing against him.

12

OLD GABE BRIDGER AND HIS men pulled out the next morning, without a Ute guide. Bridger had no hard feelings for either the Utes or for his old friends. Indeed, Bridger, Rawlins, Early, and Chardonnais had spent a goodly portion of the night reminiscing over fresh elk meat. Adams sat nearby, avidly listening—and sketching the four longtime mountain men.

"I thought his name was Jim," Adams said after Bridger and his men had pulled out that morning.

"It is," Early said.

"Then why'd you three keep calling him Gabe?"

"Nickname," Rawlins said. "Every chil' in the mountains knows Jim as Ol' Gabe."

"Why?" Adams was a little confused.

"Bridger was one of Ashley's boys when me'n Lucien come out here in twenty-two. So was another chil' named Jed Smith. Now, ol' Jed, he was a pious critter, but one tough ol' hoss, too. Son of a bitch'd go wadin' into Blackfeet with a rifle in one hand and a

Bible in the other. Anyways, he looks at Jim one day and says, 'Ye know, ol' hoss, ye remind me of ol' Gabriel of the Bible, all serious and glumlike.' Name's stuck to Bridger ary since."

"You ever seen this Jed Smith again?" Adams asked.

"Ol' coon went under," Early answered flatly. He wasn't that great a friend of Jed Smith, but he hated to see any man he liked some go under. "Down on the Cimarron. Comanches made wolf bait of him."

Adams's eyes raised. That was where Early had found him, about to be tortured by Comanches.

Early nodded. "Couldn't've been more'n a week or two after I come on ye, hoss. Mayhap the same Comanches I sent packin' was the ones made wolf bait out of him." That was another reason he was not too happy about Smith's having gone under.

Adams gulped. He did not like the thought of having been the reason, or even one of the reasons, why another good man had been killed. "Mister Bridger—Old Gabe—is rather an odd character, isn't he?" Adams threw lamely into the air.

"That's one tough ol' hoss there, boy," Rawlins said.

Talk drifted off then and so they went back to work. They and some of the Utes went out hunting again, once more taking most of the day for it.

Though it was the beginning of September, as best the mountain men could figure it, they had snow flurries that night.

"It's time we was movin' on," Rawlins said as he watched the few drifting flakes coming down. He was eager to get going, wanting to feel the icy water of a beaver stream swirling around his legs, to feel the soft fullness of a well-tanned beaver plew in his hands. He wanted to be away from people, or at least most people. He had had his fill of Taos for a while, and now even the Ute village, with its population of forty or so, was a little too crowded for him.

"If the women can finish up jerkin' that elk meat tomorrow, we can pull out the mornin' after," Early said.

The men helped out as best they could the next day, until the women told them to get out from underfoot. Then the men went and checked their supplies. While they were doing so Rawlins asked, "Where're ye fixin' to take us this year, Ez?"

Early looked at him and grinned. "Maybe up near the three forks?" he suggested. "Or a bit north?"

"Gettin' a mite close to Blackfoot country, ain't ye, hoss?"

"Ye gone scared in your ol' age?"

"What you mean in his old age?" Chardonnais interjected. "Dat chil's always been afraid of everyt'ing."

"Everything but a short, fat, frog-humpin' sack of shit," Rawlins said pointedly.

"Dat's because I 'ave a good 'eart. If I didn't, I would've made wolf bait out of you years ago."

"She-it, the only thing you can make wolf bait of, ye little frog fart, is a baby, and a real young'n at that. Hell, Standing Eagle's already bigger'n ye are."

While Chardonnais was chewing that one over in his mind, Early asked, "Ye have a reason for askin' where we're headin'? Or you just bein' a pain in the ass?"

"Since you're set and determined to drag our asses up into the heart of Blackfoot country, I say we best stop by Robideaux's post and pick us up some more DuPont and Galena."

"We brung as much as usual."

Rawlins nodded. "But we've lost some somehow. Either the Utes're filchin' from us, or a couple cans fell out of the packs somewhere on the trail."

"It ain't likely any of Strong Bear's people would've done such a thing."

"Reckon you're right. To my thinkin', though, hoss, it don't much mean shit either way. We're short on powder, and we used more lead than we figured in huntin' the past two days."

"We'll stop," Early said with a nod. "But don't figure on stayin'."

"I ain't. This ol' chil's got a real hankerin' to get down to business afore we miss all the goddamn prime plews."

"I feel de same," Chardonnais said.

Early grinned. He and the two others had been together plenty long enough to know what each was thinking more often than not.

Rawlins glanced at Adams, who appeared to be paying scant attention to his three companions as he worked. "One thing we got to do afore we pull out, Ez, is get ol' hoss there a woman." He pointed to Adams.

"He don't want one."

"I don't much give a shit what he wants," Rawlins said evenly. "I ain't fixin' to have him get his pizzle all in an uproar 'cause he's lonely halfway through the winter. He starts lookin' at Scatters the Clouds and I'll gut the ol' hoss. I reckon ye feel the same about Falling Leaf." He shrugged and grinned. "No tellin' what froggie thinks about such doin's with

Looks Again, but there's ary chance she'll get tired of him stickin' his teeny little frog pizzle in her every goddamn two minutes and she might be lookin' for a way out."

"You're just jealous dat you can't do it so often—or so good—as dis ol' chil'," Chardonnais boasted.

"Shit, Frenchie, that goddamn little thing of yours is gonna fall off one of these days. Ye know, ye cain't put the cork in and out of the jug too often afore it starts to fall apart."

"It's his cork," Early said with a laugh. "He wants to use it all up afore he sees another moon, that's his business." He noticed that Adams was suddenly listening to them. "Ye hear what we been talkin' about, ol' hoss?" he asked.

Adams nodded. "I told you all before that I don't want a Ute woman," he said stiffly. "Have no fear of me casting leering looks at your women during the winter."

Rawlins calmly pulled out his pipe, tamped it full of tobacco, and then walked to the fire to light it. He returned and sat on a pile of supplies, puffing lightly. "That ain't the only troubles I can see from this, ol' hoss."

"Oh?" Adams said tightly, still smarting from being the butt of the joke about Bloody Basket. He squatted where he was, grateful to change position. He still ached all over from the unaccustomed labors.

"Ye gonna tan all your plews, hoss?" Rawlins asked.

Chardonnais laughed a little. "What makes you t'ink dat chil' will get him any bevair anyway, eh?"

"Because, goddamn," Early growled, "he's gonna partner up with this chil'. And I can outtrap the two of ye peckerwoods all by my lonesome."

"Listen to this goddamn windbag, will ye, froggie?" Rawlins hooted. "Goddamn, boy, ye got some specie ye want to wager this ol' chil' that I'll take more plews than ye and that ass-draggin' chil' ye went and saddled yourself with?"

"Hundred bucks says you're full of shit, hoss," Early said gleefully. "Hell, I took fifty from ye already, but I can always use more."

"I want in on dis, too, *mon ami,*" Chardonnais tossed in. "I will bet you a hundred dollars, too."

"That shines with this chil'."

"Now, wait a minute, Ezra," Adams protested. "I can't let you bet all that money—against two others—for something I'm responsible for to some extent."

"Ye want in, too?" Early asked cockily.

"I'll side with you—if you think I'll be of any help to you."

"Hell, boy," Early said with a laugh, "ye hold me back too much, I'll leave your ass in a beaver stream somewhere."

Adams didn't believe him. Not totally, anyway. He nodded. "I'll take Lucien's bet, then," he said firmly.

"*Bon.*"

"That still don't solve our little problem," Rawlins insisted. "Ol' hoss there needs a woman to cook and to fix his 'skins and make meat and most of all, if he gets any plews a-tall, cure them plews."

"Abe's right, Bart," Early said, looking at him.

"But, Ezra . . . I don't want —"

"Look, hoss," Rawlins snapped, pulling the pipe out of his mouth, "ye don't have to hump her, if'n you're not of a mind to. But ye do need ye a woman to take care of ye. I sure as shit ain't gonna do so."

"Me neidder," Chardonnais said. "You are our *ami,* yes, dis is true, but we can't be your keepers. *Mais non!* It's hard enough for us in de wintair wit'out 'aving to take care of you, too."

"What've you got to say about all this, Ezra?" Adams asked stiffly. He suddenly felt as if he had been shut out by these three men, and just when he had felt he had really become one of them. Not a peer, of course, since there was still so much to learn, but at least fully accepted as a friend and as a man.

"I think the same as they do," Early said evenly. "It ain't none of our affair what ye do with that woman whilst you're in your lodge. Ye can hump her as often as Lucien does Looks Again, or ye can look on her as your sister. But there's too much work to be done up there for me'n the boys, or our women, to be able to give ye much help."

"Look at it this way, hoss," Rawlins offered, "We ain't gonna know what the hell ye do in your lodge. And, like Ez says, we don't much give a damn—"

"I do," Chardonnais said with a roguish laugh. "I want to watch to see if dat chil' does it well."

"Goddamn, froggie, you're a disgustin' thing, ye know that?" Rawlins said. Then he laughed. "'Course, ye might learn a thing or two from young hoss over there. He might shine in the robes."

"You men are filthy," Adams said angrily. "You're all despicable, vile, filthy-minded reprobates."

"Goddamn, that chil's finally found out our secret," Rawlins said with a laugh. "Damn, if he didn't."

Adams was speechless, face screwed up in anger.

"Christ, boy," Early growled, "don't ye go gettin' the sulks on us. We get enough of the melancholy and gloom from Lucien there."

"I can understand why," Adams said tightly. "Living with you two probably drives him to it."

"I think ol' hoss there jist insulted us—me and ye, Ez," Rawlins said with another laugh.

"Goddamn, I think you're right, Abe," Early agreed. "Maybe we ought to just send him packin'."

"That's an idea," Rawlins agreed.

"Out here?" Adams sputtered. "Why I'd never make it a day."

"De chil' is learning," Chardonnais said. "Now 'e knows 'ow important we are to him. Maybe he will listen to what we have to say to him, eh."

"Mayhap," Early said. "Look, Bart, we'll find ye a good woman. We ain't gonna saddle ye with a Bloody Basket." He laughed when Adams shuddered. "We'll get ye one who'll treat ye right. One who can cook good and one who can work real good."

"I expect we can find ye one who don't demand too much," Rawlins added. "'Specially in the robes."

"I will take care of dose t'ings for you, *mon ami,*" Chardonnais said brightly.

"Goddamn, froggie," Rawlins snapped, "put that thing back in your pants. Jesus."

"You just wish you 'ad one like mine."

"Like hell I do. This chil' don't want nothin' to do with a pizzle that runs him all the goddamn time."

"Besides," Early threw in, "Looks Again'll cut your balls off she catches ye humpin' another woman in the same camp. Ye remember what happened last year when ye brought that other squaw into your lodge, don't ye?"

"Mais oui! How can I forget dat?"

"As I was sayin'," Rawlins went on, almost as if he had not been sidetracked, "we can find ye one won't nag ye too awful much. But one that'll be willin' if'n ye change your mind somewhere durin' that long, cold mountain winter."

"You three aren't going to let me alone about this, are you?" Adams asked with a sigh.

"Not for a goddamn minute, hoss," Rawlins said almost gleefully. "We're fixin' to be on the trail tomorrow, boy, and we cain't be settin' here all the night whilst ye make up your mind."

"All right, then," Adams said in resignation. "Just make sure she's at least presentable."

13

"THIS HERE IS BLUE RATTLE, hoss," Rawlins said as he and Chardonnais escorted a young woman into Early's lodge, where he and Adams sat.

Adams looked rather horrified at not only the woman, but also the child in its cradleboard. "She's married!" he gasped.

"Like hell she is," Rawlins said. He and Chardonnais sat at the fire with Early and Adams. Blue Rattle went to sit with Falling Leaf. Rawlins fished a piece of meat out of the pot and tossed it lightly from hand to hand to let it cool a bit. Then he popped it in his mouth and said, "She's a widder."

"She was married to an ol' chil' named Jed Boatwright," Early said.

"Who was he?"

"An ol' hoss Lucien met back in Independence. Ol' Frenchie there went back to see his folks—or so he says. He got the melancholy come over him one time, thinkin' of the folks back east, and ye know him when he gits that way."

Adams nodded tentatively.

"He was on the way back here when he met ol' Jed, and ol' Jed joined up with us."

"What happened to him?" Adams asked with suddenly parched throat.

"Crows got him," Rawlins said flatly. "Rubbed him out whilst he was trying to protect that stumpy-ass little frog fart over there."

"*Mais oui,*" Chardonnais said sadly. "But I took care of dat asswipe of a Crow right den and dere," he added almost defensively.

"That was one goddamn humdinger of a fight. The four of us and a few Utes against Christ knows how many of them red devils. Ez there nearly got hisself rubbed out, too. Looks Again managed to sew him up, gittin' done just afore froggie's little brat popped out of her." He paused. "Little Rider—that's Blue Rattle's baby there—was born five days later."

"Maybe we got de wrong woman for dis chil'," Chardonnais said suddenly, voice harsh. He pointed at Adams. "Maybe he ain't so good for Blue Rattle, eh."

"What the hell's that supposed to mean?" Adams demanded.

"You know what de hell I mean, boy," Chardonnais growled nastily.

"No, I don't," Adams said flatly. "Maybe you better tell me plainly. And speak English so I can understand you."

Chardonnais rattled off several burning sentences in French, all of which Adams knew were not flattering to him.

"I whipped your ass once, Lucien," Adams said quietly. "I'll be glad to do it again for you."

"Take it easy, hoss," Rawlins said. "He's just gone into one of his melancholy times. It was probably brought on by all this talk about ol' Jed and how he went under."

"I don't much give a damn what brought it on," Adams snapped. "I don't need to sit here and listen to his foolishness."

Chardonnais drew his knife and swept to his feet. Adams was only a half second behind in doing the same. But both Rawlins and Early got between the two men.

"Go on outside, Frenchie," Rawlins said quietly. "There'll be no bloodshed 'tween us."

"Get out of de way, Abe, before I stick you good, eh." The French-Canadian jabbed the knife blade in Rawlins's direction a few times.

"Ye touch me with that Green River, ye stumpy little shit, and I'll make ye eat it." He paused. "Now go on and cool off. Bart ain't gonna hold this agin ye."

Chardonnais scowled at his old friend, but then whirled and headed outside of the lodge, slipping his knife away as he did. All the while he muttered, sometimes in English, more often in French.

The others sat.

"Ye know, hoss," Rawlins said flatly, "it don't shine with this chil' to have ye threaten my *amigo*."

"I'm brokenhearted you feel that way," Adams said sarcastically.

"Sass me again, boy, and *I'll* take my blade to ye."

"Have at me, then," Adams said evenly. He was scared down to his toes, but was bound and determined not to show it.

"Somethin' stuck in your craw, hoss?" Rawlins demanded.

"Yes, as a matter of fact there is. I'm sick of the three of you taking sides against me. If you didn't want me here, you should've never brought me along. Since I'm one of you—at least for this season, as you call it—then I should be treated like one of you."

Rawlins's face clouded in anger. Then he suddenly laughed. "Goddamn, hoss, that's what we been doin'," he said, still laughing.

Adams looked at him in consternation. Then he smiled. "You know, Abe, I think you're right." He paused, then asked seriously, "But how do you two put up with Lucien and his mercurial ways?"

"Best to ignore him mostly," Early said. "He'll get over it soon enough. Always does. 'Course there's always a time or two when he seems to go too far over the cliff. Then we got to beat some sense into him, since talkin' don't do no good."

"I believe you." Adams put his knife away and made a conscious effort to relax. "Now, what about . . . Blue Rattle, is that what you called her?"

"What about her, hoss?" Rawlins countered. "She's yours, if'n ye want her. She'll be a helpmeet for ye or a partner in the robes for ye, if'n ye want that."

Adams glanced over at Blue Rattle. He was surprised that he was drawn to her, since the thought of lying with a savage disgusted him. Still, she was a rather pretty young woman. She had a bright, easy smile and seemed adept at her work.

The baby troubled him, too, but not as much as he would have thought. The little fellow didn't seem to be much trouble, and had cried only once since entering the lodge. That had quickly been silenced when Blue Rattle gave him her breast.

"I don't have much choice, do I?" Adams suddenly asked, looking from Early to Rawlins.

"Nope," Rawlins responded almost gleefully. "There ain't but two more women her age in the whole damn village, hoss, and they're both married."

"Far be it from me to break up a happy home," Adams said with only a touch of sarcasm.

"Then it's settled," Early said.

Adams nodded, not quite sure how he felt. "Am I supposed to give her father something for her?" he asked. "Isn't that the way it usually works?"

Rawlins nodded. "Usually. But this ain't usual. We traded her brother some meat and a little powder and lead."

"What about living arrangements?" Adams was suddenly very uncomfortable again.

"She's got her own lodge," Rawlins said. "Ye can move in there straight off, hoss, and I'd suggest it."

"Why?" Adams asked nervously.

"Give ol' Ez some privacy. Ol' hoss there's been growlier'n an ol' b'ar for days now since he can't hump ol' Falling Leaf with ye sittin' there a-watchin' arything he does."

"I'm sorry, Ezra," Adams said, abashed. "I really am. I just never realized. . . ."

"It's all right, hoss," Rawlins said with a laugh. "Ez cain't git it up more'n once a month or so anyway, so he ain't missed much."

"Hell," Early retorted, "he's just happier'n a pig in shit that ye ain't been stayin' in *his* lodge. Then you'd find out that he cain't git it up at all. Christ, I don't know why Scatters the Clouds stays with him. Hell, he ain't humped her since she birthed Standin' Eagle."

Adams smiled when he noticed that both women—and Blue Rattle—were giggling. He figured it was over the men's statements. "All right," he said. "But I'd be obliged if you didn't bother me about Blue Rattle every ten minutes."

"I cain't make no such promise, ol' hoss," Rawlins said with a grin.

Hobart Adams was decidedly uncomfortable when he entered what was now his lodge. Well, rather, his and Blue Rattle's, he corrected himself. He stood awkwardly just inside.

"Here," Blue Rattle said, indicating a willow backrest in the honored place where he could sit and watch the entrance to the lodge. A small fire was burning in front of the backrest. A coffeepot sat on a flat rock almost in the flames; a stew pot hung from an iron tripod, where it would stay heated.

Adams tentatively went around the fire and sat. "You speak English then?" he asked.

"Little. You'll be happy here. I'm a good wife."

"We need to talk about that a little," Adams said nervously. "Sit." When she did, looking a little confused, he said, "I don't expect you to be my wife. Not in the real sense."

Blue Rattle looked blankly at him.

"You and I . . . we don't have to . . ." His voice petered out and he waved vaguely at the robes.

"No?" Blue Rattle asked, eyebrows raised in surprise.

"No," Adams said firmly. "I . . . I have a wife. Back in Taos. In the big white man's town." He knew he sounded lame, but he was not sure how much of this Blue Rattle was getting.

"I don't mind."

"Don't mind what?" It was Adams's turn—again—to be confused.

"That you got a wife in white man's stone village."

"But I do," Adams insisted. He was certain now that this was not going to work out. He should've known better than to acquiesce, he told himself silently. These Indians were entirely too free with their persons. A moment later that thought struck him as almost ludicrous. After all, Dolores had made love with him the first night they met, and he had ended up marrying her.

Maybe that was part of the problem, he thought. Or, rather, maybe he was the real problem. While he loved Dolores with all his heart, he had fallen in love with her so easily at first that he was afraid that the same would happen with Blue Rattle. On the surface, the thought of falling in love, or even just coupling with, a savage like Blue Rattle was repulsive, but he wasn't sure he could trust himself.

"I treat you good," Blue Rattle said.

"I know you would," he lied. "But I'm not interested."

Blue Rattle looked crestfallen. "You don't like me?"

"I don't even know you," Adams said in exasperation.

"Why you stay in lodge with me?" Blue Rattle asked. Sadness swept over her as she remembered the few months—the few grand, passionate months—

she had had with Jed Boatwright. She missed him terribly.

"Didn't Abe or Ezra tell you?" he asked, surprised.

"Tell what?"

"That I need a woman to care for me, to cook and repair my clothing, to cure my pelts."

"Yes. I do all that for you. But we do hump-hump, too?"

"No." Adams felt bad for Blue Rattle, but he was determined to stay true to Dolores.

Looking beaten down, Blue Rattle rose and got a horn bowl. She filled it with stew and gave it to Adams. "You must eat," she said. Then she left the lodge.

Adams ate, wondering what to do next. After finishing, he sat there waiting. Finally he rose and walked out. He did not see Blue Rattle, but that did not matter. He walked to Early's lodge and called for entrance. He went in and sat, not really surprised to see Chardonnais there.

"So, how you like my sister-in-law, eh?" the trapper asked.

"Blue Rattle's your sister-in-law?" Adams said, eyes wide.

"*Mais oui!* Didn't we tell you dat?"

"No, you didn't, damn you. Damn all of you," Adams said heatedly. "And that's not all you forgot to tell people either, dammit."

"Oh?" Chardonnais asked innocently.

"Yes, dammit. You never told Blue Rattle about the arrangement we were supposed to have."

"Well," Chardonnais said with a shrug, "I t'ink dat once you see Blue Rattle—maybe when she takes her clothes off to go to sleep, eh?—you change your mind about dis foolish idea you have."

"There's nothing foolish about it," Adams said stiffly.

"Hell, hoss," Rawlins said with a chuckle, "ain't no chil' I know's gonna turn down a roll in the robes with a woman looks like, and is eager as, Blue Rattle. Ye sure ye got all the gear ye need for such doin's?"

"Yes, goddammit," Adams hissed.

"He's got it," Early agreed. "I seen it one of them times down in Taos a couple year ago when we was gettin' fancied up for one of the *fandangos*."

"Was everything big enough?" Rawlins asked with a chuckle.

Early began to laugh a little. "Seemed to be, though I nary did check too close, ye understand. I figure the problem is that ol' hoss there jist don't know how to use it none."

The two other mountain men chortled as Adams sat stiff of shoulder and stern of face.

"Blue Rattle, she could teach dat chil' how to use dem t'ings if she is anyt'ing like her sister. *Mais oui!* She would make *un grand homme* out of dat chil'." He and his two longtime friends were laughing pretty well now.

"You three are disgusting, vile creatures, unfit for human companionship," Adams said tightly.

"*Mais oui!*" Chardonnais said, laughing all the more. "Dat is what makes de t'ree of us shine."

"Goddamn certain," Rawlins and Early agreed.

Adams jumped up and stormed out, the cackling laughter of his companions still ringing in his ears. He realized a few minutes later, though, that he had nowhere to go but back to Early's lodge or to Blue Rattle's. He went to Early's first and gathered up what few belongings he had there, including his two blankets. He would need them for sleeping. He just hoped that Blue Rattle would be more understanding about all this than the three mountain men were being. Reluctantly, he headed for his own lodge.

14

THEY PULLED OUT THE NEXT morning, heading
north. Riding at the back of the pack like he almost
always did, Rawlins had an eerie feeling. With the
exception of Adams, Looks Again's son Crow Fight,
and Little Rider, this looked a whole heap like the
procession that rode out of Strong Bear's village at
the beginning of a trapping season two years ago.

As the group's nominal leader, Early led off. He
was followed by Falling Leaf and then four-year-old
Straight Calf on a pony. Then rode Rawlins's woman,
Scatters the Clouds and, after her, their son Standing
Eagle. Following the boy was Blue Rattle, with Little
Rider in a cradleboard hanging from the saddlehorn.
Then came Looks Again, riding proudly. Crow Fight
rode in a cradleboard, too. Behind her was the cavvyard
of pack mules and extra horses, loosely herded by
Chardonnais and Adams. Then came Rawlins. It
wasn't so much that he really preferred to be just a
bit away from everyone else, it was more that next to
Early, he had the keenest senses. It seemed as if the

two of them could almost smell danger coming.

The last two seasons had been horrible in most ways, running together as they did. While the three, plus Boatwright, had caught more than their fair share of plews, Boatwright had died in the Crow attack, and their plews had been stolen. Five of their Ute friends had died as the three men tried to get their furs back. It almost made Rawlins shudder. He was not a man to be frightened by anything, but the eeriness of the trip out of the Ute village made him think.

It was colder this year than last, Rawlins thought, and there was a strong hint of winter in the air. The skies were clear, but there had been a rime of frost on the water supply that morning.

They camped on the Uncompahgre River that night and for several more, setting their traps. The plews they pulled out weren't the best they had ever seen, but they were close to prime. The four men paired up—Rawlins and Chardonnais, and Early and Adams. One pair would check the trap lines, quickly skin the beaver, and reset the traps; the other pair would watch over the camp. The next day they would switch.

They moved on a little ways when they had exhausted the first spot. Continuing to do so, they made their way slowly north through the valley. Two weeks after leaving Strong Bear's village, they came to a small log-stockade trading fort along the Uncompahgre, about four miles from its confluence with the Gunnison.

The group found only three men at the fort—the owner, Antoine Robideaux, and two clerks.

"*Bonjour, mes amis,*" Robideaux said with apparent

joy at seeing the travelers. He came out of a log building. "Welcome to my trading post."

"*Bonjour,*" Chardonnais said as he dismounted. "*Comment allez-vous?*" He and Robideaux embraced briefly.

"*Bien, bien. Et vous?*" Robideau replied.

"*Très bien.*"

"*Hola,* Antoine," Early said.

"*Bonjour,* Ezra."

"How's doin's, ol' hoss?" Rawlins offered.

"*Bonjour,* Abe." He paused, beaming. "Come, into ze dining room. You will stay some time, eh?"

"Just overnight, since we got to get back on the trail. But only if that won't put ye out none, Antoine," Early said.

"I will enjoy ze company. *Mais oui.* I like ze Utes and all, but ze are poor company for a white man. At least as a steady t'ing. And zose clerks of mine." He threw up his hands in helplessness.

Early turned and spoke to the women, who then went outside to begin setting up their lodges. There was not enough room inside the small fort's tiny open ground.

They all went into a log building whose outer wall also served as one of the walls of the trading post. It was warm inside, after the chilliness and gloom of the stormy day, and the men appreciated the coffee that a Ute woman handed them. Bowls of lightly spiced elk stew soon followed.

The room smelled of meat and herbs, wood and smoke, tobacco and humans, wet clothing and old flatulence. Large hunks of smoked meat hung from some of the rafters, as did herbs, twists of tobacco, and strings of onions and chili peppers. There were two wood tables with a bench on each side. Together, they would accommodate sixteen men, if they didn't mind being too packed in.

"What brings you to my humble place, messieurs?" Robideaux asked as he noisily slurped coffee.

"We can use a little more powder and lead," Rawlins said. He was on his second bowl of stew already.

"Some cigars, too, if you have them, Mister Robideaux," Adams said quietly.

"I do," Robideaux responded. He looked from Early to Rawlins. "And who is zis chil' you 'ave here?"

"Antoine Robideaux," Early said, "meet Mister Hobart Adams, late of New York and Taos. Bart, Mister Antoine Robideaux."

"*Enchanté de faire votre connaissance,* Monsieur Adams," Robideaux said with considerable dignity. He held out his hand. "Please to meet you, Mister Adams."

"The pleasure is mine, Mister Robideaux," Adams said as he shook hands with the Frenchman.

"Anyt'ing else you need?" Robideaux asked.

Early shook his head. "Maybe a little tobacco if ye can spare it. That ought to about do it."

"But of course."

"Ye had any trouble out here, Antoine?" Rawlins asked.

"*Mais non.* Should I have?" He was interested. If they had seen or heard something that might affect him, he wanted to know about it, and as early as possible.

"Nope. Jist askin'."

Robideaux nodded. "Ze last trouble we had 'ere, it was when ze Shoshones made a raid on a Ute village southwest of here a mont', maybe two mont' ago. Zey made off wit' twenty-two Ute ponies. Ze Utes, zey were not pleased."

"Reckon they weren't," Rawlins snorted. "The goddamn Utes go after 'em?"

"No. Zey said zey will wait till ze spring comes, zen zey will go up zere and show zem Shoshones how to raid. Me, I t'ink zey are full of shit."

Pipes and cigars were brought out and lit as the men relaxed. The snapping of the fire provided a comforting sound to them all. Robideaux brought out a jug and five tin cups. He filled the cups from the jug and passed them around.

Robideaux held up his cup. "*Bon chance, messieurs.* May you make ze beaver come, eh!"

The others agreed with the toast and drank to it.

"Where're your clerks, *mon ami?*" Chardonnais asked.

"In ze storeroom or ze trade room."

Chardonnais looked at him in surprise. Robideaux was not usually so standoffish with his employees.

"Zey are worthless, zese two. *Mon dieu!* Zey can't read wort' a damn, zey can't do figuring. Useless, ze bot' of zem."

"Fire 'em," Rawlins suggested.

"And where would I get new helpers out here, eh?" Robideaux retorted. His dander was rising. "No, I must wait till ze spring now. Zen I will take zem back to Taos or I'll send zem packing with some brigade zat comes t'rough here. And I will get me zome real clerks zen." He gulped down the whiskey in his cup and then refilled it.

The men spent the night talking, drinking, eating, and smoking. It was well past dark when they stumbled toward their beds through the light but steady snowfall.

They all were slightly hungover in the morning,

but not so bad as to really hamper them. As the women began taking down the lodges Early and his men loaded their supplies on the mules. They got what little they needed from Robideaux, paying in gold coin, and loaded that, too. Then they pulled out, once more heading mostly north along the Uncompahgre.

Crossing the Gunnison River late that morning took them more than three hours, and then they pushed on, following the Gunnison northwestward.

It took another nine days to make the junction of the Gunnison and Grand rivers, what with stopping to trap and all. They turned westward along the Grand River, and soon crossed it, which was another huge undertaking requiring several hours to get everyone and all the supplies and equipment across. They headed north, stopping to trap small streams and ponds wherever they found beaver sign. They began moving a little faster as they found a drier, less fruitful land. The country was high and stark, with low hills rising all over.

They made their way through Douglas Pass and onto the west fork of Douglas Creek. Another two days and they made the White River. They spent several days at the junction of Douglas Creek and the White River. The group used the time for resting up some, repairing gear, and trapping.

It was almost a month since they had left Strong Bear's village. It was snowing with some regularity now, though it wasn't accumulating too much, at least where they were. Temperatures were below freezing as often as not, but as yet were not intolerable or even inconvenient.

When they left that camp, they headed west

along the White River, moving from the hills to a flat, sere, barren land. They traveled swiftly now. There were few or no beaver in this area, so they had no reason to dawdle. Except for the White River, which they were roughly following, there was little in the area to strike one's interest. That, too, added speed to their journey.

In two days they reached the Green River, where they spent the night. With a fresh start in the morning, they made it across the Green with a minimum of trouble.

After two and a half days following the Duchesne River, they began heading up into the Uinta Mountains. Then they slowed again, once more taking up their sporadic traveling, stopping for a few days to trap wherever they found beaver sign.

They worked ever farther into the heart of the Uintas, trapping as they went. The temperatures were almost constantly below freezing now, and snow fell almost every day, though only once did they encounter a serious storm, which they sat out in their comfortable camp.

They eventually cut almost due north, gradually coming down out of the Uintas, and then hitting the Bear River. They followed its wavering course north and then northwest, before leaving it and turning northeast, trapping whatever ponds or streams they found, heading north.

When they came to the Snake River, they crossed it—losing a mule loaded with prime plews—and then followed it west. Finally, in early December, about three months after they left Strong Bear's village, Early pulled to a stop in a mountain meadow in a small valley along a little tributary of the Snake. Pines and aspens abounded, cottonwoods lined the stream, and there was plenty of game.

"Reckon this'll do," Early said.

None of the others disagreed.

They set about making their winter camp. They were used to the routine by now. Even Adams had become one of them. Rawlins, Early, and Chardonnais had pushed the young Easterner hard during the whole journey, especially at the beginning. There were times when he was sure he was not going to be able to make another step, but he always did.

Adams looked like his counterparts, too. Blue Rattle had made him a buckskin shirt and pants, plus buffalo-hide moccasins lined with buffalo wool. She had also made him a bear-fur coat, hat, and mittens.

Rawlins picked out the site for their lodges, and the women set the tipis up in a semicircle with the opening facing east. The lodges were close enough to make defense possible and close enough to make their work of gathering firewood and such easier. Yet they had enough distance between them so that they would have privacy when they were inside.

While the women went about preparing their homes for the rapidly approaching winter, the men went out to hunt. The next day the women were kept busy making meat while the men continued to hunt. After three days of hunting there was plenty of meat to be made into jerky and pemmican.

The women kept making meat, in addition to their other chores. While they continued to hunt, the men went back to trapping, and helped out around camp when they could.

Just before Christmas, a howling, screaming, plundering blizzard charged into the valley and shut the mountain men and their families up in their lodges for four days. When the storm finally got disgusted with not being able to dislodge these tenacious humans, it blew itself out of the valley.

The members of the group came outside for the first time in four days and looked on a white wonderland. They also found a dead horse and a dead mule. The two animals were dragged off a ways, where scavengers could feed on them without disturbing the people.

They finished securing their winter camp, making more meat and making sure a good supply of firewood was split and available. Then they all settled in to wait out the winter.

15

THE MEN TRAPPED WHEN THEY could, but that wasn't very often once the stream and the few ponds froze over. Still, there was work to be done. The women still had plews that had to be cured, and the men had to pack them into bales. Clothes had to be made or repaired, children cared for, and fires tended. The animals needed looking after to make sure they had enough forage. Minor blacksmithing was needed, and firewood was always a necessity. Hunting was a welcome diversion, not only for a slight change of scenery but also for the fresh meat. The more fresh meat they had, the longer they could stretch out their jerky and pemmican. Besides, it was far preferable eating fresh elk than elk jerky or elk pemmican, no matter how well the latter two might be made.

The closeness of living quarters and all, though, made everyone testy at times. Chardonnais, who was prone to fits of melancholy or euphoria, was affected the most. Rawlins and Early were used to

him, and so let him be when he was in one of his
strange humors. In the several years they had been
together, Looks Again also had proved to be good
for the French-Canadian at these times. Adams
still was not sure how to react when Chardonnais
suddenly began insulting him and trying to provoke
a fight. He did, however, attempt to keep his silence
and his patience.

Adams spent a considerable amount of time—
when there were no chores to be done, which was
often enough—sketching and writing. He still planned
to send some articles and sketches to Humphrey
McWalters, editor of the *New York Register*. The
money would always come in handy, and Adams was
sure people would be interested in men like Abe
Rawlins, Ezra Early, and Lucien Chardonnais.

Because of his sketches and writings, Adams
often observed his three friends closely. They were a
strange bunch, he thought more than once. He knew
Early the best, having met him first and traveled with
him for some weeks after the trapper had saved him
from the Comanches. Early was somewhat serious,
apparently an astute businessman, tough as any man
Adams had ever seen, yet with a big and generous
heart—as long as this fact wasn't thrust in his face.

Lucien Chardonnais was a fairly easy man to figure out. He was, simply, a man who was passionate
about everything. He apparently lived up to the tales
about his sexual prowess. Indeed, Adams had seen
him heading for his lodge far more frequently than
the others, and usually the sounds of lovemaking
seeped out shortly after. His passion for life was what
made him somewhat unstable of mind, what pushed
him into his occasional melancholy fits. It was still

disconcerting, however, to see just how swiftly he could go from friend to bitter enemy—and back.

Abe Rawlins, on the other hand, was something of an enigma. More than once Adams had thought him taciturn, but that wasn't the case. He was quick to laugh, quick to dally with the women, quick to fight. He did all three, and just about everything else, with a sense of gusto, as long as it did not get too complicated for him. He worried little about tomorrow, and seemed to seek no friends other than Early and Chardonnais. Yet he would step in immediately and help an unfortunate—even someone like Diego, who hadn't liked him. He was at least as tough as Early, and probably more ruthless, though he didn't seem to hate very much. He simply did what needed doing as efficiently and with as little fuss as possible. If that included a killing or two, so be it. He would get it done and go back to enjoying his life.

All three mountain men regularly insulted each other, calling each other names that would've gotten any other man killed for saying. But while all took part, Rawlins and Chardonnais were the biggest perpetrators. Early seemed to stand above it at times, and at others he seemed to be watching over their repartee like a parent.

One day while he and Early were in camp and the other two trappers were out hunting, Adams asked, "Why do Abe and Lucien always insult each other?"

Early shrugged. "Just the way they are. We all do it."

"I know you all do it, but there's something different, something almost special, in the way those two go about it."

Early glared at him for a moment, then grinned a

little. "It goes back to, I don't know, twenty-four, I think," Early said. "We was still with Ashley's brigade then. The three of us was sent out with a dozen or so other boys under Jed Smith to trap up along the Snake and its tributaries. Me and Lucien'd been paired up, since we knew each other from twenty-two. But ol' Abe there, he didn't have but one year in the mountains, so he was still some green. Because of that, Jed stuck him partnerin' with an ol'-timer, a fractious ol' fart named René DuBois."

Early drifted back over the years. Lord, they were so young then, full of fire and wildness. Even back then, Abe Rawlins was generally an easygoing man, but he hated DuBois. Had right from the start. He had even complained to Smith about him as soon as the pairing was made. He could've done it out in the open, but he was trying not to hurt the old man's feelings.

Smith had listened, then nodded. "I understand what ye're talkin' of, Mister Rawlins." He was unfailingly polite, until pushed too far. "And I can sympathize with ye. Yes, I can. But I'll tell ye somethin', ol' hoss, that ye're about the only man of this crew I figure can stomach bein' paired up with that sinful reprobate."

"What the hell's that supposed to mean?" Rawlins snapped. He hated being talked to in such a way, especially by a man not more than a year or so older than he was.

"It means that ye're about the most even-tempered feller we got here—aside from me, of course, and I got other duties to deal with. Anybody else here'd end up killin' that ol' man."

"And ye don't think I will, dammit?"

"No, Abe, I don't. Ye're a reasonable man. Ye'll put up with his nonsense and then make some jokes 'round the fire with your two friends, Ezra and Lucien. That'll calm ye down." He sounded positive.

Rawlins considered arguing, but then decided against it. He was not a man to beat his head against a wall. It was plain that Smith had made up his mind, and there would be no swaying him. Rawlins could either accept the decision and try to live with it, or he could take off. And this far from civilization, that was a plumb foolish thing to do on one's own.

Rawlins tried for the first few weeks to be friendly with DuBois. But the old trapper—his fifty-two years qualifying him as ancient to the eighteen-year-old Rawlins—was having none of it. He was lazier than any Indian Rawlins had ever met. All he ever did was plunk his rump on the riverbank and doze, or smoke his old clay pipe. Occasionally he did both. That left Rawlins with all the work, including skinning the beavers they caught in their traps.

By the time they were on the western reaches of the Snake, Rawlins was about ready to kill DuBois, but was managing to keep himself in check only with the help of his two close friends. He went out one morning, intending to trap another tributary of the Snake he had seen across the wide, fast-rushing river, a mile or so west of the camp.

"Don't you try it, boy," DuBois warned. "Such doin's can hurt a man. *Mais oui.*" He did not sound in the least concerned for Rawlins's welfare. Rawlins figured the old man just didn't want to make the effort.

"Eat shit, DuBois," he snapped. "Jist 'cause your balls're all dried up and ye got no more gumption left in ye, don't mean we all have to turn into dead sacks of shit like ye."

He walked off, not really caring if the old trapper followed him. With his rifle on one shoulder, and five traps slung over the other, he started across the Snake, about midway between the camp and the tributary, leaping from rock to rock. Then one of his moccasins hit a slick spot on a rock. The twenty-five pounds or so of traps, plus a sudden gust of wind gave him more momentum, and he fell into the water. The river's swift current swept him away.

DuBois, who was standing on the bank watching, cackled with laughter. "Hope you can swim dere, hoss!" he shouted, voice cracking with apparent joy.

"Shit," Rawlins muttered just before getting dunked. He dropped the traps but held on to his rifle. He drew in a breath whenever he could as he bobbed down the river like a cork. He banged off rocks in the roiling, foaming water, making him wince regularly.

Rawlins was a little surprised at how fast the river had pushed him the half mile to their camp. As he churned past the camp he could see men pointing toward him and yelling, but he could hear nothing but the river's deafening roar. Then he was past the camp and had slammed into another rock.

Moments later a frantic-looking Chardonnais splashed up alongside Rawlins and grabbed his shirt. "I will save you, *mon ami!*" he shouted.

"Ye goddamn, stupid, stump-humpin' idiot frog," Rawlins bellowed back.

"I come to save you!" Chardonnais reiterated.

"I don't need your goddamn savin', ye goddamn fool!"

Then the water slammed Chardonnais's head into

a boulder. He released Rawlins's shirt and disappeared under the roiling river.

"Shit," Rawlins muttered. He sucked in a deep breath and plunged his head under the water, groping wildly with his free hand. Then his shoulder plowed into another rock. The sudden jolt of pain forced him to swallow a mouthful of muddy river water.

Rawlins fought to the surface and sputtered. He managed to suck in a few good breaths before plunging into the water again. Once again he found nothing. Gasping for air in the swirling river, he dropped his rifle, barely dodged another rock, and then went under the water again, swimming a little to keep himself steady.

Just before he thought his lungs would burst, his right hand encountered rough cloth. Two more powerful strokes and he latched onto Chardonnais—at least he thought it was Chardonnais—with both hands. He surfaced, managing to haul his friend along with him.

Rawlins got an arm under Chardonnais's hairy chin and kept him sort of on his chest as they bounced along backward through the water. Rawlins kept throwing glances over his shoulder, using his free arm to push off rocks when he could.

He spotted what looked to be even rougher rapids ahead, and he fought with all his strength to get to the side of the river on the camp's side. He was making little progress. Then he saw a large boulder thrusting up out of the water. Rawlins managed to angle toward it and braced himself.

The river smashed him against the boulder, and he grunted with the impact. The seething water tried to rip him loose for another slam on the rock, but he managed to fight that off. He hung there, back and lungs aching, trying to breathe while still keeping Chardonnais's head above the water.

Rawlins glanced toward shore and saw Early galloping up on horseback. Early jumped off the horse and ran toward the river.

Rawlins frantically waved at him. Early looked up just as he entered the water, and stopped.

"We don't need another chil' in the water!" Rawlins shouted, not sure Early could hear him. The yelling hurt his lungs.

Early nodded and backed out of the river. He turned, looking frantically for something that would help. Just about then, Smith and a few other men galloped up. The always levelheaded Jed Smith had a coil of rawhide rope. Early grabbed it. He dropped the bulk of it on the ground and then threw the end. It went about five feet and fell.

Feeling like an idiot, he grabbed a rock from the many along the river and tied it to the end. Then he threw it again. He missed by a dozen yards. He tried again and yet again. On the sixth toss, the rock hit Rawlins in the head and bounced off into the river.

Irritated at the whole situation, Rawlins shook his head, but he managed to grab the rope and wrap it around his left forearm several times, then gripped it in his left fist. Making sure his grip on Chardonnais was strong, he bellowed, "Pull!"

In two minutes the other mountain men had hauled the two men ashore. Someone pulled Chardonnais out of Rawlins's protective arm and stretched him out on his back. As Rawlins sank exhausted to the rocky riverbank, he saw that Early was jerking Chardonnais up and down by the belt. Rawlins rested his head on his arms, and then heard Chardonnais vomit up a load of water. He smiled a little, relieved.

The next day, the little trapper tried to thank his friend for saving his life, making a great gushing speech of thanks.

"'Tweren't nothin', hoss," Rawlins said uncomfortably.

"But, *mon ami,* wit'out you, I would've gone under. *Mais oui!*"

"Ye hadn't of jumped in that goddamn river, you stupid stump of a Frenchman, I would've never had to save ye."

"But I was trying to save you, *mon ami.*"

"What made ye think this ol' chil' needed savin', 'specially by the likes of ye?"

"I was trying to do good," Chardonnais said sulkily.

"I know that, but when ye jumped in that goddamn river after me, ye caused me to lose my rifle. Now I'm out that, plus my traps."

"*Je suis désolé, mon ami.* I am sorry I caused you so much trouble."

"Forget about it, Lucien. It's over and done with."

"Still, dere is de matter of you saving my life. *Mais oui.* I still am in your debt for dat."

"I tol' ye, hoss, 'tweren't nothin'. Ye would've done the same for this ol' chil' had I been damn fool enough to jump in the water after ye."

"I would've tried, but who knows how I would've done, eh?"

"Ye would've made do. Same as ye would've for Ez. We're all in this for each other, hoss. No thanks needed."

"How can you say dat, eh?"

"It were easy. Now go away, you stump-suckin' little toad."

"*Mais non!* I cannot do dat."

"Ye don't, ye bandy-legged little bastard, and I'll finish up the job the ol' Snake started on ye."

"But—"

"Look, ye want to thank someone, hoss, go thank Ez. Weren't for him, me'n ye both might've gone under."

"No! I'm in *your* debt forever. Anyt'ing you ask, I will give to you. You have no rifle and you want mine? Voilà! It is yours." He held it out. "You want my horse, take de damn t'ing. And de saddle. You want my traps, take dem all. You want my woman?" He sighed greatly. "Ah, *je le regrette,* I 'ave no woman. I hope Monsieur Smit' takes us to a Shoshone village soon, eh? But if I had a woman and you wanted her, voilà! She would be yours to have. One time or every night."

"Ye want to give me somethin, ol' hoss?"

"But of course, *mon ami.* Anyt'ing. You just ask."

"Ye can give me some goddamn peace and quiet, ye fractious, stump-high bag of shit. That's what ye can give this ol' hoss." Rawlins was uncomfortable with being thanked, and Chardonnais's persistence was annoying him. He also was angry at himself for having fallen into the river into the first place, losing his traps, and then losing his rifle.

"Well dat's just fine, dammit," Chardonnais said, growing a little heated. He felt he was in Rawlins's debt and did not like that. He wanted to make things even again, and Rawlins was not cooperating. "*Merde!* You're a skunk-humping ingrate. A piece of sheep shit. *Mais non!* You are even lower dan sheep shit. Snake shit, *oui,* dat is what you are."

Rawlins's annoyance was rapidly fleeing, and a grin emerged. "That so, froggie?"

"*Oui.* Dat's what I say to you. You t'ink you are better dan dat, eh?"

"I'd rather be snake shit than a stumpy-legged little turd like ye."

Chardonnais spun and stomped away, muttering in French. Rawlins grinned, feeling a little better.

16

ADAMS SHOOK HIS HEAD in amazement. "And they've been at it ever since?" he asked.

"Yep." Early laughed. "Hell, since I saved 'em both, more or less, I was permitted to join in the fun. To tell ye the truth, though, hoss, I ain' so good at it as them two."

"How'd Abe overcome the loss of his traps and his rifle?"

"The traps was easy to replace. They weren't really his traps. His was all set out with DuBois's. He'd borrowed those others from the company's stores. He would've had to pay for 'em come the end of the season."

"But he didn't have to do that, did he?" Adams asked astutely.

"Shit no," Rawlins said with a laugh. "He just went out the next mornin', early, and pulled up DuBois's traps. He carted 'em back to the camp and gave 'em to Jed. That ol' chil' was some surprised, I tell ye."

"I expect he was. What happened then? DuBois surely must've found out."

"He did, yep. When Abe gave the traps to Jed, he told him he wouldn't be goin' out with DuBois anymore. Jed didn't see fit to argue the point. So when DuBois went out to where Abe had set his traps, he didn't find shit. That ol' son of a bitch went stormin' back to camp and was about half-froze to raise hair. He went straight to Abe and accused him of stealin' his traps."

"I take it that didn't set real well with Abe," Adams suggested.

"Ye know that ol" chil' pretty well now, don't ye. Abe jist stands up and says—with a calm face, mind ye, 'If'n ye cain't keep track of where ye lay your traps, ol' hoss, ye oughtn't to be out here with the rest of us critters.' Well, Christ, DuBois's bowels was packed then, boy, or I wouldn't tell ye.

"Well, ol' Jed stepped in and said as much to DuBois, and then told that ol' niggur that since he didn't have no more traps, and there weren't no more in the stores, that he'd have to earn his keep by actin' as a camp helper. I thought DuBois'd shit his 'skins right there."

"Whatever happened to DuBois?" Adams asked innocently.

Early shook his head. "Goddamn ol' fool allowed as it was Abe who caused him all the miseries in his life, and he painted his face black against Abe."

"Challenged him?"

"Yep," Early said with a nod.

"And Abe killed him, of course."

"Yep. He tried not to at first, but then DuBois managed to get in a lucky swipe with his knife and cut Abe. Our ol' *amigo* was plumb put out by such doin's, and made short work of that damned ol' Frenchman." Early suddenly grinned, sloughing off the gloom that had so recently befallen him. "Ol' Abe did get himself a nice rifle out of it, though."

One of the pleasures of the winter was gathering in one of the lodges and gabbing. It happened nearly every night. On one blustery evening, the four were sitting around the fire in Early's lodge, listening to the wind howling outside, buffeting the lodges. The three old partners had been regaling Adams with tales of the mountains when Rawlins suddenly looked at Adams and grinned. "Ye bedded that purty-lookin' squaw of yours yet?" he asked with no sign of embarrassment.

Adams was discomfited enough for them both. "That's none of your concern," he said stiffly.

"He ain't done it," Chardonnais said with authority. "Goddamn, I know he ain't."

"How the hell do you know?" Adams demanded.

"Did you forget, *mon ami,* dat she is de sister of Looks Again? You can't keep women from talking of dese t'ings."

"Goddamn, I am plumb ashamed of ye, Bart," Rawlins said solemnly, fighting back a grin. "Christ, Ez, how'd ye ary come up with this chil'? Ain't ye taught him nothin'?"

"Hah!" Chardonnais interjected. "Ezra teach any chil' anyt'ing? How can he do dat when he don' know dese t'ings himself? Answer for me dat question, eh."

"Shit, froggie, I forgot all about that. Reckon we cain't expect too much from ol' Bart, considerin' who he's got for a teacher."

"I hope the both of ye critters falls in a big pile of shit and drown," Early said, fighting back a chuckle. "Bart's a big boy. He ought to know what to do with a woman."

"Maybe he t'inks you will come and put it in dere for him," Chardonnais said with a hoot. "Like wit' horses."

"Shit," Early said with a roar, "if that's what the hell he's waitin' for, he's gonna be waitin' a spell. It'll be a cold day in the pits of hell afore I touch his diseased little pizzle."

Adams's face was a bright, bloody red as the three others rocked with gales of laughter. He was saved from further embarrassment when Scatters the Clouds came and took Standing Eagle from her husband and left for her own lodge. The child had crawled into Rawlins's lap a little earlier and had fallen asleep.

Adams was still rather amazed whenever he saw Rawlins with Standing Eagle. He still had trouble reconciling the mighty warrior he knew Abe Rawlins to be with the caring parent of Standing Eagle. Rawlins would play with the boy for hours. It was often rough play, Adams noted, but there was a specialness there, too, that Rawlins made no effort to hide.

When Scatters the Clouds took the child, Adams looked at Rawlins and grinned. He wanted to keep the conversation from getting back around to him and Blue Rattle, if he could. "If I had just seen you in Taos, I'd never have known how good you were with children. I'm impressed. How'd you ever—"

Adams stopped abruptly when Rawlins's face

darkened in anger. The trapper rose and stalked out
of the lodge without his hat or capote.

"What the . . . ?" Adams said. He looked at
Early, panicked. The lodge had grown as cold and
hard as the storm blowing outside, and Adams was
suddenly afraid. "Did I say something wrong?" he
asked weakly.

Early glared at him for a moment, then relented a
little. "It goes back to, I don't know, twenty-eight, maybe
twenty-nine," Early said. "We was up in Absarokas,
I think."

"Mais oui," Chardonnais added in a hoarse voice.
"It was de Absarokas." If Early was going to tell the
story, he figured he might as well help out.

Early nodded. "We had us a small winter camp
up there. Spring was still a ways off, but we was nigh
out of meat. Goddamn, but if those weren't starvin'
times. I tell ye, hoss, this ol' chil' thought we was all
gone under for certain. Anyway, we decided that I'd
stay in camp with the womenfolk—this was afore
Lucien and Looks Again hooked up—and young'ns,
whilst Lucien and Abe went out lookin' for meat.

"It was colder'n a witch's tit, hoss, and don't ye
nary doubt it neither. Snow up to a buffler's hump,
wind blowin' strong enough to knock down a lodge if
it hit the right way, but they pulled out on a couple
scrawny horses."

Early could still see the two—Rawlins tall, lean,
hard; Chardonnais short, broad, and angry—riding
out on the two horses that looked like they wouldn't
go a hundred feet. The animals hadn't had any
decent forage in weeks. Fifty feet from the lodges,
the men and horses disappeared into the swirling,
wind-lashed snow.

Chardonnais was ahead of his friend for no particular reason other than Rawlins liked riding at the rear to keep an eye on things. They rode all that day, camped that night in a small stand of trees that did little to block out the searching wind. They each ate one strip of jerky and then tried to get some sleep.

The next four days were pretty much the same. Rawlins kept them going through strength of will and little else. Both were weakening swiftly, and Chardonnais seemed to be on the verge of having delusions. It was then that his horse died right out from under him. The short, stout French-Canadian fell to the ground hard as his horse collapsed and lay dying.

Rawlins pulled up sharply and dismounted. He took one look at the horse and knew the animal would never get up again. He slit its throat to put it out of its misery. Then he walked the few paces to Chardonnais. "Best git your ass up, ol' hoss," he said.

"I am gone under, *mon ami,*" Chardonnais said weakly, though with no note of whining in his voice. "You go on and find meat for ze others. Take some to Yellow Feather."

"Ye ain't goin' under whilst I'm still on my feet, hoss." Rawlins set his rifle down, bent, and picked his friend up. He carried him to the only horse left and almost tossed him into the saddle.

"I can't stay up here, Abe," Chardonnais gasped.

"Ye listen to me, ye toad-suckin' little shitball. Ye ain't dyin' on me out here, and that's all there is to it. Now ye hold on to that saddle horn and stay up there, or I swear to Christ I'll tie ye up there."

Chardonnais's dark eyes burned with fury. "I'll

show you, damn you," he snapped. "Goddamn long-legged, skunk-humpin' son of a bitch."

"That's the spirit, froggie. Now hold on." He picked up his rifle and began to walk off, leading the horse.

"Wait!" Chardonnais screeched. "Wait!"

"What the hell is it now?" Rawlins asked, more than a little irritable.

"Take some meat from de 'orse, eh. Dat will 'elp us bot'."

"Goddamn, for a frog humper, ye ain't so dumb as others might think." Rawlins swiftly hacked out some meat. He figured he could carry maybe fifty pounds of it, if it wasn't for too long. He needed to find a place where they could bed down for the night, a place with enough wood for a fire.

Before leaving again, he pulled a long strip of buckskin from his possible bag and swiftly fashioned a rude sling for his rifle. He slung it over his back, then used another piece of the rawhide to wrap around the meat. Holding the strap in his left hand, he hung the meat over his back. He took the reins in his right hand and pushed on.

Two hours later Rawlins found something of a cave. Actually it was more like two almost flat slabs of rock having fallen roughly in a tipi shape. It was big enough for them to lie in, though, and there looked to be sufficient firewood easily available.

Rawlins spread out a buffalo robe, got Chardonnais off the horse, and laid him down on the robe. Then he went to gather firewood. He patiently built a fire, ignoring as best he could the exhaustion and cold and despair that swept over him. With the fire going, he put some of the horse meat on to cook. Then he rose, reluctant to leave the fire's warmth and the smell of the meat. "Don't ye go nowhere, ol' hoss," he said.

"Where're you going?"

"Back to get your saddle. You'll need it sooner or later. And if the wolves and coyotes ain't took all of it, maybe I can get us a bit more meat."

"Leave me here and go back to de odders," Chardonnais insisted. "Take de 'orse meat and go back."

"Eat shit, froggie." He pulled into the saddle. "Ye get to feelin' up to it, ye might gather up some more wood. And ye make sure ye fill your meatbag good, ye fractious, toad-suckin' sack of shit."

Rawlins rode off, the smell of horse meat lingering in his nostrils. Wolves were still working at the horse's carcass, but he managed to drive them off, wasting only two shots. The wolves' work, though, had made it easier to get the saddle out from under the dead animal. And there was another fifty or sixty pounds of meat that was still edible. He took it and rode back to the "cave."

Chardonnais was asleep, but Rawlins could tell he had packed away a good seven or eight pounds of meat.

Rawlins unsaddled the horse and tied it to a tree where the animal could get at some sweet cottonwood bark. With his knife, he loosened some of the bark, and the horse nibbled at it immediately.

Rawlins went back to the fire and sank wearily to the ground. Then he began digging into the horse meat himself. It tasted like hell, but it was hot, and he could feel it filling his belly with the first bite.

Rawlins wanted to spend a couple of days there so that Chardonnais could recover more, and so he could gain some of his strength back. But he decided that would not be right. They still had not found any meat, other than the dead horse, and he could not go back to camp with forty or fifty pounds of meat—which would be all that would be left once he and Chardonnais got through with it—to serve three men, three women, and two children. No, they had to push on.

They spent the rest of that afternoon there, and that night. Both spent most of it sleeping, but Rawlins awoke every couple of hours to build up the fire and then wolf down another pound or so of meat.

In the morning he ate again, and made the French-Canadian do so, too. Then he saddled the horse. "Can ye get your fat ass up in that saddle?" he asked. "Or do I have to throw ye up there again?"

"You ride. I'll follow along as best I can, eh."

"Listen, ye dirt-eatin' shitball, I ain't of a mind to argue with ye. Either get your stumpy little ass up there or I'll throw ye up there."

"Skunk-humpin' beanstalk," Chardonnais snarled. He rose, lurched to the horse, and pulled himself into the saddle.

Rawlins handed Chardonnais his rifle and hung what meat they had left over the saddle horn. He slung his own rifle over his shoulder again and hefted the saddle. Taking the horse's reins, he walked off.

Sometime before noon, Chardonnais hissed. Rawlins stopped. "Dere are elk," the little trapper whispered. "Two, maybe t'ree of dem. To your left. Maybe fifty yards away."

Rawlins nodded and eased the saddle down, trying not to make any sudden moves. He pulled his rifle off his shoulder and checked it. He stuck the butt into the snow. "Give me your rifle, *amigo*," he said. He did not look back, he just reached. When he felt his fingers close over the rifle, he grabbed it and pulled it forward. He checked that, too. He knelt, aimed, and fired. One elk went down, and four others, two of which had been hidden by trees and rocks, bolted.

Rawlins dropped Chardonnais's rifle and grabbed his own. He fired again, and another elk went down.

"You sure made dem come now, *mon ami*," Chardonnais said happily. But he was still so weak that he almost fell off the horse.

Rawlins patiently reloaded both rifles, gave Chardonnais his, and slung his own again. Then they hurried to the two elk. Butchering did not take long. Chardonnais did, however, keep insisting that he was well enough to help, and Rawlins kept ignoring him.

When he had several hundred pounds of meat wrapped in bloody elk hide, Rawlins made a simple travois and attached it to the horse. He got the meat and his friend's saddle loaded on it and pulled out, walking while Chardonnais rode.

Rawlins would allow stops only long enough to build a fire and heat some meat. The two trappers would eat, Rawlins would force Chardonnais back onto the horse, and then they moved on.

They made it back in a little more than two days. Rawlins staggered into camp, nearly spent. Chardonnais was in pretty good shape, having eaten well each time they stopped. Rawlins fell in the snow.

Scatters the Clouds hurried out of her lodge, screeching in Ute. Early and Chardonnais helped drag Rawlins inside, where Scatters the Clouds was determined to see to his recovery.

It took several days before he was aware of the world around him, and that's when Scatters the Clouds told him about their eight-month-old daughter.

"Red Butterfly is dead," she said, her voice choked with emotion, her face etched in pain.

Rawlins looked at Scatters the Clouds and felt a coldness deep down in his guts that was far worse than anything he had experienced out here in the mountains. "When?" he asked, voice clotted with grief.

"Three days after you left."

"How?"

"The cold. No food. I am a bad mother. I couldn't . . . couldn't . . ." Scatters the Clouds broke down, heavy sobs racking her body.

Rawlins put his arms around her and pulled her close. "It ain't your doin', woman," he said softly. "'Twer my fault. If I'd been able to keep meat in camp, ye would've had enough tit milk for her."

They sat there like that for some time, before Scatters the Clouds finally pulled away and went about her chores. It was several days before Rawlins regained his strength, and when he did, he saddled his horse and rode off.

"I will go wit' him," Chardonnais said.

Early grabbed Chardonnais by the shoulder. "Let him be, Lucien."

"But he saved my life, Ezra. It was my fault Red Butterfly has gone under, and I must go help Abe now."

"It weren't your doin's that put Red Butterfly under. Mayhap it was God's or the Great Spirit's. It don't much matter. Ol' Abe's got to do this."

Chardonnais nodded sadly, feeling a deep despair settling on his shoulders.

Rawlins was gone for two weeks, and he almost seemed his old self when he finally returned. But everyone could see the hurt that lingered in his eyes. It would take some years before that faded.

17

ADAMS SAT IN SILENCE, listening to the crackle of the fire. He did not know how any man could overcome such a thing, though it obviously was something most people were capable of, given the fragility of life out here.

He didn't know what to say, either, not for a while. So he said nothing. Early and Chardonnais still seemed to be far away in their minds. Adams was glad, in a way, for the chance to think.

Finally Adams said, "I don't know how to apologize to Abe." He felt like crying, but he would not let himself do that in front of these two men. "I meant no harm. I was . . . I was trying to compliment him. To be friendly."

Early looked at Adams and smiled a little. "He's long over his loss, Bart. Havin' Standing Eagle the next summer helped considerable in that. So have the years that've gone by."

"But," Chardonnais said, "he don' talk about it. *Mais non!*"

"Lucien's right. He don't ever speak of it, but ye can still see the hurt in that ol' chil's eyes every now and again."

"How do I apologize, though?" Adams insisted. He felt lower than a snake's belly and wanted desperately to make amends.

"Just let it lay, ol' hoss," Early suggested. "That'd be the . . ."

Rawlins stomped back inside the lodge and took his seat at the fire again. "Goddamn, it's cold out there. Like to froze this chil's balls right off."

Adams looked at him in surprise. Rawlins seemed to be perfectly normal again. Then he saw the pain lurking deep in the older man's eyes. "I'm sorry, Abe," he said meekly. "I didn't mean—"

"It's all right, hoss." He paused. "These two assholes tell ye?"

Adams nodded.

"So now ye know. I don't want ye to ary bring it up again, hoss, ye hear?"

Adams nodded. With a dull, sick feeling, he rose and headed for his own lodge.

Blue Rattle was feeding Little Rider. She looked up and smiled faintly. She had become used to their platonic life, though she could not say she liked it. She still missed Jed Boatwright considerably, but she was getting over it. She was a healthy woman, with a healthy woman's desires. She was a little worried by the look on Adams's face.

Adams went and knelt in front of Blue Rattle. He ran a finger down Little Rider's plump cheek. He had never really thought about having children before. He wanted them, to be sure, but he had never really thought about what it might mean. He had the sudden thought that siring a child would be the most important thing he could do. That set him thinking about Dolores, and he wanted to be with her something awful. But she was hundreds of miles away.

Adams touched the baby's face again, and this time Little Rider pulled his mouth away from Blue Rattle's nipple and looked to see what was disturbing his feeding. It gave Adams a clear view of the woman's breast, and his mouth suddenly dried. He forced himself to stand, turn, and leave. Outside in the storm, he hoped the coldness of the night would cool his boiling blood.

The winter was not nearly as bad as some others Rawlins, Early, and Chardonnais had weathered in their years in the mountains, but it seemed to want to linger on and on. Eventually, though, the winter began to blow itself out, easing its icy-fingered grip on the pleasant mountain valley.

They were all glad to see spring trying to force itself into the land, though they had no real plans to leave this little valley before they had exhausted its supply of beaver.

The winter had passed without too much trouble. Their supply of jerked meat had been more than sufficient, and there had been several periods where they could hunt. Game was not plentiful in the depths of the winter, but they found sufficient fresh meat. They had only lost one of the animals, too, a mule that had become weakened by refusing to eat. They found it frozen to death one morning.

The only real low point of the winter was that nearly all of them, men, women, and children, had suffered through at least one cold or bout with ague. All felt miserable during the course of the illness, but suffered no lasting effects.

They started setting their traps as soon as they could, and pulled in thick, prime furs. Once again they paired off—Early and Adams, and Rawlins and Chardonnais—and took turns running the trap lines and watching over the camp. Their friendly competition, pushed on by the bet they had made among themselves, once more heated up, with a considerable amount of vulgar boasting and insults.

Two weeks after they had resumed trapping regularly, Rawlins and Chardonnais were ahead on the number of furs, and neither was about to let his opponents forget it. As Early and Adams headed out of camp one morning to run their trap lines, Rawlins grinned and shouted gleefully, "Ye critters best give up hopin' to win that specie. It's as likely for a buffler to jump over these here Rocky Mountains as it is for ye two to beat this ol' chil' and that stumpy little frog over there."

"Mais oui!" Chardonnais threw in. "We can make dem bevairs come better dan anybody in de mountains."

"Suck elk snot, the both of ye," Early shot back just before he and Adams disappeared into the trees.

Rawlins and Chardonnais laughed.

"Well, *mon ami*," Chardonnais said with a huge smile, "me and Looks Again 'ave business in de lodge."

"Jesus, Frenchie, can't ye keep your pizzle in your pants more'n five goddamn minutes?" Rawlins complained, though he was laughing.

"Mais non! Non, non, non, non, non! Nevair." He

laughed uproariously as he headed for his lodge.

Rawlins sat on a log and began braiding long strips of rawhide into a rope. His fingers worked on their own, allowing him to keep his senses attuned to the camp and its environs. Standing Eagle and Early's daughter, Straight Calf, were playing some game of their own imagining outside Early's lodge. Nearby, Scatters the Clouds and Falling Leaf kept an eye on the children while working on a couple of beaver plews. The entire camp was bedecked with soft brown furs knotted to willow hoops, which dangled from every tree and decent-size bush in and around the camp.

Rawlins set aside his work for a moment and filled his pipe. Lighting it with a stick from the fire, he stuck the stem in his mouth and went back to making the rope. He kept sweeping the camp with his eyes, alert to any danger, but his eyes always came back to Scatters the Clouds.

For her part, Scatters the Clouds frequently looked at Rawlins, when she didn't have her gaze on the children. She smiled whenever her eyes and her husband's connected.

Though he and Scatters the Clouds had been together almost eight years now, she still looked as good to him as she had when he first met her. She still excited Rawlins every bit as much, too. He didn't question any of that; he just accepted it and enjoyed it, though it did surprise him a little if he really thought about it. No matter how much he enjoyed his dalliances in Taos, he always came back to Scatters the Clouds. More surprising to him, though, was that the Indian woman loved him enough to take him back each time.

Chardonnais came out of his lodge and took a seat near Rawlins. "Ah, dat was a pleasure, *mon ami*," he said with a bright smile. "But it always is."

"Goddamn thing of yours is gonna fall off ye don't give it a rest every now and again," Rawlins commented.

Chardonnais shrugged, then laughed. "I would regret dat," he said almost seriously. "But den I would use someone else's. Maybe yours. It is far too small, but it ain't been used so much."

"Ye come anywhere near my pizzle—for any goddamn reason—and there ain't gonna be enough of ye left to fill a sparrow's meatbag, ye bandy-legged little shit." Rawlins set aside the rope he was making and his pipe and rose. "But ye have given this ol' chil' an idea." He grinned and walked toward Scatters the Clouds.

The woman looked up at his approach. She smiled when Rawlins held out his hand, and took it. They entered the lodge together, and then Scatters the Clouds turned to face him. "I hoped you would think of this," she said with a lusty smile.

"Oh, ye did, did ye?"

"Yep." She pulled his head down. Just before placing her lips on his, she whispered, "No more talkin' now."

"Yes'm."

In moments, Scatters the Clouds's dress was shoved up, Rawlins's pants were pushed down, and they were thrashing around on the robes, making every bit as much joyful noise as Chardonnais and Looks Again had made not so long ago.

Scatters the Clouds gasped and spasmed moments before Rawlins did, and then they rolled so they were on their sides, still connected at the groin.

"That was good, dammit," Scatters the Clouds said soon after.

"This chil' thought so."

"So good maybe we do it again now, dammit?" Scatters the Clouds suggested.

"Ye been foolin' with Lucien?" he asked not very seriously. "That where ye got this notion of twice in a couple minutes?"

"I don't want no Lucien."

"Even though he wants to hump every quarter hour?"

"No," Scatters the Clouds said firmly. "I love you, Abe Rawlins." She stroked his cheek.

"I'm pleased to hear that, ma'am," Rawlins said honestly.

"Besides," she said with a giggle, "I couldn't stand all that damn hair on him." She almost shuddered. "It'd be like humpin' a buffler."

Rawlins laughed, which forced them to lose their connection, but they still lay in each other's arms. "So, now I know why ye really stuck with me all these years," he said in mock offense. "Jist so ye wouldn't get stuck with that hairy ol' frog out there."

"Should I have another reason?" Scatters the Clouds asked, unable to bottle up the giggles.

"Reckon not," Rawlins said agreeably. "Might be nice, though, if ye cared some for this ol' hoss."

"That'll come in time."

Rawlins laughed again. He knew she loved him, even if she hadn't told him just moments ago. He figured she knew he felt the same about her, though he had never said so to her. It wasn't his way. Not that he didn't want to; it was just that he couldn't bring himself to do so, for some reason. He didn't know the reason and wasn't all that interested in pondering it.

Another thing that surprised him was the fact that she was always waiting for him when he got back to Strong Bear's village from Taos. She was a young, healthy, strong, pretty woman, one who could not be faulted for the quality of any work she did. It would be easy for her to get a Ute husband. Or another white one, for that matter. She might take a Ute husband for the summers, he supposed, but he didn't really think so, if he even thought of it at all. He wondered only rarely how he would feel if she were doing that.

Scatters the Clouds finally pulled away. "I got work waitin'," she said as she stood. She settled her dress and then patted her slightly expanded stomach. "You don't mind that I carry another child?" she asked. She really wasn't worried; she just wanted, or maybe needed, a little reassurance.

"Nope." Rawlins rose, pulling up his pants. He did the horn buttons and then replaced his belt and weapons. "How far along are ye?"

"Three moons, maybe a little more or a little less."

Rawlins nodded and smiled. He didn't mind being a father again at all. "This'n gonna be a boy or a girl?"

"A girl, I think."

"Bueno."

Within a couple more weeks Rawlins was getting eager to be on the move. He was restless, and he decided that a little hunting would be a way to get out of the camp at least a little. Since Chardonnais was suffering another bout with a cold, he figured he would go himself.

"Let me or Bart come with ye," Early suggested when he and Adams had returned from running the trap lines.

"Rather be alone for a spell," Rawlins answered.

Early nodded, knowing that was what Rawlins would answer. "Ye sure?" he asked, playing along.

"Yep. There's nothin' to be worried about."

"I expect not. 'Cept for Crows and Shoshones."

"A few of them red devils don't scare this ol' hoss. Now, was we up in Blackfoot lands, I might reconsider jist a bit. But down here?"

"Ye remember what them goddamn skunk-suckin' Crows did two years ago, don't ye?" Early asked a little harshly.

Rawlins was not offended at the tone, but there was annoyance in his voice as he answered, "Of course I goddamn remember what them drippin'-dick Crows did. But it's too early for 'em to be on the prowl."

"Ye best hope they aren't."

"Goddamn, Ez, you're gettin' to be an ol' lady." Rawlins grinned. "Where'n hell's your adventuresome spirit got off to? Ye leave it back there in Taos?"

"I'll give ye adventuresome spirit, ye son of a bitch," Early said with a laugh. "Ye jist watch your topknot."

"I'll do that." Rawlins mounted his horse and trotted off.

18

RAWLINS HAD TRAVELED A LITTLE over two miles, he estimated, when he jumped a good-size elk cow. He dismounted and dropped the animal with one well-placed shot. He stayed where he was to reload his rifle, which he did by rote. His eyes were busy scanning the land around him. He couldn't see too far, since there were too many trees surrounding the small meadow.

When he saw nothing out of the ordinary, Rawlins mounted the horse and, towing the pack mule behind him, rode to where the carcass lay. With practiced efficiency, he began butchering the elk, placing the hunks of meat on the spread-out hide. He was most of the way through when the sudden flight of a flock of swifts and swallows stopped him cold.

He carefully wiped the knife on the leg of his blackened buckskin pants and slid it away. He rose slowly and turned. Just as he began sliding his rifle out of the scabbard, he spotted the Blackfeet.

The warriors were edging into the clearing. One saw Rawlins and charged.

Rawlins swung the rifle up and fired in one easy move. He did not wait to check his accuracy. He jerked loose the knot tying the reins to one of the horse's forelegs and jumped into the saddle. Then he raced off, leaving the meat and the pack mule behind.

He looked back only once, just long enough to see that the warrior he had shot was on the ground and not moving. He also noticed that the four other Blackfoot warriors were charging after him. Then he was back in the trees. He flattened himself on the horse's neck and let the animal run.

He headed southeast and was soon moving between two tall, imposing peaks. That brought him farther from his camp, which was his plan. He was not about to lead the damned Blackfeet to his friends, where the women and children would be in danger.

He rode hard for a while, outpacing the Blackfeet. Finally he entered a stream and followed it at a much slower pace for another mile. Then he pulled out of the stream and moved on, covering his tracks as much as possible, until he was riding on rock.

Spotting a thicket, he stopped and swiftly unsaddled and unbridled the horse. Then he forced the animal into the thicket as far as he could and tied it to the thickest branch of a nearby bush. As he worked his way back out of the thicket, he pushed branches back into place.

Back in the open, he checked his handiwork. It was not good, but he didn't figure he could do any better yet. Rawlins hoped that if the Blackfeet got this far, they would be more intent on the trail than on the sides of it. Then he shrugged fatalistically. There wasn't a hell of a lot to do about it now. That was why he had put the horse here. If the animal gave its presence away, Rawlins didn't want to be standing next to it. He might lose the animal to the Blackfeet, but that was better than losing his hair to them, he figured.

Rawlins hauled up his saddle and bridle and moved up the stream bank, until he found another thicket and carefully eased his way into it. Finding a small space, he dropped the saddle. Pulling his .53-caliber Fordney rifle from the saddle scabbard, he squatted and reloaded the weapon. He set it down in front of him and pulled his pistols.

Then he hunkered down inside the thick patch of brush and trees, stock-still. His heavy, flintlock rifle lay on the ground right in front of him, and he had his two matching pistols in his big hands. He peered out through a slight hole in the brush, watching for the four Blackfeet who were looking for him.

He estimated that only a half hour had passed since his encounter with the Blackfeet. Another hour passed before they came into view again.

The warriors were prowling around, one of them on foot, scrutinizing the ground while someone else held the rope to his pony. A third warrior had a rope around the neck of Rawlins's horse. Rawlins swore silently at that.

He cursed inwardly again when he spotted a war leader he recognized as Gray Horse. He had run into the Blackfoot before and was of the opinion that Gray Horse was the lowest sort.

He considered dropping the Indian, but realized

right off that such an idea was purely foolish. The other three Blackfeet would be on him within moments, and even if he got another one or even two of them, he'd be just as dead.

Besides, he was a fatalistic—and a realistic—man. Killing Gray Horse would serve no good purpose other than to allow him to go under knowing he had sent at least one more of Bug's Boys to the great beyond. That, in and of itself, was hardly a justifiable end. He sighed. This was not the time or place for such doin's.

With the thought of waiting the Blackfeet out planted firmly in his mind, he relaxed his muscles, if not his vigilance.

The Blackfoot who was tracking him suddenly stopped and looked around, dark face turning slowly. Rawlins held his breath, not wanting to give himself away.

The warrior pointed to a spot just to the hidden trapper's right. He said something to the others, mounted his horse, and then moved toward where he had pointed. Gray Horse and the two others pulled back into some trees across the little stream, showing their respect for Rawlins's prowess with a rifle. They might not know him for sure, but they knew he was a mountain man, and any mountain man with his own rifle was a force to be reckoned with.

The Blackfoot made his way into the brush and dismounted. That was the last Rawlins heard of the warrior, who moved like a wraith. This worried Rawlins, because he couldn't track the Indian by ear. Then came the snapping of a twig, and the trapper nodded in relief.

Rawlins placed his pistols on the ground, rose,

and moved off a ways, going every bit as silently as the Blackfoot had. He stopped, pulled out his knife, and waited.

The Blackfoot came around a bush and almost ran into him. The mountain man struck like a snake, fast and deadly, jamming the long blade of his butcher knife into the man's stomach. At the same time, his left hand latched onto the warrior's throat and locked there. The Blackfoot managed only one startled gasp before his air passage was choked off.

Leaving his blade deep in the warrior's guts, Rawlins lifted him off his feet and then tossed him up and over his shoulder. The heavyset warrior slid off the knife and crashed to the ground, on the verge of death.

"Shit," Rawlins muttered at the noise. He should have known better, he scolded himself silently. But it was too late to worry about that now. He swiftly knelt and peeled the warrior's scalp. Then he wiped his blade off on the Indian's breechcloth and slid it away.

He shoved out of the thicket and found the Blackfoot's pony. Making sure the animal was tied, he went back, hefted the body, and then tossed it across the pony's back. He cut off the rawhide string that held up the Indian's breechcloth and jerked it out from under the body. Rawlins used it to swiftly tie the Blackfoot's body down. Then he undid the animal's tether and smacked the pony on the rump. "Git goin', critter," he said, referring to the horse as well as the Indian.

Rawlins watched for a few moments as the horse ran off, the body flapping wildly, blood splattering the ground from its scalped head. "Waugh!" he muttered.

"See how ye like them goddamn doin's, ye red-hided sons of bitches."

He went back into the thicket, picked up his pistols, and squatted again, waiting once more. His thigh muscles complained at having to assume such a cramped position.

One of the Blackfeet darted out of the trees on horseback and caught the horse with the dead warrior, then dashed back into the trees.

Rawlins did not move. He was getting tired of the game, and his legs were screaming at him. He had spent too many years standing thigh-deep in mountain streams trapping beaver to want to abuse his legs by spending several hours like this.

He gave it another hour, and when he saw nothing moving across the stream, he stood. Slipping his pistols into his belt, he picked up his rifle. Then he spent another hour laboriously making his way through thickets and pine forests until he was about a half mile upstream. He crossed the rushing little cascade and ducked into the forest on the other side. It took him about as long to work back toward where the Blackfeet had been hiding.

The Indians were gone, he found out. He tracked them through the forest away from the stream for a while, until he found where they had cut back northwest, heading again toward the stream. He figured they were gone for good, since they couldn't sneak up on his haven from behind, what with that big cliff.

"Goddamn shit-suckin' red devils," he mumbled angrily. They had cost him his freshly killed meat, his mule, and his horse. And now he had to walk back to his camp, which was, he estimated, at least five miles away; maybe more. The dark bay horse

had been a good one, and he was going to miss the
animal more than just for the ride back to camp. The
horse was well trained and was used to Rawlins.
Training another would be trouble, and the trapper
did not look forward to it.

He cut some tobacco off the small twist he carried
in his possible sack and shoved it in his mouth. He
chewed slowly, letting the action remove some of his
tension. Finally he spit in annoyance and headed
back to the stream.

Rawlins walked boldly out into the open and
across the stream. He neither saw nor heard anything that would lead him to believe the Blackfeet
were still around. He got his saddle and other tack
and hauled it up onto one shoulder. Spraying the
thicket with tobacco juice, he stepped off, heading
upstream.

He finally figured the trip back to camp was only
about four miles total, but it took him almost ten
hours over that day and the next, since the journey
was up and down—far more up than down, it seemed.
He struggled up steep slopes, through forests, and
punched his way through thickets, all the while lug-
ging the heavy saddle.

Darkness settled over him while he was still a
few hours from camp. He considered pushing on, but
then decided that wouldn't be wise. He dropped his
saddle in the first convenient place he found, tossed
down his otter-fur sleeping robe, and crawled in. He
was asleep in moments.

He awoke in something of a poor humor. Being
hungry often did that to him. Still, he had faced
starvin' times before, and lots worse than this. He
saw a deer and was about to pull his rifle, but stopped.

He was in no mood to shoot, butcher, and cook, plus having to find wood and build a fire.

"Go on, get goin', ye stupid critter," he said. "This ol' chil's got a heap better things to do than make meat out of the likes of ye, goddammit."

The deer looked up, startled, froze for a few moments, and then bolted into the trees.

"Ye would've been mine, damn ye, had ye been a ridin' animal," Rawlins said. He shook his head and then laughed. The deep, rich sound was strange in the otherwise silent forest. "All right, ol' hoss, there's doin's to be took care of," he said aloud. He grabbed the saddle and pushed on.

The trek was no easier this day than it had been the last, though it was considerably shorter. The last half mile was almost flat, too, which helped, and well before midday he spotted smoke rising from the camp nestled among the pines up against a tall, formidable cliff.

He crossed a small clearing and hit the trees. As he did he whistled once like a gray jay. He paused for half a minute and repeated the call. He nodded when the signal was returned, and pushed ahead, suddenly finding a spring in his step.

19

"HEY, LUCIEN," EARLY SHOUTED when Rawlins lurched into the camp. "Look what the cat's drug in here." He stopped splitting firewood and stood watching Rawlins.

"I see dat," the short, squat French-Canadian said. Chardonnais pulled off his bright green knit cap, the top of which flopped to the side, and scratched the thick thatch of pitch-black hair with a stubby, dirty finger. "I am amaze at dis." He grinned, showing a gap where two teeth used to be in the upper left corner of his mouth. His nose was red from the cold he was suffering. "We send dat useless t'ing out to make meat. A simple job, no? Even a boy could do it. But what does de great mountaineer Abe Rawlins do? Hah! He comes back wit'out meat and wit'out his horse and wit'out de mule."

"Eat shit, ye fat little frog fart, ye," Rawlins growled as he dropped his saddle on the ground outside his lodge. It was spring, and this high in the mountains, it was still cold. In warmer weather, the mountain men and their families would often sleep out in the open.

"But what is dis?" Chardonnais said in mock incredulity. "We welcome dis weary traveler into our camp, and he calls us names?"

"I can't recall as he called me any goddamn names, Frenchie," Early said with a grin. "As I recall, it was you he was referrin' to in such derogatory terms."

Chardonnais scratched at the thick tangle of black hair that covered his swarthy face from eyebrows to past his chin. It continued down until disappearing beneath the bright red calico shirt. "I t'ink you are right, *mon ami*," he said without rancor. His and Early's kidding was only a way to mask their worry about their longtime friend.

"I'll call ye some more names, too, you fat little ball of shit," Rawlins snapped, looking at the shorter man, "ye don't close that flappin' goddamn hole in your face."

Chardonnais put a hurt look on his face. "Oh, I see," he said in mock worry, "you are de one to lose de meat, your horse, and de mule, and you don' expect me to say not'ing about it? *Sacre bleu!* But excuse me, Monsieur le Roi des Montagnes. King of de Mountains." The dark glittering coals that were his eyes sparkled with humor. They could be as expressive in menace.

Rawlins was about to make another retort when Scatters the Clouds stepped out of the lodge and came up to him, worry coloring her already dark eyes.

Rawlins nodded at her. "I'm all right, woman," he said quietly.

His two friends said nothing. They were all hard, fierce men, but they cared for their women, and had been in Rawlins's position—having to explain to a worried wife that all was well and not too much fuss should be made over them.

Adams sat smoking a cigar, watching and listening. He had been with these men for months now, yet he still found them fascinating, particularly their vulgar repartee. He was not about to speak, not while Rawlins was reassuring his wife that he was all right.

Scatters the Clouds gazed up into her husband's faded blue eyes, searching them for some moments. Then she nodded. "Are you hungry?" she asked.

"Enough to eat a b'ar right down to the claws." He grinned.

Scatters the Clouds smiled, relieved. She turned and went into the lodge.

A moment later five-year-old Standing Eagle barreled out of the lodge and bounded into his father's arms. "Pa!" he exclaimed happily.

"How's doin's, li'l hoss?" Rawlins responded, running his scratchy beard against his son's chubby cheek.

"Shinin'!" The boy giggled.

Rawlins laughed and tossed the child into the air a couple times, catching him on the way down. The boy and his father laughed.

Scatters the Clouds came out of the lodge again and stood watching her man and son playing. She had a soft, caring smile on her full face.

Finally Rawlins set Standing Eagle on his feet and said, "Git goin', li'l hoss." He gave him a light swat on the rump as the boy raced off to play. Rawlins followed Scatters the Clouds into the lodge, and Early, Chardonnais, and Adams followed him.

The men sat cross-legged around the small fire. Scatters the Clouds handed Rawlins a large wooden bowl of buffalo stew. It wasn't the best she could make, she knew, but she had been forced to make do with what was on hand. Meat still kept pretty well in the chill mountain air, but the buffalo meat she had used had been nearly a week old and wasn't the best of cuts to begin with. She worried that her man would think little of her since she could not prepare him a decent meal.

But Rawlins was wolfing down the stew like he hadn't seen food in a week instead of a day. He finished in minutes. "More," he growled. He dug into that bowl.

Early put some chaw in his mouth, Chardonnais lit his pipe, and Adams lit another cigar. They all nodded thanks when Scatters the Clouds handed them coffee. They sat silently as Rawlins bolted down his food.

After his fourth serving of stew, Rawlins set the bowl down. He belched and patted his stomach. "Them was some good vittles, woman," he said. "Shinin', they was." He poured himself some coffee and rolled himself a cigarillo, which he lit.

"Well," Early drawled, "now that you finally quit off fillin' your face, you mind tellin' us just what the hell happened?"

"Somethin' happened?" Rawlins countered.

"I t'ink I know what happened," Chardonnais said. "I t'ink Abe fell off his horse, which den ran away wit' de mule. He never did know how to ride wort' a damn."

"Might be," Early allowed with a nod. "Hell, if it was you, I'd figure you either humped them poor critters to death, or else traded 'em to some Digger Indian for a roll in the robes with his diseased wife."

"Bah," Chardonnais growled, but he grinned.

Rawlins finished his cup of coffee and sat a moment in silence, letting the tin mug dangle from an index finger. Then he explained what had happened.

His three partners said nothing during the short narrative. When he finished, Early asked, "Ye know who it was done it?"

"Only one of 'em."

Early raised his eyebrows.

"It were that goddamn festerin' son of a bitch Gray Horse," Rawlins growled.

"All the way down here?" Early was only mildly surprised.

Rawlins nodded. "Must be on the warpath early." He paused. "One of these days, I'm gonna raise hair on that bastard." Then he grinned lopsidedly. "But that can wait a spell."

"Ye didn't have no chance to make wolf bait out of him?"

"Waugh! I could've raised hair on him easy—if I wanted to get put under myself. As it were, I got two of Bug's Boys afore the others skedaddled."

"*Bon!*" Chardonnais said. As far as any of the three was concerned, it was a good thing anytime a Blackfeet went under.

The others agreed, but they were a little worried, too. They were a fair piece from Blackfoot country, and it was a little early for a war party to be riding this far south. Plus, if one war party was around, others might be, too.

"Ye thinkin' what I'm thinkin', *amigos*?" Rawlins said after some silence.

Early nodded. "We'll pull out first thing tomorrow," he said firmly. It would mean a hell of a lot of work, but it had to be done.

The rest of the day was spent in preparing to leave. Traps had to be watched, and meat still had to be made. Leaving Chardonnais and Adams behind with the women and children, Rawlins and Early went out to check and reset the traps. Then the two went hunting.

They flushed out three mule deer within half a mile of the camp. One kept his eyes peeled and gun loaded while the other shot and butchered each of the deer. Then they hightailed it back to the camp. They were not afraid—at least not for themselves. They were worried about their women and children.

The twelve people pulled out at first light the next day.

They made their way south and a little west, back the way they had come, heading for the Uintas. They moved fairly swiftly for a few days, wanting to get away from the area they had been in just in case the Blackfeet were still around.

Then they slowed, wanting to take more furs, and so following their usual pattern, staying a few days at a place, trapping until they figured they had the best of the catch from the area, and then moving on.

A month and a half later they began to move faster because the fur of the beaver they were catching was falling rapidly from prime to poor as spring set in for real.

By then, though, they were getting pretty near to the homeland of their Ute friends.

The mountain men had been following the same

yearly routine long enough to be able to judge pretty well that the Utes were back from the spring hunt. Each spring and fall, the Uncompahgre Utes headed east on an age-old trail to hunt the buffalo on the plains—and often to fight their enemies, the Arapaho and the Cheyenne. During this time they visited with their eastern relatives, but did not stay long, preferring their high-mountain home on the western side of the Continental Divide to the more barren eastern slope.

Within another week, as the small group picked up even more speed since the trapping was too poor even to bother with, they began to feel excited. The women were eager to get back to their people, to see their friends and speak their own language again. The children felt the same, since life for them in a Ute village was pretty free.

The men, however, might have felt the most excitement of all. Each year at this time Rawlins, Early, and Chardonnais brought their women back to the village and left them there. Then they headed down to Taos for a spree. After a winter of being cooped up, they were eager for a change. They might love their women, but they had a yearning for the spirited señoritas in Taos. For their part, the wives saw little wrong in this behavior. It was just the way of things, and they could do nothing about it anyway. They cared only that their men came back, which they did every fall.

To be fair, the men also enjoyed the whiskey, fiery food, and music down in Taos. There was a friendliness about the people and the place itself that attracted them. In addition, being in Taos kept them from having to go to rendezvous. They were wild enough to fit in at the rendezvous, but they had more sense than to go to the annual gathering of the mountain men and Indians, where whiskey was five dollars a gallon or more, women wanted piles of foofaraw for a fast, tepid session of lovemaking, and suppliers wanted unconscionable sums for their supplies. Rawlins and his two friends had been there before, had taken part in the wild and raucous festivities, and had ended up short on supplies and having to consider hiring on to a company again. After being free trappers for almost a decade, they could not bear the thought of working for someone else.

Adams could hardly contain his excitement. He missed Dolores something fierce and made no bones about saying so. It had been a long, long winter without her. If he had had any doubts about how much he still loved her after two years of marriage, they were gone now. True, he would miss Blue Rattle; she was a quiet, industrious woman. But he would miss her more as a sister than anything else.

So the four pushed the women and children— and themselves—across some barren flats and then back into the tall, harsh Uinta Mountains, where even now plenty of snow remained on the ground. The men loved this area, almost as much as they loved the towering spires, wind-ravaged slopes, keening wind, and tall pines of the San Juans. Such places made a man feel small, if he allowed it. The loneliness he felt in them could break a man, sending him reeling away, mind torn by the bleakness and lack of humanity. Abe Rawlins, Ezra Early, and Lucien Chardonnais had never felt such loneliness; rather, they enjoyed the quiet and the solitude.

They pulled into a mountain meadow along Uinta Creek, still in the Uinta Mountains. As best Rawlins could figure, it was approaching the first of June.

"How long's it going to be before we're back in Taos?" Adams asked.

"Three weeks, maybe a bit less, if we push it," Early said. "Ye in a hurry?"

"Yes, sir, I am," Adams said flatly. "I want to see Dolores something awful and—" He shut up when he realized Blue Rattle was within earshot. He didn't love her, but he thought her a fine woman, and he did not want to hurt her.

"Ol' hoss there's gittin' as bad as the little frog fart," Rawlins said with a grin.

"Hah!" Chardonnais boasted. "De two of you together—*mais non!* All t'ree of you—couldn't keep up wit' dis chil'."

"It don't matter," Adams insisted. "I just want to get back to Taos. We aren't going to stay here long, are we?"

"Nope," Early said. "We'll be pullin' out come mornin', just like we been doin'."

20

RAWLINS AND ADAMS WERE loading the supplies on the mules while Early and Chardonnais were saddling the horses. A light fog hung in the morning air, floating around bushes and the branches of spindly aspens, big cottonwoods, and small scrub oaks. The air, too, smelled of wetness and wildflowers, which grew heavily in the meadow, all lending a peaceful aura to the rapidly breaking-down camp.

Then the Blackfeet attacked.

They did not come in a loud rushing charge; rather, a series of arrows, silent and hungry, suddenly came zipping through the air from behind trees and brush. One thudded into the packs inches from Adams's hand. He turned white as a ghost.

Rawlins noticed that Early had gone down right away, an arrow jutting from his back. "Shit," he muttered. In the next instant he saw Chardonnais grab Early's shirt and begin hauling him toward the trees.

"Let's go, hoss," Rawlins said quietly but urgently.

He took a handful of Adams's shirt and jerked him toward the protective cover of the forest.

At the same time an arrow struck Adams in the left leg. He hissed with the sudden sharp pain, not quite realizing what had happened. It was several moments before the news reached his brain. He opened his mouth to scream in pain and fear.

"Don't do it, hoss," Rawlins said harshly, dragging Adams along. He shoved the young man hard toward a heavy bushes surrounded by thick underbrush. "Cache in there, hoss," he ordered. "Get in there as far as ye can. Keep your flappin' hole shut and don't fuck with that arrow."

"But where're you . . . ?" Adams started, but Rawlins was already gone, melting into the trees.

The trapper moved swiftly but silently through the pines and aspens and brush. He had a pistol in his right hand and his tomahawk in the left. He circled around toward where Early and Chardonnais had been—and where the women, children, and horses had been, too.

He glanced out of the trees now and again and caught occasional glimpses of Blackfeet across the meadow. Then he saw one dashing across the meadow. "Try these doin's, hoss," Rawlins mumbled as he stopped and fired the pistol. The Blackfoot went down.

"Waugh!" Rawlins growled low. Then he was off and moving again. It was a long way around this side of the meadow, which was perhaps two hundred yards long and less than a quarter of that wide, in a roughly oval shape.

Some yards on, Rawlins stopped and shot at another Blackfoot in the clearing, but missed. He could see several other Blackfeet moving in on the horses, five of which managed to get away and race into the woods. Two other warriors had edged up on the mules and tied down what packs were already on the animals. Rawlins had no idea where the women and children where. He hoped they had gotten themselves hidden well.

A Blackfoot suddenly slammed into his side, knocking him down. Rawlins managed to get up about the same time as the warrior did, and was better prepared to attack. He furiously surged in on the Blackfoot, hacking the unfortunate warrior to pieces before the Indian could mount much of a defense.

Rawlins hurried on, worry about his friends, the women, and children pushing him to greater speed. He was worried, too, about the number of Blackfeet in this war party. For all he knew, there were dozens, a not very pleasant thought.

Breathing growing ragged, Rawlins suddenly spotted a Blackfoot kneeling next to something or someone. It took only a moment to realize it was Chardonnais. The Indian was just getting ready to take the French-Canadian's hair.

Rawlins threw his tomahawk. His aim was good, but nowhere near as good as Early's, and the weapon barely clunked off the Blackfoot's side and flew off.

The warrior looked up angrily and started to straighten just as Rawlins plowed into him. They hit the ground, bounced apart, and flopped a few times. The Indian came up with his scalping knife still in hand and roared in on Rawlins.

The mountain man ducked and threw his shoulder into the Blackfoot as the warrior came at him with knife held high. The Indian's breath exploded out.

"Shit-suckin' red devil," Rawlins muttered as he grabbed the Indian—one hand on the crotch, the other around the throat. He lifted the Blackfoot clean off the ground, turned a half step, and pitched him.

The warrior's back cracked on a cottonwood trunk and he fell in a heap, groaning.

Not wanting to trust the Indian, Rawlins swept up his tomahawk and swarmed in on him. Without thought or remorse, he swung once, and almost separated the Blackfoot's head from his body. He swiftly took the scalp and threw it away. Then he ran back to Chardonnais.

The French-Canadian was unconscious, but there was life in him yet. His chest—with two arrows sticking up from it—rose and fell weakly.

Rawlins slid his bloody tomahawk into his belt and then lifted Chardonnais, trying hard not to jostle him. He trotted off a little, until he spotted a clump of fallen trees dominated by one mostly rotted cottonwood. He kicked around in the pile of rotted wood to roust out any critters that might be hidden in there. Then he gently lay his friend on the punk.

Chardonnais groaned but did not come out of his unconsciousness. Rawlins angrily snapped off the two arrow shafts as close to the body as he dared. That way they would not be seen above the clump of logs.

Rawlins moved off again, sweating from the exertion. His worry grew, too. He had seen Early go down, and he had no idea how bad his other friend was. He suspected he was in bad shape, though. With Chardonnais and Adams wounded, Rawlins was on his own, against he knew not how many Blackfoot warriors. This did not frighten him, but it did worry him, more for his friends and the women and children than himself.

He heard the Blackfeet now. The Indians were howling and yipping as they looted the camp. Rawlins moved to the edge of the clearing and watched. He spotted Gray Horse exhorting his men to get moving, to drive the horses and mules off, taking the supplies with them.

Rawlins spun and ran through the trees, hoping to be able to get to his personal gear before the Blackfeet left. If he could get his rifle, he could kill Gray Horse and have at least that much revenge for this attack.

Suddenly two Blackfeet loomed before him, grinning savagely. Rawlins did not even slow down. He simply slammed into one of them. The warrior went down, but Rawlins managed to keep his feet, stumbling ahead several steps before bringing himself to a stop. He whirled, jerking out his tomahawk again.

An arrow whistled just over his left shoulder, skimming it and slicing out a small line of flesh. Seeing the warrior nocking another arrow, Rawlins jumped behind an aspen and then dashed off deeper into the forest. He could hear the two Blackfeet coming after him. He smiled grimly. "I'll jist show these niggurs a thing or two," he muttered.

They played cat and mouse for a while, with Rawlins drawing the two Blackfeet farther and farther from the camp as he raced up and down the rugged land. In spots, he could barely move because of the thick underbrush, and knew he would have to find another way. Suddenly he jerked to a halt, teetering on the edge of a deep chasm. *Shit,* he thought, *this here is poor doin's.*

He hesitated only a few moments, though. Then he edged back from the cliff a few feet, knelt, and reloaded both pistols. Sticking the weapons back into his belt, he waited, almost patiently. When he heard the Indians coming, he grabbed a large rock, rolled it to the edge of the cliff, and then shoved it over, trying to make sure that it chipped off the cliff edge as it went. Then he screamed.

He darted behind a scrub oak, pulled out his pistols, and waited again. Moments later not two but three Blackfeet edged up to the chasm. One saw the broken ground on the edge and nodded. All three warriors laughed. They turned almost as one, ready to rejoin their fellows.

Rawlins stepped out from behind the tree and fired a pistol with each hand, killing the biggest of the three Blackfeet and the one with a bow and arrow still in hand. The latter dropped like a stone where he stood, but the former was punched back over the precipice and disappeared.

Rawlins dropped the pistols and pulled his tomahawk. "It's jist ye'n me now, ol' hoss," he said flatly.

The remaining Blackfoot gave a grim smile and smacked the head of his war club a few times. He charged, swinging the weapon loosely.

Rawlins stood his ground for just a bit, then slowly gave way. When he saw the warrior begin to tire, he stopped and then opened his counterattack.

The Blackfoot moved back, conscious of the gaping chasm behind him but not quite sure how far away it was. He could not rest his arms, though, as he continually had to fend off his opponent's slicing tomahawk. Almost without pausing, Rawlins shifted the tomahawk to his left hand.

The Blackfoot saw that and grinned, figuring he had the advantage now.

Rawlins suddenly stooped and grabbed a fist-sized rock, which he whipped at the Indian's head. The warrior ducked and fell back another step, giving the trapper time to grab another rock and heave it as hard as he could at him.

The Blackfoot once more ducked and stumbled backward. Rawlins charged him, moving fast but not too fast. "Shit-suckin', snake-humpin' chickenshit red devil," he growled, a little surprised that the Blackfoot seemed to understand him.

The warrior understood all right, and the insulting words enraged him. He forget almost everything but this tall, hard-looking enemy. He gave ground, waiting for the right moment to renew his own attack on the hated white man. Then he stumbled over his forgotten, dead comrade. He teetered on the edge of the abyss, trying desperately to keep from toppling into the nothingness.

"*Adios,* shitball," Rawlins said as he picked up another rock and threw it as hard as he could at the Blackfoot.

The projectile hit the warrior square in the chest and provided just enough impetus to send him falling to his doom in the canyon far below.

Rawlins stood a few moments, breathing heavily. Then he turned, found his pistols, and reloaded them. With his pistols and tomahawk back in his belt, he trotted off back toward his camp, a sense of dread beginning to overcome him.

As he neared the camp Rawlins slowed a little.

He could still hear the Blackfeet rummaging around. That surprised him; he figured they would've ridden off long ago. It also bothered him, but in a way, it gladdened him too. With the Indians still there, he could take more revenge for his friends, for he had no doubt that by now his two partners were dead.

He almost tripped when he heard a moan not far away. He whirled, expecting an attack, but saw none coming. He prowled a little closer and then looked under a bush to find Ezra Early lying on his stomach, an arrow still sticking out of his back.

"Well, I'll be goddamned," he muttered as he knelt at Early's side and found out that he was still breathing. "Ez, Ez, can ye hear me, hoss?" he asked urgently but quietly. He got no response. "Damn," he swore.

Rawlins heard a sound behind him. Without waiting to find out what it was, he threw himself to the side. A Blackfoot lance blade skidded across his left side, but did no real damage. As he rolled twice he hoped that the lance had not stuck into his wounded comrade, but he couldn't worry about that now. He came to a stop on his back and jerked out a pistol.

The lance suddenly came at him again and tore open the top of his right forearm. His index finger jerked reflexively on the trigger, but the lead ball went wild. As the warrior thrust the lance at him again, he managed to grab it just behind the blade and shove it to the side. That brought the warrior close enough to him that he could kick him in the knee.

The kick forced the Blackfoot to loosen his grip on the lance. Still holding on to the weapon, Rawlins rose and then thrust the back end of it at the warrior, hitting him in the stomach. The mountain man jerked the lance free and smacked the warrior on the head with it several times. Then he threw the weapon away. With a snarl of rage, he grabbed the Blackfoot by the throat and swiftly squeezed the life out of him.

As he dropped the Indian's body Rawlins heard the other Blackfeet making a last call for their friends to return. He raced toward the camp, tripping once over a log and sprawling on his face. Then he was at the edge of the clearing. The Blackfeet were riding away on the far side of the meadow, whose colorful carpet of wildflowers suddenly seemed woefully out of place. Rawlins thought he saw Scatters the Clouds and Looks Again.

"Shit," he mumbled. He burst out from the trees, racing toward where he had left his saddle and other gear. He got there and found out his saddle wasn't there. He figured the Blackfeet had gotten his saddled horse.

The Blackfeet were out of sight anyway. Almost shaking with rage and frustration, Rawlins stood and watched the Indians riding off. He finally turned and gave himself a few moments to calm down. As the surge of adrenaline in his system began to subside, he realized he was exhausted, and he hurt all over. He looked at his right forearm and decided the wound wasn't very bad.

The trapper straightened his shoulders. He faced a heap of work yet, which wouldn't get done if he continued to stand there. He ducked back into the trees again, and then made a slow circuit around the entire meadow, checking to see if any Blackfeet had stayed behind or been wounded. He found none. Nor did he find any of the women and children—or their corpses—which meant that the Blackfeet had taken them away.

Back at the camp, he cut off some tobacco and shoved it in his mouth. He chewed it slowly, knowing that the worst of the work was yet to come. He figured he'd be digging at least one grave and quite possibly three. He did not look forward to it.

Once more he headed into the woods, heading toward where he had left Adams. He had ignored the young Easterner on his earlier circuit, figuring that the young man was either alive and still holed up, or dead, in which case finding him wouldn't help much.

21

Adams was alive but rather shaken. His face was pasty white, mostly from fear, when Rawlins told him to come out from under the brush. The pain added to the ashen countenance he wore.

Rawlins, however, was not about to baby him. "Listen, hoss," he said harshly when the reporter complained about having to walk the short distance back to the camp, "Ez and Lucien're most likely gone under or'll be goin' under soon. Ye don't want to walk, hoss, ye can sit your ass down here and fix up your own goddamn leg. I ain't of a mood for such doin's."

"Ezra and Lucien're hurt bad?" Adams asked dumbly.

"Plumb bad, hoss. Lucien's got two arrows in his chest—or worse, if the goddamn Blackfeet found him after I left him. Ez's got an arrow in the back. Both of 'em look poor to this ol' chil', and I've seen my share of such things."

"You're all right?" Adams asked anxiously.

"Just a couple scratches is all, hoss."

"Anyone else hurt?"

"There ain't nobody else. Now let's get a move on."

"What do you mean there's no one else?" Adams asked in horror.

"The goddamn pus-lickin' Blackfeet got all the women and young'ns. Carted 'em off."

"You're sure?"

"Of course I'm goddamn sure." Rawlins drew in a deep breath and then let it dribble out as he tried to relax himself. "I reckon that ain't the worst thing could've happened."

"It's not?" Adams was dumbfounded.

"Nope. If the Blackfeet took 'em, they're alive. They might be in poor shape they stick with them goddamn red devils for any time, but at least they're all alive now, hoss."

Adams nodded and started hobbling next to Rawlins. He was almost fascinated by the steady wobbling of the arrow in his leg as he walked. "You sure all the Blackfeet are gone?" he asked nervously.

"Yep. 'Less'n those bastards've doubled back on us. Which ain't likely considering all the plunder they got off us." Halfway across the meadow, Rawlins said, "Go on over to what's left of our camp, hoss. I'll be back directly."

"Where're you going?" Adams asked, fear born anew inside his chest.

"Out to fetch Ez and Lucien."

"I can help."

"Go rest your leg, hoss."

Rawlins went for Chardonnais first, since he was closer. He was almost flabbergasted to find the

French-Canadian still alive. "Goddamn, you're a hardy little niggur, ain't ye, hoss?" he muttered as he knelt and lifted his friend up.

The walk back to the camp carrying the wounded trapper was interesting, considering he couldn't see the ground, and he almost tripped half a dozen times on tree roots, low-lying brush, and rocks. He finally made it back, though.

Adams, instead of sitting around feeling sorry for himself, had laid out a blanket and was rooting around for another when Rawlins arrived. He pointed to the blanket. "Put him there, Abe." As Rawlins was doing so the reporter asked, "Is he . . . ?"

"The ol' chil's still got the breath in him."

"He isn't so good, though, is he?" Adams asked, looking down on the bearded face.

"No, hoss, he ain't." Rawlins rose. "I'm goin' off to get Ez—or what's left of him." He returned a few minutes later with Early, surprised that he, too, was still alive.

Adams had managed to scrounge up another blanket. He figured the Blackfeet had not wanted it since it was worn. It had appeared to him that they had just pitched it aside.

Rawlins lay Early facedown on the second blanket. Kneeling between his two longtime friends, he looked from one to the other, a feeling of despair welling up inside him. He had been wounded as badly as they were now. So had they. But never two of them at the same time.

"What do we do now, Abe?" Adams asked.

"Wait'll Ez and Lucien're are gone under, bury 'em with what possibles we can find, and then take out after those fuckin' red devils."

"You sure that's wise?"

"I always knew ye was a chickenshit, hoss," Rawlins growled.

Adams was a little shocked, but then realized almost immediately that he shouldn't be. While Rawlins was generally easygoing, he could be as tough and vicious as any man who ever roamed these mountains. And with his wife and son gone, and his two best friends a half step from death, it was understandable that he wouldn't be too friendly. Still, the statement cut Adams.

"That's not fair, and you know it, Abe," the young man said levelly.

"It is if ye ain't fixin' to go with me against those shit-suckers."

"I never said I wouldn't go with you. All I said was the plan you just outlined was stupid."

Rawlins turned a weathered, rage-tight face toward his traveling companion, who was frightened by it. Then Adams saw in his eyes the pain that he was living with right now. Before the trapper could say or do anything, Adams hastily added, "You aren't just going to sit here and watch them die, are you?"

"What the hell'm I supposed to do, hoss?" Rawlins demanded defiantly.

"Try'n help them, dammit. You've seen wounds like this before. You've fixed them up at times, or at least you've said you have."

"But that was different, hoss," Rawlins said nastily.

"Why?"

"Because these hosses're plumb on the edge of goin' under, boy, that's why," Rawlins said with a shake of the head.

"Who's the chickenshit now?" Adams asked, voice mocking. He knew he was taking a terrible risk, but he had to try. "The great Abe Rawlins, sitting here on his ass watching the two best friends he has in the world slowly bleed to death because he doesn't have the balls to try to fix them."

Rawlins was on Adams like a cat, big, brawny hands on the Easterner's throat, squeezing.

"Go ahead, kill me," Adams squawked. "It won't help Ezra and Lucien."

Rage pulsed through Rawlins's veins as if it lived there, but his vision was all right, and he could see no real fear in the Easterner's eyes. Just worry and pain—and challenge. He released Adams and took a step back, breathing hard. He was unsure of himself, of what he should do. He had never felt this insecure before.

Adams rubbed his throat and tried speaking. It seemed to work fairly well. "Help them, Abe. Do what you can for them. Anything is better than just sitting here while they die."

"Suppose I do somethin' wrong?"

"They're not going to be any worse off than they are now—or than they'll be if you don't do anything."

Rawlins suddenly nodded. "Goddamn if ye ain't right, ol' hoss. Shit, I don't know where my brains've got off to."

"They got off to worrying about your two friends. Now come, let's do what we can for them." Adams rose. Face growing pasty white again, he grabbed the arrow still jutting from his thigh and then yanked. "Oh, sweet Jesus," he breathed as the arrowhead tore its way out. "Goddamn, if that don't hurt."

Rawlins grinned grimly. "Always does, ol' hoss." He was back to normal, self-assured again now that he knew what had to be done. He turned and built up the still-smoldering fire. He stuck his big butcher knife in the flames. Finally he turned and glanced at Adams, who was sitting again. The Easterner had tied a bandanna around his wound. "Best come over here, hoss. We might's well get ye fixed up first so's ye can help me." When Adams walked over and sat, Rawlins said, "Undo that bandage there, hoss, so's I can see what's what."

Adams gingerly untied the bandanna. Then Rawlins used his patch knife to slice open his pants a little.

"Don't look too bad, hoss," he said smoothly, keeping Adams's attention on him instead of on his wound. At the same time his hand inched out and grabbed the hilt of the knife that was in the fire. Suddenly he brought the knife up and slapped the red-hot blade on Adams's wound.

Adams screamed, and then toppled over backward, out cold.

Rawlins grinned grimly. "Sorry, ol' hoss, but that had to be done." He stuck his knife back in the fire and then prowled through the ransacked camp. He found little of use and was getting frustrated when he spotted one of the mules cropping grass. He eased up on the partially loaded animal and grabbed the rope around its neck. "Come on, damn ye," he said quietly, tugging on the rope. The mule came along rather docilely.

Rawlins hobbled the animal and unloaded it. The pack contained little, but some of its contents would help. There was some jerky and a little pemmican

left. There was also one small, but full, bottle of
whiskey. The bottle was wrapped in Chardonnais's
only extra shirt. Rawlins almost gleefully cut the shirt
into strips to be used as bandages. He also found one
beaver plew that had been shoved into a pannier.

He went back to the two wounded men. *Damn,
this is poor bull,* he thought. He took a healthy swig
of whiskey, then knelt. He cut open Chardonnais's
shirt with the man's own knife. Then he poured
whiskey on his patch-knife blade and dribbled a little
onto his wounds.

Rawlins hunched over, working with the small
patch knife to cut the flesh around the arrow shafts
jutting from Chardonnais's chest. He did not want to
cut into any vital organs, assuming none had been
damaged already, so the small knife was easier to
handle. He finally managed to cut around one arrow
and pull the head out. Then he went to work on the
other.

Rawlins lost track of the time, not really caring
about it, but he finally got both arrowheads out of
Chardonnais's chest. Then he painstakingly used a
needle and pieces of sinew he had in his possibles
bag to sew up the two wounds. He didn't think any
of the French-Canadian trapper's vitals had been
hit. Finally he made small poultices out of pieces of
the beaver plew, put them on the wounds, and then
bandaged them.

He rocked back on his heels and rolled himself a
cigarillo and smoked it down. His right forearm
burned from the wound he had recieved and from
the tenseness with which he had been working. He
flicked the corn-husk cigarillo away and turned to
Early.

The surgery on his second friend went a little easier, since there was only one wound, and Rawlins was feeling a little more confident. Before long, Early was patched up as best as he could do. Rawlins leaned back, took another long swallow of whiskey, and had another cigarillo. Then he pulled out the last of his sinew and calmly began sewing the wound on his arm. He was still doing so when Adams revived.

The Eastener groaned and sat up.

Rawlins grinned at him a little. "How's doin's, ol' hoss?" he asked.

"What the hell happened?" Adams asked, scratching his head. He had a blank look in his eyes.

"Ye decided to take a siesta," Rawlins said blandly.

"I did?" Adams was still half-blank, but recognition was beginning to filter back. "You stuck that hot knife on me," he said in accusatory tones.

"Yep."

"But why?"

"Sometimes it's the best way to seal up a wound like you had."

"Couldn't you have sewn it?"

"Could've, but I didn't have much sinew left, hoss. This is the last of it I got here."

"What are you doing . . . ? Oh, my God," Adams gasped when recognition dawned on him.

"It's got to be done, hoss," Rawlins said flatly.

"Well then let me do it."

"Eat shit, hoss," Rawlins said. "I ain't lettin' ye get your claws in me, boy. Besides, I'm almost done here." A few minutes later he did, indeed, finish. He had another jolt of whiskey.

"You did what you could for Ezra and Lucien?"

Adams asked after some minutes of silence.

Rawlins nodded. "Don't know as it'll do much good, hoss, but if any chil' in the mountain can make it, it'd be one of those two."

"You'd feel their loss greatly, wouldn't you, Abe?" Adams asked quietly. His leg throbbed, but he tried not to show the pain.

"A heap more'n this chil'd like to think about, hoss," the trapper said in a somewhat faraway voice. "Them two boys is about the onliest friends I ary had in my life. Ye couldn't go none better'n Ezra Early and Lucien Chardonnais. I'd trade places with either of 'em without a thought."

"I would, too," Adams said softly. He looked straight at Rawlins. "Or with you." He paused. "I've never had a friend the way you three are friends. I never missed it until I met you three." He paused again, waiting for a sudden burst of pain to fade a little. "And I know none of you is my close friend, but I owe all three of you a heap for all you've done for me. That's why I'd trade places with any of you who was wounded as bad as Ezra and Lucien are."

Rawlins suddenly grinned, a real grin this time. "I expect Ez or Lucien'd be glad to take ye up on that offer, could they do so, ol' hoss."

Adams was a little taken aback by the humor. Then he, too, smiled. "I expect they would," he acknowledged.

They sat in silence for some minutes, then Adams asked, "So what do we do now, Abe?"

22

RAWLINS HAD TO THINK about that for a little while. He wanted more than anything to set out after the Blackfeet right away. They had his wife and child. Scatters the Clouds was pregnant, and Standing Eagle was still only a little boy. Both were likely to suffer considerably at the hands of their captors, especially if the latter had been nothing more than a war party, which seemed to be the case.

Trouble with all that was, he could not desert his two longtime friends, the only real friends he had ever had.

He briefly considered leaving Chardonnais and Early in Adams's care, but he discarded this idea almost as soon as he thought of it. Adams was not equipped to help them—or protect them if the need should arise. Plus he was wounded, albeit slightly. Adams was not used to the mountains or the animals or Indians around here. He was a fair hunter, but being saddled with watching over two critically wounded men would be an almost impossible task for him.

"I reckon it all really depends on Ez and Lucien," Rawlins finally said. "They heal up quick, we can take out after those Blackfoot devils. They go under soon, same thing, though it won't be near as good, if ye know what I mean."

"Suppose they live, but yet take a long time to recover?" Adams asked.

Rawlins shrugged. "I ain't sure. I do know we'll be in piss-poor shape if that happens, hoss. We got no food, though there's plenty of game around here. But we've got little powder and lead. Pretty much what we're carryin' on us, since those goddamn shit-suckers got away with all our other possibles. We've got no medicines of any kind, and I sure as shit don't know about herbs and roots and such to find what we might need."

"Would it help to get them somewhere else?" Adams asked, trying to be helpful.

"I expect it wouldn't hurt none, but what're we gonna do, carry them two hosses on our backs?"

"There's the mule," Adams said hopefully.

"Might work. But there's only one mule and two of them. I might be able to carry Lucien for a spell, but I couldn't keep it up long enough to get anywhere. And I'd have a plumb hard time carryin' Ez more'n a few minutes at a time, hoss."

"How about I take the mule and go for help?"

"Where ye gonna go, hoss?"

Adams shrugged, uncomfortable in the role of potential hero. "Strong Bear's village, maybe."

"Ye ain't got the foggiest notion of where it is," Rawlins said, managing to keep the scorn out of his voice.

"You could draw me a map."

"I could," Rawlins agreed. He could see all the land in his mind's eye. The flat, rugged high prairie east of the Uintas, which gradually gave way to a more barren desertlike land to the south. The Uncompahgre plateau and the high, windy San Juan Mountains. "But I ain't gonna."

"Why not?" Adams had become a little more comfortable with the thought of actually being able to pay back Early and Chardonnais for the help they had given him.

"For one, I ain't sure you're up to that kind of trip, hoss. You've seen them mountains on the way up here. They're some mean sons of bitches. Easy to get lost in. Easy to go under in."

"I'm seasoned now, Abe. I mean, I know I've not been out here nearly as long as you or the others, but I've done well, I think, in the year almost that I've been up here."

"You're seasoned some," Rawlins agreed. "But not enough. Besides, hoss, you'd be out there alone, easy prey for any Indians who come along. Includin' the Utes. They don't know ye from my sister Sally. They'll rub ye out afore ye can even say, 'How's doin's, hoss?'"

Adams couldn't argue with that reasoning.

"And if that ain't good enough for ye, hoss, you'd also leave me alone with them two niggurs. Not such big doin's, really, but with them out like this, it wouldn't shine with this chil' to have to leave 'em to go out a huntin' and such."

"That doesn't give us much choice, does it?"

"Nope."

"How about if I stay here and you went to the Utes for help?"

Though Adams wasn't Rawlins's friend, really, he liked the young man and didn't want to hurt his feelings. Still, he was not a man known for holding his tongue when things had to be said. "Cain't trust ye," he said flatly.

Adams's face screwed up in the pain of humiliation far worse than the pain from his leg. His thoughts were jumbled. He wanted to scream, or cry, or attack Rawlins, or maybe all of them at the same time. Slowly, though, realization worked into his mind, and he nodded. "I can understand that," he said, voice choked with shame.

"Don't take it so hard, hoss," Rawlins said quietly. "It ain't ye so much as it is ye ain't had time to really get used to doin's out here. Hell, ye remember Jim Bridger, don't ye?"

Adams nodded. "He was the one came to Strong Bear's village that one time."

"Yep. Well, it was Ol' Gabe's second time up the Missouri. Same with Ez and Lucien. It were my first time out. We was all with a party bein' led by Major Andrew Henry. Well, one of the boys, an older feller named Hugh Glass, got himself tore up somethin' fierce by a big ol' b'ar. He was nigh onto dead. Well, ol' Major Henry, he didn't want to linger there, what with Indians and such. Plus he was out for plews and he weren't gonna git any settin' there waitin' for ol' Glass to go under."

Rawlins rolled himself a corn-husk cigarillo and lit it. "Well, ol' Henry asks for two boys to sit with ol' Glass till he went under, bury him, and then catch up to the brigade. Ol' Gabe and another ol' feller, John Fitzgerald I think his name was, offered their services.

"Everybody else left the next mornin', leavin' Ol' Gabe and Fitzgerald with Glass. That ol' chil' was in even worse shape. But goddamn if Glass didn't keep on livin'. After a couple days, Fitzgerald was about scared shitless some red devils were gonna git him and Ol' Gabe, so he talked Jim into takin' all of Hugh's possibles and leaving him."

"Alive and alone?" Adams asked, incredulous.

"Yep. Dug him a shallow hole and put that ol' hoss in it. Then they skedaddled. But that Hugh Glass, he was some crusty ol' bastard. After a few more days, damned if he didn't started crawlin', livin' on berries and such. He was finally able to get to his feet. It took him a couple of months, but that ol' hoss caught up to the brigade at Fort Kiowa. And I'll tell ye, hoss, ol' Glass was more'n half-froze to raise hair on them two what left him."

"Well," Adams said, "he couldn't have raised hair on Mister Bridger."

"That's a fact, hoss. He didn't do so on Fitzgerald either. He could've. Easy. But he let 'em be. Ol' Gabe was plumb ashamed, jist like ye are right at this moment. But he took learnin' from them doin's, and now ye cain't find a better chil' in all the mountains than Ol' Gabe Bridger. That ol' hoss shines, I tell ye. Plumb shines."

"Abe!" Adams shouted. "Abe, come here!"

Rawlins jumped up and ran, grabbing his rifle. He figured the Blackfeet were back, and that sent a shiver up his spine. He could not protect Early and Chardonnais while defending the camp and trying to wage battle among the trees. He skidded to a halt next to Adams. "What is it, hoss?" he asked, a little breathless.

"Look. Over there." The Easterner pointed.

"Well, I'll be goddamned," Rawlins drawled in some amazement. Not far away was a saddled horse. His horse. The one he had been using since Gray Horse and his couple of warriors got his other mount back up in the valley near the Snake.

"I thought I saw another one, too," Adams said, suddenly whispering. He was afraid that if he spoke loudly now, he'd send the horse or horses trotting off.

"Here, hoss, hold this," Rawlins said, holding out his rifle. He did not take his eyes off the horse. When Adams took the rifle, Rawlins began edging forward, moving easily toward the horse.

"Well, now, hoss," he said quietly, "me 'n ye been through some doin's together." His voice was soft, smooth, soothing. "We sure as hell have. And we can find us some more shinin' doin's. Yes, we can, ol' hoss. Like chasin' after some goddamn Blackfeet—but only after we git Ez and Lucien healed up some. Now, ye don't want to go runnin' away on me, hoss, do ye? Surely not."

The horse looked up and watched Rawlins for a few moments, as if trying to remember this man coming at him. Then the sturdy palomino went back to cropping at the grass.

Rawlins eased right on up to him and gently took the reins in his hands. He patted the horse on the neck. "Let's go, ol' hoss," he said, tugging on the reins. The horse resisted for only a moment, then shook his long mane and followed.

Back at the camp, Rawlins tied the horse to a

tree and went to check on his two friends. Adams had stayed out of the woods a little ways, watching for more horses. Rawlins went back to stand next to him.

"There's at least two more," Adams said, still whispering. "One there, and another there." He pointed almost straight ahead, and to his left.

It took Rawlins only a moment to spot them. Then he moved on toward the one. It was Early's horse and so also was fairly used to Rawlins's voice. He had no trouble taking the reins of that horse either. After speaking softly to it for a few moments, Rawlins climbed into the saddle and walked the horse slowly toward the third one. It was Scatters the Clouds's pinto pony.

While he was taking the reins to the pinto Rawlins spotted still another horse—Falling Leaf's—and he gathered that one up, too. He saw another pony, but that one took off, loping across the meadow.

"Dammit," Rawlins snapped. He wanted to just let the two he was holding go so he could chase the fifth horse, which he figured was Adams's. But that might mean the two he had would run off. Annoyed, he kept a tight grip on the reins to the two other horses and spurred the one he was riding.

It took more than a quarter hour before he ran Adams's horse down. His irritation faded as he finally trotted back to the camp. He felt almost happy.

"Goddamn, hoss," he shouted to Adams, "this sure as hell changes things for us."

"I would expect so," Adams said, walking up and taking the reins to his and Falling Leaf's horses. He walked both to a tree, where he tied them off. "You got some ideas on what to do?"

"I reckon I can come up with a couple 'tween now and the mornin', when I'm fixin' to pull out."

"You aim to head for Strong Bear's?"

"Reckon not." Rawlins dismounted, tied off the horse, and then checked on Early and Chardonnais. He poured himself a cup of coffee and then filled and lit his pipe. He sat, stretching out his long legs, relaxing for the first time since yesterday morning, when the Blackfeet had attacked.

"Why don't you want to go to Strong Bear's?" Adams asked, more curious than anything else. He also poured some coffee. When this pot was gone, they would be completely out.

"Them hosses ain't gonna be able to help Ez and Lucien. Christ, all we're gonna git there is a goddamn medicine man dancin' and singin' and castin' his secret powders about. Them're horseshit doin's to this ol' chil'."

"What about Mister Robideaux's place?"

Rawlins mulled that over for a few moments, puffing silently on his pipe. "Ye might have somethin' there, hoss." He thought about it some more. "I don't know as if he'll be able to help, hoss, but it's better'n goin' to Strong Bear's. And there ain't no place else to go out this way."

"We could try to make Taos," Adams suggested.

"Too goddamn far. I don't know how long we can expect our two *amigos* to hold up." He rose, knocking the ashes from his pipe into the fire. "Well, hoss, we got us some work to be doin' if we're fixin' to be on the trail in the mornin'."

Adams nodded and also rose. "How're we going to move Ezra and Lucien?"

"Well, it was kind of ol' Gray Horse to leave us

this one lodge here, even if they did shred it some. The lodgepoles're still in good shape, and there's enough hides from the cover that I can made a couple of travois. Shit, hoss, we're settin' purty here. We got us each a ridin' horse, a horse each for a travois for our *amigos,* an extry horse jist in case. Hell, we even got us a mule for cartin' what little supplies we can scrape up."

Adams nodded. "We're just rolling in goddamn good fortune," he said more than a little sarcastically.

Rawlins laughed. "Hell, hoss, we are—if'n ye think the starvin' poor times we was facin' just an hour ago."

"I suppose you're right, Abe." Adams shook his head. "But I sure as hell don't feel favored with good fortune."

"It's all in how ye look at it, hoss. Me, Ez, and Lucien've all faced worse times than this. Well," he added after a moment's thought, "maybe not worse times, but times jist as poor as this. And more'n once, too. Ye ain't. Jist that one time, I expect."

"That once was enough," Adams said, suppressing a shudder.

"I reckon it was, hoss. But me and our *amigos* there, well, we've seen such doin's more times'n we can count. Ye just do whatever ye can at such times. Sometimes ye shine in such times, and sometimes ye don't. Depends on whether the Great Spirit wants to smile or spit at ye." He paused. "Now, come on, hoss, let's get to work."

23

RAWLINS AND ADAMS PULLED out at first light the next morning, heading southwest, winding along on a barely visible animal trail. Rawlins rode in front, trailing a rope to the mule, which had another rope going to another horse. Ezra Early was in a travois behind that horse, tightly confined by the old tipi hides. Then came Adams, holding the rope to the extra horse and another to the last horse and another travois, in which Lucien Chardonnais was wrapped as carefully as Early was in the other.

The trail at times curled around the mountains, narrowing to a bare path with the rising stone on one side and nothing but precipices on the other. More than once Adams thought he'd pass out from looking over the edge, until he finally told himself sternly not to look over the edge anymore. That helped some, but not completely. Mostly he was more afraid for Chardonnais than he was for himself. He tried to assuage his fears by remembering that the horse pulling the wounded trapper in the travois had no more desire to go sailing over the edge into nothingness than he did. And the animal probably had a better natural survival instinct. He did wonder how Abe Rawlins up ahead of him could seem so blasé about the whole thing.

Rawlins never gave much thought to such things. He had been crawling around mountain trails for the better part of a dozen years now and he found nothing scary about them. Heights did not bother him in the least, nor did snakes, or animals, or mankind. The only things that really scared him were thoughts of losing another child or one of his two closest friends. The idea of Early or Chardonnais actually going under had never taken root in his mind, though there were a few times when he considered it a possibility. Right now, though, he was worried that neither of his *amigos* would make it.

That thought was the only thing that had really kept him from going after the Blackfeet. He had been torn, not knowing what to do about it all, but it was obvious as soon as he started thinking about it. He was about the only hope that Early and Chardonnais had to survive their wounds, but only if he got them help soon. Scatters the Clouds, Standing Eagle, and all the other women and children were either alive or dead now. If they were still alive, they most likely would continue so. They might even be adopted and mostly accepted by those Indians. If they were dead, all his rushing after them wouldn't help. If he did go chasing after revenge now, it was a fact, he figured, that both Early and Chardonnais would go under, and soon.

Thoughts of revenge were, however, always with him now, as they had been since the Blackfeet had ridden off, leaving his camp—and his life—a shambles. He would get the Indians back for this, no matter how long it took. It was that simple to him. He hoped he would be able to save Scatters the Clouds, Standing Eagle, and the others, but if not, his vengeance would be even more terrible, for tucked away in a corner of his mind, hidden by his generally easygoing nature, was a piece of Abe Rawlins that was every bit as savage as any Blackfoot could ever hope to be. It raised its vicious head only rarely, but when it did, it was a horrible thing to see.

He fully intended, too, to make Gray Horse pay personally for leading this raid. Their rivalry, if that's what it might be politely called, went back too long. It was time to bring it to an end. Those thoughts he kept in his mind, just behind his worry about his friends. They would sit and simmer steadily, until he allowed them to come to a boil of rage and hate.

Rawlins and Adams stayed that night along the Uinta River. It was a poor camp, but the trapper took little heed of it. He had spent time in such camps before; he could not be bothered by them now. They had little in the way of supplies, but Rawlins had dropped a black-tailed deer in the afternoon, so they had plenty of fresh meat. It wouldn't last long in this heat, but it would suffice for a day or two. The game was still plentiful here, so that was not a problem. Not having coffee was little more than an irritant to Rawlins.

Adams learned swiftly that complaining would get him nothing but a rebuke from Rawlins, and so he learned to keep his mouth shut. He didn't like this long push in traveling, or the lack of food and other supplies. He, too, was worried about Chardonnais and Early, and he was afraid that the Blackfeet would come back for them. His severe discomfort at the sheer precipices he had to overlook on occasion did little to improve his humor.

Rawlins was a little surprised, but quite relieved that Adams was showing himself to be a halfway decent mountaineer. He did his work without complaint, for the most part, and was mighty solicitous of their two wounded friends. And while Rawlins knew Adams was scared to death about nearly everything, he didn't let it show much or affect his willingness to do whatever needed doing.

Adams did notice the next day that they seemed to be riding almost continually downward. Granted, there were occasional flats, and even a few rises— some of them big—but in general, they headed down.

Late in the second day they were out, they came to the Green River. They were out of the Uintas now, and on the barren, wind-blasted high prairie or high desert, Adams was never sure which. He did know he felt more comfortable, though, now that he was not facing all those sheer drop-offs.

Rawlins decided that they would camp on the banks of the Green for the night. Though there was still some daylight left, he did not want to risk crossing the wide, swift Green without a full day of light ahead. He also wanted all the animals fresh.

After setting up the camp, Rawlins and Adams checked Early and Chardonnais and changed their poultices and bandages. Then they ate almost the last of the deer meat they had brought along from the day before. Done with that, Rawlins lit his pipe and strolled to the edge of the river. He stood there for some time, looking across the glistening, wide ribbon of water.

Adams sat at the fire, watching Rawlins for a while. He had lit a cigar and was trying to relax with it. But he could not, so he finally rose and joined the other man. "Something troubling you, Abe?" he asked quietly.

"What makes ye think that, hoss?"

"The way you're just standing here looking across the river. It's as if you expect trouble."

"I do."

Adams was a little surprised. "You don't think we'll make it across, do you?" he asked.

"Oh, me'n ye'll make it across, hoss. I ain't so sure about Ez and Lucien, though."

"You're trying to find the best way across, then?"

"Yep."

"Upriver maybe? Or down?" Adams suggested.

"Ain't no better either way, hoss. Not in any reasonable distance anyway."

"Then what're you planning to do?"

"Ain't sure yet. Might nary be sure neither, if ye don't leave me in peace to cogitate on it for a spell."

"Sorry," Adams said guiltily.

Rawlins shrugged. As far as he was concerned, the conversation was over.

Adams realized that after a moment and went back to the fire.

As darkness swept down on their miserable little camp, Rawlins turned and went to the fire. He stretched out, blanketless, though blankets or a sleeping robe would not've been needed anyway in this heat. He was asleep in minutes.

He was up early in the morning while Adams was still snoring. Rawlins checked on his two friends, then built up the fire and put the last hunks of meat on to cook. Then he went back to the river. The answer was no more clear now than it had been the night before. There were a few ways to do this, and he was by no means sure that any of them would work. With a shrug, he made up his mind and headed back toward the fire. He kicked Adams lightly in the leg. "Git up and movin', hoss," he said with a bit of his old humor.

Adams rolled over and muttered, "Come on back to bed, Dolores. It's too early to get up."

"Hell, hoss, if'n you're confusin' me with that purty little señora of yours, ye got yourself one hell of a problem."

"Wha . . .?" Adams mumbled, coming awake slowly and quite confused. When he saw Rawlins, he almost groaned.

"Kind of disappointin', ain't it, hoss?" the trapper said with a grin.

"Well, no, not really . . ."

"Ye lyin' sack of shit," Rawlins said, laughing. "Hell, hoss, ye ain't the only man ary dreamt of his woman."

Adams rubbed his face. "I expect not. But, damn, Abe, that dream was mighty real."

"Dreams're like that, hoss. Now git your ass up and movin'. We got us a river to cross."

"You figured out how to do it?" the Easterner asked. He looked up at Rawlins, eyes wide in surprise.

The mountain man shrugged. He had made up his mind and was comfortable with his decision. He still wasn't sure how safe it was going to be for any of them, but he had no doubts about the way he was going to proceed.

They checked on their two wounded friends and then wolfed down the deer meat. Rawlins allowed afterward that there was enough time for a pipe for him and a cigar for Adams. When those were done, Rawlins stood. "Time to move, hoss," he said.

Adams nodded and stood. "What do you want me to do?"

"Saddle our horses. Then load the mule if I ain't done with what I got to do."

As Adams walked off Rawlins knelt beside Early. "How's doin's, ol' hoss?" he asked softly, not wanting the reporter to overhear him. He didn't figure Early could hear, but he didn't think it would hurt to talk to the two wounded trappers every now and again. For all he knew, maybe it would help bring them around. He had seen—and heard of—stranger things.

Rawlins was unconcerned when he got no reaction from Early. He undid the rawhide binding the lodgepole into the travois and positioned the two poles so that they were parallel. Then he did the same with Chardonnais's, after greeting the little French-Canadian. Since both wounded men were unwrapped already, he eased each one out of the makeshift litter and onto the grass.

That done, Rawlins went and loaded the mule. It took only a few minutes, since they had so few supplies. When he was done, he saw that Adams was almost finished saddling the two horses. He waited until the other man was done and had walked the horses over to him.

They tied them to stunted, close-growing trees nearby. Then they brought the three other horses up and tied them in between the two saddled animals so that all the horses were about two feet apart.

Under Rawlins's guidance, the two men fashioned two litters between the center horse and the two unsaddled horses, one to each side. Rawlins finally went around and made sure that they were as sturdy as could be expected under the circumstances. Then he lifted first Early and then Chardonnais and carried them to the horses. He placed each in one of the litters, and then wrapped the hides around them good and tight and tied them down.

"Isn't that dangerous?" Adams asked. "Suppose they get dumped into the river if the horses spook?"

"Supposin' I loosen these bindin's and they roll out of them damn litters even if the horses don't spook," Rawlins countered. "I figure they're safer this way than they'd be the other. If the horses spook and they go down, there ain't gonna be no savin' 'em anyhow."

"I suppose you're right,"Adams said skeptically. Rawlins had explained his plan to him while they were making the litters, and the young man had some serious doubts about its viability.

"If I ain't, hoss," Rawlins said pointedly, "I'll be losin' a heap more'n ye will."

Adams smarted under these words, but then realized they were true. Rawlins would, indeed, lose more than he would if Early and Chardonnais died. It would be doubly horrible considering that it would have been Rawlins's plan that had killed them.

"Ye ready, hoss?" the trapper asked, looking across several horses' backs at Adams.

"As much as I'll ever be, I suppose," Adams said.

"Ye know what to do?"

"Yes." The Easterner's mouth had suddenly gone dry.

"You'll shine, hoss," Rawlins said quietly.

Adams nodded and climbed into his saddle. Rawlins also mounted. Each took the rope around the neck of the horse next to him. Rawlins also took the one that was around the middle animal's neck, as well as the one to the mule.

"Let's do 'er, hoss," he said.

As a unit, the two men and five horses turned. Rawlins was on the far left, trailing the mule. There was a horse on his right, then the litter with Early, the middle horse, the litter with Chardonnais, another horse, and then Adams.

They moved slowly toward the river.

24

THEY STOPPED AT THE EDGE OF the water and looked nervously at each other. Then Rawlins grinned. "Time to shine, ol' hoss," he said, then nodded.

The two men eased the horses into the water. Rawlins was glad he had the palomino under him, since the animal was used to him. The horses walked along the riverbed, but then, about seven feet out, they hit a drop-off.

Adams's horse whinnied nervously, and all the horses jerked some. Rawlins cast an anxious glance at the litters, but they held up. The horses settled down some, and started swimming.

The mule, behind Rawlins, hit the drop-off and brayed. He tugged back, wanting out of the water. Rawlins spun in his saddle, eyes red with anger. "Ye fuck with me now, ye goddamn fractious critter, and I'll put a bullet 'twixt your goddamn dumb eyes without a thought."

Whether the mule understood or not didn't matter.

He quieted down and began swimming placidly along behind the horses.

They had a few more tense moments when they started up the shelf toward the other bank. But the animals, under the shouting, whipping encouragement of Rawlins and Adams, found their footing and climbed onto the shelf, then along the slowly rising riverbed, and finally up the slick, muddy bank.

"Waugh!" Rawlins grunted. "We did it. Goddamn if we didn't. This chil' can sure make 'em come now."

Adams grinned at him, relaxing for the first time since he had heard his cohort's plan. "We push on now?" he asked.

"No, hoss. These animals need some rest after what they jist done. And I want to git Ez and Lucien back on travois."

"Can't we just leave them on these litters?" Adams asked. "They weathered that trip across the river pretty well."

"That they did. But it's too much of a pain in the ass for this chil' to get my amigos into and out of them damn litters. The time we spend with such doin's is time better spent on the trail."

"You that worried about Ezra and Lucien?"

"Yep," Rawlins said as he dismounted. "The quicker we can git 'em some kind of doctorin', the better chance they got of not goin' under. Besides, hoss, there's still the little matter of them shit-suckin' Blackfeet."

Adams nodded, some of the joy at having made it across the river diminished by the thought of revenge. Still, even he knew it had to be. He dismounted, too.

While Rawlins unwrapped Early, lifted him out of the litter, and carried him a few yards away and set him down, Adams was unwrapping Chardonnais. Then Rawlins carried the French-Canadian and laid him next to Early. Chardonnais groaned once, startling Rawlins, who then grinned. "You're some, ol' hoss," he whispered. It was the first sign of life from either wounded man.

Rawlins and Adams took down the litters and hobbled the horses. Then they turned the animals loose to graze and rest. The two checked on the wounded men, but there was little they could do at the moment.

Rawlins gave the horses an hour to rest, then refashioned the travois, put Chardonnais and Early in them, and tied them down. Then they got on the trail again. Rawlins pushed them as hard as he reasonably could, roughly following the southern side of the White River. Twenty miles on, they stopped for the night. The mountain man managed to shoot a white-tailed deer, so they ate well, but they still had to wash down their meal with river water. Adams was out of cigars, and Rawlins was mighty low on tobacco. He was also a little concerned about the amount of powder and lead they had left.

They spent the next night at the confluence of the White River and Douglas Creek. They followed the latter the next day heading south. They almost made Douglas Pass that day and camped without water that night. Their two canteens—one made from a hollowed-out gourd, the other of wood—were full, but they had no other water.

Though Douglas Pass was not difficult to travel through, it still took them most of the next day to make their way across it and down the southern side. The next day, though, they had a fairly easy downhill ride to the Grand River, where they camped.

They went through the making of double litters again and swam across the Grand River the same way they had the Green. This time, however, the mule was so fractious that in desperation, Rawlins released the rope leading to the animal. The last he saw of the mule, it was still fighting the current. Then the river swept the animal around a curve.

After a rest on the southern bank of the Green, the men pushed on, heading southeast through the valley, following the Gunnison River.

Two long days later Rawlins pulled to a stop. Adams rode up alongside him. "Well, there it is, hoss," the trapper said, pointing to Antoine Robideaux's small trading post.

"I'll tell you, Abe, there were plenty of times I never thought we'd make it."

"Waugh! Don't ye ary underestimate this ol' chil'," Rawlins said arrogantly.

Adams grinned. "All right, then, there were plenty of times I never thought *I'd* make it." He grew more serious. "Or that Ezra and Lucien'd make it."

"That fact crossed this chil's mind, hoss," Rawlins said. "But them two is still breathin', and we're here."

"Then what're we waiting for?" Adams said, spirits rising. The thought of hot coffee, bread, cigars, sugar, and other things he hadn't had for a while was enticing.

"Not a thing, ol' hoss," Rawlins said with a grin. "Not a thing." He kicked his horse into motion, and within minutes he and Adams were riding into Robideaux's post.

Robideaux came out of his log home, a smile creasing his broad Gallic face. "*Bonjour, mes amis.*

How are . . . ?" Then his face fell. "But what 'as 'appened?" he asked, worried.

"Blackfeet jumped us up in the Uintas," Rawlins said as he dismounted.

"Ze Uintas?" Robideaux was incredulous.

"Yep."

"But zat is far from their stomping grounds."

"Hell, hoss, I know that. But ye know well's I do that those fractious shit-suckers'll ride from hell to creation to raid."

"*Mais oui!* But still . . ."

"Look, Antoine," Rawlins said with an edge to his voice, "none of that means shit right now. Ez and Lucien're nearabout gone under already, and I don't know how much longer they can hold out."

"Zen why bring zem here?" Robideaux did not seem put out that they would think of it, though he did seem worried.

"Only place this chil' could think of."

"But I can do not'ing for zem here. I 'ave no medicines, no doctoring experience."

"Dammit, Antoine, ye can do somethin' for 'em. Ye don't and I'll cut your heart out and feed it to ye."

"You can t'reaten me all you want, Monsieur Rawlins," Robideaux said, affronted, "but zat will not make me a doctor." He paused, thinking. "But bring zem inside. Zey can rest in a bed for ze night. You two, also—after you 'ave a good meal."

Rawlins started to retort, but Adams cut him off. "That'd be wonderful, Mister Robideaux. We've got next to no supplies. Haven't had since the Blackfeet raided us."

"I ain't takin' the time to set here and fill my

meatbag whilst Ez and Lucien're about to go under," Rawlins snarled.

Adams turned to face Rawlins. He drew in a deep breath, then blew it out. "Riding out of here in a huff, with no food in us, and no supplies, is not going to help either Ezra or Lucien. We need to keep up our strength."

"*Mais oui!*" Robideaux interjected. "Besides, Abe, if zey are still alive after zis long, zey'll probably be all right in ze long run."

"I ain't so sure, hoss."

"I think he's right, Abe," Adams said soothingly. "And another thing. We've got to figure out where to go next. Can we make Taos from here? Or should we just try to go to Strong Bear's village? We'll need to think on that."

Rawlins sighed, trying to relax. "I suppose you two're right. Not that I like it much, but there ain't no arguin' with that reasonin'. Get some of your boys out here to help us, Antoine."

"But zere is no one but me. I will help."

"Where's your clerks?" Rawlins asked, only a little surprised. "Ye fire 'em?"

"No. Not yet anyway. I need to get supplies up here, so I sent zem down to Taos."

"You trust 'em?" Rawlins asked, more surprised.

"Not for a damn minute," Robideaux snorted. "Zey would steal me blind if I gave zem half a chance. But I sent a letter to Ceran, telling him to fire zem two clerks and to hire new ones and send ze new ones up here with ze mules and supplies."

Rawlins chuckled a little. "Them two shitballs got any brains at all, they'll have read that letter twenty minutes after they rode on out of here."

"*Mais oui!* But I am not zat stupid. No, no, no, no. I stick ze letter in amongst a bunch of ze ledger books. Zey showed no interest in zem here. I don't t'ink zey will show any interest in zem on ze trail."

"Sneaky bastard, ain't ye," Rawlins commented. "Now stop your goddamn gabbin' and come help us with our *amigos* here."

Within minutes, Chardonnais and Early were inside and lying on the clerks" beds in the small room. Then Rawlins and Adams tended the horses. When they finished with that, the two checked on their two friends again. Chardonnais showed a few more signs of regaining consciousness again, but he was still out. There was no change in Early.

"So, what happened with zese Blackfeet?" Robideaux asked as he and his two visitors sat at the small log table. His Ute woman fed them bowls of stew and the biscuits Robideaux had taught her how to make. The stew was made with fresh elk, and Rawlins and Adams dug in hungrily.

"We was attacked," Rawlins responded with a mouth full of biscuit and stew. "Them pustulent bastards first hit me up along the Snake. I made wolf bait out of two of 'em. A couple got away. Then they hit us again a week and a half, two weeks ago, up in the Uintas."

"You think zey were looking for you, eh?" Robideaux asked.

Rawlins shrugged. "I reckon so. Either that or this chil's medicine's gone plumb cold." He poured himself a second cup of coffee and slurped half of it down.

"Ze women and children?" Robideaux asked, sounding worried.

"All took by them red devils. I don't know whether they're alive or dead."

"Ah, but it doesn't matter now, does it?"

"Not a goddamn bit," Rawlins growled.

"*Oui.* You can find another woman, and ze children, zey will come, too, after a little."

"You shit-suckin' little stump of a bastard," Rawlins hissed in fury. "Ye might not think nothin' of your woman 'cause she's a Ute, and maybe ye could give her up jist like that, but that don't mean this chil's like ye. Besides, ain't no drippin'-dick Blackfoot gonna count coup on this chil' and git away with it. Them fuckin' savages took all our catch, all our plunder. This chil' aims to see they get some comeuppance for such doin's."

Robideaux was taken aback by the anger stamped on Rawlins's face. He had not thought the easygoing mountain man had such rage in him. "I didn't mean not'ing by zat," he said hastily.

"You're full of shit, froggie." Rawlins paused in his eating a moment. "It don't shine with this chil' to be so unthinkin' of my woman. Ye want to feel that way abut yours, that's your doin's, hoss. But don't ye try to make me out to be like ye in that way."

"*Pardonnez-moi, monsieur,*" Robideaux said sincerely.

They all went back to eating, this time silently. Only after they were done—six bowls of stew for Rawlins, four for Adams's and only one for Robideaux—and the trader had passed out cigars, did he ask, "You know where you will go from here?"

Rawlins shook his head. "Ain't sure yet. I'll cogitate on it tonight. Whilst we're on the trail," he added pointedly.

"*Mais non!* I cannot allow zat. *Non!* My bad manners shouldn't keep you from a bed and some measure of safety."

"I ain't so sure I can share a roof with a man I don't share thoughts with."

"Please, forget I said zem t'ings. I meant no 'arm."

"It's a good idea to stay here, Abe," Adams said. Then he had a small burst of inspiration. "Not only do we need the rest, the horses need it even more."

Rawlins nodded and downed some more coffee. Then he shut out Adams and Robideaux, letting them talk to each other while he drank coffee, puffed his pipe, and thought.

During a lull in the conversation an hour later, Rawlins finally spoke. "Ye got some supplies left ye can sell us, Antoine?" he asked. When Robideaux hesitated, he added, "I got some specie, hoss. I can pay ye."

"I was not worried about zat," Robideaux said with offended dignity. "I 'esitate only to t'ink of what I have left 'ere. Dere isn't much, but you can take what you need. You can pay me another time."

"Bein' in your debt don't shine with this ol' chil', Antoine. We'll only take what I can pay for. We ain't gonna need much."

25

RAWLINS WAS IN A FOUL-TEMPERED mood the next morning when he and Adams rode out of Robideaux's small fort. Early and Chardonnais were once again in travois. The scanty supplies that Rawlins had been able to pay for in cash were loaded on the extra horse.

They headed south, moving silently and as swiftly as they thought they could. Rawlins was still unsure of where they would go, though, even when they came to a stop that night.

"How long's it going to take us to get to Taos?" Adams asked after they had done all their work and had eaten.

"Couple weeks. Maybe a little more. If we go there."

"What do you mean, if we go there?" Adams was shocked a little. "You haven't changed your mind and decided to go to Strong Bear's village, have you?" He didn't mind all that much, he supposed,

228

though Taos would be preferable, since Dolores was there. But he had been treated well by Strong Bear's Utes, and he would not mind going back to the village. Especially since it meant he and Rawlins would be able to go after the Blackfeet that much sooner. This thought shocked him even more. Until now he had not even really considered pursuing their attackers with Rawlins. He wasn't sure, by any means, that the trapper would want him along anyway.

"No, I ain't fixin' to head to Strong Bear's," Rawlins drawled. "But I ain't so sure about Taos, neither."

"Why not?"

"Hell of a journey, hoss, though once we get to the San Luis Valley, it gets a heap easier. Still, it's some long way, and the longer we take in gettin' Ez and Lucien to help, the longer it's gonna be afore I get back after them goddamn shit-suckin' Blackfeet."

"But there's noplace else. You said so yourself."

"Well, that's mostly true. But there is one other place we can take 'em."

"Where's that?" Adams asked, interested.

"A new place Bill Bent runs over on the Arkansas. His brother Charlie said it's a good-sized place, and it's a heap closer to Taos, and I figure many a chil' shows up there at some time or another."

"What good'll that do us? Or Ezra and Lucien?"

"Bill's usually got a heap of people around him, and the ones that're with him're usually more trustworthy. Not like them shits Robideaux hired on. We get our two *amigos* to Bent's, and there'll be someone who can git 'em to Taos for us, and without puttin' 'em under in the doin'.'"

"But if we're that close to Taos by then, why not just ride all the way into town?" Adams asked.

Rawlins grinned, but to Adams it was a chilling sight, devoid of all humor and humanity. "'Cause, then, ol' hoss, I can git after them stinkin' red devils a heap sooner. I don't git on their trail soon, it's gonna be colder'n a witch's tit."

"You'd trust this Bent fellow with the lives of Ezra and Lucien?" Adams asked, fairly sure he knew the answer.

"Yep," Rawlins said without hesitation.

"Is it any easier to get to this place than to Taos?"

"I wouldn't say that, hoss," Rawlins said evenly. "It's probably a heap worse in some ways. But once we're there, we're out on the plains. From there I can ride hell-bent north and make up some time. It'll help me catch them skunk-humpin' Blackfeet a bit sooner."

"You sound like your mind's made up," Adams commented.

Rawlins thought about that for a few seconds, then nodded. "Yep, hoss, I figure it is after all."

They turned eastward the next morning, again pushing themselves as hard as they dared. That night they came onto the Gunnison River again and camped there. They followed it as best they could. A few days later, they came to Tomichi Creek.

As they were preparing to leave the following morning, Chardonnais startled them both when he suddenly said, "*Mon dieu,* why is dis chil' all truss' up in dis contraption like a papoose, eh?"

Rawlins jerked his head around, eyes wide. The voice had been soft, little more than a whisper, but he had no doubt that it was Chardonnais's. He trotted over and squatted next to where the wounded man was already encased in the travois.

Adams was only a second behind in getting there and kneeling.

"How's doin's, ol' hoss?" Rawlins asked, trying to keep the worry out of his voice.

"Dis chil' is hurting like hell, if you want to ask and to hear," Chardonnais grumbled. "How do you t'ink I feel?"

"Think ye can eat somethin', froggie?" Rawlins asked, relieved.

"*Mais non,*" Chardonnais said with regret. "Dere is much pain, and I don' t'ink my stomach would want anyt'ing in it now." He grinned, but it was a pale imitation of his usual one. "Except maybe some whiskey?" he asked hopefully.

"Ye want the governor's finest wine?" Rawlins asked dryly.

"Dat won' be necessary," Chardonnais whispered flatly.

"Whether ye thought it was or not, Frenchie, you'll have to settle for some plain ol' shit-tastin' *awerdenty.*"

"Dat shines wit' dis chil'."

"Christ, that's jist like ye, ye goddamn stump-high sack of shit," Rawlins said. "Jist wake up and the first thing ye want is a snort of *awerdenty.*"

Chardonnais smiled weakly again. "Knowing me, you would've t'ought I'd have wanted a woman, no?"

Rawlins laughed, his relief soaring. "Goddamn, I was wonderin' how long it'd take ye afore ye got around to mentionin' that. Christ, froggie, one of these days you're gonna be on your deathbed and be askin' for a woman for one last humpin'."

"Better to go under humping de hell out of some sweet mademoiselle dan to be made wolf bait of by a Blackfoot arrow, eh?"

"I reckon ye got somethin' there, Lucien." Rawlins looked at Adams. "Go fetch that whiskey of ours."

"You mean the only one . . ." Adams shut up when he caught the black look in Rawlins's eyes. He nodded, rose, and left.

"Ezra?" Chardonnais asked.

"He's hurt worse'n ye, goddamn your froggie little heart. But he's still with us. Now that you've regained consciousness, maybe he'll do the same soon."

"I hope dat is true." Chardonnais paused as Adams returned with the whiskey. He took a tentative drink with help from both Rawlins and Adams. Then he took another. He nodded, and his friends eased his head back down. "And Looks Again and Crow Fight?" he asked flatly. He did not see them around, and so he was sure they were dead.

"Them scum-suckin' Blackfeet got 'em, jist like they got ary other woman and chil' we had with us. Rode off with all of 'em."

"Dey will not have an easy time of it, *mon ami*."

"Lordy, I never thought of that," Rawlins said sarcastically.

Chardonnais ignored the comment. "Where are we?" he suddenly asked. "We are not in de Uintas no more."

"Nope. We're on Tomichi Creek."

"You come all dis way wit' me and Ezra on death's doorstep?" Chardonnais asked.

"Yep."

"Why?" The French-Canadian was flabbergasted.

He could feel unconsciousness creeping back up on him, but he wanted to hear more before it overtook him.

"Because, ye fractious sack of shit," Rawlins snapped, "I'm tryin' to get ye and Ez some help."

"Where are you going to get help way de 'ell out here, eh?"

"Figured I'd head to Bent's place. We tried Robideaux's first, but that son of a bitch weren't much help."

"Why not go to Taos?"

Rawlins explained his reasoning.

Chardonnais nodded. He was having trouble keeping his eyes open now. There was something else he wanted to tell Rawlins, but his mind would just not cooperate. Then he was out again.

Adams looked across Chardonnais's inert form at Rawlins. "Think he'll be all right?" he asked.

"Hell if I know, hoss. But I expect it's a good sign he was awake—and alert—even if jist for a little bit there. Both these hosses're tough ol' critters. If anyone can make it with wounds like them, I'd say it'd be these two skunk humpers."

Adams nodded. Then he and Rawlins went back to work.

They stayed along Tomichi Creek again that night, but moved away from it the next day as the creek curled northward. A few days farther on, they hit the Arkansas.

"Doesn't look like much," Adams commented when he saw the thin ribbon of fast-rushing river. He remembered the journey on his way west four years ago. He had crossed the Arkansas with Ebenezer Parfrey and his wagon train of goods along the Santa

Fe Trail. The river had been wide and swift there.

"Hell, boy, the headwaters of that river ain't too far from here. North and a little west. It'll git bigger all the time."

That night, while Rawlins and Adams were sitting around the fire having some after-supper coffee, Early awoke. They became aware of this when Early tried to get up and succeeded only in getting to his hands and knees before falling on his face.

Once he had lifted Early and placed him back on the travois, Rawlins explained where they were, what had happened, and what they were doing.

"Damn," Early said, his voice a faraway whisper. "Ye just leave me'n Lucien with Bart," he continued faintly. "Ye go chasin' after them goddamn Blackfeet."

"I'm gonna go get me some snake-humpin' Blackfeet," Rawlins reassured him. "Jist as soon as I git ye'n the frog over there some help."

"We'll make do."

"Sure ye will, hoss," Rawlins snorted. "Hell, Bart here don't know Pierre's Hole from his shithole. He'd have ye three lost soon's ye rode a hundred yards."

Adams was insulted, but he also knew Rawlins was right, so he said nothing.

"I'll help guide him," Early insisted.

"Sure ye will, *amigo*. And my horse is gonna fly soon's I strap a couple eagle feathers to him."

"Goddammit, Abe . . ."

"I'll tell ye what, ol' hoss," Rawlins said with a touch of humor, "I'll wrassle ye for it. Ye win, and I'll leave ye'n Frenchie with Cap'n Adams here. I win, ye shut your flappin' hole and ride along like a good chil'."

"Ye drive a hard bargain, Abe," Early said, and then fell unconscious again.

Five days later they approached the rickety-looking little log fort William Bent had used for several years until the new place opened farther down the Arkansas two years ago. During the first two of those five days, both Early and Chardonnais had awakened several times and then fallen into unconsciousness again shortly after. Then, though, they began taking in a little nourishment and were awake for longer periods.

Since it was late in the afternoon, Rawlins decided to stay at the small, abandoned fort. He was annoyed, beginning to think he should have gone straight to Taos after leaving Robideaux's. They would've been there by now, and his two friends would be getting help. He would've been on the trail of the Blackfeet by now, too.

Both Early and Chardonnais complained as loudly as they could when Rawlins carried them into one of the small log buildings. They kept up the commentary as Rawlins turned to leave. Rawlins suddenly whirled, eyes flashing in anger. "Shut the fuck up!" he roared. "The both of ye!" He turned and stomped out.

Adams had heard, and looked at Rawlins in surprise when Rawlins came outside again. But he said nothing when he saw the look on his face. He did go check on Early and Chardonnais a few minutes later, though, making sure they were all right. Both were asleep.

After eating, Rawlins took a torch and went into the cabin that held the two wounded men. Adams followed along with bowls of weak stew. Early and

Chardonnais seemed not to hold Rawlins's earlier explosion against him. They just took to wolfing down the food and then asking for more.

When Adams went out to comply with their request, Early said, "What're ye fixin' to do now, Abe?"

"Get ye troublemakin' goddamn critters to Bent's and then head on off after them stump-suckin' Blackfeet," Rawlins growled flatly.

"Now listen to me, ye thickheaded snake humper," Early said as forcefully as he could. "Ye leave the two of us here with Bart. If it'll make ye feel any better, go out and do some huntin'. We can make meat here. We got a roof over us, and some walls around us to keep out the savages. We don't need to get on the trail, so Bart won't get us lost. We shine here, sure as hell. Soon's me'n Lucien can travel some, we'll head down to Taos ourselves. We'll get us outfitted and then come on up and save your worthless ass."

"*Mais oui!*" Chardonnais added. "Just like we always do."

"Eat shit, ye peckerless little frog." He sat in thought. It might be feasible, but he'd never be able to live with himself if something happened to them because he left them in inexperienced—or incompetent—hands. He was sure Adams was the former; he wasn't certain about the latter.

"I can handle it, Abe," Adams said quietly.

Rawlins nodded. "I expect ye can, ol' hoss, but such doin's don't shine with this ol' niggur at all." He paused, then said, "I'll cogitate about leavin' ye two here, too. We'll talk more about it in the mornin'."

Rawlins was almost finished with breakfast the next morning when he made his decision. "Bart, ol' hoss," he said, "we got shit to git done. We're going to Bent's."

26

ABOUT MIDAFTERNOON OF THE next day, a large brown splotch hove into view over the horizon. From a distance, it sort of looked to Rawlins as if a section of Taos had been moved onto the plains in the middle of nowhere. As he and his small entourage drew closer the brown muddle slowly coalesced into an adobe fort.

An hour or so later they rode in through the wide double doors into the *placita*. Rawlins had noted the round bastion on the left side as he rode in under the small guardhouse directly over the gates.

The place resembled an anthill, with Mexican laborers scurrying around, shops going full tilt, mountain men lounging around yarning and gambling, Indians wandering in and out.

Rawlins was taken aback by all the activity. He never expected such an out-of-the-way place to be so busy. He wondered where he should stop, since he had no real clue as to the whereabouts of Bill Bent.

Bent solved the problem himself by stepping out of a room in the rear left-hand corner of the fort. He moved out from under the small portico and shaded his eyes against the glare of the sun. "That you, Abe?" he asked, coming forward with a small grin on his face. Then he spotted Early and Chardonnais. "Good, sweet Jesus, Abe, what's happened to your *amigos*?"

"Goddamn Blackfeet," Rawlins said, coming to a halt. "I figured they were gonna go under for certain, but they seem to be hangin' on." He and Bent shook hands. "Bill," the trapper added, indicating Adams, "a new *amigo*, Bart Adams."

"How's doin's, ol hoss?" Bent said, taking stock of Adams. He was not quite sure what to think. The young man was nearly as tall as Rawlins, but had nowhere near his breadth of shoulder or musculature. He looked city-bred and soft, despite the buckskins and other accoutrements of a mountaineer.

"Shinin'," Adams said, feeling a little self-conscious about using the mountain slang. He was little impressed with Bill Bent. After the stories he had heard, he expected a man seven feet tall, a giant in size as well as in deed. What he was, though, was a short, swarthy individual with a hard, sharp-featured face. There was not much to set him apart from most other men.

"You're that feller headed out here with Parfrey's band of cutthroats a few years back, ain't you?" Bent asked. "The one they left out in the Cimarron to die. The one who up and married ol' Don Francisco's purty little daughter?"

"I am," Adams said. Then he ventured, "You seem to know a lot about me, Mister Bent."

"Call me Bill, hoss." He laughed, adding, "There ain't much that goes on in Taos that I don't know about." Seeing Adams's look of surprise, he said, "Hell, either one of my brothers, or Ceran—you know Ceran Saint Vrain?—or some of my workers are always runnin' between here and Taos. They keep me well informed."

Adams nodded, understanding.

"Hey, goddammit, Bent, don't stand there with those two assholes jawin'," Early shouted. "Come get me out of here."

"Don't listen to that ol' hoss," Rawlins said loud enough for Early to hear. "He's been a right pain in my ass since he took that goddamn arrow. Damn Blackfeet learned how to shoot some, we wouldn't have to stand here listenin' to his goddamn whinin'."

"Well," Bent said, "I could have a couple of Cheyennes come in here and finish up what the goddamn Blackfeet weren't able to."

Rawlins looked like he was pondering that for a bit, but Chardonnais bellowed, "Get de 'ell over 'ere and let us loose from dese damn contraptions!"

"Or what?" Rawlins asked innocently.

"Or I'll tell everybody here about dat time down in Taos when dat señorita's pa almost caught you wit' her and—"

"Ye see, Bill, what I got to put up with?" Rawlins complained. "Goddamn, if they ain't the two most tryin' hosses this chil's ever seen." His worried eyes betrayed the joshing tone, though.

Seeing that look, Bent said, "We best get them two under cover and have 'em looked at." He called to a few laborers and directed them to take Early and

Chardonnais into a room across the *placita*. Other laborers took away the horses.

Rawlins, Adams, and Bent followed as the two wounded men were carried into the room. Bent knelt and looked at first Early and then Chardonnais. Then he stood. "Jesus, Abe, they're in plumb bad shape."

"Don't ye go gettin' the undertaker ready just yet," Early growled, but his voice had weakened considerably. The short exchange of words outside had tired him.

"Same wit' dis chil'," was all that Chardonnais could manage.

"You two just shut your traps," Bent ordered. "Get comfortable. I'll have someone come in here soon and see if they can do anything to save your cantankerous ol' hides."

Bent, Rawlins, and Adams went outside. "They look plumb bad, Abe," Bent said.

"Tell me somethin' I don' know, hoss," Rawlins growled.

Bent nodded. "Come on, let's go get some coffee. You hungry?"

"Ye ary known me to not be hungry?" Rawlins retorted.

Bent led them across the *placita* to the room he had left when Rawlins rode into the fort. It was a fair-sized dining room with several long wooden tables with benches. Bent took one of the tables and the other two men sat.

"Charlotte!" Bent bellowed. "Charlotte. Get out here."

"I's a-comin', Mister Bent," a short, very round black woman said, coming from a small room at the back. She stopped. "You got comp'ny." She whirled and went back where she came from. In moments she was hustling back into the dining room with a large tray containing a coffeepot, cups, bowls of stew, and a plate of biscuits.

As Charlotte set the items on the table Bent said to her, "Two ol' *amigos*'re in a room across the *placita*. They're hurt bad. You got somethin' to use as a poultice that might help 'em?"

"I think so, Mistah Bent. I'll see to it directly."

The three men fell to eating quietly. Afterward they sipped coffee. Rawlins lit his pipe.

"What happened, Abe?" Bent asked.

"A few Blackfeet jumped us just afore we was to leave our winter camp up near the Snake."

"Jumped *you,* you mean," Adams corrected.

Rawlins shrugged. "I made wolf bait out of a couple of them shit-suckers. Then Ez decided we'd best hit the trail afore them goddamn Blackfeet came back with a large war party." He paused to eat a cookie. "Well, shit if them hosses didn't hit us again whilst we was up in the Uintas on the way back to Taos. That's when Ez and Lucien caught them arrows. Skunk-humpin' sons of bitches made off with all our plunder, plus all the women and children."

"What the hell're you doin' way over here?" Bent asked, surprised.

"We went to Robideaux's, but he wasn't no help. Then I figured to hit your place here, since that'd not take me so far south as Taos."

Bent nodded, understanding that Rawlins wanted to get after the Blackfeet.

"So here we are. Now, if'n ye can spare me some

supplies and a mule, I'll be hittin' the trail."

"You can have what you need," Bent said without hesitation.

"I'll pay ye," Rawlins said. It was a point of pride with him not to take anything for free. He always wanted to pay his way. "Ceran's got some specie banked for me down in Taos. Take what I owe ye from that."

"I ain't worried about the money, Abe," Bent said, unconcerned about helping a friend. "But I suggest you wait till mornin', ol' hoss. You've been on the trail a long time."

"Time's awastin'," Rawlins said flatly.

"Hell, it's been several weeks already. Another couple hours ain't gonna make you no difference." He paused. "You plannin' to chase after someone in particular? Or just go kill whatever Blackfeet you can find?" This was said in a tone that indicated that it wouldn't be all that bad a thing.

"I got someone in mind. An ol' shit-suckin' chil' named Gray Horse."

"You mentioned him before," Adams interjected. "He was leading the small war party that attacked you the first time."

Rawlins nodded. "Ye got a good memory for such things, hoss."

"Didn't you have a run-in with that chil' sometime back?"

"Yep." The word was cold.

"Well, what happened then?" Adams asked guilelessly.

Rawlins scowled, not wanting to think about it or talk about it. Then he sighed. "We was up in Blackfoot country, back in 'thirty. We knew we was takin' a

chance settin' our traps up there, but we figured we
had some powerful medicine."

"Damn fools," Bent muttered.

"Reckon so," Rawlins said almost agreeably.
"Gray Horse and three or four other of them red devils
tried runnin' off our horses one day."

Rawlins had been the one in camp that day
watching over things. All of a sudden the horses
bolted. He jerked his head up and glimpsed an Indian
driving off the small herd. He grabbed his rifle and
let a shot fly. He hit nothing, but he hoped it would
alert Early and Chardonnais that there was danger in
the camp.

He watched for only another second, seeing
which way the thieves were driving the horses.
Then he spun and ran for the woods. He did not feel
it necessary to tell any of the women what to do.
Empty rifle in his left hand, he charged into the
forest, running as hard as he dared. He leaped over
fallen trees, clumps of brush, rocks, whatever was in
his way, dodging branches all the while.

The Blackfeet were driving the horses northwest,
through a long open meadow that curled around
back toward the north. By cutting through the
woods, Rawlins hoped to be able to catch up to them
as they headed north.

He was still running full out when he saw the
first of his horses. Then he spotted a big, painted
Blackfoot warrior on his horse. Still charging, he
dropped his rifle. As he burst out of the trees he
jumped. His legs almost went around the midsection
of the Blackfoot on the horse, and both men toppled
off the side of the animal, each landing with a heavy
thud.

"Waugh!" Rawlins growled as he surged to his feet. "How's them doin's, ol' hoss?"

The Blackfoot—who Rawlins would later learn was Gray Horse—grinned viciously and charged. So did Rawlins. They slammed into each other with a mighty crash and struggled for advantage.

Gray Horse reared back to head-butt Rawlins, but the mountain man jerked his head out of the way, so most of the Indian's shot missed. Rawlins used the chance to latch his teeth onto Gray Horse's ear. He clamped on it good and then tugged at it, growling and jerking his head like a puppy with a piece of meat.

Gray Horse slammed a fist into Rawlins's ribs, and the mountain man snapped his head back. But he brought the Blackfoot's whole ear with him. He spit the bloody thing out.

Rawlins grinned viciously, his face smeared with Blackfoot blood. "How ye like that shit, hoss?" he taunted, neither knowing nor caring whether the Indian could understand him.

Gray Horse charged again, still having made no sound despite the pain Rawlins knew he must be in. The Blackfoot ripped out a war club and swung it at Rawlins's head as he charged.

Rawlins ducked, the stone head of the club whistling within an inch of his head. Then he grabbed Gray Horse's legs and straightened up, flipping the warrior up and over his shoulder.

Gray Horse landed hard, and as he tried to get up Rawlins whirled and kicked him under the chin. Gray Horse's head snapped back. Rawlins swarmed in and stomped on the warrior's genitals. Gray Horse's face paled.

"Goddamn shit-suckin' red devil," Rawlins mut-tered as he pulled his butcher knife. "We'll jist see how ye do after losin' your hair, hoss." He grabbed a handful of the Blackfoot's long, greasy hair, put a fist on Gray Horse's chest to hold him down, and then bent to take the scalp.

"Shit, goddammit, son of a bitch!" Rawlins suddenly yowled as he involuntarily straightened from the impact of the arrow low in his back.

Gray Horse lashed out with his feet, knocking the trapper's legs out from under him. Rawlins fell in a heap, cursing again. He felt himself fortunate, though, that he fell on his side and not on his back, which might have driven the arrow clean through him.

Rawlins got to his feet just in time to have another Blackfoot jump off his horse onto him. He went down again. The arrow shaft snapped off. Feeling himself weaken just a bit, Rawlins scrambled up and managed to get his tomahawk out. He was off balance, but he whipped the tomahawk out mostly blindly, surprising himself a little when the weapon bit into Blackfoot flesh.

Rawlins straightened, ignoring the pain in his back, and then saw the other Blackfoot who had attacked him. The warrior was about ready to crush his head with a stone war club. Rawlins thought everything was moving very slow, giving him time to see the Blackfoot's snarling, painted face, the careful part in his hair, the small, individual feathers on the haft of the war club.

Then the Blackfoot's face went blank and he fell weakly against Rawlins, knocking him down. A moment later the mountain man heard the crack of a rifle. As he shoved the warrior off him he saw two other Blackfoot helping Gray Horse onto a pony. Gray Horse and one warrior raced off. The other helper scooped something up from the ground before leaping on his pony and thundering off after the others.

27

"THAT STUMP-SUCKIN' RED DEVIL'S had his face painted black agin me ary since," Rawlins said to Bent and Adams. "Goddamn if he ain't." He grinned a little. "'Course it ain't done him no good."

"You've encountered him between then and this latest time, then?" Adams asked.

"Hell, yes," Rawlins said with a laugh. "Next time was a couple weeks later. Gray Horse and a bunch of his fractious toad humpers tried to take our horses again. And goddamn if they didn't get 'em all that time, too. I ended up walkin' some distance afore I run into Chester Hamm. Ye know him, don't ye, Bill?"

Bent nodded.

"Chet give me a couple of horses and enough plunder that I could trade for some with the first band of Crows I found. Goddamn if that weren't a pain in my ass. Nearly lost our spree down in Taos that summer, dammit."

"You did all this while you were wounded?" Adams asked skeptically.

"Well, hell yes, hoss," Rawlins said, feigning offense. "Lost me enough blood to fill two big buckets. I was some hurtin' ye understand."

"You think you can pile the shit any higher?" Bent said with a laugh.

"I suppose I could," Rawlins said, also laughing. "But I ain't of a mood. To tell ye boys the truth, I had good medicine in them doin's for goddamn certain. That arrow nary touched no vitals. Ez cut it out and sewed me up. I were good as new in a couple weeks—jist about the time them red devils come on us again."

"Ye think that toad humper was lookin' for you up on the Snake?"

Rawlins shook his head. "He was as plumb surprised at seein' me as I was seein' him. I think he and a few of his shitballs jist got of a mood to do some raidin' and rode out of their village. They come on me by chance." He paused for a swallow of coffee and winced. "Goddamn, this coffee's some poor doin's, Bill. What the hell're ye makin' it out of?"

"Coffee beans, buffler balls, and a touch of skunk piss," Bent said with a laugh. "Dick!" he called loudly. When a tall, handsome black man came out of the kitchen, Rawlins said, "Bring us a bottle, ol' hoss."

Soon the three men had filled their tin mugs with whiskey. Rawlins drank some and smacked his lips. "Now, that plumb shines with this chil'." He grinned and drank some more before refilling his cup. "That time up near the Snake was by chance," he continued, "but that other time sure as shit wasn't. Them flat-faced sons of bitches must've trailed us into the Uintas."

"Took 'em long enough to find you," Bent said.

"I expect they took those two I put under back to their village to say their heathen prayers over 'em afore they laid 'em to rest. Even if they buried 'em on the trail, they still would've had to go back to their village to get more warriors. There was only four, maybe five of 'em up near the Snake. There was a pisspot more of 'em when they come on us in the Uintas."

"That'd account for it," Bent said with a nod. "Well, Abe, drink up. We'll go get you some supplies. That way you can ride on out of here come first light."

"That shines with this chil'," Rawlins said before draining his cup.

"Do you think you might let me have some supplies, too, Mister Bent?" Adams asked. "It'd have to be on credit, I'm afraid," he added, abashed at having to reveal his poor financial state. "I'll pay you back as soon as can, though it might be a while."

"What do you want supplies for?" Bent asked, surprised.

"He's got to get back to Taos, Bill," Rawlins said. "I tol' him you'd be able to see that he did. I expect he can ride down there with a few of your boys makin' a regular trip."

"I can do that," Bent said with a firm nod. "And don't you worry none about the supplies, hoss. You can feed from the stores my men bring with 'em. If you still feel a need to pay for it, you can do some work on the trip. That'll earn your keep for you."

"I'm obliged, Mister Bent," Adams said sincerely. "But that's not what I meant." He turned to look at Rawlins, wondering at his newfound hatred for the Blackfeet. "I'm going after the Blackfeet with you," he added flatly.

"Like hell you are," Rawlins growled.

"Don't be foolish," Bent threw in. "You're still too new to the mountains. You'd be more of a hindrance than a help."

Adams never took his eyes off Rawlins's. "If I get to be a hindrance, you can leave me on the trail. I'll follow along or turn back as I see fit." His voice was filled with determination.

"Bill can use your help here. And Ez and Lucien need you more than Bill does, both here and in Taos."

"I'm going with you, Abe," Adams said firmly.

"What the hell's got ye so all-fired up, hoss?" Rawlins asked, surprised at the gumption Adams was showing.

"I owe it to Ezra to help get the ones who did this," Adams said adamantly. "And, goddammit, I owe it to you and Lucien, too, what with all the help you three have given me."

"Ye sure there ain't somethin' else?" Rawlins asked suspiciously.

"There is something, yes, though it's only a small part of the reason."

"And what's that, hoss?"

Adams was suddenly uncomfortable. "I keep thinking about Blue Rattle and Little Rider," he finally said defensively.

"That plump little Ute finally humped her way into your good graces, eh, hoss?" Rawlins said, suppressing a chuckle.

"You're a crude and profane man, Abe Rawlins," Adams said seriously. "And your offensive accusations disgust me, as they would any decent man."

"Shit, hoss," Rawlins said, finally breaking into a laugh, "where'd ye ary git the notion I was anything close to a decent man?"

"Regardless, I'd be obliged if you were to keep your vulgar thoughts to yourself."

"What the hell's wrong with this chil'?" Bent asked.

"We brung Blue Rattle along for him," Rawlins said with a mischievous grin. "They set up house-keepin' in a lodge, but goddamn if ol' hoss here ain't ary humped her."

"You're joshin' me," Bent said in surprise.

"Like hell I am, hoss."

"You mean he's got himself a purty squaw keepin' his lodge for him, cookin' for him, carin' for him, doin' all the wifely things—except one—and he ain't took advantage of her givin' and good nature?"

"That's a plumb goddamn fact, Bill," Rawlins said, shaking his head in wonder. "He went and married that purty señorita down there in Taos, and he aims to keep his pecker dry. Savin' it jist for her, I reckon."

"That's the most god-awful thing this ol' hoss's ever heard," Bent commented.

"This ol' chil's been thinkin' it's some queersome all along. Hell, me, Ez, and Lucien figured that once he was away from his señora, and saw what a Ute woman could do, he'd fall into her graces. But god-damn if he ain't got a stiffer backbone than this ol' chil' figured on."

"Appears to be about the only stiff thing that hoss's got," Bent said with a laugh.

Adams's face reddened in embarrassment as Rawlins joined in the laughter.

When the laughter died down, Adams said gruffly, "Now that you two've finished talkin' about my personal life, I—"

"What makes ye think we're done jawin' that one over?" Rawlins asked, looking serious. Then he burst into laughter again.

"Laugh all you want, Abe," Adams said stiffly. "I'm still going after the Blackfeet with you."

Rawlins stopped laughing and looked squarely at Adams, whose jaw was tight with determination. "What about Dolores?"

"She'll keep." He thought himself horrible for saying that, but at the moment that was the way he felt.

"That don't sound like the ol' hoss I know," Rawlins said skeptically. "Ye sure ye ain't holdin' somethin' back on us?"

Adams's face pinked up again. "Yes," he mumbled.

"Well, out with it, hoss," Rawlins said loudly. "'Less'n ye want us to git ye an audience first?"

"Don't you dare," Adams hissed.

"Then tell it, hoss," Rawlins encouraged him.

"Damn you, Rawlins," Adams snapped. Then he grinned sheepishly. "The only way I was able to get Dolores to agree to let me go on this harebrained venture in the first place was for me to allow her to visit some of her family deep in Mexico." It was the first time he had admitted this to anyone.

"Why, ye sneaky little critter, ye," Rawlins said with a laugh. "Pretendin' to be *el grande hombre* in the *casa*—the big man in the house—whilst ye really had to wheedle your way on this adventure."

"I didn't have to wheedle," Adams muttered.

"Mayhap not, *amigo*. But won't she be waitin' for ye? Hell, you'd be a fool to disappoint her again."

"I don't think she'll be back in Taos for some weeks yet," Adams said.

Rawlins nodded, but sat in thought. Finally he said, "I still don't know, hoss."

"I can be of help against the Blackfeet, Abe," Adams insisted.

"I ain't so sure I can trust ye, hoss," Rawlins said bluntly. "Ye ain't fought Indians but what? Once, maybe twice? Ye still got too many principles for this ol' chil'."

"I'll do whatever the hell is necessary," Adams snarled.

"Let me think on it, hoss," Rawlins said. "I'll let ye know jist afore I pull out in the mornin'."

"I'm not that goddamn stupid, and you know it," Adams snapped. "I won't be played for a fool. You give me that line of shit, and then you'll ride on out of here without even waking me." He caught the faint smile on Rawlins's lips, but he was not amused. "I'll tell you something, too, Abe—you pull out of here without me, and I'll follow you."

"Don't be so sure about that, boy," Bent said. It was clear that he was friends with Rawlins, but not with Adams. He would help the Easterner if that didn't interfere with his helping his old friend.

"Unless you keep me bound and gagged from now until you let me off in Taos, I'll get away and follow Abe. Even if you do tie me all the way to Taos, I'll just leave as soon as I get there. It might take me a while to find Abe—and the Blackfeet—but I'll do so, by God."

"Jesus, Abe," Bent said with a grin, "this ol' hoss here sure has been learnin' from you and the others. Goddamn, he's nearabout as craptious as you three."

"Goddamn, I think you're right, Bill," Rawlins said, not sure how he felt about this. "It still don't make me trust him full like I do Ez and Lucien."

"I don't expect you to trust me as much as you do them," Adams said heatedly. "Jesus, Abe, you three've been together what—twelve years? You're more like family. Almost like some old married couple—together so long you're almost the same."

"Goddamn, Abe," Bent said with a hoot, "I didn't know that Lucien'd got so familiar with you and Ezra."

"It did seem odd to me, too," Adams threw in recklessly. "Some of the sounds that came out of their lodges at nights. My God, it must've been a bacchanal there half the time."

Anger clouded Rawlins's face at first, but then he couldn't help the grin that crept up and then began spreading. "'Leastways we're dippin' our peckers in somethin','" he said with a whoop. "That's better'n the doin's of some other hoss I know."

Adams colored again, but shot back, "That's the best you could do? Jesus, a long, skinny fellow and a hairy little Frenchman. That's reprehensible."

"I expect it would be," Rawlins said with a laugh, "if'n it were true, which ye goddamn full well know it ain't, ye fractious little fart."

Adams was almost taken aback. Not so much at what Rawlins had said, but at the fact that he had said it. Rawlins seemed to be treating him—with free-flowing insults—the way he always did Early and Chardonnais.

Finally seriousness returned, and Rawlins still looked doubtful about bringing Adams along. Seeing this, Adams said quietly, "I don't know what I can do here and now to prove myself to you, Abe. And I don't know why you don't trust me at least some. Hell, I fought well even though I was scared half to death when the Apaches attacked us that time outside Santa Fe when you and the others were teachin' me to fight an' all. And I didn't back down when the Blackfeet came at us up in the Uintas. I held my own through the whole goddamn winter, and you should know that."

"Goddamn, hoss, but ye put up a good argument. Still, it don't shine with this ol' niggur to go takin' along a pilgrim."

"I'm going after the Blackfeet, Abe. Count on it. And if it'll help me prove my mettle to you, I'll challenge you here and now. I didn't let Lucien get away with this kind of shit a few years ago, and I'll be damned if I'll let you get away with it now."

"Ye mean that, do ye?" Rawlins asked harshly.

"I do."

"Tomahawks. In the *placita*," Rawlins said, shocking Bent.

"When?" Adams countered, rising.

"Right goddamn now." Rawlins pushed himself up. "After ye, hoss."

Adams turned and started walking toward the door. Rawlins followed him and suddenly leaped at him with a shout.

Adams was startled, but he reacted swiftly, swinging around with an arm up to block a blow, if necessary.

It wasn't. He kept moving, grabbing Rawlins's buckskin shirt. He spun and slammed Rawlins up against the wall.

He was about ready to paste Rawlins in the face when the mountain man grinned. "We leave at first light, hoss," he said.

Adams dropped his fist and nodded.

28

I~~T WAS ALREADY HOT WHEN~~ Rawlins and
Adams rode out of Bent's Fort the next morning,
though it was barely past dawn. The two men rode
abreast, each leading an extra horse and a loaded
mule. Rawlins also led another extra horse. Adams
emulated Rawlins in riding with his new rifle lying
across his saddle in front of him.

The two men rode at a good pace northwest
across the broad sweep of rising prairie. The Rocky
Mountains hunkered on the western horizon, kind of
grayish purple in the low light and haze of the fresh
morning.

They had only been out an hour when Adams
asked, "Aren't we going to try to get some help from
the Utes?"

"No time," Rawlins snapped. "Them shit-suckin'
Blackfeet've got more'n a month's head start on us.
We take the time to git to Strong Bear's and call for a
war party, them goddamn red devils're likely to be in
Canada or something."

Adams was rather surprised. "They'll for certain be back in their village anyway," he said tentatively.

"Yep."

"So why not get some help for when we find them? We'll not be able to attack the whole damn village. Not unless you're suicidal, which I don't think you are."

"Raisin' my own hair don't shine with this chil'," Rawlins growled.

"So why not get some of the Utes to help us?"

"Like I said—no time."

"But—"

"I'd like to get to Scatters the Clouds and the others afore them snake-humpin' bastards put 'em all under."

Adams paled. "You think they'll do that?" he asked, worried.

"Ye nary can tell with them critters. Any of our women or kids give them Blackfeet any shit, them bastards'll think nothing of partin' their skulls for 'em. And if they ain't adopted or married into the band, they'll be in bad shape. We head for Strong Bear's and it'll add another two weeks, maybe more. Besides, them Utes ain't much for seekin' war."

"I thought they were good fighters."

"They are, but they don't live for war like many of the other tribes do. You mess with 'em, you're askin' for a heap of trouble, since they're about the toughest bastards this chil' knows. Still, they'd rather set up there in the San Juans mindin' their own business instead of huntin' down errant Blackfeet."

"Doesn't that bother you?" Adams asked.

Rawlins shrugged. He cut some tobacco and

shoved it into his mouth. Around the wad of tobacco, he said, "It sort of makes sense to this chil'. Ye got to live out here all the time, where it's hard jist to keep alive, why go lookin' for trouble? Long's you're tough enough to kick some ass when it's necessary."

Adams nodded, not quite appeased, but unwilling to press the point.

They spent the night in a dry camp about thirty miles northwest of Bent's Fort. The next night they lucked out and found a little water in Squirrel Creek. About due north, another dry camp followed, but the next night they made it to Cherry Creek, which still was running some.

They followed along Cherry Creek for another full day, spending the night along the creek before it turned more west. The two men kept moving almost due north and came on the sluggish, wide, and extremely shallow South Platte River, which they followed until the river made its large curl toward the east.

Not wanting to waste any time, Rawlins pushed them hard, and they made thirty, sometimes forty miles a day. The going was relatively easy, since the land was mostly flat. But above the Platte, things got more arid. Most of the creeks and streams were dried up, and the gullies hadn't seen decent rain in a while from the way it looked.

By the time they reached the Medicine Bow River, where they made their camp somewhat earlier than usual, Rawlins was worried some about the animals and considered spending an extra day there, but then decided against it.

They went up the Little Medicine Bow, still heading north, and hit the North Platte. It, too, was running slowly and shallowly, but it provided enough water. Then came two more days and nights with no water.

Adams was beginning to get desperate about the lack of water when they came to the Powder River, a real, rushing, full-of-water river. He drank until he thought he would empty the river. Then he sat back, feeling bloated. He belched loudly, and then grinned sheepishly. "I thought for a while there we weren't going to make it," he said seriously.

Rawlins winked. "Me, too." Then he, too, grew serious. "I been in worse times, though, boy," he said quietly. "There's been times when me and Ez and Lucien went and cut the ears of the mules so's we could drink their blood jist to have somethin' wet goin' down our gullets. But such doin's don't shine with this ol' chil' nonesoever. Hell, there was one time we had to drink buffler piss we squeezed out of its bladder after we shot that goddamn critter."

"That's repulsive," Adams said with a shake of the head.

"Mayhap, hoss, but you'd go and do it, too, was times bad enough, and don't ye doubt it." He paused. "I was more worried about the animals this time, though. Them critters go under, we're gonna be in some sorry shape, hoss."

"Don't remind me." Adams rolled over and stuck his face in the water again to drink. When he was finished, he asked, "Where the hell are we?"

"Absaroka—Crow country."

"Don't you hate the Crows?"

Rawlins shrugged. "Some, I reckon. Not so much as the goddamn Blackfoot, but after the Crows went and rubbed ol' Jed out, my feelin's toward them critters ain't the most neighborly. Still, they've never caused me and the boys too much trouble, and I can usually deal with 'em given half a chance. 'Course, they're notional critters sometimes, and ye cain't nary trust 'em. Bastards'll steal anything they can. Christ, there was one time I remember, one of the boys we knew from the ol' days with Ashley was with some Crows. He took his pecker out to piss, and by Jesus if the goddamn Crows didn't steal that, too." He waited a second before he burst into laughter.

Adams laughed, too. "You had me going there for a while on that one," he said.

"I expect I did, hoss. But them goddamn Crows are the biggest goddamn thieves this chil's ary met. And I aim to keep away from 'em if I can."

"Think it's possible?"

Rawlins shrugged. "Might be. Since it's summer, a good many of the Crows'll be up in the Bighorns tryin' to stay cool. 'Course, like most other Indians out this way, they're down on the flats here as often as not to hunt and make war and such."

"Where away do we go now?" Adams asked.

"Northwest for a spell, then . . ." Rawlins shrugged.

Adams could pry no more information out of him, and he wondered about that. He could not know that the Blackfeet covered a lot of territory, and like most Western Indians, lived in small bands more often than not. All Rawlins had to go on was a vague general area where the Blackfeet generally called home.

Crossing the Powder River in the morning, they headed northwest. They roughly followed the base of the Bighorn Mountains, with the peaks casting long shadows over them in the afternoons. They crossed Crazy Woman Creek and Clear Creek and the Little Bighorn River.

After curling around the northern edge of the Bighorn Mountains, they headed more westerly. When they came to the Shields River, they turned northwestward again, passing close to the Crazy Mountains on the east.

A few days later they followed a valley between the Big Belt and Little Belt mountains, along a river. Finally they reached the Missouri River. They made a camp, and after eating, Rawlins sat pondering what to do.

The only thing he was certain of was that they would have to cross the Missouri. Beyond that, he didn't know. The Blackfeet could be anywhere, he knew, and all he could think of to do was to just start looking.

It took three and a half more weeks, but Rawlins and Adams finally found the village they were looking for. They had encountered numerous Blackfoot camps, all of which had to be checked. The two men also had to make sure they were not seen, either when checking the villages or when they were riding across the vast expanses of plains.

Rawlins was growing more frustrated and angry as the days passed. He knew that with each passing day, Scatters the Clouds, Standing Eagle, and the others were liable to be one day closer to death—if they were not dead already. His rage built as he thought of what the women and children must be undergoing. He had done all he could to get this far in the trail of the Blackfeet, but it had not been nearly enough. Early and Chardonnais seemed to be still too close to death, the women and children were suffering unspeakable horrors, so much time had passed, and here he was sitting in a camp north and west of the Missouri River having no clue as to where he could look for the Blackfeet.

Making it all the worse was the fact that their supplies were running low. They were just about out of coffee and flour. They had to rely on hunting for all their meat, which added to their problems. Few of the Blackfeet had guns, and if some of the tribesmen heard a gunshot in the area, they were almost certain to take a look for the source. Rawlins had to be mighty careful about when and where he did his hunting.

Adams kept his silence for the most part, knowing that the more he spoke, the worse Rawlins would get. He also kept his mouth shut because he was turning morose. He worried almost constantly now about Blue Rattle and her child. It was not as if he had come to love her because she had been taken captive. It was more that he felt responsible, that he could've prevented it. He had been her protector, or at least he was supposed to have been her protector, and he had failed in his duty. That alone was enough to make him determined to gain back all the women and children.

One day, along about midafternoon, Rawlins spotted something on the horizon. It took only a few moments for him to realize that several Indians were coming, and up here, it was almost certainly Blackfeet. He pointed. "Time to cache, hoss," he said quietly.

Adams looked, paled, and then nodded. "We run?" he asked.

"Nope. Such doin's'd raise too much dust. We'll head into that coulee over yonder there." He pointed again.

They rode slowly toward the deep depression in the prairie, then they dismounted and hobbled the animals. Rawlins took his Fordney rifle and climbed up the steep side to the rim of the gully. He stretched himself out on his stomach, rifle ready.

The rim of the coulee was the highest point for some miles, so Rawlins had a clear view of the approaching Blackfeet. He was concerned that the Indians might ride right up on their position, but he eventually realized that they would miss them by sixty or seventy yards.

Rawlins rolled to where he could look down into the coulee. "Hoss," he called. "Hoss, listen to me." When Adams looked up, he said, "Try'n keep those goddamn critters quiet. Them goddamn Blackfeet're gonna be passin' fairly close to here."

"How many are there?" Adams asked, trying to whisper and holler at the same time.

"Eight. Looks like a war party, too, rather than hunters. They spot us, we're gonna be in a heap of trouble, especially if their raidin's gone well and they think their medicine's strong."

Adams nodded. He wasn't sure how he was supposed to keep five horses and two mules quiet, but he vowed silently to do whatever he could.

Rawlins came back around to watch the Blackfeet, rifle ready. As the Indians rode slowly by just to the north, he gritted his teeth in anger. It took all the willpower he possessed to keep from killing Gray

Horse, who was with the band of Blackfeet. It would be so easy, the mountain man figured, though it would certainly lead to his own death. That, and one other thing, were all that kept Gray Horse alive. Rawlins had realized in a split second that he could follow the Blackfoot warrior straight to his village. It would not be easy, but was definitely possible.

When the Blackfeet had ridden by, Rawlins half ran, half slid down into the gully. "I just saw that shit-suckin' Gray Horse," he hissed. "I'm fixin' to follow that son of a bitch."

"You're crazy, Abe," Adams said.

"Mayhap, hoss, but I ain't fixin' to spend the rest of my days lookin' for that goddamn camp."

Adams nodded. He was still scared all the time, but he seemed, at least to himself, to be getting used to living that way. "Let's go."

"Not quite so fast, hoss," Rawlins said grimly. "I ain't fixin' to ride right up Gray Horse's ass, ye know. We'll let them red devils git a little farther down the trail. Then we'll follow 'em nice and easy. So set and relax your bones a spell, hoss."

29

RAWLINS AND ADAMS KEPT THEIR distance from the Blackfeet warriors and rode slowly so as not to stir up too much dust. They made a cold camp that night, watching the little flickering glimmers of light coming from the Blackfoot camp and wishing they could make a fire.

They were up early, with Rawlins trying to figure out when the Blackfeet would pull out. He certainly didn't want to ride into the awakening camp by accident. But he was too fidgety to wait very long, and soon he and Adams pulled out, moving slowly and cautiously, heading northwest.

He need not have worried. The Blackfeet looked to have been gone since shortly after Rawlins and Adams had awoken. They picked up speed a little, but Rawlins would climb up every rise in the land, going on hands and knees the last few yards, then peering cautiously over the top, checking out where the Blackfeet were.

The thick clods of clouds overhead and the general grayness that had come with the morning also helped conceal them somewhat. Rawlins figured they would have rain by evening.

The warriors came to a river and turned westward, generally following the water's ragged course. The land rose more as afternoon approached and they made their way into the mountains. About the same time Rawlins started seeing an awful lot of Blackfoot sign, and he figured they were close the Gray Horse's village.

Rawlins spotted a thin trail leading off away from the river and turned into it. Since an animal path was there, the Blackfeet most likely would not look too closely at it and see that some human-led animals had gone that way.

They followed the trail as it wound upward and then curled toward the north. The trees were thick, bunched close along the side of the trail. The underbrush was heavy, filling in much of the space between the lodgepole pines, aspens, and mountain ashes.

Shouting drifted on the warm air up to the two mountain men, giving them direction. When Rawlins figured he was about opposite the camp, though higher on the mountain, he stopped and poked into the brush, looking for a place. He then moved slowly up the trail, occasionally stopping to seek a suitable site.

The mountains were growing more rocky and the foliage thinned some in the stony soil. Then he found a cave about ten feet off the trail, dug into the side of a mountain, facing away from the Blackfeet camp.

Rawlins nodded. "This'll do us fine for now, hoss," he said as he led his horse into the cave. Soon all the animals were inside the cave. Rawlins and Adams unsaddled the two horses. The Easterner unloaded the mule while the trapper took a look around. The cave was, he figured, fairly secure. It could not be easily seen from the trail, and while he figured the Blackfeet knew about it, he had seen no reason to believe that they used it for anything. He was satisfied.

Rawlins prowled around some more and almost fell off a rock ledge, but managed to grab a twisted tree that hung out over the abyss at a crazy angle. "Goddamn, hoss," he breathed, "ye best watch yourself." He found, though, that if he sat on the ledge, he had a fairly good view of the Blackfeet village. He took his hat off and set it beside him.

Adams joined him a few minutes later. "Nice view," he commented.

Rawlins just grunted.

"Aren't you worried about being seen?" Adams asked.

"Hell no," Rawlins snorted. "Ain't no one down there gonna be able to pick us out sitting way up here in these ol' buckskins. Not unless they're lookin' for us, and lookin' mighty damn hard." He paused and squinted at Adams. "'Course, ye keep that goddamn cigar goin' and you'll make it a hell of a lot easier for them critters."

Adams suddenly looked horrified. He swiftly mashed the cigar out on the rock ledge. "I never thought," he said sheepishly. Then he sighed. "I'll never learn all there is to know out here."

"Mayhap nobody ever really does, hoss," Rawlins said quietly.

Adams was surprised at these words, but did not follow up on them. "You sure they can't see us?" he asked nervously. He felt terribly exposed on this rather barren slice of hanging rock.

"I doubt it, but ye should remember this. There ain't but one guarantee out here, hoss. Death. That's the only thing ye can be certain of. It might be that you'll have strong medicine and live long enough to die of old age in your bed somewhere back in the settlements—"

"Doesn't sound much like you approve of that notion."

Rawlins shrugged. "That ain't where this chil's stick floats, hoss."

"Why not?" Adams asked, surprised again. "I'd've thought anyone who's lived such a hard life as you have'd be pleased to die an old man in his own bed somewhere."

"The dyin' of old age ain't the problem, hoss. It's the doin's in gettin' there. It don't shine with this niggur to have his eyes go out on him and have all his teeth drop out. Nor would I find it shinin' bein' half-crippled-up with rheumatiz. I'd as soon have a Blackfoot arrow send me to my just rewards." He grinned. "Only not jist yet. This chil' ain't done with livin' by a long shot, hoss." He laughed. "And I want somebody to get that critter afore he can take my hair. I ain't fixin' to meet the Great Spirit with my skull shinin' through."

"Doesn't the idea of dying scare you, Abe?" Adams asked seriously. "It does me."

"Tell ye true, hoss, I ain't ary thought much on it. I don't suppose I am scared of it. Cain't see why I—or any other hoss—should be. Hell, it's gonna happen to everybody sooner or later, whether ye go out fightin' some goddamn Blackfeet or if ye set in your house all the day long ary day of your life. Might's well enjoy life whilst ye got it."

"Do you believe in heaven and hell?"

Rawlins shrugged again. "Cain't rightly say jist what I believe in about the hereafter. The Utes and other Indians got some intriguin' notions on that. But, then, so do the pious Christians. All I'm sure of about any of this, hoss, is that I'm gonna live my life the fullest I can. Then, if there ain't ho heaven or no happy huntin' grounds, I won't've missed nothin'."

"What if there is a heaven? Or worse, a hell?"

"Then this chil's ass deep in a suckin' swamp and no help in sight." Rawlins laughed softly again. He wondered, though, why Adams troubled himself about such things. He supposed most men were afraid of dying, but it had just not been in him to dwell on such a thought, and he couldn't understand why others did.

It began to rain softly and some thunder rolled over the mountain behind them. The only concessions Rawlins made to the weather were to put his big felt hat back on and swiftly wrap the lock of his rifle in a piece of fur.

Adams did the latter, too. "Do you think they're all down there?" he then asked, suppressing a shiver.

"Cain't say. I've seen Scatters the Clouds and Blue Rattle. I ain't sure but what I've seen Falling Leaf, too."

Adams's eyes widened. "You've seen them? And never reacted?" He was amazed.

Rawlins shrugged. "Nothin' I could do by gettin' excited now, except maybe bring attention to us."

"Do you think they're all still alive?" Adams looked sharply at his companion and could see the anger deep in the mountain man's eyes.

"Well, at least some of 'em are, 'less'n my eyes are gone bad all of a sudden. Cain't say about all of 'em, though."

"What're we gonna do?"

"Goddamn if ye ain't a question-askin' hoss." He paused to spit some tobacco juice down into space. "We're gonna wait, hoss," he finally said.

"How long?"

"Till I say so. Now shut your trap and give my ears a break, hoss."

Just before darkness fully descended, Rawlins finally rose and went into the cave. He set his rifle down, then pulled his pistols, one at a time, emptied them, cleaned them briefly, and then reloaded them. After sticking the pistols back into his belt, he pulled on his capote. While the day was still rather warm, the temperature was falling, and Rawlins wanted to keep the rain away from his weapons if at all possible.

Rawlins looked at Adams, who had been watching his companion in curiosity. "Saddle our horses," he ordered. "You've seen those simple rope reins the Utes sometimes use?"

"Just the one rope around the animal's lower jaw?"

"Yep. Take some of that rawhide rope we got and do that with the three other horses—and the mule."

"What're yo going to be doing?" Adams was a

little insulted that he was being assigned such routine chores.

"This chil's gonna pay a little visit to the shit-suckin' Blackfeet down below."

"At night? In the rain?"

"Rain never kilt nobody that I know of. Hell, boy, it's a blessin' in disguise. It'll allow me to go wanderin' around there pretty much unmolested. Was it a nice night, there'd be Blackfeet crawlin' all over that camp."

"But at night?" Adams prompted again.

"Ye think it might be better if'n I was to wait till daylight and then walk on down there and ask them critters to give us back our women, young'ns, and all our plunder?"

"Well, no, but . . ."

"Jist quit your frettin', hoss. I ain't back by day-light, ye take your horse and you tear ass as fast as ye can southward, like all the goddamn Blackfeet in the western lands was on your tail." He grinned. "Because, ol' hoss, they damn well might be."

"Why don't I go with you?" Adams asked. For some reason, he suddenly looked forward to fighting. He could not explain it. If he had the time, he would've pondered such a thing. But there was no time, and he realized, he had no inclination to mull this over.

"You're still a pilgrim, hoss," Rawlins said flatly. "I can move through that village without no one seein' me. I doubt ye could do the same. Besides, ol' hoss, I get the women and young'ns out of there, we're gonna need to have those animals ready to go. We'll need to make tracks."

Adams nodded. He didn't like the idea of staying behind to wait with the animals, but he understood

Rawlins's reasoning. He watched as the mountain
man began heading out into the rain. Just before he
got outside, Adams said, "Good luck, Abe."

Rawlins looked back and grinned. *"Gracias,
amigo."* Then he was lost in the darkness and rain.

Rawlins knew where he was going, had plotted
out his route and committed it to memory while he
had been sitting on the rock ledge. Now he moved
with confidence and swiftness. His only real worry as
he approached the village were the dogs. Damn near
every tribe he had ever encountered had a pack of
dogs. He hoped the rain would keep them inside the
lodges, or uninterested if they were outside the
lodges.

Another thing that Rawlins had noted from his
post on the ledge was the lodge in which Scatters the
Clouds was living. He had seen her go into and come
out of it half a dozen times. The same with Falling
Leaf. He had spotted Blue Rattle once, but could not
tell where she way staying. He had seen no sign of
Looks Again, which worried him.

Soon he was down off the peak and moving
across the flat meadow. There was very little thunder
now, but the rain was coming down fairly hard and
he figured it would mask any noise he made.

He kept away from the horse herd for now, not
wanting to spook the animals and give himself away.
He went around the entire village, which took him a
little time, until he was finally standing at the rear of
the lodge he figured Scatters the Clouds was in. He
whistled like a gray jay, and then did so again. Then
he waited.

He was beginning to think that Scatters the
Clouds had not heard him or that she was not in that

lodge when she came strolling outside and around the tipi. They embraced briefly, which allowed him to hide his wince of pain and annoyance at the sight of her bruised face.

"Where's Standing Eagle?" he asked urgently.

"Inside the lodge."

"Ye all right? And Standing Eagle?"

"Yes. Both."

"How many warriors're in there?"

"Two. Bear Robe, and his son-in-law, War Walker."

"Women and young'ns?"

"Two women. No children except Standing Eagle."

Rawlins nodded and stood thinking. He figured the Blackfeet would be going to sleep soon, and he decided he could do his work then. "Go on back inside, but stay ready. Pretend to sleep. When you're sure them shit-eatin' Blackfeet're asleep, stick a knife through the lodge hide toward the back here where I can see it."

"Then you'll come to get me?"

"Ye and Standing Eagle both. And the others, too, if I can. Where are they?"

"In several lodges. Once I'm safe, I'll show you."

Rawlins nodded again. He kissed Scatters the Clouds and then sent her on her way with a light tap on the rump, and the warning, "Don't ye go doin' nothin' foolish now, woman."

Scatters the Clouds headed back into the lodge with a much lighter heart. She would be free soon, she and her son. That was all that mattered to her now. She even calmly suffered a slap from War Walker, who looked smug after punishing her for being gone so long.

30

RAWLINS WAS NOT VERY FOND OF squatting in the rain in the dark. There was too much chance that someone might come along. Though the rain and darkness hid him somewhat, it also hid others; someone could easily walk up on him and cause a ruckus before he was aware of it.

What with his precarious position, it seemed to take hours before a knife blade suddenly popped through the hide of Bear Robe's lodge. The mountain man grinned grimly as he rose.

Rawlins slipped around the side of the lodge and in through the flap, closing it swiftly behind him. He froze as someone rustled in his or her sleep. In the dimness that was broken only by the orange glow of the dying fire's embers, he could see Scatters the Clouds huddled with Standing Eagle near the rear of the lodge. They had warm coats on and were ready to go.

Rawlins stood there a moment more, deciding whether it was best just to slip out or if he should "dispatch" the Blackfeet. War Walker shifted in his sleep, almost waking. That made up Rawlins's mind for him.

He pulled out his butcher knife and glanced at Scatters the Clouds. She nodded, letting him know she thought he was doing the right thing. Rawlins moved up until he was next to War Walker. He considered the young warrior the most dangerous of the sleeping Blackfeet, and the young man's wife the next most dangerous. Bear Robe looked old and worn-out, and his wife even more so. Even if they did react to what he was doing, Rawlins figured that at their age they would not present much of a problem.

Though he was not pleased with his task, Rawlins felt no remorse as he plunged his large knife to the hilt in War Walker's smooth chest.

The warrior jerked awake and half rose. His eyes widened as he saw the devilish white face just above his. Then he gasped and sank back, dead.

His wife also woke at the sound and activity. The surprise and shock of what she saw held her speechless a moment. Then, as she opened her mouth to scream, Rawlins jerked the knife free of War Walker's chest and whipped out with it, opening a long gash across the woman's throat. She gurgled, and her hands desperately clutched the spouting wound in her neck. Then she, too, fell over.

Bear Robe and his elderly wife still snored in blissful ignorance as Rawlins turned toward them. They died in blissful ignorance, too, as the mountain man swiftly slit their throats. He felt only a momentary pang of conscience as he ran the blade across the old woman's wrinkled, flabby neck.

Rawlins cleaned the knife off on Bear Robe's

blanket and slid it away. Then he waved to his wife and son. They came to him. "Where're the others?" he asked in a whisper.

"Falling Leaf and Straight Calf are three lodges left of here, toward the horses. Looks Again is . . . she is dead. . . . She would not do what a warrior named Yellow Ghost wanted, so he . . ." Her pained voice trailed off.

"Jesus fuckin' Christ," Rawlins breathed. What little remorse he felt for killing the old man and his wife quickly fled. There was no Blackfoot who deserved to live, he figured. Not with the way they treated people. He sighed. "Anybody else dead?"

Scatters the Clouds nodded into the darkness. "Little Rider. He was too much trouble, so a goddamn warrior named Big Talking dashed him to the ground." Since she was Little Rider's aunt, she was filled with grief, but she was managing to keep it under control. There was much that had to be done.

"Crow Fight?"

"He's all right. He's in Yellow Ghost's lodge, feeding at White Sleeve's breast."

"Not for long," Rawlins said grimly. "How about Blue Rattle?"

"She mourns," Scatters the Clouds said simply. She knew that Rawlins would understand.

"Where's she?"

"Across the goddamn camp. In Big Talking's lodge. I'll show you."

Rawlins nodded. "We'll git all of our people back, woman, don't ye worry. When we git Crow Fight back, ye let Blue Rattle take him. She'll have plenty of milk for him, and mayhap it'll help take her mind off'n her grief."

"It is good," Scatters the Clouds said.

"You doin' all right, woman?" he asked, patting her bulging stomach.

"Yes." She knew her pregnancy would slow her down, but she was still able to move fairly well, despite being in her eighth month. She was determined not to let it interfere with her escape or freedom for the others.

Rawlins nodded toward the door. Scatters the Clouds and Standing Eagle moved swiftly toward the flap. The pregnant woman went out first. If anyone was around, they would not think it too suspicious if a captive woman came outside of the lodge. She took a quick look around, then called softly to her husband and son.

The two males came out, and Scatters the Clouds pointed across the camp. Rawlins nodded and they all moved in that direction. As they walked, he asked, "How many people in Big Talking's lodge?"

"Too many. At least six."

"Shit. You'll have to git Blue Rattle. Go in as quiet as ye can, wake her gentle, and then git her out here."

Scatters the Clouds saw no need to respond.

When they got to Big Talking's tipi, Rawlins squatted on one side of the entry and Standing Eagle on the other. The trapper had his tomahawk in one hand and knife in the other, just in case.

Scatters the Clouds crept inside as Rawlins waited tensely. Within two minutes, though, she and Blue Rattle crept out. Rawlins breathed a sigh of relief. They all moved away from the lodge, then squatted in a small circle.

"How many people're in Yellow Ghost's lodge?" Rawlins asked his wife.

"Just Yellow Ghost, Red Water, and . . . Crow Fight."

Rawlins nodded. "Ye think ye can get Falling Leaf and Straight Calf like ye did Blue Rattle?" he asked his wife.

"Yes." Scatters the Clouds's voice was determined.

"*Bueno*. Ye do that. Blue Rattle, ye come with me. I'll take care of that shit-suckin' Yellow Ghost and his harlot. I want ye to git Crow Fight and carry him with us."

Though she was still deeply grieving for her own child, Blue Rattle understood the importance and reasoning behind Rawlins's order. She nodded.

"Where is Yellow Ghost's lodge?"

Both Scatters the Clouds and Blue Rattle pointed.

Rawlins nodded again. "We'll meet over there near the mountain, yes?" He pointed.

There were murmurs of assent.

"Standing Eagle, ye go with your ma, hoss. Ye wait outside the lodge, keepin' an eye on things while she goes in for Falling Leaf. Ye got that, boy?"

"Yes." The boy's eyes were wide, and he was terribly solemn.

"*Bueno*. Let's go."

Rawlins and Blue Rattle moved off in one direction, Scatters the Clouds and Standing Eagle in the other. At Yellow Ghost's lodge the mountain man stopped, breathed deeply a moment, then nodded.

Blue Rattle went inside first, moving silently. Rawlins followed her, moving as if he were a specter, a vengeful wraith, a bad spirit of the night. The Indian woman moved straight toward where Crow Fight slept in a cradleboard propped up against a tree stump. Rawlins headed for Yellow Ghost and Red Water.

As Blue Rattle lifted the cradleboard Crow Fight gave out with a healthy squawk.

"Shit," Rawlins breathed as Red Water sat up abruptly, ready to feed the child she had adopted. Her eyes opened and focused just in time to see Rawlins's tomahawk descending. She did not have time to make a sound as the hand ax split her head and face. She fell back, dead.

Her death woke Yellow Ghost. Rawlins had just managed to yank the tomahawk free of Red Water's mangled head. Before he could use the weapon against Yellow Ghost, the Blackfoot had caught that wrist.

Yellow Ghost jerked Rawlins forward, snapping his own head in order to butt Rawlins in the face.

Rawlins grunted and jammed a thumb into Yellow Ghost's right eye. He didn't know how the Blackfoot was able to withstand the pain of this and still slam a fist into Rawlins's side. But he did.

Both men were in an awkward, semisitting position, unable to get enough leverage to fight, so Rawlins ground his thumb even deeper into Yellow Ghost's eyeball.

The Blackfoot hissed, but gave no other indication of pain as he pounded Rawlins in the ribs a few more times.

"Goddamn son of a bitch," Rawlins muttered through clenched teeth. He pulled his left hand back and then slammed the heel of it into Yellow Ghost's forehead with all the strength he could muster in his position.

The Indian's head snapped back and his grip on Rawlins's wrist lessened a little. Rawlins snatched that arm free and then rocked back onto his heels. As

Yellow Ghost fell the mountain man swung at his head with the tomahawk. He missed.

Yellow Ghost popped halfway back up and slammed Rawlins in the kidney with the back of his upper arm, knocking the mountain man forward and onto his face. The Blackfoot began pounding the back of Rawlins's head with punches. Once again he could not get too much leverage, but he had enough so that the blows hurt.

Rawlins shoved himself onto hands and knees. As Yellow Ghost's other hand groped for his genitals, Rawlins smashed him in the mouth with an elbow, shattering a few teeth. The Blackfoot moaned and slumped back again.

Rawlins rolled out of the way, spun, and came up on his knees. As Yellow Ghost rose and turned, ready to charge, the mountain man swung the tomahawk mightily.

The sharp blade caught the Indian on the side of the neck, and almost took his head off. Blood spurted wildly and the torso and loose head flopped in their death throes for a few minutes. Finally the remains of Yellow Ghost were still.

Rawlins still sat on his shins, and he looked over at Blue Rattle. As soon as the baby had made some noise, the woman offered her breast, which had quieted him. "It is good," she said as the child continued to nurse. "What you did, it is good."

Rawlins nodded and rose. He cleaned off his tomahawk and slid it back into his belt. "We best get movin', Blue Rattle," he said quietly.

The young woman nodded and pulled the baby from her nipple, cooing to keep him quiet. She set the cradleboard down and did up her dress. She rooted around for a few moments until she found a blanket coat, which she pulled on. Then she pulled Crow Fight from the cradleboard—there had been no time to do so before—and slung the cradleboard across her back. She picked up Crow Fight and held him against her breast again, inside her coat, where the child would stay dry and warm. Ready, she nodded at Rawlins.

"Ye go first," he said.

Blue Rattle understood and complied. She saw nothing untoward and called to Rawlins to come out. Then they moved swiftly toward the designated meeting place. Scatters the Clouds, Standing Eagle, Falling Leaf, and Straight Calf were there, looking worried but ready for anything.

"This way," Rawlins said as he led the way away from the village. Seventy-five yards or so on, he stopped. "There's a little trail here," he said, pointing. "It's some steep, but ye can do it." He wasn't so sure about Scatters the Clouds, despite his confident words. "When ye git to a flat spot and see a big maple lyin' half across a boulder, ye go right. About fifty yards on is a cave. Ye probably cain't see it in the dark, but make a wee bit of noise. Bart's there waitin' for ye."

"Where're you going, my husband?" Scatters the Clouds asked.

"See if'n I can git us a couple more horses. We got enough for everyone—barely. But I expect them shit eaters're gonna be huntin' for us come first light. We don't need a bunch of tired animals."

"We'll make do."

"Jist go. I'll be all right." He kissed her and stalked away. When he was several yards away, he began trotting, heading across the open. The rain was still pouring down, and it made the ground slick, so he had to watch his footing.

As he neared the horse herd Rawlins slowed and then stopped. In the occasional flashes of lighting, he looked around, trying to see if there were any horse guards. He finally spotted what he thought was one. The man was standing there looking over the horses while he urinated.

When the warrior was done, he wandered among some of the horses, petting and talking to them. Rawlins decided that the man had just needed to urinate, and while he was out here he would take a look around to make sure everything was all right.

Scrunched over, Rawlins worked his way swiftly toward the Blackfoot, coming up from behind him. The warrior seemed oblivious to anything but his horses.

Rawlins realized there was no great need to kill this man, but he was resolved to take as many of the hated tribe out as he could. He slipped out his knife and slid up behind the warrior. One of the horses snuffled a little, but the man paid little heed. Rawlins suddenly slapped his left hand across the man's mouth, pulled his head back, and ran the blade along the exposed throat.

He held the Blackfoot up until the death throes ended, then dropped the body and slid his knife away. He moved toward the nearest horse, which looked at him nervously. Rawlins pulled several short sections of horsehair rope out of his pocket. He slipped the loop of one around the horse's neck. He did the same with three other horses, then tugged them gently.

The mountain man moved swiftly, towing the ponies back the way he had come. When he reached the spot where he had left the women and children, he mounted one pony and then rode, going the long way to reach the original trail he and Adams had taken up to the cave.

Twenty minutes after killing the Blackfoot near the horse herd, Rawlins gave his gray-jay whistle softly.

Scatters the Clouds waddled out of the cave to greet him.

31

"I WAS BEGINNING TO THINK YOU'D been captured," Adams said as Rawlins entered the cave with the horses. It had suddenly become mighty crowded in the cave.

"Them red devils ain't gonna git this ol' chil', hoss." Rawlins pulled off his hat and slapped it against his thigh, sending out a cascade of water. He looked at Adams. "Ye heard?" he asked.

"About Looks Again and Little Rider? Yes." His face was etched with hate and grief.

"Best get these ponies reined quick, hoss," Rawlins said quietly.

"We're leaving?" Adams asked. "Now?"

"'Less'n ye want to wait till mornin', when them red devils wake up and find them corpses I left down there. Them shit-suckers're gonna be after us as soon as they find out, so we best git as much head start on 'em as we can."

"Did you have to kill some of 'em?"

Rawlins cast a withering glance at the young man. "Ye got no stomach for fightin' red devils, *amigo,* ye should've stayed back at Bent's place. This ain't no time to go gittin' squeamish. Now see to them ponies." His voice had grown increasingly harsh as he spoke these words.

"But I still think it would've been better if you hadn't killed any of them," Adams said adamantly. "I'm not being squeamish, but if you hadn't killed anyone, they probably wouldn't be interested in chasing us."

"That so, hoss?" Rawlins asked, anger rippling through the words. "Since when did ye become a goddamn expert on the toad-humpin' Blackfeet?" He waited for a response, but got none. "Ye hear what them bastards did to Little Rider? Or to Looks Again? Ye want to be the one tells Lucien his woman was carved into wolf bait 'cause she wouldn't willingly lay with a skunk-humpin' Blackfoot? Huh? Ye think them shit-suckers're fine human bein's after they took poor little ol' Little Rider and smashed his brains against the goddamn ground 'cause he was cryin'? Don't fuckin' talk to me about havin' mercy on them shit-eatin' dog-humpers." He was raging. Though quiet, it was pure, unadulterated rage nonetheless.

Adams was taken aback by the vehemence in Rawlins's words. He had never seen him like this. He wanted to protest, to tell Rawlins that he was wrong, but he couldn't, not in the face of such fury. He turned and began working with the horses.

Rawlins went to the small nook they had found in the cave and where they had built a small fire. There was a little meat cooking, and the last of the coffee was in the pot. He had some of each, then shrugged and finished off both.

As Adams worked on the ponies a picture of Dolores suddenly popped into his mind. He almost smiled when he realized that in his conjured-up vision of his wife, she was pregnant. This faded into a picture of Dolores and a child, walking down a street in Taos. Then Dolores was grieving over a coffin—a small, child's coffin.

"Oh, dear God," he whispered. He glanced over his shoulder at Blue Rattle, who was nursing Crow Fight. Suddenly he understood. His grief was as deep as Blue Rattle's, his rage as hot as Rawlins's. He hurried with his work, wanting to get away from here, not because he was afraid, but because he wanted the surviving women and children to be safely away from the bloodthirsty Blackfeet.

As soon as Adams was done, Rawlins rose and poured the dregs of the coffeepot onto the fire. "Blue Rattle," he said, "ye take my horse. That way ye can hang Crow Fight from the saddle horn. I'll take that chestnut we brung with us," he added, pointing. "Everybody else jist git mounted and let's ride."

Rawlins helped Scatters the Clouds onto a small, wiry pony, then got mounted himself. "I'll lead the way, hoss," he said. "And I'll need ye to bring up the rear."

Adams nodded solemnly.

"Jist make sure ye keep your eyes peeled for the goddamn Blackfeet. And, goddammit, make sure ye keep your powder dry."

Adams nodded again, almost awed by the responsibility invested in him.

"Scatters the Clouds, you and Falling Leaf divvy

up the extra horses and mules between ye and lead
'em." Rawlins rode out of the cave, through the curtain
of brush and down the narrow little trail.

The trail was slick with mud and wet rock, and
with the pitch-black of the night, traveling down onto
the flats was a real adventure, but they made it with
still an hour or two before dawn, as best as Rawlins
could tell.

The trapper kicked his horse into a mile-eating
trot, heading southeast. He looked back frequently to
make sure the others were following. As far as he
could tell in the darkness, they were.

About the time the sun vainly tried to poke
through the thick, gray clouds, Rawlins called a halt
to let the horses rest a little.

"Think they're coming after us yet, Abe?" Adams
asked.

"Doubt it, hoss. But it ain't gonna be long now."

"You think we can outrun them?"

"Not a goddamn chance, hoss. Especially if
they're gonna be half-froze for our hair like I figure
they will."

"Then what . . . ?"

"We're gonna go a different way, hoss. There's
more'n one path through these goddamn mountains.
With this rain coverin' our tracks damn near as fast
as we make 'em, there's a good chance we can throw
them red devils off."

"If we can't?"

"Ye don't really need me to answer that for ye, do
ye, hoss?"

"I suppose not," Adams said sourly.

Rawlins made himself wait a full quarter hour
before he had everyone on horseback and moving

again. A few miles farther on, he turned them southwest, heading for Rogers Pass. They made it across the summit of the pass and partly down the other side of the mountain before he halted them for the night. He found another cave that was large enough to accommodate the humans, the horses, and the mules.

People and animals alike were exhausted, but there was work to be done yet. Rawlins had risked a gunshot a couple hours earlier, so they had fresh meat, but firewood had to be gathered, and the animals had to be cared for. While Blue Rattle rested with Crow Fight, Scatters the Clouds and Falling Leaf—assisted by the children—took care of the firewood while Rawlins and Adams saw to the horses.

Supper, such as it was, was a rather dismal affair. There was no coffee or even tea. They had no biscuits or bread. All they had was meat from the elk Rawlins had shot. It had been an old bull elk, and the meat was stringy and tough. It did help fill them, though.

They made it to the bottom of the mountain by the next night, after another day's worth of riding in the intermittent rain. Rawlins found them a small clearing surrounded by a thick stand of aspens, cottonwoods, and pines. There was a creek nearby, with fresh water.

Rawlins took a look around at his bedraggled group. Scatters the Clouds, being so far along in her pregnancy, was having trouble getting around, and was tired and sore from the long, hard traveling. Despite her more than adequate care of Crow Fight, Blue Rattle was still so racked by grief that she was almost useless. Falling Leaf was the healthiest of the three women, but she had circles under her eyes, her skin looked almost gray, and she was mighty listless. The two older children—Standing Eagle and Straight Calf—were not in bad shape. Young as they were, they were pretty resilient. Adams had bags under his eyes, and he slumped in whatever he was doing. Rawlins didn't want to see what he himself looked like. He couldn't be in much better shape than the rest, though his indomitable will would drive him until death, if that seemed necessary. Still, he could see that the others could not keep up with him. Though it worried him to think of it, he announced that they would stay at this pleasant little spot not only that night, but the whole next day and night, too. He assuaged his conscience by telling himself that the animals needed rest even more than the people. This was partly true. If the animals started dying on them, they would be in serious trouble.

While Adams tended to the animals and the women set up something of a camp, Rawlins mounted his own horse and rode off, looking for game. It took nearly an hour, but he finally jumped a doe, which he brought down. So they ate well for the entire time they stayed in that camp.

The rest did them all much good, and when they rode on again, it was with considerably raised spirits. It was a mixed blessing, however, that the sun had finally come out. On the one hand, it made their traveling a little easier; on the other, they would leave a trail for the Blackfeet to follow. Rawlins could only hope that the Indians had been misled and had continued southeast after he had turned his people toward Rogers Pass.

Two days later he knew the Blackfeet had not
been fooled. Either that or they had learned of their
mistake and had ridden hard to make up for lost
time. Either way, Rawlins began to feel like they were
being followed. His hunches were often correct, so
he dropped back until he was riding next to Adams.

"Head on up to the front and lead things, hoss,"
he said.

"Me lead? Why?" Adams was flabbergasted.

Rawlins shrugged. "I think them red devils're on
our trail. I want to ride back a bit and check."

"What good'll that do?"

"Depends on how far behind they are," Rawlins
said with a shallow grin. "If they ain't too close, we
might still be able to shake 'em."

"What do I do?"

"Just ride. Like ye been doin'. Keep your eyes
open for Indians."

"What if I see some?"

"I expect you and the others'll be made wolf bait
of, hoss." The mountain man pulled a twist of tobacco
from his pouch and cut off a chunk and shoved it into
his mouth. "I'll be back with ye afore dark, hoss, so
don't get your balls in an uproar over nothing. Ye find
a good spot to camp, pull up."

Adams nodded. His mouth was dry and his palms
suddenly sweating. He looked up the line of slowly
riding women and children. Then he turned back to
say something to Rawlins, but the mountain man was
already out of sight around a bend in the trail.
Nervously, Adams trotted up to the front of the line
and then slowed his pace to that of the others.

Rawlins rode back about two miles and then
forced the chestnut up a steep hill. The horse bucked

and jumped, but finally made it to the crest, puffing hard. The trapper dismounted and stood next to the animal, patting its neck.

The position gave him a commanding view for miles around, except for where tall peaks intruded. He stood there for more than an hour, watching, waiting. Finally he was rewarded—a term he would have thought entirely inappropriate if he had thought of it—when he spotted a slight movement far off in the distance. He watched a little longer before he began leading the horse down the hill. He didn't need a spyglass to tell him the Blackfeet were, indeed, on their trail. Fortunately, the Indians were far enough back not to present a problem just yet.

Rawlins skidded and slipped down the hill, finally falling on his buttocks and sliding several feet. "Shit," he grumbled as he stood and rubbed his derriere with his free hand. He had his rifle and the reins in the other. Then he was back on the ground and he mounted the horse, whistling as his almost scrapped-raw buttocks hit the horse's solid back.

When he caught up to the others, they were still riding. Rawlins trotted right up alongside Adams. "Didn't find no place to stop, hoss?" he asked.

Adams shook his head. His hands, where they were wrapped on the saddle horn, were white-knuckled from tension.

"Probably jist as well." Rawlins pointed. "Turn us up that way, *amigo,* and then push a little faster."

"They behind us?" Adams asked, once more afraid and hating himself for it.

"Yep. But not too close. I figure I still got a couple tricks up my sleeve."

"Aren't you going to take your position back here again?" Adams wanted to be relieved of the duty. Or so he thought anyway.

"Nope. I'm gonna ride in the rear—jist in case, hoss."

Adams was suddenly glad he was at the front of the column. He led off, turning south and east, heading for MacDonald Pass. They stopped well before they reached the pass and camped in a canyon that night. They pushed through the low canyon the next day, in the shadow of a couple of massive peaks to the south.

Instead of going east the short distance to the large valley and following the Missouri River south, Rawlins turned them southwest into a small canyon. They followed that for two days, until they hit Boulder Creek.

During that time Rawlins would explain the day's travel to Adams and let the young man lead while he himself stayed at the rear. He also frequently rode back a few miles and found a high spot from where he could watch their back trail. Sometimes he spotted the Blackfeet. Whenever he did, it was clear that they were closer.

They followed Boulder Creek southeast and then mostly south, before cutting away from it, heading east. They went past another giant peak and then cut south.

For two weeks Rawlins had been using all his skills and strength to keep them ahead of the angry, ever-nearing Blackfeet, fleeing from cave to forest, canyon to pass.

He finally began to realize he could not keep this up much longer. The next morning Rawlins pointed up into the mountain they had come around. "That's where we're headed, hoss."

Adams looked at him in surprise. "What for?"

"We got no choice, hoss. Them Blackfeet're gettin' too goddamn close. It won't be long afore they've caught up to us. It's time to make a stand. And this way we git the choosin' of where we make it."

32

THE SMALL GROUP WORKED FURIOUSLY to put up breastworks of earth and logs. Even Standing Eagle and Straight Calf joined in, dragging small tree branches and sometimes rolling rocks to be put onto the hastily fashioned defenses. The only ones not working were Scatters the Clouds, who had found the work too strenuous in her condition, and the baby, Crow Fight, who slept in her arms.

A tall, slanting, rugged cliff behind them would prevent the Blackfeet from getting up there. Trees were plentiful and grew close together, offering some protection, but the real benefit of this was in keeping the Blackfeet from making a concerted charge at them. With only three rifles—like his partners, Rawlins always carried a spare rifle, just in case—and seven pistols among them, they were vastly out-armed by the twelve or fifteen Blackfeet Rawlins believed were after them.

The horses were tied to a picket rope between two stout trees right at the base of the cliff, under an overhang. Between the thick stand of trees and brush on one side and a promontory of rock jutting out from the cliff, the animals were protected on three sides.

The people were in among the trees, looking out over a small—no more than ten yards by ten yards—area where the trees were more widely spaced. Here, they were still safe from any Blackfoot charge, but did not have too much cover. The fault of their position, from Rawlins's perspective, was that it gave the Blackfeet some places to hide. Still, the Indians would not be able to charge on horseback.

"This is all for naught, isn't it?" Adams asked, puffing from the exertion as he and Rawlins worked next to each other.

"I expect," Rawlins answered. "These doin's are some poor bull to this ol' chil'." He half grinned. "But like I told ye afore, hoss, I'd rather die of a Blackfoot arrow than wastin' away from age. 'Course, I was figurin' on gittin' jist a wee bit older afore such doin's, but we cain't always pick the time and place when the Great Spirit calls to us."

"You're a cheerful son of a bitch, aren't you?" Adams retorted grumpily.

"That I am, hoss," Rawlins said with a lopsided grin. The mountain man was pretty well fatalistic about it all.

A few hours later they finished the breastworks. Rawlins surveyed things. "Well, hoss," he said, "it ain't exactly Bent's Fort, is it? But I expect it's about the best we can do."

"So now we just wait?" Adams was tense and worried.

"Yep. Though I suppose ye could go on out there,

hoss, and encourage them Blackfeet to hurry up and
get it over with."

"I'd rather wait," Adams said dryly.

The day dragged on, hot and dry. It was quite
dull just sitting there waiting. At least it was before
Scatters the Clouds went into labor. When Falling
Leaf came to tell him the news, Rawlins quickly went
back to see how his wife was doing. "Damn, ye Ute
women sure know how to pick the wrong time for
such doin's."

"Damn right," Scatters the Clouds grunted. When
the contraction ended, she smiled weakly. "I'll be all
right."

"Can Blue Rattle tend to ye?"

Scatters the Clouds nodded.

"Good. I'm gonna keep Falling Leaf with me'n
Bart so's she can reload for us, if'n them Blackfeet
come along."

She nodded again, preoccupied with another
contraction. Rawlins took that as his cue to leave.
These doin's weren't for a man to be involved with.
He left Blue Rattle there, with Crow Fight asleep in
his cradleboard, and little Straight Calf. He took
Falling Leaf and his son, Standing Eagle, with him.
Falling Leaf knew what was required, and she sat quietly, mending a dress for her daughter. Standing
Eagle was a heap harder to keep settled, so Rawlins
finally told him to go get several of the small gourds
they used for a variety of purposes. At the same time
he asked Falling Leaf to begin building a fire—"close
enough for us to git at, but not too near that powder."

When Standing Eagle returned with a few
gourds, Rawlins sat and pulled the stoppers out of
the tops. He picked up one of the three cans of gun-

powder sitting nearby. Lead balls were piled up, too, as was patching material. All of it was to be used for reloading as quickly as possible when the battle began.

Rawlins filled the five small gourds with gunpowder. He was tempted to do more, but he didn't want to use up too much gunpowder. He closed the can of DuPont gunpowder and set it down. He added several lead balls to each. Then he told his son to go and get the small—and only—bottle of whiskey they had. While he was waiting Rawlins pulled off five of the whangs from his pants. When Standing Eagle returned, the trapper dripped the thongs into the whiskey and set them aside to dry.

"Bombs of some kind?" Adams asked.

"Yep. Ain't sure they're gonna work, but with us bein' outnumbered by seven or eight to one, we got to try'n even the odds a wee bit."

Adams gulped. "Seven or eight to one?"

"That's right, hoss."

"Goddamn, we really are in deep trouble, aren't we?"

"That's right, ol' hoss. And like ye figured afore, we ain't got a peon's chance of freedom of comin' out of this alive. But this ol' chil' ain't jist gonna give himself up to them goddamn skunk humpers. Hell, no. This chil's gonna make some of them goddamn Blackfeet come for goddamn certain. I'm fixin' to make wolf bait out of as many of them niggurs as I can, hoss. Ye should be thinkin' the same."

"Looks like I don't have a hell of a lot of choice, now does it?" Adams responded. He suddenly felt a little calmer, as if knowing he was going to die soon had filled him with a reasoned fatalism.

"Nope."

Two and three quarter hours after leaving Scatters the Clouds with Blue Rattle, Rawlins became a father for the third time. He heard the baby yelling, and he smiled sadly. He waited several more minutes, wanting to make sure the women's work was done.

"Ye watch over things here a bit, hoss," he finally said, standing. He walked off to where his wife was already cradling her child against her bosom. He knelt next to her, and she held the child out for him to see. "Goddamn, if he ain't some now," Rawlins said of his son as he ran a big, blunt finger along the tiny infant's wrinkled cheek. "Ye got a name for him?"

"He-Who-Came-While-Waiting-for-the-Blackfoot-to-Come."

Rawlins mulled that over a bit, since she had said it in Ute. "Waiting for the Blackfoot," he said aloud. He smiled a little, not wanting Scatters the Clouds to see in his eyes his knowledge of their impending doom. "That shines with this ol' chil', woman. Damn if it don't."

Rawlins rose and walked back to the breastworks, where Adams still sat, along with Falling Leaf and Standing Eagle. "A son," he said as he sat.

"That's goo . . ." Adams's smile turned sickly and froze on his face. "I'm sorry, Abe," he finally said.

Rawlins nodded.

"What's ol' hoss there sorry about, Pa?" Standing Eagle asked with all the seriousness of a just-turned-six-year-old.

"Nothin', li'l hoss," Rawlins responded. He suddenly felt the weight of his often reckless life. He didn't much care about dying, though he certainly would have put it off for some time had he been given a choice. But he had never really thought about Scatters the Clouds and Standing Eagle dying. He did, of course, know that it could happen at any time, but it had never seemed like a real possibility. Not until now. And now his newborn son might be dead before he lived more than a day or two. Of course, there was always the possibility that the Blackfeet would capture the infant and raise him as a Blackfoot. Rawlins wasn't sure what was worse, having the boy die within the next couple of days, or having him spend his life as a hated Blackfoot.

Rawlins felt the pieces of buckskin fringe he had dipped in whiskey. They seemed dry enough. He set each one so that part of it hung into a powder-filled gourd, the rest hanging outside. He shoved the stoppers back in as tightly as he could.

Then they waited some more. When dark arrived, they ate swiftly and silently. Rawlins told everyone to go to sleep. He kept a watch. He neither saw nor heard anything, and as the new day marched onward toward afternoon, he was beginning to think that they might possibly have thrown the Blackfeet off their trail.

That notion died a quick and sure death when he heard horses coming just as the sun was about at its highest point in the sky. "They're comin', hoss," he said. "Don't fire till ye got a certain shot."

Adams nodded. His mouth was too dry for him to speak, yet he still felt sort of calm.

"Falling Leaf," Rawlins called over his shoulder, "go'n git Blue Rattle. Tell her we'll need her here to help with the reloadin'. Tell her to leave Crow Fight with Scatters the Clouds and Waitin' for the Blackfoot.

Go stay with your ma, Standin' Eagle."

The mountain man leaned his extra rifle on the breastworks just to his right and laid his four pistols along the top. Seeing this, Adams placed his three pistols on the breastworks, too. They waited some more.

It was a full three quarters of an hour more before Rawlins detected some movement between the trees. He rested his rifle on the breastworks and took aim, waiting some more.

When he finally made out three Blackfeet coming on foot, leading their ponies, searching for sign on the ground, Rawlins pulled back the hammer of his rifle to full cock. Just then, Waiting for the Blackfoot wailed once, loudly.

The three oncoming Blackfeet jerked their heads up and began talking and gesticulating wildly toward where Rawlins and the others were holed up.

"Hold your fire, hoss," Rawlins said. "Roll over here and give me your rifle." He took a sighting on one of the Blackfeet. "Time for ye to go to the happy huntin' ground, shitballs," he muttered, and then he fired.

One warrior went down. Rawlins dropped his rifle and snatched up his extra. He quickly aimed and fired at one of the two Blackfeet who seemed frozen. That warrior dropped, too.

As the mountain man tossed that rifle down for reloading and grabbed Adams's, the third Blackfoot swung onto his pony and whirled. Rawlins shot him in the back.

"Waugh!" he muttered as the Indian toppled off his horse. "That's makin' 'em come now for goddamn sure."

Things grew very silent. For more than an hour the soughing of the wind through the trees was the only sound. Then the thudding of more horses floated up to those who were waiting. And soon after, shadowy figures began flitting through the nearby trees.

Suddenly two Blackfeet charged, on horseback. They were lying low on their ponies, presenting a mighty small target. And having to cover little distance, they made it fast.

Rawlins fired and hit a Blackfoot pony in the chest. As the horse fell, throwing its rider and skidding along, the trapper tossed his rifle to Falling Leaf and grabbed a pistol. As soon as the warrior rose he shot him with the pistol.

Adams had glanced at Rawlins when the charge began. Scared again, he looked at the rushing horse. He spotted the other pony going down and realized that Rawlins had shot the animal. He did the same, figuring that if it was good enough for his companion, it should be good enough for him. Out of the corner of his eye, he saw Rawlins gunning down the Blackfoot, and he tried to do the same. He missed his first shot and tossed the pistol behind him. He grabbed another and aimed. But he could see nothing at first. Then he spotted the Indian flat on the ground, crawling back toward the cover of the trees.

"Don't waste another shot!" Rawlins yelled. "Let him be—unless he gits up and runs."

Rawlins saw Blackfeet massing deep in the trees and figured they were about to make a concerted charge despite the less-than-appropriate terrain. "Grab a couple of them bombs, hoss, and git ready."

"What do I do with them?" Adams asked as he

picked up two of the powder-filled gourds.

"Light the wick with a burning stick or something and then toss it when them red devils charge."

They did not have long to wait before the Blackfeet rushed them, darting between the trees.

Rawlins lit the fuse on one of his primitive bombs and tossed the thing. It fell and lay sputtering, then went out. Adams had followed suit, and his bomb suffered the same fate.

"Jesus goddamn Christ," Rawlins mumbled. He grabbed a pistol and fired at the bomb. He hit it, and the thing exploded just as a horse was riding over it.

The Blackfoot pony's belly was shredded, and the animal crashed to the ground, pinning its rider. The bomb had also broken at least one leg on each of the horses on either side. Those ponies went down hard, whinnying in fright and pain. Their riders also fell, but got up and began running back the way they had come, each getting picked up by a friend who was still mounted.

Adams saw Rawlins shoot at the gourd-bomb, and he nervously laid a pistol across his protective works and aimed carefully. He was as surprised as anyone when he hit the bomb. The blast knocked one pony down, sending its rider sailing. That warrior landed on his neck, which snapped. He was out of the fight.

The only problem was that by the time Adams had set off the explosive, two horses were already past it. He managed to shoot one of those two warriors, but the other leaped his pony over the breastworks and galloped toward the cliff—and the horses.

"You aren't getting away with that shit, you dumb savage," the Easterner muttered as he jumped up and ran after the Blackfoot, after taking a swift glance to make sure no other warriors were around.

Rawlins blasted two more Blackfeet with pistols, but he was about to be overrun. Two warriors leaped their horses over the low barrier, one of them throwing his lance down, hoping to pin the mountain man with it.

But Rawlins had rolled out of the way, grabbing his last two pistols. He fired once from each hand, hitting both warriors, who tumbled down. He looked back over the breastworks. The other Blackfoot had run for cover, at least for now. The mountain man rose and pulled his tomahawk as he headed for the two he had just shot.

33

RAWLINS SAW THE BLACKFOOT heading toward the horses—and toward Scatters the Clouds and the two babies and two other children. "Shit," he cursed. Then he saw Adams running for the warrior as hard as he could. Rawlins was about to join the younger man, but one of the two Blackfeet he had shot suddenly jumped up in front of him, swinging a war club.

Rawlins managed to duck out of the way and knee the warrior in the stomach. He grabbed the Indian's hair and jerked him up. He was about to cleave the warrior's head with his tomahawk when the man sort of jumped forward. Rawlins stepped back a pace and let him fall. There was a tomahawk stuck in the man's back.

Rawlins glanced up and saw the other warrior he had shot charging at him, enraged at having accidentally killed his friend and wanting revenge.

The Blackfoot had a knife in hand. Rawlins braced for the attack and swung the 'hawk. The blade chopped halfway through the Indian's knife arm.

Rawlins shoved the warrior away and finished him off in a moment. He looked toward where Adams had chased the Blackfoot. Then he glanced back at where the other Blackfeet were. He was in a dilemma. If he went back to help Adams and Scatters the Clouds, the main force of Blackfeet might attack and easily overrun them. If he went back to the breastworks, there was the likelihood that Adams, Scatters the Clouds, and the four children would die. In either case, all of them were done for.

He decided after a few moments to go back to the breastworks. If they were all going to die anyway, he wanted at least one chance to dispatch Gray Horse. The wily Blackfoot war leader had stayed hidden the whole time his warriors were attacking, but Rawlins figured that if the others broke through the light defenses here, then Gray Horse would be coming. The trapper figured that if he could stay alive that long, he could take his enemy with him to the happy hunting ground, or wherever it was he was going when he was dead.

After taking his position again—with all his guns reloaded by Blue Rattle and Falling Leaf—Rawlins kept watching over his shoulder. He figured that once the Blackfoot killed Adams, gray House might stampede the horses out here, or he just might come sliding quietly up to kill him. Rawlins wasn't about to get killed from behind before he killed Gray Horse. Not if he could help it.

Suddenly one of the babies yelled loudly, and Rawlins started. He wanted to head back and take

care of that goddamn Blackfoot, but as he looked
forward he could see that the other warriors were
about to charge again. He did a swift toting up of the
Blackfeet he and Adams had killed, and came up
with eleven. He thought only a few should be left,
but there certainly seemed to be a lot of them massing out there. He shrugged. It didn't matter whether
there were four Blackfeet or four dozen. He was in a
tight spot.

As Rawlins gathered the last three homemade
bombs close to him, a sudden burst of wailing broke
forth from back by the horses, and he knew it was
Scatters the Clouds. His heart grieved for her, and
for his sons, but he could do nothing. So he waited,
gaze flicking from the trees and the Blackfeet out
in front of him, to the horses and Lord knew what
behind him.

Adams thought he would never catch up to the
galloping Blackfoot. But the Indian had spotted
Scatters the Clouds and the children. He pulled up
sharply, figuring to kill the insufferable half-breed
brats, take the woman, and then ride off with her and
all the white men's horses and mules. There weren't
too many of the animals, but they would add to his
own herd. He would even add to his status in the
tribe by returning to their owners the several horses
the white men had stolen.

Black Buffalo slid off the pony, jabbing his lance
into the ground nearby. He would not insult the
weapon by using it to kill little ones. His buffalo-jaw
war club would serve just as well. He tied his shield
to a buckskin thong that dangled from the hunk of

buffalo robe he used for a saddle. Then he headed toward the woman and the four children.

Black Buffalo was pleased to see that the woman was new with child. It meant she was fertile, and would bear him many sons. She was more than pleasing to the eye, and with her milk-heavy breasts, she was intriguing as well.

Scatters the Clouds had risen when she saw the Blackfoot. Swiftly she had slung Crow Fight's cradle-board onto her back then pulled out her knife. She stood with Waiting for the Blackfoot in one arm, cradled against her breast, and her knife in the other. Having given birth the day before, she could not run, or even maneuver very well, and even if she could, there was noplace to go. For the children, however, it was a different story.

"Run, children, run," she said in Ute to Standing Eagle and Straight Calf.

Straight Calf started to obey, but Standing Eagle stood his ground. He, too, had a knife, and was, in his little boy's mind, quite prepared to defend his mother and this unattached female. He vowed to sell his life dearly, making the Blackfoot pay in blood.

Black Buffalo stalked forward, laughing at the sight of the little would-be warrior. He suddenly lunged one step in Standing Eagle's direction, then stopped. He was impressed that the boy had shown no fear. "You would make a good warrior someday," he said in his own language. "Maybe I'll let you live and we'll find out." He knew the boy could not understand him, so he smiled.

Standing Eagle was having none of it. He growled at the Blackfoot and brandished his knife.

"Maybe I won't, though," Black Buffalo said in

Blackfoot, "if you keep on defying me." He stopped in front of Scatters the Clouds, whose face was expressionless. Suddenly his right hand darted out and snatched Waiting for the Blackfoot out of Scatters the Clouds' arms. He suffered a deep cut on the other arm from the woman's knife. With a sneer, he pitched the day-old infant away.

Waiting for the Blackfoot squalled, then fell silent suddenly as his tiny body thudded into the jutting base of the cliff.

Scatters the Clouds set up a frightful wailing and jumped at Black Buffalo, her knife slashing wildly.

Black Buffalo blocked the knife with his war club and backhanded the woman a good blow, knocking her down. He no longer desired to take her back to the village, not if she was going to be this much trouble, so he moved in to finish her off with the brutal-looking war club.

An enraged Adams suddenly slammed into him as hard as he could. The Easterner had been afraid to shoot the Blackfoot, since he was so close to Scatters the Clouds and the children, so he had pulled out his tomahawk, and when he saw the warrior so casually fling little Waiting for the Blackfoot against the rocks, he jumped at him.

The two tumbled to the ground. The Blackfoot was surprised at this attack, but his fighting instincts were superb, and he lost no time in scrambling to his feet. When he saw his enemy, he grinned evilly. Hobart Adams did not impress him in the least.

Adams was frightened, but he maintained control of himself as he got up. Black Buffalo looked fierce, especially with that wicked war club in his left fist, but once he took a little more objective look at him, his fear began to drizzle away. Oh, he suspected that the Indian was indeed fierce, but he was fairly small. Adams figured him to be five-foot-six at most, and not all that heavy. He was well built, but slim, with well-defined muscles. What worried Adams most was that he knew that the Blackfoot had been raised all his life to fight.

The two men began to circle each other warily, looking for a weakness. Adams half suspected that Black Buffalo was toying with him. That made him angry. It also made him think of Rawlins up at the breastworks all alone, ready to face a Blackfoot onslaught that was surely imminent. Adams decided he needed to finish this up fast, but he didn't really know how.

Little Standing Eagle suddenly darted in on Black Buffalo and slashed him across the back of one thigh with his knife. The warrior whirled like a cat and smacked Standing Eagle hard across the face, sending the boy sprawling. He began turning again to face his real enemy when he felt Adams's tomahawk split his face open from just over the left eye diagonally down past the nose. Black Buffalo crumpled.

Adams was shaking a little from the frightful wound he had just dealt. He had had to look closely at it as he pulled his tomahawk free. He wanted to vomit, but would not allow himself to. As he stood, the tomahawk dripping blood and brain matter onto his moccasin, he saw that Scatters the Clouds was already cradling Waiting for the Blackfoot in her arms again. Her wailing had stopped, but she was moaning low in her throat.

Adams looked at Standing Eagle. "Those doin's

shined, li'l hoss," he said with a nod. "You keep watching over the others." He turned and ran as he heard gunfire.

Rawlins was as ready as he could make himself when the Blackfeet charged. Moments earlier, mostly on a hunch, he had thrown the three bombs out across the area in front of him. When the Blackfeet began their rush, he calmly fired a pistol at one bomb. He casually flipped the weapon to Falling Leaf, picked up another, exploded the second bomb, and then did the same to the third.

Several Blackfeet went down, but others kept coming, firing arrows. Rawlins shot until all his weapons were empty, and by then the Indians were swirling all around him. He jumped up on the breastworks, pulled one warrior down off his horse, and split the man's skull with his tomahawk.

Three Blackfeet jumped on Rawlins, and they all tumbled to the ground inside the mountain man's camp. With a roar and a bellow, Rawlins fought to his feet and went wild, hacking at anything that moved.

One warrior headed for Blue Rattle. The woman stuck her bare hand into the fire, grabbed, and flicked a handful of embers into the Blackfoot's face. The warrior howled, and Falling Leaf leaped on him, jamming her knife in his heart.

Another Blackfoot grabbed Blue Rattle from behind and started dragging her off. Adams came running up, slammed to a stop, and buried the tomahawk in the Indian's back, using both hands for power.

As Blue Rattle fell she saw several more Blackfeet pouring over the breastworks. She dove forward and scooped up one of the cans of gunpowder. She flipped it into the fire. A moment later it exploded, sending shards of tin flying around the area. Three Blackfeet fell with the blast. All rose again, but they were dazed and bleeding. They staggered off.

Adams pulled out one of pistols he had stuck in his belt and blasted a warrior at close range, but then he was hit with an arrow high in the chest on the right side. He fell, and a Blackfoot suddenly jumped on him. He grappled with the warrior, fighting desperately. They rolled and twisted, snapping off the arrow shaft in the doing, before coming to a stop with the Blackfoot on top. He was about to mash Adams's head with a rock when Blue Rattle stabbed him in the back three times. The warrior fell forward onto Adams's face.

Rawlins was still fighting like a wild man. He chopped and hacked and punched and kicked. He bit when the need arose, and more than once he lifted a Blackfoot up and threw him at others. He was splattered with blood—both his own and the Blackfeet's. He felt no weariness, though, despite his many hours without sleep and his tribulations. Rage was driving him now. Rage and adrenaline. And hate. And a survival instinct that went deeper than even he knew.

All the while he had his mind set on Gray Horse. He could not distinguish one Blackfoot from another, and he might not've been able even to recognize friends in the state he was in. But he knew he would know Gray Horse if that Blackfoot war leader came along. He had not seen him, though, and that pumped up his rage even more.

Rawlins had no idea how many Blackfeet he had killed, wounded, or simply thrown aside, but it seemed to him as if there was no end to those warriors.

They kept coming at him, no matter how many he dispatched, or thought he dispatched.

Waugh! he thought. *Bring on the whole goddamn Blackfoot nation. I'll wipe 'em all out, goddamn, shit-suckin' red devils.* And he fought on.

Rawlins suddenly heard a few gunshots and wondered where they came from. Adams couldn't have fired, he knew, nor could the women, since none of the weapons was loaded. He thought that perhaps the Blackfeet had somehow come on some guns, or were using for the first time guns they had kept hidden during the assaults. That didn't seem likely, though.

Things became even more puzzling a few minutes later, when there seemed to be fewer and fewer Blackfeet coming against him. He sank his toma-hawk into another warrior's side, and as the Blackfoot stumbled away and tried to climb on his pony, Rawlins realized he was virtually alone.

He looked around, almost in a daze. He saw something—or rather someone—familiar, but he couldn't put his finger on who or what it was. He kept turning in a slow circle.

Falling Leaf and Blue Rattle were sitting, breath-ing heavily. They were covered with dirt and dust, ashes, gunpowder, sweat, and even blood. They looked half done in.

Adams was standing at the breastworks, watch-ing the Blackfeet race off. Suddenly he saw an Indian making his way through the trees. He bent and grabbed a pistol. His hands shook as he poured powder into it and then loaded in a ball. He pulled back the hammer and started to aim.

"Whoa, hoss!" Rawlins bellowed. He jumped off

the breastworks and ran the few yards to Adams. Apparently the young man hadn't heard him, and so Rawlins plowed into him. The pistol went off, but the ball hit only the ground a few feet away.

Rawlins rose and offered his hand to Adams. "Sorry, hoss," he said as he pulled him up. He turned and pointed. "Them're Utes from Strong Bear's band." They both watched as four Ute warriors came out of the trees, followed by Ezra Early and Lucien Chardonnais.

34

"Ye sure are one messy ol' cuss," Early said to Rawlins as he slid off his horse, walked up to his friend, and briefly hugged him.

"*Mais oui!*" Chardonnais threw in. He hopped off his horse with a bounce. "He nevair tidies up anyt'ing. It's always us, me and Ezra, who 'ave to come in and clean up after dat ol' fool."

"Me'n ol' hoss over there was doin' some fine. We didn't need no interferin' from the likes of ye shit-balls. 'Specially some little turd of a Frenchman."

"It's good to see ye, ol chil'," Early said with a smile.

"Same here, ol' hoss." Rawlins turned to Chardonnais. "Cain't say the same to ye, froggie."

"Dere is somet'ing wrong?" Chardonnais asked.

"Sure is, hoss." Rawlins sat on the breastworks. The exhaustion was catching up to him now. He reached out and grabbed the small bottle of whiskey. "Set, Lucien."

Chardonnais sat, looking at Rawlins with worry

316

in his eyes. The American took a drink and then handed the bottle to his friend, who also took a long pull. "Best tell it to me quick, *mon ami,*" he said as he gave the bottle back.

Rawlins looked around. The Utes had tied their horses and the several pack mules to trees and were moving through the camp taking scalps. Early stood on the other side of the breastworks, leaning on the muzzle of his rifle. "Looks Again went under," Rawlins said flatly.

"*Mais non!*" Tears seeped from Chardonnais's eyes. He was the most emotional of them all, and no one thought less of him for the tears.

"*Mais oui,*" Rawlins said in low, monotonous tones. "Some shit-suckin' Blackfoot warrior put her under when she wouldn't do what he wanted."

"She was like dat," Chardonnais acknowledged. "And Crow Fight? Is he gone under, too?"

"Nope. But Little Rider is. Blue Rattle's been takin' care of Crow Fight for ye whilst we been on the trail."

Standing nearby in pain, Adams suddenly blanched. "Oh, my God," he breathed. When everyone looked at him, he said, "I got bad news for you, too, Abe."

"Tell it," Rawlins said, voice dead. He figured Adams was going to tell him that his wife and both children were dead. He had already come to grips with that likelihood.

"A Blackfoot killed Waiting for the Blackfoot," he said, no life in his voice. "I got the one who did it, but I was too late to save the infant." He felt like he wanted to die.

Rawlins nodded, then his eyes widened. "The others're all right?" he asked in surprise.

"They were when I left them." Adams was puzzled at Rawlins's reaction.

"Who is dis Waiting for the Blackfoot?" Chardonnais asked just before blowing his nose loudly in an old bandanna.

"He were my new son," Rawlins said. "Born jist yesterday."

"Ah," Chardonnais said sadly, "I am feeling sorry for you. You 'ave my sympathy."

"*Gracias, amigo.* But my loss ain't no worse'n yours."

"But it is. . . ." Chardonnais protested mildly.

"Ye don't seem none too put out, ol' hoss," Early said, "that ye jist lost a newborn chil'."

"I'm mournful, Ez. Don't ye think not. But to tell ye the truth, hoss, I was plumb certain that Scatters the Clouds, Standin' Eagle, and Waitin' for the Blackfoot had all gone under. When I heard it was only the least one—who I ain't even really met yet, if ye know what I mean—I was some relieved. Besides, after this little ruckus here, I'm plumb worn-out. I'll save my grievin' till I can do it properly."

Falling Leaf finally stood and went to Early, hugging him roughly. Blue Rattle went to Adams and looked at his wound.

"Goddamn," Early said, trying to be a little light-hearted to maybe break the gloom that had spread over the camp, "ain't it just like Bart there to be the one gets stuck with a Blackfoot arrow. We just can't keep him out of trouble no matter where we take him."

"That's a fact," Rawlins said dully. He looked at Early. "Come on. Straight Calf's with Scatters the Clouds and Standing Eagle."

Early looked around. The Utes were moving

about, roping Blackfoot ponies. Chardonnais was sitting, working himself into one of his well-known melancholies. Early hoped it wouldn't be too deep a one or last too long. He was in no mood for it. "You go on and see to your woman and all, Abe," he said. "Send Straight Calf back here."

"Ye sure?"

Early nodded. "Besides, I got to doctor Bart here. Knowin' him, if I don't do it soon, he'll fester up on us and he'll be no end of goddamn trouble then."

Rawlins nodded and walked away. When he got to Scatters the Clouds, she was still sitting on her shins, rocking back and forth with the baby in her arms. Crow Fight was crying softly in the cradleboard on her back. Standing Eagle and Straight Calf sat nearby, eyes wide.

He looked at Straight Calf and winked, though he didn't feel it much. "Your pa's here, missy," he said. "Go on and see him and your ma. Go on now."

Straight Calf jumped up and ran, face full of smiles.

Rawlins squatted next to Scatters the Clouds. "Come, woman," he said softly, "we need to bury the chil'." He almost choked on the words. "We had to do this once afore, and we got through it. I figure we can git through this time, too."

But Scatters the Clouds just continued to rock and moan, releasing small, animallike sounds.

Rawlins gently pried the baby away from her. Holding the baby in one arm, he rose and pulled Scatters the Clouds up with him. With a solemn Standing Eagle following them, they made their way into the forest and found a relatively soft spot under a towering pine. Rawlins knelt, still holding the baby, and began chopping at the earth with his knife.

Scatters the Clouds came and took the baby's body from her husband. He looked at her, uncertain, but she nodded. She would be all right—eventually. She would have to grieve awhile, and that was understandable, but Rawlins was sure now she would get better.

He went back to his digging and soon had a small hole. They lay the blanket-wrapped baby in the hole. Teeth clenched to the point of hurting his jaw, Rawlins covered the little body and tamped the dirt down, then piled rocks on the grave. He stood. He didn't really know any prayers, so he said simply, "Great Spirit, I know this ol' chil's got no right to go askin' Ye for anything. But if'n Ye can see Your way clear on it, I'd be powerful obliged was Ye to take my little chil' into Your kingdom, whatary Ye call it. He nary had much of a chance, what with bein' only a day old and all, and I figure he's owed somethin' of a chance in Your kingdom." He paused, then tacked on, "Amen."

Then the family walked back to the others. Blue Rattle and Falling Leaf took Scatters the Clouds aside and chatted with her. Both the others had known the kind of grief she was experiencing.

"How's ol' hoss there?" Rawlins asked as he sat on the breastworks again. His grief was there, too, a small but solid and immutable ball of it somewhere in his stomach. He would not let it out now. He couldn't afford to. There were still things to be done. He would care for his mournfulness in his own way and time.

"Full of piss and vinegar. He'll be all right in no time."

Rawlins nodded. "And Lucien?"

"I am all right now, *mon ami,*" Chardonnais said as he sauntered up. Much of his usual cockiness was gone, but he seemed to be more like his normal self.

"He ought to be," Early said with a flat laugh. "He's just spent the past ten minutes hackin' a couple of them Blackfoot bodies up."

"Your grief'd be a hell of a lot better served, froggie, if'n ye was to hack the shit out of some live Blackfoot."

"I will kill Blackfeets. *Mais oui.* Whenever I find dem I will kill dem."

"That's good, Frenchie," Rawlins said. "I suggest we start soon."

"What's dat?"

"I said we ought to start killin' the skunk-humpin' goddamn Blackfeet soon."

"Why?" Early asked.

"Them shit-suckers still got our all plews and other plunder," Rawlins grumbled.

Adams was sitting nearby, favoring his right arm. "Is that so bad?" he asked. His three friends always seemed to have enough money when they needed it, and he figured they should be able to weather this latest travail without too much trouble.

"It means we ain't got shit, hoss," Rawlins growled. "We lost all our plews year afore last. We come out all right last season, but it didn't make up for another loss like this. And we ain't got near enough specie with Ceran to cover much. Goddamn, Ez, I ain't about to hire on to no goddamn fur company because some snake-humpin' goddamn red devils stole our plunder."

"I ain't real fond of that idea neither," Early said. "We been on our own too long for such doin's."

"Den we go get our t'ings, no?" Chardonnais asked with a cold grin.

"Yes," Early and Rawlins answered in unison.

"When do we leave?" Adams asked.

"First light," Early answered, back in charge again. "Ye have a problem with that?"

"No, sir. Just asking."

"Speaking of askin' things," Rawlins said. "Jist how'n hell'd ye boys get up here and come on us when ye did?"

"I ain't tellin' no goddamn story," Early huffed, "till I fill my meatbag."

"We ain't got much, hoss," Rawlins explained with no guilt.

"Runs Back got an elk and two deer earlier today." He turned and called to Falling Leaf and told her where she could find the meat.

As the three women walked off Rawlins asked hopefully, "Ye got any coffee? We ain't had none in some days, and this ol' chil's got a powerful hankerin' for some."

"Sure do."

Within minutes, meat was sizzling over a built-up fire and coffee was being made. And before long everyone was wolfing down baits of elk and deer meat and pouring down coffee.

Once they were done and leaning back with pipes or cigarillos, Rawlins said, "All right, Ez, your meatbag's full. Now tell your tale."

"Ain't much to tell, ol' hoss. Me'n Lucien got to be feelin' right pert there at Bent's Fort, and we was wonderin' what ye and Bart was up to. Lucien there, well, ye know how the hell he is, was botherin' all the Mexican women at the fort—most of 'em wives of workers there. Bill even went out and got him some Cheyenne to pleasure him. Goddamn fat cow she was, too. Must be the ugliest goddamn Cheyenne ary lived. You've seen Cheyennes. Men and women're handsome folks, but this'n. Tell ye the truth, Abe, I wouldn't've humped her with your pecker. That's how bad she was."

"Christ, froggie, ain't ye got no shame?"

"She wasn't dat ugly."

"She weren't, huh? Lord, I tell ye, Abe, she would've scared off a buffler stampede. And fat. Jesus, it'd take two, maybe three full buffler hides just to make her a dress."

"You're a disgustin' ol' fart, froggie, ye know that?" Rawlins offered.

"*Mais oui*," Chardonnais said with something of a chuckle. "But you are still jealous of me."

"Reckon I am," Rawlins said in even tones. "I got to admire anybody who can hump a woman that fat and ugly and then brag about it."

The men almost laughed. Their grief and anger was still too deep to allow them too much humor, but they could laugh a little.

"Anyway," Early said, "it was gettin' so bad that Bill kind of politely suggested we ought to take leave of his place. We got some supplies from him—cheap, too; I think he did that to help us get out of his fort and stop causin' trouble. We headed for Strong Bear's, not knowing where else to go. Neither of us was in a humor for *fandangoin'* down in Taos."

"Ye mean ye two shitballs missed me?" Rawlins said in feigned shock.

"Ye and Bart both," Early said honestly. "By the time we got to Strong Bear's, we decided that we were comin' after ye two to see if we could be of any help. Runs Back, Bull Nose, Buffalo Heart, Iron Wolf, and Slow Foot said they'd come along.

"We had no idea where you'd be, so we headed up toward the Belt Mountains. We took the valley between the Big and Little Belts until we hit the Missouri. We found some Crows and talked to them. They said they'd seen a couple of white men heading south. Said they'd seen a heap of Blackfoot ridin' after 'em."

"That was us all right," Rawlins said. "I finally spotted 'em on our trail, but I only counted maybe fifteen."

"I think at that point they'd split up and were lookin' for ye in a couple places. We found other Crows who'd seen the Blackfeet, and so we followed 'em that way for a while. A couple bands of 'em got back together maybe a day's ride north of here. The Utes picked up the Blackfoot tracks there and followed 'em. We almost went too far south, which is what the Blackfeet did. But they doubled back. I guess they missed where ye turned off. If'n we had missed it, too, we'd be buryin' all ye folks now, instead of sittin' here chattin' with ye."

"I suppose I'm supposed to be some thankful for that?" Rawlins asked sarcastically.

"Wouldn't hurt none," Early said with a small smile.

35

WITH THE UTES AND THE women and children, the mountain men rode north after the Blackfeet. They had sufficient supplies, good hunters in the Utes, and plenty of animals. They each put aside their grief as much as they could and let their anger push them along.

Right from the first night, Chardonnais began to show an extraordinary interest in Blue Rattle, but she rebuffed his advances, preferring to stay with Adams. The French-Canadian became so persistent that Adams felt he had to talk to him.

He thought about what he would say all day while they rode, but when it came down to it, nothing made sense other than to make it short and plain. "Blue Rattle doesn't appreciate your attentions, Lucien," he said quietly after supper that night.

"I want to hear her say dat to me."

"She has. Several times."

"I never hear dat," Chardonnais insisted.

"Then you've either gone deaf, or you're too damn foolish to understand," Adams said flatly.

Chardonnais's eyes turned into dark, glittering coals. He still had his knife in hand from eating, and he ran a thumb along the side of the blade. "Another word, *mon ami*," he said coldly, "and you won't care no matter what she says to me."

"You don't scare me, Lucien," Adams said quietly. "Maybe one day you did, but no more. Not after I helped Abe stand off half the goddamn Blackfoot nation. You want to come at me with that knife, have at it. But don't make any wagers that I'll be the dead one when it's all over."

Anger suffused Chardonnais's face, and he began to rise.

"Set your ass down, froggie," Rawlins growled, "or you'll be facin' the two of us."

"You turn against an old friend like me?" Chardonnais asked, surprised and shocked. He looked at Rawlins.

"I ain't so much turned agin ye, Frenchie, as I have built up some respect for ol' hoss over there. It weren't for him, Scatters the Clouds, Standing Eagle, Straight Calf, and Crow Fight'd be lyin' buried next to Waiting for the Blackfoot back there. Besides, he's right. Blue Rattle don't want ye. Jist 'cause she's Looks Again's sister don't mean she wants to move into your lodge now."

"But dis peckerless sack of shit don' use her for what women are supposed to be used for. He don'—"

Adams moved so fast that Chardonnais didn't know what hit him as the Easterner slammed into him, wounded shoulder and all. Then he was on top of Chardonnais, his knife at the French-Canadian's throat. He was in a blind rage almost. "You ever, *ever* say things like that to me again, my friend, and I'll cut your throat without thinking about it. You understand that?"

"Oui."

Adams sat there a few moments more, then rose and turned to walk back to his seat. He half expected Chardonnais to attack him from behind.

The little trapper had thought of it, until Rawlins said, "Don't do it, froggie." Chardonnais scowled at him and retook his seat.

"Why don' you hump dat Blue Rattle, eh?" Chardonnais seemed to be over his anger already, which all the others had expected. He was like that, changing moods in the blink of an eye. "Are you afraid of her or somet'ing?"

"No, I'm not afraid of her. What I do—or don't do—with Blue Rattle is none of your concern," Adams said sourly. He was still enraged at the other man and couldn't understand how his moods could swing from fury to joy in moments.

Chardonnais nodded, accepting it. He still thought there was something wrong with Adams, but the Easterner wasn't the only strange man in the mountains.

The altercation stayed on Adams's mind for a while. He was not sure why he had not made love with Blue Rattle. She was certainly willing enough; she had made that plain on more then one occasion. Most of the reason, he supposed, was Dolores. Adams thought it would be insulting to her if he was to suddenly bed down with an Indian. He was unwilling to admit, though, that he thought there was something wrong with such an arrangement, a feeling that was hard to discard. He went to sleep that night still wondering.

Knowing where they were going this time, the group made it to the Blackfoot village in just under a week and a half. Rawlins led the way up the side trail and to the cave. It was crowded inside with all the people and animals, so they took some of the animals into the woods across the trail and tied them to trees with enough rope to allow for grazing.

"You got any idea what ye want to do now that we're here, Abe?" Early asked.

"Well," Rawlins drawled, "I think them shit-suckin' Blackfeet figure their medicine's gone shit poor. There ought to be some way we can encourage that feelin'."

"I expect we can. But how?"

"I'll need to think on it some."

In the morning Rawlins went to the small ledge. He watched the village for a while, until he spotted an older Blackfoot who had the look of a chief about him. He had been hoping to spot Gray Horse, but since the attack on the camp a week and a half ago, the warrior seemed to have disappeared. Rawlins shrugged. Maybe this would serve his purpose just as well, he concluded. With the mistiness that still hung in the trees, he was not worried about his powder smoke being seen.

Rawlins moved up until he was kneeling and aimed. He fired, and the old chief fell a moment later. Blackfeet came running out of their lodges, or stopped what they were doing and looked around. "Waugh!" Rawlins said with a tight chuckle. "How do ye like them doin's?"

Twice more during the day, Rawlins shot a suspected chief down in the village, each time filling the Blackfeet with consternation.

"What now?" Early asked as the four whites and the five Ute warriors gathered at the fire in the cave to eat.

"I think we got them niggurs spooked real well about their poor medicine," Rawlins responded, "and this chil' thinks it's time to put an end to all this."

"We attack dem in their village?" Chardonnais asked.

"'*Mais oui!*' as some goddamn frog fart I know would say."

"When and how?" Adams asked.

"Just afore dawn. We'll have a couple of the Utes scatter the horse herd. The noise of that ought to rouse those red devils. The rest of us boys'll be waitin' for them Blackfeet to come runnin' out. I figure that once we make wolf bait out of a few of them shit-suckers, they'll figure their medicine's gone so bad that they'll give us back our plunder."

"You want us to kill whoever comes out of the lodges?" Adams asked, horrified. "Includin' women and children?"

"Ye ain't forgot, have ye, what them peckerless scum did to Looks Again, or Little Rider, or Waiting for the Blackfoot, have ye, hoss? Or what they was plannin' to do to Scatters the Clouds, or any of the rest of us?"

"No, but . . ."

"Ye ain't got the balls for these doin's, hoss," Rawlins snapped, "stay up here with the women, young'ns, and the animals. We'll take care of these doin's."

"I'm coming along," Adams said flatly. "I'm just

not happy with the idea of slaughtering women and children."

"Such doin's don't shine with none of us, hoss. But what's got to be done's got to be done. Ye don't do your part in it, and that damn well might mean one of the others of us'll be made wolf bait of."

"I'll do my part."

They all went to their beds soon after, wanting to be ready for battle. Adams lay there a little while, listening to the sounds of lovemaking from Early and Falling Leaf and Rawlins and Scatters the Clouds, as well as the snores, farts, burps, and other assorted noises from the rest of the men. Blue Rattle rolled to him, her hands reaching for his manhood. Adams froze, then relaxed a little.

A shrill war cry split the misty darkness just as dawn was trying to edge into the valley. Then Bull Nose and Buffalo Heart began running off the Blackfoot horses. The thundering of hundreds of hooves rattled off the mountains behind them.

Blackfeet began pouring out of their lodges, right into a withering fire from the mountain men's rifles and the Utes' arrows. Several warriors fell dead. The others stopped, milling around in confusion and worry.

"Ye Blackfeet best move on," Rawlins bellowed. "I'm the chil' who comes in the night and leaves corpses behind."

Chardonnais had to stifle a chuckle.

"And I'm the chil' who whupped your asses down in Crow land. Ye best run for your lives, goddammit. Go!"

Chardonnais was still trying to keep from laughing, and none of the others knew if the Blackfeet understood a word Rawlins had said. Then Blackfeet—men, women, and children—fled. They knew their medicine had gone completely bad, and to stay here any longer would mean defeat and death for them all.

Soon the village was empty. Or so it seemed. As sunlight began burning the mist off the valley, Gray Horse shoved out of a lodge. He was tall, his black hair long and flowing, covering his missing ear. He wore a long buckskin war shirt, fringed buckskin leggings, and a blue blanket breechcloth. He had a painted shield on his left arm and a lance in his right hand, point upward. He stopped and planted the butt of the lance on the ground. A war club dangled from a buckskin thong from his left arm. A feathered bonnet sat on his head. And a withered, tanned human ear hung around his neck from a rawhide thong.

Chardonnais began to bring his rifle up, but Rawlins stopped him.

"You want de honor, eh?" the French-Canadian said. "I can agree to dat."

"I just want to see what ol' hoss's got to say for himself—before I make wolf bait out of him."

"You!" Gray Horse thundered, pointing his lance point at Rawlins. "I challenge you," he said in such heavily accented English that he was barely understandable.

"Challenge me?" Rawlins snorted, leaning onto his rifle. "Ye challengin' me? Ain't ye the one who hid whilst his warriors was gettin' rubbed out by the dozens? The chickenshit chil' who runs away whenever things git tough, leavin' his people to die? The shit-suckin' ol' hoss whose medicine's so poor even ol' squaws don't want nothin' to do with ye?"

"Are you afraid of Gray Horse that you talk so much?"

"I'd be more scared of your toothless ol' grandma."

"Then face me. Man-to-man."

"Toss away the lance, shitball. Then me'n ye can go at it with war clubs and 'hawks." When Gray Horse obliged, Rawlins handed over his rifle. "Hold this, froggie, whilst me'n Gray Horse there *fandango*."

"You sure you want to do dis, *mon ami?*" Chardonnais asked, taking Rawlins's rifle.

"After five years of lookin' for this son of a bitch?"

"He's a big fellow."

"Ain't near as big as that big goddamn Crow Ez run into a couple years ago. Ye jist quit your worryin', Frenchie, or all that black hair of yours is gonna go white on ye, and I don't think I could stand such a goddamn hideous sight." He walked toward Gray Horse.

The Blackfoot now had his war club—an awesome-looking weapon with a wood handle with a tomahawk head and three knife blades—in his right hand. He still wore the shield on his left arm.

Rawlins pulled out his own tomahawk as he walked. He took his knife in his left hand. He stopped about ten feet from Gray Horse. "Your move, hoss," he said quietly.

Gray Horse crouched and moved forward, the war club moving very little in his hand.

Rawlins also crouched, and waited. Gray Horse was about the same height as he was, but weighed perhaps twenty pounds more.

Gray Horse danced in toward Rawlins, war club flicking out now and again, here high, there low, now from the side.

Rawlins gave way slowly, concentrating. As he had suspected, Gray Horse was very good with that war club, and he did not want to get rubbed out by underestimating his opponent and overestimating himself. He made a few tentative moves with his tomahawk, but Gray Horse easily blocked them with his shield.

Gray Horse kept coming, his war club probing, testing. He started an attack one way, then quickly reversed himself and managed to scrape the blades of his war club against Rawlins's left upper arm. The mountain man did not even flinch, though the slight wound did annoy him.

Each time Gray Horse came at him, Rawlins learned a little more about the Blackfoot and how he handled his war club. Trouble was, he didn't see much fault, and had little opportunity to spring his own attack. He figured he was going to have to create his own chance. This turned out to be a lot easier than it sounded.

Instead of giving way straight backward, Rawlins began moving to his right. The sun was fully up now, and he hoped to use that to his advantage. He suddenly went after Gray Horse, his tomahawk raised high.

The Blackfoot followed the blade up with his eyes and caught the sun in them. He swung his shield up swiftly but not before he was momentarily blinded. He suddenly began swinging his war club wildly, planning by sheer momentum to keep Rawlins from taking advantage.

Rawlins knew he had only a moment before Gray Horse's eyes were back to normal. He also knew that he would not be able to trick the warrior twice. He swiftly made an X of his knife and tomahawk and brought them up to catch Gray Horse's war club.

Once he did that, he kicked Gray Horse in the left kneecap. The Blackfoot sagged toward that side. Rawlins whipped the tomahawk from the X and slid it backhanded across Gray Horse's midsection, tearing open the Blackfoot's stomach.

But Gray Horse wasn't quite ready to give up the ghost. He dropped to the ground and used both legs to kick Rawlins's feet out from under him. The mountain man landed hard on his buttocks, and he swore. He dodged a blow at his head as Gray Horse rolled toward him. Rawlins half rolled and jammed his knife into the side of the Indian's neck. As he pulled the blade free Gray Horse kicked him in the side and knocked him away.

Rawlins rolled a few times and then came to his feet. His face was tight with anger as he thought about Waiting for the Blackfoot and Looks Again and Little Rider. "Time for ye to head to the happy huntin' grounds, shitball," he murmured.

He came in fast and hard on Gray Horse. The Blackfoot made a fairly strong swipe with his war club, but Rawlins batted it up and away, then jerked his knife upward. The blade sank into Gray Horse's right armpit, and the Blackfoot dropped his war club.

It was but a moment more before Rawlins plunged his knife into Gray Horse's heart, and a few moments more before he took the Blackfoot's scalp. He turned and walked back toward his friends.

"Goddamn, but that chil' took a heap of killin'," he gasped. Then he sort of grinned. "Let's go through their lodges, *amigos,* and take back our plunder," he added.

36

THEY FOUND MOST OF THEIR plews, as well as some the Blackfeet had stolen from others. They got just about all their other gear back, too. While they were looking through the Blackfoot lodges Bull Nose and Buffalo Heart brought the Blackfoot ponies back. A number of them were used for carrying plews and other equipment. The Utes would take the rest of them home.

Once they had all the animals loaded, Runs Back went to the cave and got the women, children, and horses. Two hours after Rawlins had slain Gray Horse, they were ready to leave. They pulled out and rode all day, figuring to put themselves beyond reach of the Blackfeet for now—if the Blackfeet were even considering trailing them, which didn't seem likely.

After they had eaten supper that night, Chardonnais asked, "So, what do we do now, *mes amis?*"

"Shit," Early said, "it's gettin' nigh onto fall, and we're up here already. It'd be nice if'n we could just stay up here."

"We can't do that and ye goddamn well know it, hoss," Rawlins snapped. "There's a heap of things we'll need for winterin'."

"That's a fact, but there ain't much chance for us to get to Taos for supplies and then back to the mountains before the fall hunt."

"There's Bent's Fort," Rawlins suggested. "It ain't much closer'n Taos, but at least there we won't have to go through all the shit we do in Taos to trade in our plews. It's also out on the flats, where we can make better time."

"What do ye think, Lucien?" Early asked.

"I t'ink it's a good idea. I also t'ink we better make tracks or we'll nevair find any bevair."

Early nodded. "Then that's what we'll do."

"I ain't so sure now that's a good idea," Rawlins said. When his partners looked at him in surprise, he said, "Ye'n Lucien're still feelin' the effects of your wounds some." Over Chardonnais's protest, he said, "I could see it in ye both whenever ye did anything. But there's another reason, too."

"And what is dis grand reason?" Chardonnais demanded. He did not like being told he was not completely healed.

"The women and young'ns'll slow us down. Me'n Bart can make the trip a hell of a lot faster, just the two of us."

"I reckon ye could," Early noted. "But there's a heap of hostile territory to cover between here and there. Hell, ye got the Crows, who ain't been entirely friendly to us in a couple years. Plus ye got the

Blackfeet, maybe, and for sure the Snakes, the
Arapahos, and the Cheyennes."

"Damn, I forgot about them Cheyennes," Rawlins
said with a grin. "They might still be pissed after
Lucien humped that fat ol' squaw into submission."

"That they might." Early laughed. Then he grew
serious. "There's a heap of danger."

"When ain't we faced a heap of danger?" Rawlins
countered.

"What about Bart? He's wounded, too. And a lot
fresher wounded than me'n Lucien."

"Ye see him lay about for several weeks waitin' to
go under?" Rawlins said. "I did see ye'n Lucien doin'
so."

"Ye got a point there, *amigo*." Early paused. "Ye
all right for such a trip, Bart?" he asked.

"I am," Adams said firmly.

Early thought for a while, then nodded. "Me'n
Lucien'll go with the Utes back to Strong Bear's. We'll
wait for ye there."

"Shines with this chil'," Rawlins agreed. "Me'n
Bart'll split off from ye the next day or two and head
down toward the flats. We can make better time that
way."

Three grueling weeks later Rawlins and Adams
spotted the fort. They stopped a moment, and Rawlins
caught his companion looking wistfully toward Raton
Pass.

"Go on," he said quietly, jerking his chin toward
the pass—and Taos beyond it.

"No," Adams said with a shake of his head. "I owe
you and the others too much to leave now. Besides,

I don't think I could make it back on my own."

"Sure ye can, ol' hoss. Ye can make 'em come with the best of 'em these days. Ye shine, boy, ye plumb do. Go on, your woman's waitin' for you."

"What about you, though? You'll need help getting the supplies back to the others."

"I'll make do."

"You certain?"

"Yep."

Adams nodded. "Before I go, though," he said, "I've got somethin' to give you." He rummaged around in his possible sack for a moment and came up with his sketching pads. He tore out a couple of sheets and held them out to Rawlins. As Rawlins took them Adams said, "I've never seen Red Butterfly, of course, but Ezra told me the story about her and described her to me."

Rawlins looked at the two drawings—one of Red Butterfly as she was just before she died, and the other of Waiting for the Blackfoot. Tears sprang into his eyes. It was the first time he could remember crying since he was eleven years old and his father had slapped him upside the head for misbehaving.

"I don't know what to say, ol' hoss," he mumbled, only partly embarrassed by the tears. He was more embarrassed because he thought he was unworthy of such a gift.

"You don't need to stay anything, Abe. It's small enough a payment for all you've done for me." Adams smiled, pleased that he had elicited such a strong reaction with his drawings. "Now, I expect to see you and Ezra and Lucien down in Taos next summer. No more of this ridin' all over the mountains hunting for lost plews and such."

"That shines with this chil'." Rawlins finally tore his eyes away from the drawings.

"*Adios, amigo,*" Adams said with a tip of the hat. Then he turned his horse and headed south.

Rawlins watched a moment, then he looked at the pictures again. He would have to find some good, hard leather covers to put these treasures in. Scatters the Clouds would love them, he knew. Still holding the drawings, he headed for the fort a mile or so away.

JOHN LEGG is a full-time writer and newspaper editor who lives in Arizona with his family. This is his ninth book for HarperPaperbacks.

PEOPLE OF DARKNESS

An assassin waits for Officer Chee in the desert to protect a vision of death that for thirty years has been fed by greed and washed by blood.

TALKING GOD

A grave robber and a corpse reunite Leaphorn and Chee in a dangerous arena of superstition, ancient ceremony, and living gods.

SKINWALKERS

Three shotgun blasts in a trailer bring Officer Chee and Lt. Leaphorn together for the first time in an investigation of ritual, witchcraft, and blood.

A THIEF OF TIME

When two corpses appear amid stolen goods and bones at an ancient burial site, Leaphorn and Chee must plunge into the past to unearth the truth.

THE FLY ON THE WALL

A dead reporter's secret notebook implicates a senatorial candidate and political figures in a million-dollar murder scam.

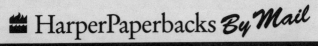